MIKE NEMETH

PARKER'S CHOICE

A ROMANTIC MURDER MYSTERY

PARKER'S
CHOICE
FIREBIRD BOOK AWARDS SECOND-PLACE WINNER FOR THRILLERS
MIKE NEMETH
FINALIST FOR THE AMERICAN FICTION AWARD
ROMANTIC MYSTERY and DIVERSE & MULTICULTURAL MYSTERY

Life is a sum of all your choices.
— Albert Camus

Every love story is a tragedy
if you wait long enough.
— Margaret Atwood *The Handmaid's Tale*

All the devils are here.
— William Shakespeare *The Tempest*

For my soulmate,
Angie Nemeth,
whose inspiration, enthusiasm,
and boundless encouragement
made this book possible.

ALSO BY MIKE NEMETH

FICTION

DEFILED (2016)
THE UNDISCOVERED COUNTRY (2017)
THE TWO LIVES OF EDDIE KOVACS (2022)

NONFICTION

128 BILLION TO 1
Lies, Damned Lies, and Statistics

THREE YEARS AGO

The doorbell camera alerted Parker to Meredith's arrival. On his phone he watched her pose for the camera, an eye-catching confluence of tanned, sweeping curves, long blonde hair, and sapphire blue eyes. Wearing a red, V-neck sundress that exposed two inches of cleavage, her sexual magnetism radiated like heat waves off a blacktop road. He opened the door and Meredith walked into his arms as though she were his lover arriving for a romantic evening.

Awkwardly, Parker extricated himself from her embrace. He led her to the dining room in his cramped beach bungalow where the papers to dissolve their partnership in Advanced Fraud Analytics, LLC were laid out on the table.

"Where's your wife? I know she doesn't like me."

"She's visiting her mother in Lakewood."

"Ah." Meredith couldn't suppress a smile. "Then no interruptions as we haggle over our company's demise."

Parker motioned to the papers. "Look, it's sad that it's come to this, but we've burned through all our investors' cash and we don't have enough paying customers to keep us afloat."

She shook her head, and her long hair flew off one shoulder and onto the other. "The big banks think they can build this in-house and the small banks have someone's nephew cook something up in his garage. But I think you're giving up too soon, Parker. You know how good I am at convincing investors to give us money."

What Parker knew was that Meredith was expert at setting honey traps. He had fielded complaints from investors who felt they had been extorted. And his wife, Paula, had given him an ultimatum: "Choose her or me. You can't have us both."

"It's time to get off the investor-schmoozing merry-go-round and kill our 'baby,'" Parker said.

"And do what? Hard to imagine you in a nine-to-five job."

Parker had no intention of slaving in someone else's boiler room but first he had to dance with the devil. He pushed the papers toward Meredith and said, "It's a fair deal. You're relieved of all company debts and obligations and indemnified against any lawsuits; in return, I retain full ownership of the fraud detection algorithms and computer programs. Okay?"

She tapped the stack of papers with her ruby nails but did not take a seat. "Let's do this outside. It's such a lovely evening."

Parker had prepared for this contingency. He swept up the legal documents and carried them to the pebbled glass table in his lanai. Beyond the screened wall, a swimming pool dominated a backyard that ended in a gentle slope to the Intracoastal Waterway. The sun was a dying ember on the horizon, so Parker turned on the underwater pool lights. It wasn't a romantic gesture; he wanted a little indirect lighting.

"Do you have any wine, Parker? May as well make this pleasant."

He hesitated, wondering if this was a ploy to have his hands occupied when he returned. He had no weapons in the house. "White or red?"

"White if you have it."

He nodded. "You can read the documents while I'm pouring the wine."

When he returned to the patio with a chilled glass of Chablis and a sweating bottle of Tecate, he found Meredith standing at the edge of the pool with her back to him. Her dress and lacy bra had been discarded haphazardly. She stepped out of red thong panties and flipped them with her foot onto the Cool Crete surface surrounding the pool. Naked, she grinned at him over her shoulder.

"Come on in," she said. "Let's have some fun before we do business." Then she dove into the pool.

Unwilling to get into the water where he'd be less mobile, he squatted at the edge of the pool and extended the glass of wine to her. She waded toward him, her breasts parting the rippled water like the prow of a ship plowing through ocean waves. With her eyes she gave him permission to gawk, but she couldn't resist a quick glance over her shoulder at the waterway. He followed her gaze and saw it then, a white Boston Whaler silently drifting up to his dock. He had thought the odds would be in his favor, and now they weren't. He set the drinks on the Cool Crete and rose into a sprinter's crouch. Madeleine realized she had lost the element of surprise and made a grab for her purse at the edge of the pool, but Parker was quicker. He snatched the unusually heavy bag and tossed it into the deep end of the pool. Then he kicked her clothes into the water.

Meredith shrieked, "Help! Rape!"

A rangy man in military fatigues, wielding a double-barrel shotgun, leapt onto the dock and advanced toward the pool like a Marine assaulting a beach.

"Get the fuck off my property," Parker barked.

Meredith screamed, "Kill him! He raped me!" She climbed out of the pool and dashed into the house.

The man raised the shotgun with one hand. "I always wanted a reason to kill you, Parker."

Bent at the waist, Parker hustled into the protective shadows at the side of his house and cowered behind his hot tub.

"It's another one of her cons, Hardy" Parker said. "You're being set up."

Hardy's response was a single blast of the shotgun, splattering the wooden frame of the hot tub with buckshot. Duncan Hardy, Meredith's ex-husband, moved stealthily and purposely around the far side of the pool, his back to the wooden boathouse beside the dock. The terror Parker felt was what an antelope feels when it is about to be eaten alive by a pride of hungry lions. He took shallow breaths through his nose to mask the sound of his breathing as he listened to the blood coursing through his carotid artery—whoosh, whoosh. Where the hell is my backup?

In the crepuscular light, Parker saw her then. She emerged from her hiding place in the boathouse and assumed the shooter's stance she'd been taught at the gun range. She gave the hunter no warning, just fired her compact Beretta once, and the man crumpled onto the Cool Crete surface with a thud and a rush of expelled air. That hadn't been the plan. She was only supposed to balance the threat Parker suspected Meredith had posed. She wasn't supposed to shoot anyone. It's so easy to get these things wrong.

A scan of the house's back windows revealed no sign of Meredith. Parker put a finger to his lips—don't talk—and motioned for the woman to hurry into the shadows. The wounded man moaned softly, and Parker's quick check confirmed that he was semi-conscious and neither moving nor watching. Parker took the woman's pistol and shoved her toward the neighbor's property. The snowbirds who owned the place were away enjoying the mild Canadian summer during the Florida off-season.

"Run," he whispered.

She loped into the darkness. He counted to twenty—one Mississippi, two Mississippi, three Mississippi—then he dialed 9-1-1.

PRESENT DAY

His briefcase packed for his business trip, Parker hurried down the back corridor of the office building in Technology Park in the Atlanta suburb of Norcross. He had a plane to catch. Overly friendly to his new colleagues, he said hello to everyone he passed until he reached the office of Jack Shaw, the CEO and majority stockholder in Shaw Technology. He waited for a tall brunette in a short skirt and high heels to leave Shaw's office and then peeked around the doorjamb. Shaw sat alone at his desk, readers low on his nose, scanning a document. Shaw's white teeth peeked through a carefully groomed two-week beard that matched the trimmed white hair on his head. The white halo and Caribbean-blue eyes turned the man's long, weathered face into something patrician and hip at the same time. Known in the insurance business as "Gentleman Jack," Shaw was reputed to be a man of southern charm and manners.

Parker rapped a knuckle lightly on Shaw's door and said, "Do you have a minute, Mr. Shaw?"

"Sir!" The word came from behind Parker, from Shaw's head of human resources, Carolyn Burke, who doubled as Shaw's executive assistant. An attractive woman with an ample bosom and a heavily made-up face, Carolyn stood in an oversized cubicle, surrounded by the filing cabinets that held the company's employee records. She fancied herself Shaw's gatekeeper and the employees referred to her as Shaw's "work wife."

"You need an appointment," she said.

Parker ignored her and stepped across the threshold into the large office. To his right, two leather couches were arranged parallel to a low coffee table and in front of two bookcases that flanked a large rectangular picture. It was a yellowed group photo of perhaps thirty people dressed for business and standing outside a colonial structure with an overhead sign that read:

Shaw – Ross Insurance Agency

Columbia, SC

1976

The picture was dated a year after Parker's mother had graduated from the University of South Carolina and a year before Parker's birth.

"Mr. Parker, right?" Shaw said.

"That's right."

"I've got it, Carolyn," Shaw said.

Shaw unfolded his six-foot, two-inch frame and strode quickly to Parker's side, his rangy body in a forward lean from the hips. Although he was a couple of years beyond the traditional retirement age, Shaw exuded the energy of the athlete Parker knew him to have been, an intermediate distance hurdler at the University of South Carolina.

Parker took a step toward the picture to get a closer look, but Shaw wrapped an arm around Parker and turned him away from the picture and toward the opposite wall where the two largest trout Parker had ever seen were mounted on either side of a whiteboard whose wooden doors were closed.

"Do you fly fish?" Shaw asked Parker.

"No, too sophisticated for me. I'm a cane pole and worm sort of guy."

"Like Huckleberry Finn."

They chuckled together. Shaw pointed first to the one on the left, then to the one on the right. "The brown I caught in the Cache la Poudre River in Wyoming. The rainbow I caught right here in the Hooch, below the I-75 bridge. Maybe we can do it together sometime."

"Sure, I'm always ready for a new adventure."

Shaw skillfully guided Parker back through the doorway and into the corridor, beside Carolyn. Parker felt he was getting the bum's rush.

"I'm glad you stopped by," Shaw said. "I just took a call from a woman named Meredith Walker who was looking for J. Parker Braun, her former business partner in Florida. She called HR, and Carolyn passed her to me. She was looking for you, wasn't she?"

Parker's stomach did a summersault. "Probably wanting to catch up for old times' sake. I dropped my adoptive father's name out of spite when he and my mother separated." He manufactured a disarming smile. "My mother called me Johnny but I've always called myself Parker, my middle name and my mother's maiden name. I'm still getting used to being *Mr.* Parker."

That was a lie. Karl Braun left Parker's mother when Parker was twelve years old. Shaw's blue eyes betrayed his disbelief. "I told her I'd pass the message to you and she said not to bother. Said she just needed to verify employment."

Shaw waited for Parker's reaction with raised eyebrows.

"That woman has trust issues." Parker feigned a chuckle. "The terms of our partnership dissolution prohibit me from using our intellectual property in my future jobs, but I'm doing nothing like fraud detection for IBS. What did you tell her?"

"I explained that you work for our partner, India Business Services and merely office in our building." Shaw frowned. "It disappointed her when I said she'd have to contact IBS HR in Chennai, India. Spewed some very imaginative profanities."

"She has rough edges."

Carolyn took Parker by the elbow. "You have a plane to catch."

"After work on Friday we'll have an employee meeting and I'll introduce you and your colleague, Steve Goldblum, to my staff. They're worried you might be auditors or IRS agents."

They laughed together again and Parker resisted Carolyn's pressure on his arm.

"You know we have a connection of sorts? My mother, Alice Parker, was a Gamecock, a cheerleader, in fact, while you were on the track team." Parker shrugged bashfully. "I Googled you."

"I'm flattered. Sorry to say I don't remember her."

"She passed away a few months ago. No warning."

Genuine sadness fell across Shaw's features like a curtain dropping over a stage. "My condolences for your loss."

"Thanks. My uncle, Hugh Parker, was in the Risk Management course of study, around the same time as you. He still lives in Columbia, where he was an underwriter at Colonial Life. Since your father was an agent, you might have crossed paths with him."

"Ah." Shaw sounded as though he had stumbled upon the solution to a riddle. "My father's agency was in Property & Casualty insurance, so we didn't represent Colonial Life. I got my start in his agency, but I went into business for myself when I recognized the need for a shared call center that served agents. When that became a success, I bought American Insurance Software here in Atlanta, Terry Horan's company. About a year and a half ago, we added Alexi Petrov's artificial intelligence team." Shaw stroked the silky hairs on his chin. "Don't believe I ever knew any Parkers."

Parker stifled a reaction. "Well, thanks for making room for me and my colleague."

"My pleasure. Your boss, Kumar, asked me to take care of you guys as part of our partnership. If you need anything, just tell Carolyn."

"Sure, glad to have met you."

"Good, good." The men shook hands.

Carolyn pulled on Parker's arm. "They're waiting for you in the parking lot. Don't miss that airplane."

Parker hustled toward the front entrance, wondering how track star Jack Shaw could have failed to meet cheerleader Alice Parker at the University of South Carolina. His bigger worry was how Meredith Walker had found him. To elude Meredith and obscure his past, Parker had truncated his name from John Parker Braun to John Parker, the name on his birth certificate, and fled from Florida with his wife, Paula, to hide in an upper-middle-class Atlanta suburb. "It's like we're in the Witness Protection Program," Paula had said. The ruse had apparently failed.

Two men and two women formed a picket line outside the main entrance to the New England Indemnity headquarters building in Hartford, Connecticut, a city that called itself the insurance capital of the world. At least one hundred years old, the brick-and-mortar building had been designed to engender trust, stability, and solvency. One pair of picketers strolled leisurely down the street as the other pair marched up the street. At a prescribed boundary, the teams reversed field and converged in the center like soldiers marching on a parade ground. A woman in jogging pants and a T-shirt emblazoned with the company logo led the down-the-street team. She carried a sign that read "American Workers Unite Revolt." On her co-worker's sign, the New England Indemnity logo was encircled by the words "Unfair Labor Practices." A small crowd, some with signs—"Bring American Jobs Home"—had gathered on the lawn to heckle visitors as they ascended concrete steps leading to the double doors.

Parker and his colleagues, Sabrina Mitchell and Terry Horan, watched from the street until the picketers moved away from the entrance. As soon as the path was clear, Terry took a step up the walkway, but Sabrina grabbed his arm. "We shouldn't cross the picket line."

Shaking her off, Terry said, "We're not scabs, we're visitors. Parker needs to see what his job is doing to these people."

Ducking their heads to evade eggs thrown by protestors, they hurried up the walkway and climbed the steps to the doors as the picketers hurled insults at their backs.

"Traitors!"

"Pimps for Indians!"

"You've sold your country!"

In the lobby, the tall brunette Parker had seen in Shaw's office stood beside the security desk. "Get a move on, Terry, we're running late. Sign in here."

Terry shambled toward the desk, and his colleagues followed. Terry was thick as a football lineman and seemed broader because of his generous red mane and bushy orange beard. As he stepped up to the desk, he jerked a thumb over his shoulder. "I don't believe you've met Parker. He's the head of analytics for our partner, India Business Services."

Parker extended a hand, and the woman gave it a perfunctory shake. She wore an electric blue dress that ended two inches above her knees with a five-inch slit up the front to facilitate walking in her red four-inch heels. "Denise Davison. I manage sales for Shaw Technology. Call me Dennie."

"Pleased to meet you, Dennie," Parker said as the Mitch Ryder song, *Devil with a Blue Dress On,* played in his mind.

Dennie waited for the guests to sign in at the security desk, then rode the elevator with them to the third floor. She led them through an open floor of cubicles, arranged in rows interrupted by load-bearing pillars. Small American flags were stuck in the corner posts of cubicles; posters proclaiming, "America First!" were taped to several pillars. The insurance company employees talked to neighbors over the cubicle walls or gathered in small groups in the aisles. Phones rang and went unanswered. Indians in Western dress, jeans and polo shirts, milled about on the perimeter. Like Dennie, Terry and Sabrina worked for Shaw Technology, which meant that the Americans were their customer, but Parker and the Indians worked for IBS. The partnership was intended to provide insurance companies with cheap offshore administrative resources from IBS using sophisticated software from Shaw Technology.

"Why isn't anyone working?" Sabrina said to no one in particular.

"The New England Indemnity people are on strike," Terry said. "They have to teach the Indians how to use my systems so their jobs can be moved to India, but the Americans refuse to train their replacements. The New

England Indemnity staff filled forty flip chart pages with diagrams of their subjective and discretionary decision-making processes, but your *Indians*," he said directly to Parker, "want to create an assembly line in which their workers can mindlessly follow a script— step one, step two, step three. The Americans are sure the Indians will never do the job properly."

Sabrina surveyed the bizarre scene and laughed.

"What's so funny?" Parker said.

Sabrina motioned at the inert workers. "You don't see the irony in pissed-off white folks losing their jobs to brown folks?"

Parker flushed with embarrassment. "It may be ironic, but it's not funny."

Dennie scanned the room as though surveying the charred remnants of a burnt house. "You here to break this impasse?" she asked Parker.

"Ah, no, I'm just the numbers guy."

"Well, your numbers are another problem you can fix."

"I've brought new numbers," Parker said.

"We're late, let's go see the claims guy," Dennie said.

Smiling, Terry said, "That should be fun."

Dennie led the way to the office of Thomas Cahill, the senior executive responsible for claims. Alexi Petrov, Shaw's Director of Artificial Intelligence, waited outside the office, but before they could enter as a team, Parker's cell phone vibrated in his pocket.

He stopped and checked it: a call from his wife, Paula. "I have to take this."

Dennie scowled at him, and he gave her an apologetic shrug of his shoulders. He moved down the hallway and leaned on the wall. "I can't talk, Paula, I'm working."

She was crying. "She found us, Parker. She spray-painted, 'You can't hide' on our front door."

Parker knew who Paula meant by "she." He motioned to his colleagues to go ahead without him. Dennie gave him a disapproving look but led the team into Cahill's office and left him his privacy.

"Meredith is behind bars, Sweetie. Neighborhood kids probably did it." Parker hoped he was right.

"Neighborhood kids don't know we're hiding. You were supposed to protect me but I'm not safe here."

"Take a picture of the door, then call the police. Let them see it before you wash it off."

"Can you come home tonight?"

"You know I can't. We fly to Iowa tonight. Kumar will be there."

"We? Is she with you? You take her everywhere."

Again, he knew who Paula meant by "she." "She doesn't work for me, Paula. She goes wherever she wants."

He heard Paula's sniffles. "Call the police, Sweetie," he said. "I have to get into my meeting."

In Cahill's office, Dennie introduced Parker as IBS's head of analytics. The moment he met him, Parker dubbed Cahill "Mr. Square." The claims executive had a square body topped by a square head with a half-inch flattop haircut. With his sun-damaged tan, Cahill resembled a Marine drill sergeant who spent his days outdoors berating recruits. Cahill shook hands with a vise-like grip and offered Parker a side-railed chair in front of a desk that appeared to be fashioned out of raw lumber. Dennie stood beside Cahill, Terry took the other chair, and Sabrina moved to a couch and sat primly on the front edge of the cushion. Alexi leaned nonchalantly against the window ledge.

When everyone was settled, Cahill said to Alexi, "I called this meeting because your artificial intelligence system can't match the results of our rookie adjusters, much less our experts."

The Russian stood up straight and swept long blond hair behind one ear. "We conducted a trial, human versus machine on hundreds of closed cases, and my system outperformed your best adjusters three to one."

Cahill gritted his teeth. "Alexi, I'm telling you, the damned system is unusable. Check your work and tell me where you've gone wrong."

"We haven't gone wrong," Alexi said. "Your database has been corrupted." Alexi looked directly at Terry. "It is sabotage."

"Say what?" Cahill asked.

Parker intervened before the Russian started World War III. "I'm here to tell you about an enhancement to Alexi's system. After he fixes your database, we'll refine the system's decision making with advanced analytics, and the system will outperform your experts."

"Explain how that works, please," Cahill said.

"Sure." Parker simplified the explanation. "Alexi's base system, out of the box you might say, applies your rules to each decision as a singular occurrence, but we'll borrow a theory from the Israelis that precision can be increased by comparing decisions to historical results. In other words, did the rule produce a positive outcome. Each rule in the system will carry a probability for producing a positive outcome, and that probability will be adjusted with each actual result. As more results are recorded, the probabilities become more accurate over time."

"Sounds like gobbledygook to me. I thought analytics was about finding a golden needle in a haystack of data," Cahill said.

"That's just slicing and dicing, breaking data down to find interesting factoids. But if the information isn't actionable, it isn't analytics. Analytics draws inferences and calculates a probability that the inference is correct. It's a new technique called machine learning."

"The machine learns?" Cahill spat the words as though he had bitten into a rotten apple.

"The machine learns faster than humans do. It learns which rules are most likely to produce a positive outcome."

"And what exactly is your definition of a positive outcome?"

Alexi jumped in. "Savings compared to the average settlement for similar claims across the country. I have a database of court awards in all US jurisdictions for every kind of damages plus a database of the economic value of all occupations in the event an injured person can no longer perform that job. My system will use the data to compute settlements."

"That's what we need," Cahill said.

The cheer of a crowd outside the window prompted six heads to turn toward the window. Above the roar, a voice shouted, "Burn, baby, burn!"

"What the hell?" Cahill said.

"Here we go," Sabrina said.

As one, they rose and moved to the windows. Cahill's office overlooked the courtyard behind the building where outdoor tables with umbrellas clustered around a fountain. Employees milled about in nervous groups, watching a woman in an American flag sweatshirt drop a stack of flipchart pages onto the flagstone pavement. Beside her, a fiftyish woman held up a can of charcoal lighter fluid and a box of wooden matches so the crowd could see her tools. The crowd cheered louder. She handed the matches to the American flag lady, who removed one match from the box and made the "raise-the-roof" motion with her hands. The crowd resumed chanting, "Burn, baby, burn."

"Holy shit!" Dennie gasped. "The New England Indemnity processes are diagrammed on those flipcharts."

The older woman soaked the pages with lighter fluid as the chanting became more frantic. The American flag lady threw her head back in a cackle, struck the match, and dropped it onto the pile of pages. With a whoosh, the pile became a pyre.

Cahill's assistant threw open his office door. "I've notified security and called 9-1-1," she said. "What else?"

"I'll fire them and have them removed from the premises," Cahill said. He rushed out of his office to play sheriff outside.

In the hallway, Dennie ordered Alexi to repair his database. As he slunk away, Alexi said, "It is sabotage."

Turning to Parker, Dennie asked for the new savings projections. "I have to get this clusterfuck back on track."

Parker dug in his briefcase for the report and handed it to her. "You won't like the numbers. Neither will they."

"Jesus, you're freakin' useless." Dennie spun on her heel and stomped away.

As they rode the elevator to the ground floor, Parker said, "Quite a mess."

"Inevitable," Terry said. "Dennie makes outrageous promises to make a sale, and then IBS throws Americans out on the street."

"The worst part is that Alexi gives insurance companies the excuses to screw people out of their payouts after they've lost arms and legs." Sabrina grabbed Parker's arm. "And now you're going to help him."

Parker pulled his arm away, flustered at having to defend himself. "Your insurance premiums pay for the lawyers who will fight your claims in court. Advanced analytics will eliminate human bias and manipulation, resulting in settlements that are objective and fair."

Terry gave him a disgusted grunt. "Hope that helps you sleep easy."

"It's the only big hotel in town," Terry said. "All our competitors will be staying here so watch what you say in public."

"Will the employees at Midwestern Assurance cooperate with us if we win the bid?" Parker hoped he wouldn't witness another revolution like the one in Hartford.

"Yeah," Terry said. "These are salt-of-the-earth Midwesterners. They'll train their replacements and walk away hanging their heads in shame over losing their jobs."

"What will become of the people who are displaced?" Sabrina asked.

Terry ran both hands through his thick hair, smoothed his beard. "Crown Bluff, Iowa is a town of about three hundred thousand, but there are only two major employers: Midwestern Assurance and that cereal plant we passed on the way from the airport."

"Yeah, it smelled awful," Sabrina said.

"Some of the white-collar workers here will end up working at that plant. Others will return to family farms. Too many of these people will become burger-flippers."

"There are major insurance companies in Minneapolis and Chicago. Maybe they can relocate," Sabrina said. "I moved from California to Atlanta for my job."

"You're one of the lucky ones," Terry said, "Stanford MBA and all. Single, no kids—"

"There's nothing 'lucky' about being a black woman in corporate America," Sabrina said.

"Don't get huffy. I'm just saying that not everyone is as mobile or as qualified to make a move."

"The theory is that new industries will soak up the surplus workers," Parker said.

"This isn't the Industrial Revolution, Parker." Terry's voice carried a tinge of anger. "There's no soft landing for displaced workers in America today. Manufacturing and factory jobs are gone. Customer service and call center jobs are gone. When you get laid off in the globalized economy, you drop out of the middle class."

Parker wondered if a white ex-con and a black woman should feel guilty about having good jobs. Sabrina might not feel lucky to have a job, but he did. "I need some sleep," he said.

"Me, too," Sabrina said.

"Aw, come on, let's have a nightcap," Terry said. He pointed to the lobby bar on their left.

Dragging their wheeled bags, Parker and Sabrina headed for the bank of glass elevators. Sabrina waved goodbye without looking back.

As the elevator rose toward the tinted glass ceiling twenty stories above the atrium lobby, Sabrina said, "When he called me 'lucky', he meant I tick the boxes for gender and ethnic minority."

"If you were an illegal alien, you'd have hit the trifecta, but Shaw took a chance on you."

"You are such a shit." She punched him in the gut playfully but harder than necessary.

Sabrina got off on the sixth floor, and Parker rode to the ninth. In his room, the red message light on the plastic hotel phone blinked at him. He pushed the buttons and heard his boss, Kumar: "Breakfast at 7:30. Don't be late."

***

Dressed in his usual Florida uniform of boat shoes, worn-out jeans, and faded t-shirt, Parker slipped into a seat across from Kumar at precisely 7:30. Kumar stabbed a chunk of cantaloupe with his fork and, without raising his head, looked at Parker through his eyebrows, as though the cantaloupe might escape if he didn't watch it closely. His compact body and the hint of Mongolian ancestry in his eyes and cheekbones made him appear fearsome even when solicitous.

"Get yourself some food." Kumar pointed the cantaloupe at the buffet line on the far side of the room where Parker saw Sabrina waiting in line for an omelet. "Most important meal of the day."

Important enough for Kumar to pile pineapple, strawberries, watermelon, honeydew melon, and cantaloupe on a plate alongside grapes and blueberries in a cereal bowl. At the several meals Parker had eaten with Kumar, he had noted that his boss always ate vegetarian with his Indian subordinates out of respect for their religious beliefs and steaks with his American customers to fit in.

"I never eat breakfast. Slows me down."

Kumar wiped his lips with his napkin, turned Parker's coffee cup right side up, and poured for him from a silver barista decanter.

Subramaniam Patek—Mani, for short—was the first of Kumar's retinue to make an appearance. Tall for an Indian man and stiff as a factotum in a vampire movie, Mani came past the hostess stand and headed for their table. Kumar gave him a one-handed stop sign, and he changed course, confused and disappointed. Dennie arrived in the dining area with Alexi and his assistant, Karen Del Monte. This morning, Dennie wore skinny jeans, her trademark patent leather red high heels, and a loose, silky top that shimmied and shimmered as she walked. The threesome chose a semi-circular booth with three place settings.

Slicing a square of pineapple, Kumar said to Parker, "Your savings projections for New England

Indemnity in Hartford aren't useful. Dennie chose not to reveal them."

"The numbers are accurate. New England Indemnity will take a one-time sugar pill that lowers their labor costs and creates a new normal. The senior execs will be expected to deliver cost savings year-over-year, but the additional savings will never materialize unless you cut your profits."

Kumar dropped his utensils on his plate with a clatter. "If your analytics can't help me sell these deals, why do I need you?"

Kumar's head of offshore operations, Chandra, an Indian facsimile of Santa Claus, lumbered their way with an elastic smile on his cherubic face. Kumar rerouted him with a backhanded wave and waited impatiently for a reaction from Parker.

Parker took a sip of tepid coffee. "Someone has to tell the emperor he has no clothes."

Kumar jerked back in his seat and lowered his smoky gaze at Parker. Then he burst into laughter. Chandra and Mani looked their way with envy, like children spurned by their father.

"Wrong answer. Without your business card, you'd be shining shoes in an airport."

Parker ignored the insult. After his stint in prison, it was impossible to intimidate him with anything less than a threat of bodily harm. "I promised Cahill, the claims guy, that I'd add machine learning routines to Alexi's artificial intelligence system and that will produce better outcomes to offset the static labor savings."

With a perfunctory shake of his head, Kumar rejected the idea. "You get your assignments from me, Mr. Parker. Alexi doesn't need your help, but I need savings projections for moving work to my operation in India. Fix your numbers and get them to Jim Kilmarten, New England Indemnity's chief administrative officer. Make him happy if you know what I mean."

"I know what you mean. I just thought I could turn Cahill into a good reference."

"We don't need that old buzzard." Kumar popped a grape in his mouth then picked out the seed with his fingers and wiped them on the tablecloth. "Peter Thorndike of Golden West will join us this afternoon to give us a glowing reference during our presentation."

Abashed, Parker slumped in his seat. Meredith's words, uttered on that fateful night three years ago, echoed in his mind—he wasn't suited to working nine-to-five for a corporation. Conceding Kumar's control over his life, he said, "I look forward to hearing Thorndike's speech."

"Mandatory attendance at the reception this evening, please. Put on your sales hat and schmooze. They'll want to talk about our numbers."

Parker had hoped to sneak away and fly home this evening to comfort Paula.

Kumar noted Parker's hesitation. "Change into business clothes before the prospect sees you. You look like a beach bum." When Parker still didn't move, Kumar said, "Today, if you please." He waved a speared strawberry at Parker, dismissing him.

Parker rose and saw Sabrina alone at the least desirable table near the buffet line. Her table had three empty chairs. Terry had not come down for breakfast. *Probably hungover.* As Parker maneuvered toward Sabrina's table, he watched Kumar's subordinates scramble to camp at the boss's table.

***

Parker changed into his IBM-blue business suit and yellow power tie. He was about to leave his room when his cell phone rang.

Paula again: "I'm scared, Parker. Meredith killed my cat."

"Gator?" He had wanted a dog, but Paula had insisted on a cat. "Less work," she'd said, "but just as much love." To make nice, she'd allowed him to name the cat after his college mascot.

"He probably got into a fight with a raccoon or a bobcat. I told you not to let him outside."

"Can a bobcat nail him to our front door?"

Parker's stomach dropped. Meredith wasn't behind bars. "Did you see her do it?"

"I saw her car leaving the cul-de-sac." Paula's words were slurred; she had been drinking. "It's big, black, and shiny and has tinted windows."

"Go to Jordyn's apartment, Paula. I'll be home in the morning."

"Jordyn doesn't need her mother sleeping on her couch. Come home tonight."

He took a deep breath and braced for a bad reaction. "I can't. There's a reception. I've been ordered to schmooze the prospect."

"Oh, God, you're having an affair. I hear it in your voice when you talk to that black chick on the phone."

"What you hear is me being courteous to a female colleague."

Paula had worried about the time he'd spent with Meredith, had worried about Meredith's brazen flirtations in public. He had insisted that he'd never encouraged her. "Well, you don't discourage her," Paula had responded. Now Paula's insecurities were caused by Sabrina.

He heard the catch in her throat that presaged an emotional diatribe. "I should never have let you drag me up here. I'm calling the cops again. They practically live at our house."

"Good."

"When I see her, I'm not going to ask questions. I'm just going to shoot her ass."

"Let the cops handle it, Paula."

He gave Paula a moment, but she was quiet. "Paula…Paula?" He wasn't sure if she had hung up or passed out. He dialed Jordyn's number and reached her voicemail. *Probably in class.* "Go get your mother and make her stay at your place tonight. Don't let her talk her way out of it. She's in danger."

Scared now, Parker called his lawyer, Tim Morrison.

"I'm glad you called," the lawyer said. "You were on my list."

Emotionally cranked up, Parker said, "Me first. I need a protective order against my former business partner, Meredith Walker. She got out of prison somehow and she's harassing us. Paula's come unglued." He told Tim about the spray paint on the front door and the dead cat.

"She's what we need to discuss. You may want to hold off on legal action," the lawyer said. He paused for effect, then disclosed the bombshell: "A Florida court has finally issued a judgment in the civil suit she filed against you before she went to prison. You've been ordered to pay her half of the proceeds from the sale of your company's intellectual property."

"That's bullshit. When our startup ran out of capital, she refused to sign a dissolution agreement. I kept the four hundred thousand dollars from the sale of the intellectual property because those algorithms were my damn invention, Tim."

"Well, the judge doesn't care who invented the stuff. You were partners, so he says you owe her half. Her Georgia lawyer contacted me this morning. If we go through the courts, he knows how this will go: we'll waste time arguing that the property was yours to dispose of; a Georgia judge will uphold the Florida ruling but will order mediation; then we'll drag our feet, and it will take months or even years for Ms. Walker to get any money and all the while her lawyers will suck her dry. So, he's preparing a settlement agreement. Let's see what they offer before we start a war."

"Too late. Paula reported her to the police. Twice."

"Don't do anything else till we see their offer."

Parker shivered as though he had walked outdoors in a Wisconsin winter. He couldn't tell Paula about this turn of events or her collapse would be complete.

"That money is sunk into Paula's riverfront mansion." The house he never should have bought. Before he bought the house, he could have paid Meredith, and they could have scraped by. Not now.

"Maybe Meredith will take the house in trade."

***

When Parker entered the ballroom, Terry was the only person there, serving himself a soda at the refreshment stand at the back of the room. "Too bad there isn't any alcohol. I anticipate a disaster," he said.

Soon Kumar arrived, and the Midwestern Assurance employees drifted in and took their seats.

Roberto Gonzalez, the CFO who had recently been hired away from a brand name competitor took the stage and welcomed IBS and Shaw Technology to the competition. He introduced Nancy Maddox, their new chief administrative officer who had worked for a major player in Chicago and then explained the reason for the competition. Midwestern Assurance must outsource "everything but the kitchen sink," he said. "We have to move at least fifteen hundred jobs." Their big-city competitors had already outsourced their operations to India, cutting administrative costs by forty percent. The new sheriffs in town intended to change overnight the culture of the sleepy little company in America's Heartland, and they expected savings equivalent to those of their big-city competitors. Then he turned the microphone over to Dennie.

She introduced her colleagues and walked the audience through the agenda. Parker was first to speak. He enjoyed public speaking and was good at it, sprinkling his dry subject matter with witticisms, encouraging feedback and questions, maintaining eye contact with the audience.

Today Parker's savings projections for the movement of jobs to India failed to meet the prospect's expectations because wages in the semi-rural Midwest were lower than those paid by their major competitors in big cities.

Dennie paced nervously while Kumar maintained his optimistic demeanor. Sitting in the center of the front row and flanked by Gonzalez and Maddox, Kumar chatted, smiled, and assured the Midwestern Assurance execs that the best was yet to come.

Kumar had invited Jack Shaw to sit with royalty, but the dapper man chose a seat at the end of the back row nearest the lobby exit. He wore pressed beige dress slacks and a blue blazer over a white polo shirt with a Pebble Beach golf logo on the left breast.

Parker sat at the end of the front row for easy access to the stage, and Terry sat beside him, kibitzing. Sabrina,

Parker noticed, had selected a seat at the end of the last row on the opposite side of the room, a mistake, he thought, to separate herself from the team. She looked every bit the part of a Stanford MBA, dressed in a business suit, her hair parted in the middle, slicked down, and gathered into a big bun at the base of her skull.

Alexi took the stage, and in the thick Russian accent that lent credibility to his theories, he explained how his expert systems worked. Gonzalez and Maddox listened attentively. Alexi asked Karen Del Monte to join him at a computer desk on the stage, he the magician and Karen his distracting assistant.

Karen opened the claims app and her computer screen, mirrored on the large screen over her head, displayed a long list of errors. The crowd fidgeted in sympathetic embarrassment.

Terry leaned towards Parker. "They're such fuckups."

In desperation, Karen closed and reopened the app and was presented with a banner screen that read: "System Failure."

"This isn't the right version," Karen stammered.

"They're such fuckups," Terry said again.

Alexi asked the audience for patience as Karen searched for the right version of the demo. Meanwhile, Alexi summoned Peter Thorndike to the stage. Confidently, Thorndike, the claims executive from Golden West Insurance, climbed three steps to the stage.

Unlike the grizzled veterans of field adjusting who managed claims for most companies, Peter Thorndike was young, energetic, and enthusiastic about what artificial intelligence could do for claims management. Lithe, with a shaved bald head, he carried twenty thick manila folders onto the stage and plopped them down on the computer desk. He slapped a palm on the top file. "These are the claims cases in which we saved millions because of Alexi's system. We call them victory files."

An appreciative murmur rose from the crowd. The audience gave Thorndike it's rapt attention as he explained how Alexi's software was used at his company. When he displayed the statistics for the overall experience with Alexi's AI app at Golden West Insurance, the murmurs became impolite taunts. The statistics showed GWI was losing money by using the AI system.

Thorndike glared at Karen. "Those are the wrong numbers."

Karen rose and averted her red face as she trundled down the steps. She never stopped as she rushed out the far end of the room, toward the bathrooms. Sabrina followed her.

Gonzalez climbed onto the stage and grabbed the microphone. "I think we all understand the principles embodied in the AI applications, so there's no need to watch a broken demo. I'm sure Mr. Thorndike can supply the correct numbers in written form." He reminded everyone that the cocktail reception would start momentarily in the atrium and called the session to an end.

After all the witnesses were gone, the IBS and Shaw teams gathered around a seething Kumar. "Fire that woman, or I'll fire you," he yelled at Alexi.

"It's sabotage," Alexi said. He shook the thumb drive containing the demo at the staff. "I'm gonna find the one did this and strangle him." Alexi looked at Parker, then Terry.

Parker shook his head. Terry shrugged. At the back of the room, Dennie and Gentleman Jack conversed in hushed voices. Shaw left via the doors to the atrium and Dennie went the other way, out the door to the restrooms.

Kumar harangued his team for another ten minutes before dismissing them. Parker hurried out the door to catch up with Jack Shaw, but the old man had become a ghostly specter.

In the atrium on the ground floor, a band stage had been set up, and a local cover band played classic rock music. Circular cocktail tables filled most of the open space, leaving a small area as a dance floor. Midwestern Assurance employees milled about and mixed with staff from several competing vendors. Parker and Terry stood in a long line leading to a portable bar that served free booze to the invited guests.

"Don't guess we'll win this bid," Terry said.

"Strange how you knew it was going to be a disaster."

Terry shrugged. "What can I say? They always fuck up."

As they reached the bar, Sabrina joined them, her hair unpinned and shaken out. They ordered drinks then found an empty table. Their Indian colleagues had disappeared. The Midwestern Assurance staff did not approach Parker for explanations of the numbers.

"Did you catch up to Karen?" Parker asked Sabrina.

"She tested those demos this morning and they worked perfectly."

Sabrina and Parker looked at Terry, who shrugged.

The band played a slow song, and Sabrina coaxed Parker onto the dance floor.

He held her at a respectable distance, but her spicy perfume shot up his nose and pierced his brain like the mustard served in Chinese restaurants. Sabrina leaned close, her lips to Parker's ear. "Do you see the guy Dennie is dancing with?"

Wearing her signature heels and a form-fitting dress, Dennie was the center of attention on the dance floor. "Yeah."

"Stop gawking." Sabrina gripped his face with her hand and turned it back to her. "He's one of the Midwestern Assurance execs."

"So?"

"Are you always this articulate? When Karen and I came out of the restroom, Dennie and that guy were in the alcove trading spit like they meant it."

Parker chuckled. "Terry said Dennie would do anything for a sale, but I don't think a roll in the hay will erase the image of those bad numbers on the screen in our presentation."

"There's more to it. He gave her the proposal from American Systems Corporation, red with gold lettering. They're our toughest competitor."

"Oh. Does she know you saw her?"

"No, we ducked back into the restroom, and I cracked the door to spy on them. We should tell Mr. Shaw."

As he and Sabrina slowly rotated on the dance floor, Parker searched the crowd for Jack Shaw and didn't see him. He thought it odd that the CEO wasn't lobbying the prospect execs, smoothing over the afternoon debacle. Parker had last seen him conversing privately with Dennie.

"Not yet. Never play a trump card until it can win a trick."

When the slow music stopped, and the band cranked up "Should I Stay or Should I Go?" by The Clash, Sabrina moved toward their table, but Parker grabbed her hand and kept her on the floor.

"You can dance fast?"

"Is that a slur against white men?"

"It's not a slur if it's a fact, white boy. Who taught you?"

"My mother. She said if I wanted to impress southern girls, I either had to go to church or learn to dance. I chose dancing."

"You're smooth, for a white boy. You even have rhythm."

"I'm a reasonably good athlete. Played baseball at the University of Florida."

They didn't sit down until the band took a break. Abandoned, Terry had retreated to the bar. Dennie and her dance partner had disappeared.

They rode the elevator together, Parker wiping his brow with his handkerchief. When it stopped on Sabrina's floor, she exited, then glanced back over her shoulder. "That was fun."

"Yeah," he said, as Sabrina sashayed down the hallway.

When he reached his room and began to undress, he realized he hadn't turned his phone ringer back on after the presentations. He had missed three calls from Paula. Braced for her reaction, he rang her back.

"What have you been doing all night, Parker?" Paula said.

"Schmoozing the prospect," Parker lied.

"Yeah, I'll bet. Well, you might want to know that Meredith was here, at the house."

"You saw her?"

"No, I heard her clomp, clomp, clomp across the deck."

"Probably a deer. Did you check it out?"

"Hell, no, I didn't check it out. I set the alarm and locked myself in the bedroom with my gun."

"I thought you were going to shoot her on sight."

"Don't be a dick, Parker." She disconnected.

When he landed, Parker rushed home to find Paula braced against the kitchen counter, treating her hangover with the hair of the dog that bit her and a handful of aspirin.

"I buried Gator in the flowerbed," she said.

"What did the cops say?"

"Oh, they were very helpful, said they'd be right over if anything else happened. They're like janitors; they clean up the mess but they don't prevent the mess."

"Well, now I'm here."

Paula pulled her pistol from her jeans pocket and waved it at him like a gunslinger in an Old West bar. "I can take care of myself."

"Didn't sound that way last night."

"It's a holiday. Go play golf or something," Paula said.

"I have to catch up on email." Parker hid in his office.

After their eighteen-month separation, while Parker served time, he found it impossible to talk of anything important, and she lost the capacity to have fun. All that remained were the dry mechanics of everyday life, like chalk dust on an erased blackboard. They passed the day in tense silence until Jordyn joined them for dinner. Then they retreated to the back deck.

Parker drank from a glass of watery iced tea and tried to ignore Paula as she sipped her third glass of white wine. "It's only wine," Paula said. *I think you've had enough*, the common refrain of those who love—and think they can manage—an alcoholic, danced behind Parker's eyes but never reached his lips.

Nightfall arrived on cue, friendly white clouds in a faded blue sky replaced by black splotches on an indigo backdrop. Few stars penetrated Atlanta's summer haze, and a yellow crescent moon offered little illumination, creating a perfect canvas on which to paint a masterpiece with fireworks.

Parker and Paula sat on cushioned chairs, the evening humidity oiling their skin like a cheap moisturizer. In the darkness, Parker sensed Paula crossing and uncrossing restless legs and waving an impatient hand in front of her face to chase away gnats and mosquitos. A mixture of cigarette smoke and *Obsession*, once an irresistible aphrodisiac for him, infiltrated the aroma of his cigar. With a bobby pin, Paula secured a clump of her unruly red hair.

Random trees and bushes in the Corps of Engineers' right-of-way at the bottom of their yard blocked their view of the Chattahoochee River, although they had paid a premium to live on riverfront property. The gates of the Buford Dam, twenty miles upriver, were open, releasing Lake Lanier water to generate power. As it passed their house, the river ran fast, rose above midstream boulders, and flooded the vegetation on the lower banks. A boisterous Fourth of July crowd at Jones Bridge Park, eighty yards away beyond a thicket of bushes, trees, and underbrush, drowned out the sound of the rushing water.

After an uncomfortably long silence, the first fireworks erupted over the river. A large globe of silvery-white shards briefly lit swaths of lawn alternating with shadows cast by swaying pines. Parker saw a ghostly apparition emerging from the trees in the lower right corner of the yard. As quickly as the vision appeared, blackness erased it as the sound of the explosion drifted downriver.

Parker jerked to his feet and waited for the next volley of fireworks. First came an explosion of blue and green sparks, followed by a red eruption like a vase of roses painted on the sky. In the dimmer light, he saw her, closer, waving something white and rectangular in her left hand. Rising from her chair, Jordyn yelled something, but Parker couldn't understand her words over the two concussive booms. He saw Jordyn reach for the switches on the house wall that controlled the backyard lighting. One by one, she flipped the switches for the deck lights, the corner spotlights, and the marina lights along the stone path to the firepit. None of the lights illuminated.

In a series of white explosions, he saw the ghost again, moving toward the firepit. He dropped from the deck onto the lawn then hesitated, thinking he should run to the garage to get a baseball bat.

Paula realized that something was wrong. "What is it, Parker?"

"Meredith is here! Get inside."

Paula rose uneasily, knocking over her chair and spilling her wine. In a panic, she fumbled with the door handles before getting one door open.

Jordyn said, "Wait, Dad, make her come up here."

He gave Jordyn a one-handed stop sign. "I've got this."

Fireworks erupted at a faster pace, flashes illuminating the backyard like a strobe light on a '70s disco dance floor. Meredith waited for him next to the tall chimney of the firepit.

They stood two paces apart, the tall, fit man and the petite, voluptuous woman. Her long-sleeved blouse covered a pair of cutoff denim jeans—not the proper garb for crawling through a thicket, as evidenced by the red welts on her fleshy thighs.

"Get the hell off my lawn!"

She waved a document at him. "I've brought a settlement agreement. We know you have cash, and I'll take what I can get."

"The lawyers will handle things."

She jabbed a red-painted fingernail at him. "I can't wait here in Atlanta any longer. Sign the agreement tonight, and I'll be out of your life forever."

"How much?"

"I'll give you a cash discount—one hundred fifty thousand dollars."

Reflexively, they craned their necks to watch a rapid succession of fireworks until the echoes faded, and a single firecracker went off directly behind Parker. He whirled to see Paula in a marksman's pose, her right hand bracing the left hand that pointed a pistol at Meredith.

"That bitch is shooting at me!" Meredith shouted.

Palms outward in the common peacemaker pose, Parker yelled at Jordyn, "Take that gun away!"

Meredith and Parker flinched when a brick in the wall of the firepit chimney disintegrated, and a ricocheting bullet zinged past them. He whirled around to see Paula was pointing her gun toward the bushes at the side of their yard. Someone else was shooting at them. Instinctively, Parker ducked as a second shot exploded. The shot was barely distinguishable from the overhead fireworks, but he saw the plate-glass window in the open half of the French doors shatter and drop in a cascade of slivers.

Meredith's screams prompted Parker to turn her way and see her pull a small chrome pistol from the back of her shorts. As she aimed at Paula, he dove at her and made a perfect tackle, right shoulder into her midsection. They went to the ground, and her right knee caught him on the chin and stunned him. Stuck under Parker, Meredith writhed like a coyote caught in a leg trap, and he lost his grip on the hand that held her pistol. She extricated herself with a swinging kick to his forehead. He struggled to his hands and knees as she ran toward the bushes. After she disappeared, Paula loped past him and plunged into the bushes. He hobbled after her, but Jordyn sprinted past him. "I have a flashlight." She waved it at him.

Jordyn entered the thicket at the bottom of the yard, following in the footsteps of Meredith and Paula. Instead of following the three women along the river, Parker angled away from the river toward the parking lot, where Meredith must have had a getaway car. Traveling at this angle, he stood a chance of cutting off the retreat of the person who had fired the high-caliber gun at him and Paula.

Inside the thicket, the light from the fireworks was fragmented by the canopy of trees. Rapidly exploding fireworks drowned out all sounds of movement. The air was redolent with the smell of cordite as five people with three guns felt their way toward or away from one another in a leafy cocoon.

Fearing that Meredith's accomplice could ambush him, Parker proceeded carefully, hands in front of his face to protect his eyes against whipping bush limbs. As he struggled through the dense thicket, a high-caliber cannon boomed, back toward the river and closer to the park, the route the women had taken. A small caliber shot responded immediately. He stood transfixed in the thicket, the fireworks accelerating into a crescendo of bangs and booms distorting more sounds he thought were gunshots. Rather than move toward the shots and the people with guns, he continued through the tangled underbrush, vainly hoping he could reach the parking lot before Meredith and her accomplice.

By the time he emerged from the thicket, the fireworks show had ended, and cars crept toward the exit, slowed by the mingling crowd leaving unhurriedly on foot for nearby neighborhoods. From above, Parker imagined the scene would look like an amoeba writhing under a microscope. There was no sign of Meredith, no sign of Paula or Jordyn in the roiling mass of sweating humanity. He saw no one lugging a high-caliber weapon. He called Paula's cell phone and reached her voicemail.

Years ago, the children who had then lived in their house had trampled a crude path from the backyard to the park. He trotted down the line of trees toward the point where the old footpath met the park pavilion. He knew Paula was somewhere in the thicket, possibly wounded, possibly… Unwilling to let Jordyn find her mother lying in a pool of blood, he plunged into the thicket. Long overgrown, the path wound haphazardly along the top of a steep bank that canted sharply downward to the raging river. He flinched when his cellphone rang—Jordyn.

"We're back at the house. I'd come and get you, but I don't want to leave Mom alone."

He shuffled slowly toward the house, the path no longer illuminated by fireworks; he found no bodies, encountered no shooters. He was surprised to emerge at about the point from which Meredith's accomplice had ambushed them. The accomplice knew the way through the thicket, so why did Meredith take the hard way and come out at the bottom of their yard? *To position herself where her accomplice could get a good shot at me.*

Jordyn and Paula stood in the darkness, Paula leaning on her taller daughter.

"What the hell were you thinking?" he asked Paula.

"You didn't stop that bitch, so I had to."

Jordyn held Paula's Beretta Tomcat out to her father. He took a handkerchief from his back pocket and used it to grip the .32 caliber gun. Jordyn shot him a scornful look. She knew exactly what he was doing. He ejected the seven-round clip and found two available rounds. Counting the live round in the chamber, four bullets were missing. Paula had fired one shot at Meredith from the deck, and perhaps a shot at Meredith's accomplice, which meant she'd fired at least two more times in the thicket.

With his free hand, he grabbed Paula's shoulder and shook her. "Did you shoot Meredith?"

"Stop it, Parker! All I did was trip over a root and land in a bush."

Jordyn knocked his hands off her mother's shoulders. "We need to get her in the house and treat her cuts." She wrapped an arm around Paula and helped her onto the deck and into the house.

Puzzled by the fact that the backyard lights hadn't worked, Parker climbed onto the deck and checked the spotlight above the French doors. The bulb turned easily in its socket, and the light came on. The spotlight on the other end of the deck also lit when he screwed the bulb tightly into its socket, and the backyard shadows surrendered to bright light. *Someone had loosened the bulbs.*

He stepped down off the deck onto the stone walkway to the firepit and tightened the bulbs in the marina lights as he went. The small lights soon lit the path with a muted glow. Someone had tampered with all the outdoor lights. *The attack had been planned. The lights had been loosened by Meredith clomping across the deck last night.*

The document Meredith brought lay on the lawn, next to the fire pit chimney. He picked it up and read it. Meredith and her lawyer had proposed a settlement of one hundred fifty thousand dollars, in exchange for which the pending lawsuit would be withdrawn. Meredith's lawyer had convinced her that a fractional payment was better than slogging through the civil court system. Had she not been drunk, Paula would have insisted he sign it to get Meredith out of their lives.

He joined the women at the kitchen table and evaluated Paula's injuries: scrapes on both knees and both elbows, a bloody gash on the top of one foot, a red abrasion on her cheek. Mud clung to her bare legs, and twigs hung from her disheveled hair.

Meredith had barely been scratched by her trip through the bushes; Paula looked like she had been in a fight with a bobcat.

While Jordyn retrieved antiseptic and bandages from a bathroom, Parker collected a broom and a dustpan from the garage and swept the deck. Among the glass shards, he found two .32 caliber shell casings. Paula had fired two shots from the deck, and therefore two shots in the thicket. He reentered the house to find Paula smoking another cigarette and sipping amber liquid from a cocktail glass. A bottle of Scotch, half-empty, stood at Paula's elbow.

"Where the hell did that come from?" Parker said. Over the past three weeks, he had found liquor bottles stashed in the dishwasher, in an ornamental urn in the family room, and in the guest commode water basin. It had become a game of hide-and-seek: Paula hid the bottles, and Parker found them.

When he outwitted her, and she couldn't find her hidden bottles, she screamed: "You made me this way!" He admitted that he'd contributed to her descent by selling her little store—she'd called it a gallery for her artwork, but mostly, she framed family pictures and cheap movie posters—for less than the value of the inventory and moving her to Atlanta a few months ago. She said she hated Atlanta—"All that traffic and no ocean, Parker." He had also removed her from the cloying influence of her mother, the only person who could comfort her or control her. It was all too much for her fragile sobriety.

Jordyn blamed him too. After one fight, she had confronted her father. "She was fine in Florida. Then you dragged her away from her support system, and now she's a drunk again."

Paula drained her glass and poured another double shot as Jordyn swabbed her knees.

"If you hurt her," he said, "we have to know before the cops get here."

Paula glared at him with hooded, jade-green eyes. "Did you find any dead bodies out there?" His silence was his answer. "Then get off my ass. Someone shot at us in the backyard, and I shot back. End of story."

"You shot first. We're not in Texas, Paula. You have to wait for the intruder to cross the threshold of your house before you shoot them."

Paula waved his sarcasm away with one long-fingered hand and took another sip of Scotch. "It's our word against hers."

"Well, now you are too drunk to give a statement," Parker said.

"Fuck you."

There's nothing quite like the disgust alcoholics feel for the people who think they can help them, Parker thought.

While Jordyn bandaged Paula's knees and elbows, Parker held the casings up for Paula to see. "You took two shots from the deck and two more in the thicket. Who did you shoot at?"

She gave him the coquettish look pretty women use to get out of trouble. "No one. I never saw anyone."

It was useless to talk to Paula when she was drunk. Parker wiped the casings with an oily rag and carried them to the front door. No cops lurked in the cul-de-sac. Lights glowed from neighboring homes, but no nosy neighbors were on the street. Moving swiftly, he walked down the driveway and casually dropped the damning evidence into a storm drain. Then he prayed for rain. In that moment, he may have become an accessory after the fact to murder. What choice did he have if his wife had killed his worst enemy?

Back inside the house, he carried the pistol into the laundry room and hid it in a space above the cabinets where he stashed his rare port. Finally, he covered the gaping hole in the French door with a piece of plywood.

"When the cops come," Parker said, "there was no shooting in our backyard. We have no idea what happened in the woods out there."

Jordyn scowled at him. "You think you can lie to them again? Why can't we tell them the truth this time?"

"As a convicted felon, I'm not supposed to have a gun in the house."

An insolent smile tugged at the corner of Paula's perfectly formed mouth; two pronounced vertical ridges under tiny nostrils that made her upper lip into a wave with two sharp crests. "Good thing I had one, or you'd be dead." Paula saluted Parker with her glass.

"She's right and I have proof." Jordyn pulled her cell phone from the back pocket of her jeans—the favorite phone storage location for all women, and probably the origin of the term "butt dial"—and pulled up her photo gallery. She handed it to her father and said, "Swipe left."

The first picture was dimly lit, Parker and Meredith beside the firepit chimney. He swiped. Meredith pointing her finger at something over Parker's shoulder, pointing at Paula, who had just taken a shot at her. He swiped, his anticipation growing. Parker and Meredith ducking because her accomplice had shot at them. He swiped. Meredith holding her pistol high and broadside in her right hand, making identification easy. The picture was well lit by a fireworks explosion overhead. He swiped. Meredith aiming the pistol over Parker's shoulder. Somewhat grainy but usable. The pictures were date- and time-stamped, starting with 10:02 p.m. on July fourth.

No crime goes unrecorded today. "Don't tell anyone you have those pictures."

"You want to go with 'There was no shooting in our backyard,' but these pictures prove it was self-defense. When the cops come, I'll show them the pictures. If I have to, I'll testify to taking these pictures."

"That's the last thing I want. If Meredith is dead out there, your mom will be facing the death penalty."

"She's not dead," Paula said. Her words were slurred.

Parker pulled Jordyn into the dining room. Hands on hips, she waited for his interrogation.

"Did you see what she did out there?"

"Mom? No."

"Where did you find her?"

"On the path, ten or fifteen yards from the pavilion. I didn't see anyone before I found Mom."

"Did you hear the shots?"

She exhaled. "I heard two shots, like a big dog barking followed by a yappy small dog. Close together, big dog first."

"I heard several small-caliber and a couple high-caliber."

Jordyn's brown eyes—eyes she'd inherited from him—clouded over as she reconstructed her report. "There were two gunshots, Dad, and a lot of fireworks and firecrackers."

Parker knew the difference between the echoing crack of fireworks and the flat, truncated punch of a bullet breaking the sound barrier. "You heard just one small caliber shot, and your mom didn't shoot at anyone, and yet two bullets are missing from her gun. How do you explain that?"

Jordyn gave him a rock-hard stare. "Maybe the clip wasn't fully loaded."

They stood there in a stalemate, Parker fending off the one thought he couldn't ignore—that Paula had shot Meredith and maybe her accomplice too. Since they didn't find any bodies in the thicket, the wounded assailants would be at a hospital, giving the cops damning statements. The cops would be at their door soon. Jordyn crossed her arms over well-defined swimmer's muscles and shifted from foot to foot. "You should put ice on your forehead."

"You should leave while you can."

"Want me to delete the pictures?"

"No. Save them in case we need a Hail Mary."

It didn't occur to Parker until after he had bathed Paula and put her to bed that the police had not shown up at their door. Maybe none of shots had hit home after all.

Parker arrived early at his office on Friday morning for a hastily scheduled meeting with Kumar, who had flown into Atlanta the night before. Sitting at his desk with his office door closed, Parker called his lawyer, Tim Morrison. The call was a ruse. If Meredith had been harmed, he wanted the cops to discover that he had no idea that something untoward may have happened on the Fourth of July. Parker had made his choice, and his choice was to protect his wife.

Tim listened impatiently to Parker's story. As though it were good news, Parker told the lawyer that Meredith had hand-delivered a settlement proposal last evening that was almost acceptable. Tim was distressed that Meredith's lawyer had allowed her to deliver the document outside of legal channels.

"Maybe her lawyer didn't know she would do that," Parker said. "We can save time if you let her lawyer know we'll settle for a seventy-five-thousand-dollar cash payment. I don't have as much money as they think."

Tim stifled his professional ire and promised to make the counteroffer immediately. Parker thanked him and hung up.

"One problem down and one problem to go," he muttered to himself.

The phrase "dead man walking" echoed in his brain as he ambled down the hallway, assuming Kumar would conduct a firing squad in retaliation for the poor performance in Iowa. He slowed as he approached Shaw's office and stopped when Carolyn appeared in Shaw's doorway.

"They're in Jack's conference room," she said with obvious distaste. "Keep the connecting door shut. Jack has meetings."

Parker tried to crane his head around Carolyn for another look at the old group picture on Shaw's wall but Carolyn blocked his view. He gave her a joyless smile and moved to the conference room portal to face his colleagues.

Kumar camped at the head of the table, his jacket over his chair, his alligator briefcase open in front of him. Dennie held her usual diet soda and sat beside Alexi and Kumar's supernumerary, Mani, on the far side of the table. Sabrina leaned against the glass outer wall. On the whiteboard, a diagram had been written in dry-erase marker:

Automation (ST)> Outsourcing (IBS)> Analytics (IBS)> Artificial Intelligence (ST)

Parker recognized the diagram as the joint strategy for the partnership, the strategy that would shrink the American middle-class workforce. As the analytics guru for IBS, Parker was at the heart of that strategy.

Parker moved to the nearside seat beside Kumar and pulled out the chair beside it. He signaled to Sabrina, who pushed herself away from the wall and moved to the proffered seat with the sinuous grace of a runway model. She pulled red readers off her head and perched them on her nose, opened a spiral notebook, positioned a Mont Blanc pen on a blank page, and cleared her throat. Kumar gave Parker an impatient look, then waved at Dennie to begin.

Dennie crossed her legs right over left, exposing eight inches of bare thigh. One shoe dangled precipitously from the bare toes of her swaying foot. "Midwestern Assurance has asked us to revise our proposal. They recognize that we had technical issues with the demo."

"Sabotage," Alexi said. "Won't happen now that I have guard on lab door. You see Ilya? Jack hired him, keep my code safe."

Parker shrugged. "Yeah, I've seen him. He looks like Frankenstein's Monster. Did you remember to give him a brain?"

"Fuck you."

"Let's talk business," Dennie said. "I know what we have to propose to win the Midwestern Assurance deal."

"How do you know?" Parker asked.

Dennie's sipped her diet soda. "Sales intuition."

"We've made two sales together to Shaw's customers. This third sale will give Dennie the references she needs to attack the open market," Kumar said.

"We're negotiating with ourselves," Parker said. "Our competitors will make counterproposals, and we don't know what they'll propose."

Dennie's hands curled into fists on the tabletop. "That's the beauty of it. Midwestern Assurance has down-selected just one other supplier besides us— American Systems Corporation, ASC. The numbers ASC presented in Iowa are final. We're the only bidder getting a second chance."

"We've been invited to present our revised numbers to Midwestern Assurance at the insurance convention in New Orleans, the week after next," Kumar said.

"But we don't know what numbers we have to beat," Parker said. He looked at Dennie to gauge her reaction. She didn't skip a beat.

"I know the number," she said.

Parker looked her in the eyes. "Amazing. Hope you didn't have to do anything, uh, unnatural, to get this information."

She jumped out of her chair and threw her soda can at Parker. It struck him in the chest and deposited cold liquid in his lap.

"Sit down!" Kumar shouted as he slapped the table with both hands.

Dennie didn't sit.

Parker leaned back and nonchalantly shook soda drops off his hands. "So, what's the number?"

Dennie's words sounded like the hissing of a King Cobra. "Fifteen percent savings in labor arbitrage upfront and a five percent improvement year over year in labor cost, plus a twenty percent reduction in claims payments."

Parker's laugh was impulsive, derisive. "We can't get close to those imaginary levels."

Dennie shoved her hair behind her ears. "If we had good references, I could win with less, but our references are shit, no thanks to your projections for New England Indemnity."

Kumar waved Dennie into her seat before she could find something else to throw at Parker. "We'll do call center support from Manila instead of Columbia to save money," Kumar said. "Alexi will generate the claims savings with his AI apps." He gave the scrawny Russian green card holder a reluctant smile.

"Sounds like you have a plan," Parker said. "What do you need from me?"

"I need year-over-year process savings, of course."

"You already have my numbers," Parker said. "They're in our original proposal."

"They're not good enough. We're getting a second chance, thanks to Dennie. But there's a catch: Midwestern Assurance has given us a set of test cases we have to use to prove our numbers are valid. I've asked Mani to lead proposal preparations in support of Dennie, and I've brought over a guy named Ravi to run the numbers for your team, Parker."

"I don't need help, Kumar. Steve and I can run the numbers."

"You tend to be pessimistic, Parker. Ravi will run the numbers first. You'll vet them when he's done."

Sabrina spoke up, emboldened by Parker's objection. "The numbers come to me first, and I put them in the proposal. If I like them."

"When our numbers are ready, we give to Dennie," Alexi said.

"Jack won't agree to that," Sabrina said.

"Jack is fully aware of how we're doing this one," Kumar said.

Alexi gave Sabrina a smug look. "We make numbers, you get from Dennie."

Parker wondered how much Shaw had been told, how complicit he was. "Sure," Parker said. Although his exposure to Indian culture had been brief, Parker had adopted their use of a desultory "sure" to indicate reluctant agreement.

"It's agreed then," Kumar said. "Mani will give Ravi a couple of IT guys to help with the technical stuff."

"Why do we need Parker at all?" Dennie said.

"Because no one believes numbers coming from a saleswoman," Kumar said. "Parker has a reputation as a brilliant analytics guy. As chief science officer, he'll validate Ravi's numbers and then present them to the Midwestern Assurance executives in New Orleans."

Parker played along. "When I see Ravi's numbers, I'll let you know what I think."

"It will be a few days before we have new numbers," Alexi said.

Kumar adjourned the meeting, and the two women left with Alexi and Mani, but Kumar pushed air toward the floor with one hand, the signal for a vehicle to slow down.

"You have to decide which team you're on, Parker. Pick a side. If you don't need this job, you can pick the other side." He gave Parker a stern look.

Parker said, "I need this job, but—"

"Alright then." Kumar cut him off. "You're part of a global revolution now, Parker. Once upon a time, we enslaved our fellow man to increase productivity. As we became more civilized, we domesticated animals to do man's work. During the Industrial Revolution, we created machines to mass manufacture goods instead of tedious handcrafting. And at every paradigm shift, we found a way to employ humans in more satisfying and more valuable work. Now we're training computers to do the tedious work, and we'll find new jobs for humans. You can't stop the march of technology." Kumar leaned back and manufactured a pedantic smile. "With your criminal record, you wouldn't even have a job if it weren't for me."

When he'd been a student at the University of Florida, Parker had imagined a life shared with his college sweetheart, joyfully immersed in esoteric numbers. Now he was married to a woman who resented their circumstances and whose disease was beyond his capacity to ameliorate. Worse still, he had a criminal record and a record of failure as an entrepreneur. Parker nodded at Kumar and left.

As Parker passed Carolyn in the hallway, she said, "Pee your pants, little boy?" She pointed at the dark stain on his crotch.

"You wanna change my diaper?" He winked at her.

Back in his office, he found Terry Horan leaning his considerable bulk against a windowsill. Sabrina helped herself to a Snickers from the stash in Parker's desk drawer and perched on the corner of his conference table.

"I'm not going to let them steal those jobs," Terry said.

Parker suspected the sort of thing Terry had in mind, suspected Terry had been responsible for the sabotage in Hartford and the demo failure in Iowa.

"Calm down," Parker said. "I'll get to see what they're doing in a day or so."

Terry pushed himself away from the wall and looked at Parker with disappointment in his eyes. "Fifteen hundred Americans will lose their jobs. Think about that when you cash your precious paycheck." He left.

Sabrina tossed her crumpled candy wrapper in Parker's trashcan and slid off the conference table. "I can't be part of a fraud."

"We won't know it's fraud until we see their test case results."

"How else can they hit Dennie's numbers?"

Parker had to admit that was a good question. "We need to find the ASC proposal. It's probably in Dennie's office."

"We can't get caught in there; she carries a gun."

"What? How do you know that?"

"I saw her check it with TSA in Iowa. But, I have a gun too. Probably for a different reason."

Maybe I should borrow it, sleep with it under my pillow. "Seems like everybody has a gun except me."

"Stick with me. I'll protect you," she said.

Sabrina left him to languish alone in his office, waiting; waiting for his lawyer to call; waiting for the cops to come; waiting for Alexi and Ravi to produce fake numbers; waiting for Paula to love him again. His glass wall overlooked a shaded picnic area beside a duck pond. Despite its visual allure, the area was unusable by employees due to an invasion of ferocious geese that coated the ground with slick droppings and stole sandwiches out of the hands of lunching humans. He watched the geese peck at the crumbs under the picnic tables, preoccupied with the singular purpose of finding food. He envied their focus. Several times he meandered down the hallway, past Jack's Shaw's office hoping for a glimpse at that group picture, but each time, Jack was engrossed in a conversation with staff members. Finally time ebbed away and the employee meeting was about to begin.

***

One hundred eighteen Shaw Technology employees filed into the second-floor hall that had once housed a dance studio. Senior managers filled the first two rows of folding chairs below the raised stage while junior employees milled about or gravitated to the portable bar at the back of the room. Beer, wine, and soft drinks were dispensed at no charge to employees.

As the employees waited for Shaw to appear, the atmosphere became restless in the occupied rows and boisterous in the back of the room, around the bar. Whispers of "Where's Shaw?" filtered backstage where Parker and Steve Goldblum waited to be introduced. Steve was a hulking, ponderous man who stood six-foot-five and weighed close to three hundred pounds with a huge head, a full beard, and a mop of black curls. He was affectionately known as "The Wookiee," Chewbacca to Parker's Han Solo. Steve should be the future of human evolution, Parker thought, bigger and stronger bodies with ever larger heads to hold ever larger brains. Unfortunately, he was sure that computers and robots would nudge mankind's evolutionary path in the opposite direction—smaller bodies, atrophied muscles, and shrinking brains as humans would no longer have to perform manual labor or think for themselves.

Several minutes later, breathless from hurrying up the stairs, Shaw took the stage and the noise level abated. He introduced Parker and Steve as employees of IBS, Shaw's partner, and asked Parker to briefly explain the role of analytics. The Shaw employees were only mildly interested and asked Parker no questions.

When Shaw began to review his company's quarterly results, Parker and Steve retreated to the bar at the back of the room. Sabrina leaned nonchalantly against the wall between the bar and the exit, a common pose for her. Parker tossed his paper cup into a trashcan and grabbed Steve by the arm. "Follow me." The Wookiee obediently followed Parker toward the door.

Sabrina raised one eyebrow. "Where are you going? Don't you want to hear how Shaw Technology is doing?"

"I want another look at a picture." Parker gave her a mischievous grin. "Come along and join the party."

The three of them slipped out the back door of the dance studio and down the stairs to the first floor.

Parker positioned The Wookiee under the staircase where he could see anyone descending to the first floor. The Wookiee squeezed into the crevice, rolled into a ball the size of a small boulder.

"Perfect. Just text me if anyone comes downstairs."

Parker positioned Sabrina in the center of the bullpen, a spot with a clear view of Shaw's office. "Text me if anyone comes close."

"What are you doing?"

"The picture is in Shaw's office."

"You can't go in there!"

Parker gave her a lopsided Han Solo smile. His head on a swivel, he approached Shaw's office door as though it were a dangerous snake and gently tried the handle. The door was locked.

Sabrina hissed at him, and he waved her quiet. He crept down the hallway to the entrance to Shaw's private conference room and tried that handle. It gave. Carolyn had forgotten to lock the door after Kumar left the building. The door hinges squeaked as he squeezed into the room, so he left it ajar for his escape. As he waited for his eyes to adjust to the dark, his cell phone pinged. A text from the Wookiee: *The big Russian bodyguard came downstairs.*

Avoiding the table and chairs, Parker tiptoed through the conference room and eased into Shaw's office. He turned on the light and recoiled in shock. A picture of the South Carolina Gamecocks' mascot now hung between the bookcases, leaving a bright border of clean wallpaper where Shaw's picture of his father's staff had once hung.

Parker looked around the office and saw no picture standing against a wall or a chair. He opened the sliding double doors of a closet and found a blazer and a spare shirt hanging inside but no picture. *Shaw doesn't want me to see that picture. He was late to the party because he took the time to move it.*

He moved to Shaw's desk and picked up an acrylic "tombstone" paperweight—the sort of trophy Wall Street bankers commission to commemorate IPOs—off a neat stack of manila folders. The inscription commemorated the joint sale of software and services by the Shaw/IBS partnership to the Golden West Insurance Company. It was dated a year ago. The top folder was labeled "ST/IBS Partnership Agreement."

He riffled the papers in the folder and found one contract with addenda. The signatures weren't wet; the documents were copies. As he flipped through pages of boilerplate, his phone pinged. Sabrina: *Get out now!*

Impulsively, Parker pulled his shirttails out of his pants, laid the folder against his belly under the shirt, and shoved it down the front of his pants. He wanted Shaw to know he had been in his office and had seen that the picture had been moved. He placed the tombstone on top of the remaining manila folders, moved to the light switch, and flicked it off. As he gave his eyes time to adjust to darkness and his heart to stop racing, someone tried the locked office door then inserted a key.

Parker zipped into the adjoining conference room, closed the communicating door, navigated table and chairs without tripping, and peeked out its back door. Sabrina gave him a two-handed signal to crouch and, waving an arm, led him between cubicles and up the center hallway. Glancing back, Parker saw that Shaw's office door was open and the light was on. Sabrina tugged on his hand, and they scurried into Parker's office, locking the door like little kids hiding something scandalous from their parents.

Parker switched off the lights and put a finger to his lips. Standing with their arms and hips touching, their backs against the door, Sabrina smelled fresh as a crisp fall morning. She hadn't worn perfume to the office. A minute later, someone tried his doorknob, surreptitiously, like a burglar would have done it. They held their breath and waited, but the burglar didn't knock or try the knob again.

The Wookiee texted: *All clear.*

Parker crept to the chair behind his desk, and Sabrina sat across from him. He pulled the chain on his banker's light and adjusted the articulated arm until the light was just above his desktop. He slid the folder out from under his shirt and began reading.

"I thought you were looking at a picture in there," Sabrina said.

"It's gone. Shaw moved it after I showed interest in it, and that makes me suspicious. I took this instead: the contract for the ST/IBS partnership."

"Oh." She pulled a pair of red-railed readers out of her expansive natural hairdo.

When Parker found the meaningful sections, he paraphrased them for Sabrina: "IBS has purchased one-third of Shaw Technology stock from Jack Shaw. The money from the stock sale is earmarked for Alexi's artificial intelligence work."

He handed the contract to Sabrina, who murmured as she read. "Upon the third sale of IBS outsourcing services to a Shaw client, IBS will be granted a warrant to buy another third of Shaw stock from Jack Shaw." She sat back. "The additional stock will make Kumar the majority owner of Shaw Technology. This is Shaw's exit strategy."

"Midwestern Assurance in Iowa would be the third sale." Parker paused, thinking. "And Dennie expects to be the next CEO if she can make the sale."

Sabrina flipped through the remaining pages, then stopped abruptly. "One last provision: If three sales aren't made within one year, Kumar can terminate the partnership and require Shaw to repurchase the stock at fair market value. Shaw is out of time."

Sabrina stuck the readers back into her hair and dropped the contract on Parker's desk. He locked it in his center desk drawer. "Let's rejoin the party. Maybe no one will notice we've been away."

The Wookiee was sitting on the stairs.

"Thanks for the warning. Ilya almost caught us," Parker said.

"Not Ilya. I followed Ilya to Alexi's artificial intelligence lab, and he said, 'No one allowed.' I go, 'Looking for Alexi,' and he goes, 'Beat it.'" He looks like Russian Mafia, not as tall as me but thick as a wall, you know? So, I came back to the stairs and that's when I saw Dennie. She took a look in Mr. Shaw's office and then tried your door and then she went back upstairs."

"Alexi thinks he's being sabotaged. Dennie must have noticed we were missing so we can't go back upstairs. Let's slip out the front door and head home."

***

At home, Parker checked the alarm system—the green "safe" light was glowing. The doors to the deck were locked and secure. He didn't expect another intrusion. Meredith was either mulling his counteroffer or she was dead. Upstairs, Paula had passed out in their bed, a vodka bottle spilling its contents onto his pillow, her pistol on her nightstand. He hid the bottle, gazed for a minute at Paula's snoring form, then trudged to the family room to sleep on the couch.

While they sipped coffee in the morning shade on their back deck, Parker told Paula about his meeting yesterday with Kumar.

"Will you get fired?"

"Not yet," Parker said. "Kumar needs me to present the phony numbers to a prospect."

"Will you do it?"

Déjà vu, Parker thought, entangled again in corporate fraud. "Not sure yet."

"We need the damn job, Parker. If we go bankrupt, you can live with your girlfriend, but I'll end up in a cardboard box under a bridge."

Parker's tiresome denial hung in his throat as two men appeared from around the corner of their house. They'd expected a visit, of course, but not at seven o'clock on Saturday morning. Getting no response at the front door, the cops had walked around to the back of the house. Paula reflexively gathered her terrycloth bathrobe around her chest and held it tight under her chin. The cops flashed their badges and apologized for the intrusion.

The big black guy introduced himself as Detective Rawlings and his white partner as Detective Conroy. Rawlings appeared to be a former athlete going soft around the middle. Conroy had the look of a habitual jogger, wiry, with a twitchy demeanor. Probably hadn't been a detective long enough to be cynical and bored.

"We're investigating a missing person report," Rawlings said. "We have a few questions if you don't mind."

Missing person. They haven't found her body.

"Of course," Parker said. "Who's missing?"

The detectives eased closer to the railing on the side of the deck. They made no attempt to climb onto the deck. Parker, experienced in such matters, surmised that this would be an exploratory first encounter.

"Your business partner," Rawlings said, his round face immobile.

"The one who caused you to change your name from Braun to Parker," Conroy said.

"Former business partner, and Meredith wasn't the reason I changed my name," Parker lied. "I have a professional reputation to protect, and I didn't want customers to find my criminal record when they googled my name. You guys know I've been to prison, right?" Acting like he wasn't hiding anything from them.

Conroy and Rawlings traded looks. "We know a lot of things, Mr. Parker," Rawlings said. "We know about Ms. Walker's lawsuit." He cupped his chin with his right hand, stared with eyes the color of chocolate M&Ms, alert to any sign of fear.

Parker gave them a mirthless chuckle. "Like I said, the name change wasn't for the purpose of hiding from her. She found us easily enough and hired a lawyer."

"You reported her, accused her of harassing you," Conroy said to Paula. The young detective reminded Parker of a pit bull on the attack.

"She painted a lurid message on our front door," Paula said. "Then she killed my cat." Paula's southern drawl didn't conceal the contempt she felt for Meredith.

Parker sensed the need to soften Paula's accusations. They sounded too much like a motive for violence. "We can't be sure it was Meredith. Our dispute will be worked out in the courts." He smiled inwardly at his use of the future tense. Cops pick up on references to a missing person in the past tense. He learned that from his "friends" in prison.

Rawlings skipped ahead a few pages in his mental questionnaire. "Have you seen Ms. Walker?"

"Yeah, the other night, the Fourth of July."

Before Rawlings could swallow his surprise and follow up, Conroy said, "Where was that?"

"Right here," Parker said. "She delivered a settlement offer." He picked up the document off the side table and showed it to the cops. "Wanted me to sign it on the spot. It's a good offer, but I told her I had to discuss it with my attorney. We made a counteroffer yesterday."

That statement had the desired effect on Conroy, who was momentarily speechless. Rawlings cupped his chin again, as though it might drop off without support. "Did you go over that offer with her in your house?"

He wants probable cause to search the house. "No, she left it with me, said she had to run," Parker said and stifled a chuckle.

"How did she get here?" Conroy said. "Did she drive?"

Always tell them as much of the truth as you can, Parker, and they'll believe your lies. Another lesson from his cellmates. "She came out of the bushes at the bottom of our yard. We were out here watching the fireworks."

"She didn't want you guys to catch her trespassing on our property," Paula said.

Rawlings turned to look at the dense thicket. "And which way did she go?"

"Back the way she came, through the bushes toward the park," Parker said.

Rawlings's ability to appear expressionless was starting to unnerve Parker. "Why didn't you report her?"

"She was just trying to resolve our dispute," Parker said. "Like I said, it's a good offer."

Tired of the slick responses to his questions, Rawlings took a different tack. "Mind if I ask how you got that bump on your forehead?"

Involuntarily, Parker touched the bruise and winced. "I was under my car trying to find an oil leak. Bumped it on the way out."

"Uh-huh."

Conroy scurried to the front of the deck and used his smartphone to snap a picture of Parker. When he pointed the camera at Paula, she shrieked, "Hey!" and held out a hand to block the detective's view. She still had Band-Aids on her knees. Without makeup, the scratch on her face was a fading crimson swath.

Rawlings smiled. "And you, Mrs. Parker? Did you get into a fight with your trespasser? Maybe she threw something at you and broke that window."

Paula came half out of her chair, but Parker pulled her down. "Nah," he said. "I was practicing chipping balls into a bucket on the porch and bladed one right through the window."

"Uh-huh."

"Let me ask you the obvious question. Who reported her missing? They'd probably know she had been here and where they were supposed to see her next." *I'm not as stupid as I look. She had an accomplice.*

"It was her boyfriend in Florida, Professor Wade Gilbert. You know him, don't you?"

"Yeah, he gave us a hand with our company. Back in the day. But I didn't know Meredith was out of prison until she showed up here, so I didn't know they were dating. Guess he's next man up."

After Meredith had been released from prison, Professor Wade Gilbert had been lured away from his wife and kids by a woman who emitted vibrations that were instinctively detected by the antennae of like-minded men.

"He told us where to find her hotel room, but she's not there."

"How long has she been missing?" Parker asked.

"Depends who you ask. Gilbert hasn't heard from her since Monday, July first, but the desk clerk at the hotel said she was there on Tuesday and Wednesday, and you say she was here on Thursday."

"Sounds like she doesn't want to talk to the professor." Parker knew that cops get suspicious when people being questioned offer alternative solutions like *maybe she's on her way back to Florida.* "After I sign the settlement, she'll turn up to get her check."

"Did you ever see her with anyone else?" Conroy asked.

Do they know she had an accomplice? "Nope."

Conroy fidgeted while Rawlings thought about it. Finally, Rawlings took a long shot. "Mind if we take a look inside?"

Parker laughed out loud. "You know this isn't my first rodeo."

Rawlings snorted. "Okay, Mr. Parker. Thanks for your help. We've issued a BOLO, so I'm sure we'll find her soon." He handed Parker a business card and walked away, down the side of the house. Conroy hesitated, looked unhappy about leaving without someone in handcuffs.

Parker gave them a couple of minutes before walking through the house to a front window. They pulled away in separate unmarked cars, one beige and the other light blue. So they weren't partners.

Parker freshened their coffee and rejoined Paula on the deck.

"Was that legal?" she asked. "Taking pictures of us?"

"Maybe. They'll use them to get a search warrant."

"They'll come back?"

"Over and over until they find Meredith."

"Shit." She made the word sound as if it had three syllables.

Paula walked away as Parker read the cop's card:

Derrick Rawlings
Detective Sergeant
Fulton County Sheriff's Department

Parker's house was in Gwinnett County. *Why would a Fulton County cop question us? Because Meredith's hotel room was in Fulton County.* Conroy hadn't supplied a "business" card, so Parker guessed that he belonged to a Gwinnett County department, and the two departments were cooperating.

The pop of a champagne cork alerted Parker to hurry back to the kitchen, where he found Paula making herself a mimosa in a crystal flute. "Want one?" she asked.

"Do you need that?"

"Yes, honey bear, I do. First Meredith torments us, then you have an affair, and now the cops are up our ass, so I definitely need this." She gulped the drink and refilled her glass.

Parker had long known this moment would arrive. Paula had promised to attend AA meetings, dutifully had left home in the evenings to attend meetings at a church. But Paula was unable to describe her fellow alcoholics or recount any of the shared testimonies. She hid behind a credible cloak of confidentiality that frustrated Parker and caused him to suspect she wasn't attending the meetings. Shamefully, he'd tried to follow her to a meeting, but he'd lost her trail on residential streets in Dunwoody, nowhere near the meeting location. She had driven to a bar, parked on an incline, and neglected to put her gear shift in park. While she was in the bar, her car had rolled backward into a pickup truck. The barkeep found ID in the glove compartment and called Parker. Parker rescued her and bribed the pickup owner, who was as inebriated as Paula, to take cash instead of calling the police. He'd known then that she would never achieve sobriety in Atlanta, but he had deferred their inevitable confrontation.

He lunged for the champagne bottle but Paula clutched it to her chest and whirled away from him.

"You need to stay sober so you don't fuck up the next time the cops question you," Parker said.

Paula's green eyes became hard as stones. "When Meredith turns up alive, I want an apology." Paula loaded ice in a pewter bucket, jammed the champagne bottle into it, and stormed through the French doors to the back deck.

At this point in the progression of her disease, the implements of drinking lent her lifestyle a measure of grandeur. Parker had heard that alcoholics generally fell into one of two categories: happy drunks and violent drunks. Paula was the violent variety. When inebriated, she became argumentative, redressing old wounds and assigning guilt for past transgressions. If Parker disputed her recollections, she resorted to physical violence. She had once slashed him from calf to ankle with a ballpoint pen and, in another argument, raked his face with her sharp fingernails.

With a glass of iced tea—Parker never drank alcohol in his wife's presence—he sat in the other lawn chair, and together they watched the sunset in silence until Paula said, "I know you don't believe me, but I didn't shoot anyone."

"Of course not," he said. "Two bullets just evaporated. Happens with small guns."

"Damn it, Parker! I can't stand it when you call me a liar."

"I'm trying to help you," he insisted. "Maybe we can claim self-defense."

"Okay, Parker, I'll admit it. The gun went off when I tripped, and the bullet went straight into the ground."

Making progress. "And where did the fourth bullet go?"

Paula pushed her unruly hair behind her ears, tilted her head back until her chin pointed at the sky, and took a deep breath. "Maybe the magazine wasn't full."

Had she gotten that idea from Jordyn? "Maybe."

He didn't know if Paula was lying or if she had been too drunk to know what she had done in the thicket. All he could do was wait for the other shoe to drop. How did he feel about his wife, the putative murderer of a woman who just wanted what the courts said she was owed? He felt protective. They had been through a lot together and he owed her his protection no matter the circumstance.

After becoming intoxicated, Paula stumbled up the stairs to the master bedroom to sleep it off. He didn't chase after her. He retreated to his office and called a repairman for the window.

***

After the window repairman replaced the pane in the French door, Parker spent the lonely afternoon cleansing computers and cell phones of all text messages and email notes except those that were privileged communications with his lawyer. The messages he deleted included Paula's angry threats to kill Meredith.

Since Paula hadn't reappeared, Parker's dinner consisted of a peanut butter and jelly sandwich with a glass of milk, eaten at the tall bar table in the kitchen. The local news played on the countertop TV. In Atlanta, as in most major cities, local news is a litany of murders, drug busts, apartment fires, and deadly car crashes on the overburdened arteries that bring suburbanites into the city to work each day. The news had migrated from newsprint to electronic and digital delivery, but the old bromide still applied: if it bleeds, it leads. Of course, political scandals occasionally lightened the mood.

Tonight, the drone of bad news was interrupted by an on-the-scene report. A red banner proclaimed: **Missing Woman Found Dead**. Standing in front of emergency vehicles with their lights flashing, a reporter announced that trout fishermen had discovered a body washed up on a small island in the Chattahoochee River behind the Martin's Landing housing development in Roswell. The shot expanded to include Fulton County Detective Sergeant Derrick Rawlings. The reporter fired questions, and Rawlings deftly deflected them.

Reporter: Is it the Florida woman who was reported missing on the Fourth of July?

Rawlings: The missing person report was made on the third of July. Yesterday her hotel room was found to be vacant.

Reporter (unabashed): And is the body hers?

Rawlings: We're awaiting identification by next of kin.

Reporter: Do you suspect foul play?

Rawlings: The coroner will give us that answer.

Reporter: How long has she been in the river?

Rawlings: The coroner will give us that answer.

Reporter: Where did the body fall into the river?

Rawlings: The coroner's report will help us figure that out.

Reporter: Could it have been in Gwinnett County?

Rawlings, patience exceeded: We'll have more for you as the investigation progresses.

Rawlings walked away, and the camera pulled back for a broader shot of the dramatic scene. Paramedics pushed a gurney loaded with a green body bag through the crowd of cops and onlookers and slid it into an ambulance. A voiceover from the studio inaccurately reminded viewers that a Florida woman, engaged in a legal dispute with her former business partner, had been reported missing on the Fourth of July. Her former business partner, the announcer said, lived in Gwinnett County.

The media had already decided that Parker was a suspect. Rawlings would be next to reach that conclusion. Paula had been sure Parker wouldn't find a body in the thicket because Meredith fell into the water. After Paula had shot her.

A quick intake of breath alerted him to Paula's presence. She stood behind him, her bushy red hair matted with perspiration to the right side of her head, a look of surprise and confusion on her pale face as she watched the TV over his shoulder. His face betrayed an accusation as he looked at his wife.

Although he had feared Meredith was dead from the moment the cops had listed her as missing, a wave of nausea washed over him. He rushed to the guest bathroom to hang over the toilet bowl and dry heave until his stomach muscles knotted and ached. The nausea resulted in part from the graphic depiction of the body bag with Meredith's body in it and in part from fear of what the coroner would find in the autopsy. Holding his stomach with both hands, he shuffled back into the kitchen and sat at the table.

Paula stood over him. "You grieving for that slut?"

Taken aback, he was ready for a fight if that's what she wanted. "Don't guess I'll have to apologize to you since Meredith won't be coming back for her money."

"You don't believe me? You bastard!" She slapped him across the face, and he recoiled.

Rubbing his face, he said, "You're going to get caught."

"I'm not going to get caught," she said. "I'm innocent, don't you get it?" Then she was on him, pummeling him with clenched fists.

Bobbing and weaving, he bounced to his feet and wrapped his arms around her, stopping her flurry of punches. She went limp, and as soon as he relaxed, she sucker-punched him and ran through the living room. "You can sleep on the couch tonight," she said as she ascended the stairs.

The ploy of kicking a man out of bed had always baffled him. Who anointed wives to be bedroom landlords? And why was he being punished when it was Paula who had murdered Meredith?

Meredith. She had the connections to prospective investors and the contacts in the industry to get his science into the marketplace. "I'll do anything to get the money," she had said at their first lunch meeting, and he knew what she meant, but, desperate to make a success of his idea, he had formed the partnership that would haunt him for the rest of his life.

The cops would need a positive identification of the body before doing an autopsy, and they'd need a cause and manner of death before asking a judge for an arrest warrant. That meant the cops would have to wait for next-of-kin to arrive from Florida, which meant he had a day or two to dispose of Paula's gun. The bridge over the Buford dam, where Lake Lanier was over one hundred feet deep, seemed a good spot. He resolved to drive out there in the morning.

Paula's mother, Lillian, skipped Sunday church services to arrive early morning, driven overnight from Lakeland, Florida, by her brother Melvin. Rain streamed from the heavens when they pulled into the driveway. Parker waited under the peaked portico over his front porch as Jordyn met Lillian at the car with an umbrella. Arm-in-arm, they shuffled up the walk, the elderly lady whispering in her granddaughter's ear. Parker had been annoyed when Jordyn had shown up unannounced and uninvited for Sunday breakfast, delaying his plan to take Paula's gun for a swim. Now it was apparent that she and her grandmother had arranged their rendezvous.

"What are you doing here, Lillian?"

"I've come to rescue my daughter." With a nod, Lillian eased past Parker, and Jordyn headed upstairs.

Lillian declined offers of food and drink, so Parker directed her to the family room, where Paula had camped after gagging on the waffles Parker had prepared. Lillian grasped her daughter's elbow and led her down the hallway to Parker's office and closed the door behind them, excluding Parker from the intervention. He and Paula shared a southern heritage, but they came from different branches of the tree. His parents were a Charleston debutante and a carpetbagger from Wisconsin. Her family were gritty Florida crackers—pecan growers and watermelon farmers. Their ideas about southern etiquette and comportment often clashed.

Uncle Melvin accepted a glass of iced tea and a towel to dry his bald head. He took a seat at the kitchen table and made a sincere effort to avoid eye contact as though looking at Parker was tantamount to consorting with the devil. Both men heard the sobs that seeped into their consciousness through the closed office door as the rain seeped into the lawn. Uncle Melvin never spoke a word. The tension numbed Parker's limbs, and inertia glued him to his chair.

Jordyn came downstairs with two suitcases and a small carryall filled with Paula's clothes and toiletries.

"Where are you taking her," Parker said.

"Back to Florida where she belongs."

He sidled up to his daughter as she set the suitcases at the front door. "Take her gun with you to Florida," he whispered. "Throw it off the Sunshine Skyway bridge."

"No way. I'm not going to prison over your fight with a psychopath."

As she started away, Parker tried to grab her arm, but she pulled loose and sauntered into Parker's office without knocking, a courtesy not extended to Parker. Uncle Melvin had his eyes closed, either dozing or praying. Parker trotted to the laundry room and retrieved the putative murder weapon. Tiptoeing, he crept up to the waiting luggage and stuffed the gun into one of Paula's suitcases.

Feigning nonchalance, he took a seat beside Paula's uncle and watched his office door. When it finally opened, he hustled down the hallway, wanting to comfort his wife, but she brushed him aside. "Now you can be with your girlfriend."

"There's no girlfriend," he said to Paula's back, hoping Lillian would believe it.

"I'm never coming back, Parker," Paula said.

"You're going to leave me holding the bag?"

"There's no bag. I didn't do it."

Lillian gave Parker an evil look and dragged her daughter toward the foyer. Without hugs or goodbyes, Lillian, Melvin, Paula, and Jordyn slipped out the front door and down the walk to the car. As Parker trotted behind, drenched by the steady rain, an old orange Japanese sedan sped away from the cul-de-sac and up the street, its mufflers singing a tune like a machine gun. It didn't belong to anyone in his upscale neighborhood.

The suitcases went into the trunk. Then Jordyn helped her mother into the car, cop-like, a gentle hand on Paula's head as she ducked into the backseat. All that was missing from that scene were handcuffs. Jordyn slipped into the driver's seat and started the engine.

Lillian rolled down her window. "I'll send you the bill."

What the hell did that mean?

***

As soon as the rain subsided on Sunday afternoon, Parker's doorbell sounded, followed by heavy pounding on his front door. He didn't need to understand the words they were shouting to guess who was calling on him. The speed with which the cops were pursuing him made Parker's head spin, like that girl in "The Exorcist." He opened the door and there they stood: Frick and Frack.

One beige unmarked cop car rested at the curb, and a Gwinnett County Sherriff's cruiser was parked in the driveway, two uniforms leaning against the hood, waiting for the show to start. All four policemen smiled at Parker, enjoying the moment of intimidation that is every cop's psychological reward for doing dangerous work. Three local TV vans, the ones with satellite dishes on top, came sprinting down the street toward his house.

"How can I help you, Detectives?" Parker said, although he knew why they had come.

Conroy waved a document folded loosely in thirds like the title to a piece of property. "We have a warrant."

Conroy canted his head and watched for a reaction. His poker face intact, Rawlings waited without moving a muscle. Parker's fingers turned to icicles. Blocking the doorway, he held out a hand. "Can I read it, please?"

Expecting to walk through the door without resistance, Conroy bumped chests with Parker, knocking him back a couple of steps. With a small victory smile, he placed the warrant in Parker's hand.

The warrant was narrow in scope: the cops could search Parker's home, car, and property for firearms and the personal possessions of Meredith Walker. The only evidence the cops had was Parker's admission that Meredith had been in his backyard on the Fourth of July and a few pictures of suspicious injuries and property damage. Not enough probable cause for the judge who signed the warrant to allow a broader search. Parker knew, however, that they were searching for firearms because Meredith had been shot. He considered calling his lawyer and asking him to come babysit him, then decided against it. The moment you ask for a lawyer, the cops assume you are guilty and they become infected with tunnel vision. He handed the warrant back to Conroy, shrugged his assent, and moved aside.

"Do you have any weapons, Mr. Parker?" Rawlings said. "Tell us where they are and we won't have to tear your house apart."

Parker congratulated himself for giving Paula's gun a ride in her suitcase. "I'm a convicted felon, Detective. I own no weapons."

"What about the pistol your wife owns?"

Parker must have looked surprised because Rawlings explained, "We checked gun sale records in Florida. Paula Braun—that was her name before you changed it to Parker—bought a .32 caliber Beretta Tomcat three years ago. Nice little pocket pistol, easy to hide, easy for a woman to use. Still have that one?"

Parker pretended to be unaffected. "She needed a gun to protect herself while I was in prison. After I was released, she sold it."

Rawlings twitched slightly. "You happen to have a bill of sale for your wife's gun? Something we can trace?"

Parker flipped his hands palms up. "We've moved several times, Detective. I'll have to look through my records."

"Uh-huh."

The uniformed cops climbed the stairs. Conroy and Rawlings followed Parker into the kitchen, where Parker poured himself a glass of orange juice. He offered juice to the cops.

"No, thank you," Rawlings said.

"Is your wife at home?" Conroy said.

"No, you just missed her. Her mother's been ill, so she went to see her in Florida. Lakeland."

Conroy's narrow brow knitted, drawing sandy hair close to his vague eyebrows. More jurisdictional complications. "When will she be back?"

Parker shrugged. "In a few days, I hope."

Conroy made a note in a small spiral notebook, the kind Joe Friday carried.

Rawlings made a slow circuit of the kitchen, sliding his hand along the granite counters. "Heard the news?"

"Yes, it's tragic. We worked together for a number of years."

"Yeah. Don't guess you'll have to pay her the money you owe her." He canted his head like a dog when it is confused by its master's command.

They've settled on the lawsuit as the motive for murder. Nonchalantly, Parker made his way through the French doors to the back deck. Only neophytes or characters on bad TV shows follow the cops around asking questions. *Am I under arrest? Am I a suspect?* He had no choice but to play it cool.

"I see you've fixed the window." Rawlings pointed at the French door.

"Yeah, the plywood didn't keep the mosquitoes out." Parker sat in a lawn chair and tried to appear calm. He heard the uniforms in the house slamming cupboard doors and rattling pots and pans. Conroy stepped onto the deck and asked for his car keys. Parker told him they were in a dish in the foyer, and the wiry cop rushed back inside. Parker heard him yell, "Bring in the blue lights and spray every inch of this place with luminol."

Whether a check for blood evidence was legal during a narrow search Parker didn't know, but he thought negative results might actually be exculpatory.

Rawlings said, "Did you hear any shots fired when Ms. Walker was here?"

Parker delayed by taking a sip of his orange juice. "The fireworks were going off right over our heads. We wouldn't have heard World War III if it had happened in those woods."

"Uh-huh."

The uniforms came around the house and reported: they had found nothing incriminating in Parker's car. The taller of the pair, with biceps straining his short sleeves said, "Who's hiding the liquor bottles? You or her?"

The cops had been disciplined enough to use a step stool to run their hands through the space between the cupboards in the laundry room and the roof beams. If Paula's gun had still been there, they would have found it.

"My wife overindulges," Parker said. "Those are mine."

"I left them on the washing machine for you."

"Thanks." Parker knew that spouses often hid the alcoholics' bottles instead of throwing them away so that the alcoholic could find them and violate their spouses' trust. It was a means of dominating the person with the disease. But in Parker's case, the bottles he hid were his own rare and expensive ports. Paula never found his bottles; she had her own hiding places.

Rawlings motioned for Parker to follow him into the kitchen, where Conroy snatched Parker's glass from his hand. "I'll take this to the lab, thank you," he said.

"We don't need his prints," Rawlings said. "Mr. Parker is in the system. Anything in here?"

Conroy reluctantly handed the glass back to Parker. "Nothing, Sarge."

Rawlings nodded and said, "Thanks for your cooperation, Mr. Parker." He walked through the house, and Parker followed him.

At the front door, the shorter uniformed cop shuffled a stack of mail. Parker slapped the envelopes out of his hand, and they landed on the floor. The cop backed up with his hands in a surrender position and said, "Just doing you a favor by bringing it inside."

Conroy and the uniforms laughed, but Rawlings remained stoic as he pushed his colleagues through the front door.

"We'll be back," Conroy said over his shoulder.

"We'll have a party," Parker said to their backs. "I'll furnish the donuts."

The media parasites climbed aboard their vans, no arrest to witness today. He gathered the mail and tossed it onto the foyer table. Then he checked his cell phone, which had vibrated while the cops searched his house. He played the voicemail message and heard his daughter say, "That was a dirty trick, Dad. What if Smokey had stopped us and found it?" Jordyn was smart enough not to say "gun" on a recording. Jordyn would keep her mom company for a couple of days, and then she'd need a way back home. "Mom says she'll call you later. She's not in the mood to talk to you at the moment."

He pushed the *Call Back* button and was routed to Jordyn's voicemail. In the sing-songy voice conspirators use to convey a thinly veiled meaning, he said, "I need a sales receipt for that thing your mom sold years ago. You know the thing. Then you should enjoy all the water around you down there. Maybe take a boat ride or a walk across a bridge and leave all your troubles behind. Know what I mean, Jellybean?"

He walked back to the laundry room where the step stool was still positioned in front of the washing machine on which stood three liquor bottles. He replaced them on the rough wood planking beneath the roof. Then he made his way onto the deck and contemplated the inscrutable thicket. No matter how he replayed the events of the Fourth of July, they made sense only if Paula had shot Meredith, who'd fallen into the river. They still made no sense unless Meredith had had an accomplice who'd witnessed the murder. What Parker needed was professional help to find the witness before the cops did.

So he called Ron Gardner, a private investigator in Florida who often worked for Parker's Florida attorney, Vince Romeli. Ron had helped Parker and Vince when Parker had stood trial for a crime he hadn't committed. Parker told him about Meredith's demise.

"It's a sad way for it to end, but now you're free, my friend," Ron said.

"That's exactly why the cops up here suspect I killed her."

Parker walked him through the events on the night of July fourth but didn't mention that Paula had shot at Meredith from the back deck or that she had fired two more shots in the thicket.

"You didn't shoot Meredith or throw her in the river, so it's Paula or Jordyn we're protecting." Ron's raspy smoker's voice reminded Parker of the actor Nick Nolte.

"Paula is who we're worried about. She had a gun."

"And the cops don't know she had a gun?"

"They know she owned a gun but don't know she had it that night. Meredith had an accomplice who hasn't come forward."

"And you want me to find him before the cops do?

"Yeah."

Ron was silent for a moment, then said, "Here's the deal: I'm not licensed in Georgia, so I'm just your fishing buddy, up to console his old friend in a time of stress. My visit has nothing to do with the police investigation. Got it?"

"Yes. Understood."

"Okay, I'm on a job now, but I can get there sometime Wednesday."

"Jesus, we could all be in jail by then."

"Best I can do, buddy."

Parker pulled into the Shaw Technology parking lot and Sabrina climbed into his car. With a grunted "Good morning," he headed for the Interstate highway to Columbia, South Carolina, where they were to meet Kumar's second-in-command, Mani Patek. Parker was apprehensive about this meeting. His first two onsite visits in Connecticut and Iowa had shaken his resolve to work hard for IBS and keep a job he desperately needed. His Meredith/Paula/police problem consumed his thoughts so he couldn't think of anything to say to Sabrina until she broke the ice.

Playfully, she opened the center console, pulled everything out. "It's time I got to know you, now that we're work pals." She pushed things around until she found his iPod. She scrolled through the artists and whistled. "Lots of Motown."

"Back when music was music."

Her eyebrows danced on her forehead. "You about to criticize a unique form of black culture?"

"If you mean rap, it's not in danger of being appropriated by me."

Scrolling through his playlist, she snorted. "You have David Clayton Thomas and Joe Cocker. They *sound* black." She plugged the iPod into the sound system. She queued up the Supremes and coaxed him into singing duets. After that, they rocked along with The Temptations and Aretha Franklin, dancing in their seats. The SUV seemed to roll in rhythm and Parker temporarily forgot his problems. Until they reached Shaw's Columbia office and walked into the bullpen.

A line of employees had formed outside a glass-walled conference room. Some employees wore shocked expressions; others sobbed quietly.

"Peterson. Blankenship. Jones. Atkinson. Quintana. Day. Schulze. Nielsen. Carroll ..." As Carolyn Burke called the names, the selected employees walked to the gallows in chilling silence, the only sound the sniffles of a black woman with tears streaming down her face. "Carroll. That's me, Jasmine Carroll," she said.

Carolyn waved at her to get in line.

Parker handed Jasmine his handkerchief and watched the uncalled employees who seemed to intuit the logic of it, calculating the probability that their time was near. Parker had figured it out: the fired employees were black and brown women. White women continued to answer incoming calls.

Her eyes dry but red-rimmed, Jasmine gave the handkerchief back to Parker. "I've been here fifteen years, and now you do this."

Parker wanted to deny any role in the proceedings, but Sabrina touched his arm, and he kept his mouth shut.

"We're sorry, Jasmine," Sabrina said.

Carolyn watched the parade with dead eyes as she prodded the condemned through the doors to the large meeting space at the far end of the floor.

"It's like cows at a slaughterhouse," Parker said to Sabrina, "herded through the narrow gap to meet the man with the stun-gun, the thing Chigurh used in *No Country for Old Men*."

A woman in a nearby cubicle heard him and spoke up. "That's why we only bring in what we can carry out in one box. Too embarrassing to make two trips to the parking lot."

Mani approached them with a scowl on his face. "You shouldn't be watching this shit. You've got work to do." He shepherded them into the conference room beside Jack Shaw's office. The connecting door was closed, no way to know if Shaw was in his office or part of today's operation.

"Why are they losing their jobs?" Sabrina asked.

"The seats are moving to the IBS center in Manila," Mani said. "Cost savings."

"You call them seats?" Sabrina said. "These are real jobs and real people."

"They are seats because they are shared by three shifts. We calculate our cost per seat, not per associate."

"These people make barely more than minimum wage," Parker said. "How can it save money?"

"In Manila, the cost is even lower, and they are better educated and speak better English than these people in South Carolina." He pronounced it *Car-o-leena*. "We're taking the seats that require a neutral accent to support national accounts. The ones that service local agents will remain here where they appreciate the southern dialect."

Beads of perspiration formed on Parker in multiple places at once: his forehead, his underarms, under the collar of his shirt. He removed his jacket and used his handkerchief to blot the beads on his forehead. "I just want to do my job and get out of here," he said. "What do you need from me?"

"Mr. McPherson and his team leads will join you after the announcement. You," he pointed to Parker, "work with them to predict call volumes, call arrival times, and call length. That will help us run Manila efficiently. This place too."

Mani turned to Sabrina. "Your job is to prepare a press release, something to explain this change to the locals before the employees talk to the press." Then he turned on his heel and left.

"Just when you think slavery has ended, you realize that the master has invented a new way to do it," Sabrina said.

"What?"

"Once upon a time, we brought the slaves to the work, now we send the work to the slaves. The new slaves work for peanuts, and the old slaves are dumped on the street."

Parker didn't have time to respond as a ruddy-faced, overweight man of about forty came into the room. He leaned on the table and said, "What a day."

"Are you Mr. McPherson?" Parker said.

"Call me Scoot. Everyone does."

"Are they being treated fairly? Severance and so forth?" Sabrina said.

"Ain't nothin' fair about losing your job," Scoot said.

"Of course. I mean—"

Parker talked over the top of her. "I'm sorry for the bad timing, Scoot, but I need to talk to your team leads, and then I'll get out of your way."

"You're the efficiency expert, right? Know all about my operation."

"No." Parker shook his head. "I'll build analytic models of your call traffic. You might see ways to better align your staff."

A heavy sigh came from the overburdened man. "Alright. I know this ain't your fault. You need the ones that are stayin' or all of 'em?"

"All of them, Scoot. They want models for Manila too."

"Ah sincerely hope y'all sleep better tonight than I will." Scoot left to retrieve the team leads.

Parker walked around the table and put an ear to Shaw's office door.

"What are you doing?" Sabrina said. Her voice conveyed her fear that Parker was about to embark on new mischief.

"If Shaw's in there, I want to ask him why he's allowing Kumar to move these jobs. It's not in the contract."

Hearing no noises, Parker cracked the door and peeked inside. The office was empty, so he stepped into it. Through windows on the far wall, the Gamecocks' football stadium loomed large in the near distance. On the wall beside the door hung more mounted fish, but they weren't trout. They were saltwater fish of some kind. Turning in the other direction, he saw it—the group picture he had seen first in Shaw's Atlanta office. It now hung behind Shaw's desk in the Columbia office.

Leaning through the doorway, Parker said to Sabrina, "See what people are doing out there."

She hesitated. He jabbed a finger at the conference room door. Shaking her head in amazement at Parker's pranks, she walked to the door and peeked into the bullpen.

"They're packing up their desks. Some are moving in a line toward the outer doors. No one coming our way."

Parker hurried behind the desk to have a close look at the picture. Jack Shaw was easy to spot, the tallest person in the picture, in the back row next to men who must have been the agency's namesake owners. Parker leaned toward the picture, examining the faces more closely. The short woman in the first row, fourth from the left, the woman with wavy dark hair, blazing eyes, and a confident look on her face, looked like his mother. He placed a finger on her face, as though to feel her presence.

Alice Parker had never been a shy, retiring young woman. If Jack Shaw had somehow failed to meet her at the university, he couldn't possibly have failed to know her or known *of* her when she worked for Jack's father. A sudden chill crawled up Parker's spine and clutched his brain. The picture was dated the year before his birth and, therefore, his birth father could be one of the young men in this picture.

Alice Parker had never hidden the fact that her husband, Karl Braun, wasn't Parker's birth father. "I will tell you no lies," she had said. Braun adopted Parker and he was a good provider and a caring guardian for young Parker and his brother, but Parker yearned to understand why his real father was not in his life. His mother may not have told Parker any lies, but she hadn't told him the honest story either. "Marriage was out of the question," was all his mother would say. Her reluctance to reveal the identity of his birth father became a source of lifelong discord between them. "You aren't defined by your father's identity," she had said. "You'll be defined by the choices you make in life."

And then another thought broke the ice in his brain: Jack Shaw knew the identity of Parker's father and hid this picture to keep Parker from finding out.

Parker lifted the picture off the wall and took it back into the conference room, where he handed it to Sabrina along with the keys to his car. "Get in line and carry this out to my car. Put it in the trunk."

Sabrina's eyes grew wide. "Why me?"

Parker gave her a don't-play-dumb look. "You'll fit in with the others. They aren't firing any middle-aged white men."

Her shoulders slumped. He placed a hand on the small of her back, above her narrow waist, and gently pushed her through the door. She got in line between two black women carrying cardboard boxes. None of the fired employees gave Sabrina a second look as she filed out the door.

***

"Where are we going?"

"It's time you met the family."

Sabrina laughed and gave Parker's shoulder a playful push. "Is this a joke?"

"Uncle Hugh is my mother's only surviving relative, in fact, the only relative I ever met. You'll like him."

He turned onto leafy Pendleton Street and into the lot beside Brookhaven Terrace, a white, multistory colonial perched among sleepy willow trees that was now an upscale retirement home for the well-to-do elderly. They walked up the sidewalk and through the oaken double doors. Patti, the nice receptionist, recognized Parker. "Something for your uncle's room?"

She meant the picture he had stolen from Shaw's office. "Something like that."

"He's in the great hall," she said. She pointed to another set of double doors.

Brookhaven Terrace was the converted antebellum mansion of a wealthy merchant, and the great hall—airy, marble floors, frescoed ceilings—had been the man's ballroom. Parker hesitated on the threshold; he'd felt a cold draft, as though he had been touched by a spirit, and he shivered. His mother had died unexpectedly in a room on the third floor just three months ago, and her memorial service had been conducted in this room. That was the last time Parker had seen his estranged half-brother, Luke Braun, and the encounter had been unpleasant. Luke had declined the opportunity to eulogize his mother.

"You do it. You were her favorite," Luke had said.

"She had two kids, Luke."

"She should be happy I showed up."

"You're right, your father only bothered to send flowers."

So, Parker delivered the eulogy, lauding Alice Braun's courage, praising her undaunted optimism, entertaining the mourners with funny anecdotes that revealed his mother's pluck and resilience.

"Parker." Sabrina shook his arm. "Are you alright?"

With his mother's passing, Parker had no way to find his birth father. *It doesn't matter, it doesn't matter, it doesn't matter,* he had told himself. But, of course, it still mattered.

"I haven't been here since my mother's memorial service," he said.

They stepped into the room, and Parker scanned the crowd. This morning the great hall was filled with well-dressed seniors drinking after-breakfast coffee and socializing. Parker's uncle sat in an electric wheelchair at a square table-for-two with his gal friend, Arlene. Hugh could walk but jetting about in the wheelchair was more fun than shuffling around with a cane.

Parker pointed to him. "That's him."

Sabrina linked her arm in Parker's and patted his shoulder. When Hugh noticed Parker approaching, his eyes lit up like candles on a birthday cake, then clouded over at the sight of Sabrina hanging on his nephew.

Parker nuzzled Arlene's powdered cheek and stooped to hug his uncle. "You guys look good." Arlene was a shapely bottle blonde who wore a bit too much makeup, and Hugh was tall and slender, cleanshaven and clear-eyed, with trimmed silver spikes on his head.

"Paula didn't come along?" Hugh asked.

"Business trip," Parker explained. He swept a hand toward Sabrina. "This is my colleague, Sabrina Mitchell."

She pranced forward like a proud African queen, and Parker wondered if she was being intentionally provocative. Sabrina had her hair under a measure of control, her kinky curls pinned above her ears but bushy on top and in back. Hugh and Arlene gave her appraising smiles and courteously shook Sabrina's hand. Sabrina turned circles, taking in the opulence and ambiance.

A black waiter in a white waistcoat and black bowtie offered to find chairs and tea.

"We can't stay, have to get back to Atlanta," Parker said. "But I have quick question for you." He rested the picture on the table in front of Hugh. "Did you know these people, back in the day?"

A positive nod, pursed lips. "Knew of them. They were in a different end of the business."

"Tell me if I'm imagining things, but is that my mother in the front row?"

Hugh leaned forward; Arlene craned her neck. "That's her. While she was living with Norman," he said.

For Sabrina's benefit, Parker said, "Norman was my uncle's best friend. That's how my mother met him."

Sabrina's lips made a perfect O.

Hugh said, "She worked there even after she graduated. Most interns were just for the summer. Then she up and quit. Surprised everyone. 'Course we know why she left..." He let the words die in the air.

Again, for Sabrina, Parker explained, "My mother got pregnant but wasn't married, which was a scandal back then. Her Charleston socialite parents banished her to an unwed mother's home, where she was supposed to put the baby up for adoption. She didn't stay there. She ran away and had the baby—

me—in a private hospital. My grandparents disowned her and never figured out who paid the hospital bill."

"Norman!" Hugh said. "But his parents wouldn't let him marry Alice, and our parents certainly wouldn't have blessed a marriage to Norman. In their eyes, he was beneath her."

Sabrina's mouth formed another perfect O.

"Recognize anyone else in the picture?" Parker asked his uncle.

Hugh squinted and moved his finger across the glass. "Old Man Shaw. Old Man Ross. And this one," he pointed to a tall young man, "was Shaw's kid. He's still around, I think."

"Yeah, he has an office over by the football stadium. Did you know him when you were at the University?"

A barely perceptible shake of Hugh's head. "He was in Alice's class, I think. A couple of years behind me." Hugh took a moment to recall what he remembered from years ago. "The kid chased all the skirts. 'Course he was a good catch—handsome and wealthy—so the girls chased him too." Hugh craned his neck to look over his shoulder. "See that old bitty with the purple hair?" He pointed to a woman on the other side of the Great Hall.

"Yeah—"

"She worked for the kid, I think, but now she's got bats in her belfry."

"Isn't that a nice coincidence. I'll just say hello to her." Before Hugh could object, Parker walked between tables and introduced himself to the woman who said her name was Irene. He asked her about her days at Shaw's insurance agency, and she perked right up, like a desert flower after a rare rainfall.

"I was his private secretary for fifteen years," she said.

"Jack Shaw's secretary?"

"No, Buford J. Shaw. Didn't want anyone calling him Buford. Went by John."

"Ah, Old Man Shaw. Do you remember Alice Parker?"

"Couldn't miss her. A firecracker, that one."

"Did she hang around with Jack Shaw?"

Irene ducked her head and snickered. "It's a secret," she whispered.

"It's okay. You know she passed away."

"Of course. I was at the service." Indignant that Parker would have thought she had breached social etiquette. "Well…it was all hush-hush, but I knew about the baby."

Was Irene implying that Jack Shaw is his father? Is that why Jack appeared genuinely sad at the news of Alice Parker's passing? Old Man Shaw must have paid for his mother's stay at the hospital to protect the family reputation.

"She ran away before anyone knew she was pregnant. Is that how you remember it?"

"Of course. Caught the three of 'em arguing about it, and then she was gone. It was a secret."

Maybe they'd given Alice some money to go to Florida, where she'd raised young Parker. Irene didn't have bats in her belfry; she just knew something Hugh didn't want to believe. He kissed Irene on the cheek and returned to his uncle's table.

"She was nice, Hugh." Parker hefted the picture, preparing to depart.

"Why do ya wanna know about the old days?" Hugh asked.

"Because Jack Shaw denied knowing my mother."

"Where'd ya find the picture?"

"On Jack Shaw's office wall."

Hugh and Arlene hugged Parker and politely waved goodbye to Sabrina.

***

"What are you going to do with the picture?" Sabrina asked.

"I'm going to hang it back on Jack's Atlanta office wall, of course."

"That should get a rise out of him. Now where are we going?"

"I never leave town without having shrimp-and-grits at the Blue Marlin restaurant. They're the best in South Carolina." Parker pronounced it *Car-o-leena*, mocking Mani.

They parked on Gervais Street and walked a block to the restaurant. Parker suppressed an impulse to take her hand, an irresistible urge to experience her as one might a work of art.

"One hell of a place your uncle is in. Must cost a fortune," she said.

"He was an executive at Colonial Life. Knew how to invest his money."

A few steps later, she said, "Didn't see any black folks. Except for the waiters, of course." She stared straight ahead.

Parker cleared his throat. "You didn't see any Jews or Catholics either."

"Would you consider that discrimination?" Still not looking at Parker.

"Hugh would say that he can afford to live where he wants and with whom he wants. In his mind, other folks are free to have their own places where white protestants aren't welcome."

"He's exercising white privilege, Parker."

"No, Hugh is exercising financial privilege, which, by the way, most white folks don't have the money to exercise."

"You're glad you're white, aren't you?"

That stopped him and he turned to look at his colleague. He had never thought of being born white as a bit of good luck. "I have to admit it's easier to live as a white person."

"There ya go. White privilege isn't an economic condition, it's the freedom to live without the fear of racial bias."

"I get it." Parker held the door of the restaurant for her. They were early for dinner and took a private booth. He insisted she try the house specialty.

After the waiter departed, she folded her hands on the table. "You shy away from talk about race."

"I only know what it's like to be me. Seems stupid to offer opinions about things I don't know. White people can't possibly know what it's like to be black."

She gave him a derisive laugh. "Hang with me, and you'll find out."

She waited for the server to set their bowls of grits, thick with cheese and topped with shrimp, in front of them. She waved her spoon at Parker. "I know what you're doing with that picture, looking for your father. Your uncle thinks your dad was his friend, Norman, but you aren't convinced."

"I know he's wrong. When my mother passed, I put her affairs in order and found the record of a paternity test done at the private hospital. Norman's parents had insisted on the test and were relieved, I imagine, when he failed the test. My birth certificate lists my father as 'Unknown.' Someone else picked up the hospital bill, and the secret of my birth father's identity went to the grave with my mother."

"Do you resent her for not revealing who your father was?"

"I'd hate to admit to resentment, but she did leave a hole in my heart."

"Did she ever marry?"

"Oh, yes. Karl Braun wasn't a bad guy—very German, cold and stern. My mother was a different story, a political radical and a free spirit with no respect for rules. That drove Karl nuts. They had one boy together, my half-brother Luke, and he raised Luke his way, and my mother raised me her way. It drove them apart, and I always felt I was at fault somehow. Karl left her when I was twelve and went back to Milwaukee or somewhere up north."

"So, you did grow up without a father. You were lucky to be close to your mother."

"I don't think close is the right word for it. She was warm and supportive, but she never shared her feelings or any secrets."

"And now she's gone but you think you can fill that hole in your heart with Jack Shaw."

"Irene said that Jack and his father argued with my mother about the baby, which was me. Maybe Jack's embarrassed to admit that they wanted her to give the baby up for adoption, then paid her off and banished her from Columbia. Why else would he deny he knew any Parkers?"

Sabrina covered Parker's hand with hers. "If Jack is your father, we'll figure it out." She shook her spoon at him. "You may not know your real father, but there's no doubt that you're white European of some kind."

"I doubt I'm German like my stepdad. They love rules, and I hate them."

"Already knew that about you. Tell me something personal I don't know."

He pretended to think about it, as though he were forming a profound answer. "Mustard, rice, pepper, and lime."

"Huh?"

"Condiment, starch, spice, and fruit. White Europeans prefer ketchup, potatoes, salt, and lemon. I'm not like them."

She laughed an appreciative belly laugh. "Sorry, white boy, you're stuck with your ancestors."

"And so are you. What's your story, Sabrina Mitchell?"

Sabrina's eyes swept over his face, then around the dining room in which half the tables were occupied by black couples, then back to Parker's face where her eyes met his. "I've traced my roots to a man named Musa Oyawale, who arrived in South Carolina from Nigeria in the eighteen-twenties. The importation of slaves had been illegal since 1808, but they were still being smuggled into the country. The Virginia man who bought him called him Moses and paired him up with a woman he named Esther. Real God-fearing, Old Testament kind of guy. Now I'm getting the last laugh. I've filed to get my ancestral name back—Oyawale means 'the river goddess has come home.'"

"That's beautiful," he said. "The name 'Mitchell' came from the man who bought Musa, I suppose."

"No, Chester Woodhouse bought Musa off the boat. Samuel Mitchell came later when he bought one of Musa's daughters and had children with her. A lot of black people today have the blood of slave owners in their veins. Tommy Jefferson wasn't the only master who couldn't keep his hands off the help." A gleam in her eye, she snapped her fingers. "You know that's the solution to our racial problems. Black men can't keep their hands off white women, and white men find black chicks irresistible. In a few hundred years humans will come in just one flavor—mocha—and no one will know who had been white and who had been Black."

That made Parker laugh. "Well, I applaud you for claiming your real name. We're not all that lucky. But who is this stylish, articulate business executive I'm having dinner with?"

A self-deprecating smile formed on her lips. "All behavior I learned along the way. I'm a farm girl at heart. After the Civil War, my forebears were sharecroppers until they migrated to California and became farmers in the Central Valley. Farming is like walking on a treadmill. It puts food on your table, but what you make this year is reinvested so you can do it all over again next year. We weren't poor, but sometimes it felt that way. I went to public schools."

"And Stanford."

"Scholarships and a bunch of loans, or it would never have happened."

"And after that?"

She took a deep breath, exhaled slowly. "I don't think I've managed my career very well. I blame it on Silicon Valley, the lure of instant wealth. I worked for a succession of failed startups, then copped out and went to work for a large technology firm where there was a tinted glass ceiling if you get my drift."

"I do. Now you're a long way from home."

"Thought I'd try being a big fish in a small pond. And I wanted to experience the South. It's not what I thought it would be, more of an anthropological experiment."

"Find any interesting specimens to study?"

A raucous laugh erupted. "What you think I've been doing for the last fifteen minutes?"

***

Once they were on the interstate, Sabrina plugged in Parker's iPod again and played more Motown music, but the effervescent mood of the morning's drive couldn't be recreated. After several miles, she gave up on the singing and dancing. "Were you going to tell me about your past problems with the law?"

"HR was supposed to keep that a secret."

"Fat chance of that."

"Afraid to be with me?"

She rolled her eyes. "Some sort of white-collar crime is my guess. All those numbers you cook up."

"No, I shot a man." Sabrina caught her breath, an audible, reflexive, fearful intake. He smiled inwardly at his attempt to shock her, a test. "Assault with a deadly weapon. The prosecutor wanted attempted murder and kidnapping, but the judge threw those charges out."

"Kidnapping? There's got to be more to the story."

"Oh, yeah, lots more. I disarmed a woman to keep her from shooting me. Her accomplice was about to take a shot at me, but I got the drop on him and shot him."

Her whole body shook, and her head teeter-tottered on her neck. "Sounds like self-defense to me. Did you have a bad lawyer?"

"He was okay, a friend." Parker decided to tell her the official version that anyone could find in the trial transcripts. "Their story was that he was preventing rape and that I shot first. My bullet lodged in his L3 vertebra, right at the beltline, and he was paralyzed from the waist down. He said he'd been shot in the back by a coward. My story was that he stalked me and shot first intending to kill me, so I defended myself. We claimed protection under Florida's "no duty to retreat" law—you've probably heard it called "stand your ground"—but it didn't work. He said his gun went off when fell and the jury sympathized with the crippled Navy Seal and Iraq war hero who was trying to rescue a damsel in distress."

"Are you bitter about that?"

"Hell, yes! Official estimates are that four to five percent of the people behind bars are innocent, but I'd say it's more like twenty percent. It wasn't the first time the justice system got it wrong and it won't be the last."

She nodded in agreement. "Mostly black men," she said. "Slavery has evolved into incarceration."

Parker snorted. "Believe me when I tell you that a prosecutor in pursuit of a conviction could give a shit less what color the defendant is. Once I was charged, I was a chunk of meat thrown to a voracious predator. Your people just give them more opportunities."

"My 'people' are easy targets for racist cops." She fell silent for several miles. "Who was the woman? The one you supposedly kidnapped?"

"My former business partner, Meredith Walker." He paused, afraid Sabrina would connect the dots to the body from the Chattahoochee River, but she waited for the rest of the story.

"We were supposed to sign an agreement to dissolve our partnership, which would have left me the intellectual property. She was there to kill me so the company assets would be hers."

"Did they arrest her for attempted murder?"

"No. When the cops arrived, they found Meredith wrapped in a towel and hiding in a closet, claiming I had tried to rape her. They retrieved her purse from the bottom of my pool and found a loaded pistol in it. She said it was obvious she had needed it for protection."

Sabrina looked out the passenger side window and remained silent. Some women, Parker knew, were attracted to dangerous men, while others were repelled. He wondered which Sabrina would be.

Several more miles passed before she sat up straight and looked at him. She had made up her mind, but she let his past drop and probed a different dimension of Parker's character. "

You should devote as much energy to stopping these people as you do to finding your birth father."

Maybe Sabrina was a spirit, a nagging conscience that had become corporeal and inhabited his work environment. "Stopping what people?"

"Kumar and Shaw. They're ruining people's lives, and we're helping them."

"You mean Kumar and Dennie, not Shaw."

"You want to exempt Shaw because he might be your father? He made the deal with Kumar; he hasn't stopped Dennie; he didn't lift a finger to prevent his people from getting fired today. I have to stop all of them, Parker." She looked dead serious. "Or I'll have to resign."

Parker blew air, a deep sigh. He didn't want to argue with her. "I wouldn't blame you. I don't have that luxury."

They lapsed into silence for the last hour of the drive, Parker sorting through the problems he faced—marital problems, Paula's drinking problem, work problems, financial problems, and the mystery of what had happened in the thicket.

He stopped behind Sabrina's car in the office parking lot. "Thanks for the company."

She opened her door, then leaned back in. "I'm not afraid to be with you." Before he could think of a witty retort, she strutted around the front of his car, her backside swaying to some rhythm in her head.

At home, sleep eluded him as thoughts about Paula and Sabrina battled for prominence in his mind. Paula was right to be wary of Sabrina, but she was wrong to mistrust him. That's where the argument stood when he nodded off.

Craving coffee, Parker looked for his favorite cup, a logo mug that was the last remnant of his days at the company he co-founded with Meredith. It wasn't in its usual place on his desk or on his conference table or on his credenza. He walked to the breakroom, thinking his shared assistant, Tanya, may have washed it and left it on the drying rack. It wasn't there. Someone had misappropriated his personal mug. He took a standard Shaw Technology cup from the cupboard and made black coffee. Then he began returning calls he had missed yesterday.

Minutes later, Sabrina entered his office without knocking, noted that he was speaking on the phone, and closed the door behind her. She set a cardboard tray on his conference table and offloaded two Starbucks coffees, a cheese Danish for him and a blueberry muffin for herself. Then she took a seat and waited for him to end his call.

"I thought about it all night," she said.

Not sure which "it" had cost her sleep, Parker uncapped his coffee and smiled. Vanilla latte. "How did you know?"

"Tanya told me it's your usual Starbucks."

"It's nice to have a good assistant. So, what kept you awake last night?" Parker knew what kept him awake and hoped Sabrina didn't have the same nightmares.

"The woman they pulled from the river."

Uh oh. "What about her?"

"Is she the one who tried to kill you? The one who got you sent to prison?"

"Yes."

A sharp inhale. Sabrina had put two and two together. "Did you have an altercation with her? Was it an accident?"

He was mentally sorting through possible answers when Tanya stuck her head in the door to interrupt them. "You have a visitor in the lobby, Mr. Parker. Code Blue if you know what I mean."

Parker wasn't aware there was a color-coding system for visitors, but he interpreted Code Blue to mean his visitor was a cop. Sabrina reached the same conclusion. She closed the door, leaned against it, folded her arms, and crossed one ankle over the other.

"Did you do it?"

"I had nothing to do with it, Sabrina." Fearing he wouldn't return, he slipped into his navy blazer, gathered his briefcase and car keys. "If they let me go, can you pick me up at the police station?"

"Won't your wife do that?"

He motioned for her to move away from the door, but she held her ground. "She's gone to her mother's house in Florida."

"Oh." Sabrina's chest rose and fell as she considered the question. "Yes. I'll pick you up."

As he walked through the bullpen and down the hallway to the lobby, Parker got plenty of side-eye from his coworkers. News of his visitor had spread throughout the company like a wildfire in a California canyon.

Rawlings waited in the lobby, feet spread and hands clasped in front of his groin. The receptionist hovered behind her counter, awestruck, soaking up the drama that rarely enlivened work at Shaw Technology.

As Parker approached Rawlings, Jack Shaw came through the front doors and identified the unknown visitor as a cop. He stopped and looked from Parker to Rawlings and back again. "Everything okay here?"

Parker reassured him with a nod. "Yeah, all good."

Shaw gave him a doubtful look. "When you're done here, come see me."

"Sure." *He wants to talk about the picture.*

Shaw slipped through the inner doors to the office.

To Rawlings, Parker said, "Now what?"

"I need you to come with me to the Fulton County Medical Examiner's office."

Parker played dumb, something he had become quite good at. "Are we talking about the body you pulled from the river? I've resigned myself to Meredith's death."

"Why I'm here is we don't have a positive ID yet."

"You're asking me to ID her? Why not her family?"

Rawlings shouted like a drill sergeant. "Do I need to use the handcuffs?"

An audible gasp escaped the receptionist's lips.

"No, let's go," Parker said to Rawlings. Without handcuffing or reading the prisoner his rights, the detective followed Parker as he moved toward the outer doors.

The recovery of Meredith's body had been broadcast by all the local TV channels and made the front page of the morning newspapers. Connecting the dots between a pissed-off business partner, a visit by a detective, and a dead body was child's play for Shaw's nosy employees.

One beige unmarked cop car rested at the end of the front walkway. Knowing how police transportation worked, Parker stopped beside the back door. The detective opened it, and Parker climbed in. Sitting behind a screen that separated the driver from the prisoner, between locked doors that couldn't be opened from the inside, Parker felt as though he was back in jail already.

"Won't take long. Just confirm we pulled Meredith from the river," Rawlings said.

Parker grunted. They both knew who the medical examiner had on a slab.

Rawlings turned on the radio, and the car filled with gospel music. "That's the Ebenezer Baptist Church choir, where Dr. King preached. Heavenly, ain't it?"

Parker thought praying might just be his last resort.

Rawlings parked illegally in front of a two-story, Georgia-red brick building just south of the downtown gaggle of high-rise hotels and office buildings and opened the back door for Parker. Without a word or change in facial expression, the detective waved a hand at waist level, a signal for Parker to follow him through double glass doors and down a hallway to a set of stairs that emptied into a cold, dimly lit basement. Parker shivered as nervous perspiration evaporated off his skin. Solid steel doors interrupted yellow tile walls above a floor of poured concrete. Rawlings led the way down another hallway and around two corners before stopping. On either side of the hallway, large windows with embedded blinds hid grisly scenes. Further down the hallway, just out of earshot in a recessed alcove, Meredith's son, Cole, sat on a plastic chair.

Parker was shocked by the kid's appearance: the chubby, bullied teenager had grown into a young man. The baby fat was gone, replaced by solid muscle. He was well-groomed in the current style with short caramel hair that stood up in front, like prongs springing from the top of his forehead. He wore black, horn-rimmed glasses. A backpack, stuffed two feet thick, rested against the legs of his chair.

"You already have family to make ID." Parker hissed at Rawlings. "Why'd you drag me down here?"

"The problem is, he refuses to do it alone."

"You want me to hold his hand?" Disbelief cloaked Parker's question like gravy on mashed potatoes.

"That's the idea. You know him, and you know her. Help the poor kid out."

Although Parker had socialized often with the kid and his mother, the two had never developed a warm relationship, and after Cole's father, Duncan Hardy, was shot and his mother, Meredith, went to prison, the kid had developed a searing-hot hatred for Parker. Rawlings sounded compassionate, but he had an ulterior motive—he could not advance his case without a positive ID. And after that, did they expect him to confess to the murder, or would they simply arrest him on suspicion?

Just then, a tall, skinny guy carrying a clipboard and wearing pale blue nursing scrubs and a color-coordinated hairnet stepped out of the door beside the window on the left. To Rawlings, he said, "We're ready when you are."

Rawlings gave Parker a not-so-gentle shove toward Cole. The kid jumped to his feet, his lips trembling, face flushed, fists clenched at his side.

"First it was my dad, and now it's my mama! You're a monster, Parker."

Rawlings stepped between the two men, a smirk on his usually placid face. "Stay calm, young man. Mr. Parker will make the identification, and all you have to do is sign the form."

"It's back to prison for you, Parker." Cole pointed around Rawlings, at Parker.

"This way, Mr. Parker," Rawlings said. He nudged Parker toward the window.

They're making me knot my own noose. "Okay, okay." Parker stepped up to the window, and Cole stopped short in front of the door. Rawlings moved to the end of the corridor to speak on his phone, probably letting his team know that an arrest was imminent. The attendant stepped inside and a moment later opened the blinds.

The body lay on a gurney under a white sheet. The attendant caught Parker's eye and inclined his head in a question. Parker nodded. Carefully, the attendant pulled the sheet back to expose only the face. The body had been in the water for forty-eight hours before being refrigerated, and under the garish fluorescent lighting, her face was a bloodless gray. Blonde hair was matted to her grotesquely swollen head. She had traveled twenty-four miles over rocks and submerged trees and suffered bruises on her forehead and right cheekbone and a gash on her chin. Her lips were blue. Death is a mask, but Parker recognized her, nonetheless.

He pushed Cole away from the door. "Don't look."

Parker opened the door and went inside the freezing room.

The attendant yelled, "You can't be in here!"

"Does she have a tattoo on her right butt cheek? Monarch butterfly?"

The guy looked nonplussed. "I didn't do the examination."

At the head of the gurney, Parker stooped to inspect her sallow complexion, a deception to catch the attendant off-guard. Without warning, Parker yanked the sheet down, exposing her upper body to the waist.

"What the hell?" the attendant screamed. He tried to pull the sheet up, but Parker held it fast.

A bruise on this body's ribcage and many abrasions were visible, but the wounds that caught Parker's attention were a small red hole on her right arm, near the shoulder joint, and a rupture the size of a silver dollar on the back of the arm. Three inches of elastic skin and fatty tissue remained connected on the side of her arm, creating a tunnel through which a bullet had traveled.

Facially, this woman looked like Meredith, but none of her wounds obscured her identifying characteristic: A-cup breasts on a chest the color of Elmer's glue. Without makeup, nail polish, gaudy jewelry, and flashy clothes, Meredith's excessively augmented breasts and deep tan would still have identified her.

Drawn to the commotion, Cole came through the door and stopped at the foot of the gurney. For a moment, the kid stared at the incongruous vision of a half-naked body, then his shoulders slumped, and his eyelids drooped, betraying his loss of innocence.

"This isn't Meredith Walker," Parker told the attendant. "This is her sister, Grace."

The attendant staggered away from the gurney. Cole collapsed to his knees, hands over his face. His glasses clattered to the floor as he sobbed silently. His pain was evident, raw, and heart-wrenching to witness. The scene was too invasive and too intimate for Parker, as revolting as being spattered with someone else's blood.

"You'll have to retype that form," Parker said, pointing to the attendant's clipboard. "Grace Anne Walker is her name. Her nephew can give you her birthdate."

Parker moved behind Cole and placed his hands on Cole's shoulders. The kid leaned back to rest his buttocks on his heels, drawing strength from Parker's kind gesture. The attendant took the opportunity to cover the body.

"I'm so sorry, Cole. I know what she meant to you."

After several minutes of rocking and shaking, Cole rose unsteadily, his benediction complete. They left the body in the attendant's care, left the cold room, and started down the hallway. Rawlings approached them; two uniformed cops lurked behind the detective.

His arm around the boy, Parker walked Cole toward Rawlings. "You've got the wrong woman. That's Meredith's sister, Grace."

"Who?"

They brushed past Rawlings and eased around the two uniforms. "We'll wait upstairs. The attendant can bring us a corrected form, and Cole will confirm the ID. You'll need to let her parents know."

Rawlings's deadpan expression was replaced by pure shock, his case destroyed. He had the wrong body and no motive.

Rawlings didn't let them loiter in the lobby. Following standard police procedure, the cops took Parker and Cole to separate interview rooms and questioned them simultaneously. Parker's interview was brief: yes, he was certain that it had been Meredith at his house on the Fourth of July; no, Grace hadn't been with Meredith; no, he didn't know Grace was in Atlanta; and, no, he hadn't seen or spoken to Grace since he had moved to Atlanta. Reluctantly, the cops released him, and he made his way to the deserted lobby to wait for Cole and fathom the absurdity of Grace Anne Walker playing gunslinging backup to her rowdy sister. Paula shot the wrong sister, if there was a right one, and that made Meredith a witness. So why didn't she go to the cops and tell her story? Only one reasonable explanation occurred to Parker: Meredith was still in the water. The one positive note was that the cops did not have a bullet and would not be able to tie Grace's wound to a specific gun.

He sat on a plastic chair in the lobby and called Tim Morrison. "I think it's time to lawyer-up, Tim. Meredith is missing, and I just identified her sister as the woman the cops pulled out of the river. I've been questioned twice and doubt that's the end of things. Know anybody who's good at this stuff?"

"Good God, Parker. My partner, Connor O'Brien, does the criminal work for our firm. Let me see if he's available." Tim put him on hold.

A few moments later, Parker heard the clicks that meant his call was being transferred.

"Tim says you need representation," Connor O'Brien said with an Irish accent, the sharp edges of which had been filed smooth by years in the American South.

"I hope I don't need it, but it would be a comfort. There's a Detective Rawlings at the Fulton County Sherriff's Department who had me identify a dead body this morning. Seems he'd planned to arrest me, but the body turned out to be someone else."

"Okay, Mr. Parker, I'll take the case, seeing as how you're already a client of our firm. I'll need a retainer of ten thousand dollars to start. If you're charged with a crime, I'll ask for a lot more."

"I'm sure you will." Parker had spent a fortune on lawyers the last time he had been arrested.

"'Course it's all tax-deductible if I get you a not guilty verdict."

"Really? I didn't know."

Parker flushed at the sound of the lawyer's laugh. "I'm pulling your leg, mate. In America, you pay to prove your innocence. Your police aren't as careful about who they charge as the coppers are in Britain. Why I came here, good for my pocketbook."

"America is the land of opportunity."

Parker related the same story he had told Rawlings and asked the lawyer to get the background on the dispute with Meredith from his partner, Tim Morrison. O'Brien promised to call when he had news of note.

Cole finally emerged, shell-shocked and bedraggled. He chose the plastic chair farthest from Parker's seat and began a two-thumbed percussion riff on his cell phone's keypad. Parker moved in front of him and hovered. "What are you doing?"

The kid looked up and blinked slowly behind his thick glasses. "Changing my flight. They're holding her body for autopsy, so I have to stay here another day or two."

"Where are you going to stay?"

"What do you care?"

Parker grasped the kid's elbow, levered him to his feet, and dragged him out of the building where a gaggle of news reporters waited. The carnivorous TV crews encircled their prey, reminding Parker of the tropical fish in Hawaii that attack snorkelers and tear the little bags of food out of their hands.

Parker answered shouted questions by saying, "It's not the missing Florida woman. Detective Rawlings is holding a news conference inside."

Like radio-controlled airplanes, the reporters banked and then dove through the doors of the morgue. Parker dragged Cole up the street, away from smokers loitering on the sidewalk. Then he grilled the kid.

Cole brought Parker up to date: he was a senior at the University of South Florida in Tampa; Grace lived in St. Petersburg with his father; Meredith had rarely been around since her release from prison, but Grace doted on him and on his father. Professor Wade Gilbert, Meredith's latest boyfriend, had convinced Grace to drive up from Florida the previous Tuesday, July second, to find Meredith and bring her home because she'd been out of touch. The cops had pressed Cole about Grace's plans, but Cole couldn't add to what they already knew.

"Did your aunt bring a gun with her?"

Cole blinked rapidly behind his coke-bottle-bottom lenses. "My dad's gun is missing."

"His military-issue Colt .45?"

Cole nodded. The .45 would make a loud boom. Cole's aunt was a maladroit accomplice for Meredith; Grace Anne Walker was an accountant for a hospital, not a marksman. That explained why no one got hit by a .45 caliber slug. Ergo, Paula shot at the sister who had shot at her. Boom-bang, self-defense. Unless Meredith was still in the water.

"You can stay at my place until they release your aunt's body," Parker said. "We'll have her embalmed here, and then we'll fly her to Florida. Your father can make the arrangements down there."

"Feeling guilty?"

Parker did feel guilty, about Cole's father and about Paula shooting the wrong sister. "I had nothing to do with this, Cole, never saw your aunt. Let me help with Grace's, ah, arrangements."

Cole examined his shoes and shuffled his feet. "I don't need your charity, Parker. I can pay you back out of the life insurance. I'm her beneficiary."

"Sure, kid."

Cole deftly hit keystrokes on his smartphone to order a car from a shared ride service, and shortly, a compact car pulled to the curb. On the ninety-minute drive through the height of rush hour, Cole called his father. Cole and his father were close, but his features were his mama's—the same blue eyes and bone structure, a somewhat effeminate face that, in a decade or two, would become a sensitive face. That's when he'd have success with women. On the phone, he and his father spoke few words but cried many tears. Cole did not reveal that he'd be staying at Parker's home, which his father would have prohibited. Duncan Hardy, who was alone most days while Grace worked, assured Cole he would be fine for a couple of days. After they disconnected, Cole called the VA nurse who visited his father regularly. She promised to look in on him until Cole returned.

At the office parking lot, they transferred to Parker's car and drove to his house. Parker poured a glass of orange juice, which Cole declined, and walked onto the deck. Cole followed him.

His head on a swivel, Cole admired the grounds. "Mama said you were rich."

"I'm not really," Parker said. "The bank mostly owns this place."

Cole pointed to the thicket. "Is that where it happened?"

"The cops think so," Parker said.

Cole complained of fatigue, a common symptom of grief, and said he needed a nap. Parker directed him to the guest suite upstairs.

***

Parker had intended to go back to the office, to parade through the bullpen to advertise his innocence, but he was stalled by the ringing of his cell phone, a Florida number he didn't recognize.

"Did you ask my mother to do this?" Paula snarled.

"Do what? Your mother doesn't speak to me."

"Then it was Jordyn, that little bitch. I walked right into their trap."

"You shouldn't have gone with them to Florida. You should have stayed with me."

"Not that trap. I asked my mother to come and get me. She said she'd give me a place to get back on my feet. Turns out that's a St. Pete rehab."

Paula's mother had coerced, berated, and shamed Paula into rehab when their marriage had been on the rocks as Parker's company failed. Now Lillian had summoned the energy to make it happen again. That explained Lillian's cryptic farewell. Parker felt shame at not having done it himself.

"They're trying to help you, Paula."

"At least it's a place run by the Methodist Church. Everyone likes Methodists because they're not Catholics, and they're not Baptists either."

Parker didn't know how to express his relief without upsetting Paula so he allowed an uncomfortable silence to separate them. Then Paula said, "Are you glad I'm gone so you can fuck your girlfriend?"

Her voice betrayed no emotion, making her accusation all the more ominous. Based on her perfectly symmetrical features and her peaches-and-cream complexion, one would think Paula a sweet southern belle, but then those artful lips part, and the invective flows, profanity a flimsy veneer of toughness to hide her psychological fragility.

"Dammit, Paula, I'm not having an affair."

"You're lying, Parker, and you'll regret it."

"Your drinking has ruined our marriage. You have to get sober."

"I should have divorced you while you were wearing pinstripes."

"That would have saved us our current mess, wouldn't it?"

"Fuck you. I'll figure out how to escape."

Parker forced himself to calm down. "How long do you have to stay?"

"Till I'm sober, imbecile."

Parker recoiled, then decided that maybe he deserved some abuse. "Ah, sure. I mean, how long is the program?"

"Twenty-eight freaking days. It's already been a nightmare, filling out forms, stripping for a physical, peeing in a cup. It's demeaning."

"Hang in there, Paula. It will be worth it."

She sucked in and exhaled smoke. At rehab, they let you substitute one addiction for another. "I've gotta go," Paula said. "Group therapy session. Should be a barrel of laughs."

"Wait. Have you heard from the police?"

"Nope. We can't have cell phones in here, might arrange for someone to break us out, so Jordyn is holding it for me. We're allowed one call today, like we've been arrested, then no more calls for the first two weeks."

"The police will ask you about your gun."

She paused to think about his warning. "Well, they'll have to wait for visiting hours. It's just like prison."

"They recovered Grace Walker's body from the river."

A long pause, a smoker's hacking cough. "Good," Paula said. "She was evil."

"Did you shoot them both?"

"Go fuck your girlfriend for all I care," Paula said. The line went dead.

Depressed by the condition of his marriage, Parker decided not to go back to the office. He pretended to relax in a lawn chair on the deck, a cigar in one hand, a dishrag to wipe the stinging sweat from his eyes in the other. What he tried to imagine was Paula, drunk as a sailor on shore leave, firing two shots in the thicket and splashing both sisters in the river. She had taken lessons with the pistol at the firing range, but two-for-two—in the dark—was a prize-winning score.

The repeated ringing of his doorbell shook him out of his reverie. On wobbly legs, he walked to the foyer. He was surprised and pleased to find Sabrina on his porch.

"You weren't arrested." Sabrina exhaled a theatrical sigh that could have been heard in the cheap seats.

"A sad case of mistaken identity."

"Thank God."

No, he thought, just another of God's cruel tricks. He led Sabrina through the house, offered her refreshments. She accepted a glass of orange juice.

Sabrina marveling at the crown moldings, the chair rails, the granite countertops, the Sub-Zero appliances, the Mexican tile floors, and the French Provincial furniture. "Helluva place, Parker."

He grimaced. "You'd be even more impressed to see my credit card bill. It's all on there."

She laughed. "What's she like?"

"Who?"

"Your wife. How did you meet and all that stuff?"

Why do women always ask? Men are afraid to ask about a woman's former lovers. "College sweethearts. We met at a fraternity–sorority mixer. She's a redhead," he said, as though that explained everything. "Feisty and a little flaky, free-spirited, no respect for rules."

"Like your mother."

"Really? Dime store psychology? I'll have you know I was attracted to her mind. She's very bright in an unconventional way—art history major."

Sabrina looked around the room. "Did she paint the pictures on the walls?"

"That's how she spends her time." And how she resists the urge to drink.

"She's talented."

"Yes, that was an attraction for me."

They sat in his office, in his visitors' chairs, Parker determined to shift attention away from his personal life. "Did you find the ASC proposal?" he said.

"No, I couldn't get into Dennie's office, but I found something almost as good: the Midwestern Assurance testbed. I have their current processing metrics and five hundred closed claim files." Sabrina sounded almost giddy with excitement. "We can run our own numbers."

"How did you manage that?"

"Ravi didn't want to put them in the company SharePoint where anybody could see them, but he didn't know how to create a Google drive, so Steve did it for him. Ravi wrote the password on a sticky note for his IT guys. When they went to lunch, I snooped around and found that one of the idiots had the note stuck to his computer screen, so I stole his password." Breathless, she paused.

"Can they figure out that you accessed their data?"

Sabrina looked surprised; hadn't thought about the digital fingerprints she may have left behind. "I'll have to ask Steve. I don't know about those things."

"Okay. Now what?"

"Now Steve runs the projections, and we see what an honest proposal would be. When you get Ravi's numbers, you call bullshit."

He reminded himself that calling bullshit didn't turn out so well last time. "Okay. Save the projections in a secure file, somewhere offsite. Don't give Ravi any more help, and don't talk to anyone."

"Okay. Should we work from here?" She looked hopeful, like she would have enjoyed hanging with him at his house.

"Hell, no. Meredith's kid is staying here." He pointed to the ceiling. "He came to ID his mama, then it turned out to be his aunt. He's staying here until they release her body."

"Oh."

When his overworked doorbell rang yet again, he assumed Rawlings was back to arrest him. Sabrina made a small sound, like a cornered mouse, but followed him out of his office. When they reached the foyer, they found Jordyn dropping the two suitcases Paula had taken to Florida, now empty.

"Hey. Welcome home." He walked straight to Jordyn and gave her a bear hug that she tolerated but did not return. "I'm glad you're back. It's been lonely around here."

Looking over his shoulder, Jordyn said, "You don't look lonely. Is that her, the girlfriend Mom told me about?"

Parker dropped his arms, gave Sabrina an apologetic look. He waved a hand back and forth between the women. "This is Sabrina, my work colleague. Sabrina, this is my daughter, Jordyn."

The women evaluated each other, like animals in the wild. Friend or foe?

To Jordyn, Parker said, "In case you and your mother haven't heard about it, we now have women in the workplace."

"I should go," Sabrina said.

"Don't run away on my account," Jordyn said. "I only came to get some more things for Mom. I'm driving Grandma's car back tomorrow."

Trying to be reasonable, Parker said, "Grandma doesn't need her car."

"No, but Mom needs the support," she said, twisting the knife in his back. "She's in rehab again."

Parker slumped in defeat. Jordyn had always protected her mother from his awkward attempts to wrestle calm from chaos. "Yes, she called me earlier."

"I should help Steve," Sabrina blurted. "You've got your hands full here."

Parker didn't try to dissuade her. She climbed into her car, cranked it, and gave him a wave as she drove away.

To Jordyn, Parker said, "You've heard the news? They pulled Grace Walker's body out of the Hooch last Saturday."

Jordyn smiled innocently and ran a hand through her long auburn hair. "Yeah, one down and one to go."

Parker grabbed her upper arm and marched her into his office where they wouldn't be heard by Cole. "Did you take care of that other problem?"

"Mom sold it to Uncle Melvin months ago." She handed him a backdated bill of sale. "But there's a problem: Melvin carried the gun into the pecan orchard to kill snakes, but then he lost it out there somewhere."

"You gave it to him! I wanted you to drown it."

Jordyn recoiled. "I thought it was a better lie if he actually had the gun."

Parker understood Jordyn's tactic. She had distanced herself from the murder weapon, but anyone could find the damned thing and link it to the incident in the thicket. "Does your mother know what to say if the cops question her?"

"Yeah, she'll be fine. They've called her cell phone several times, but I haven't answered the calls. They can do their own legwork."

"They know she went to her mother's house in Lakewood so they'll find her soon enough."

He tossed the sales receipt into his desk drawer. Protecting Paula had become a dicey proposition but he had another idea to cover up the fact that Paula had a gun on the Fourth of July. "You have your mother's cell phone with you?"

Jordyn nodded.

"Load the two pictures of Meredith with her gun onto your mom's phone."

"You're complicating things, Dad."

"Don't you see? Your mom didn't have a gun that night. She didn't shoot at Meredith; she took her picture."

"Oh my God. Lies on top of lies. Are you going to give the phone to the cops?"

"Never play a trump card until it can take a trick."

"Huh?"

"Not until I have to. If they ask for it, you can tell them I have it. They'll need a warrant."

Jordyn texted the two pictures to her mother's phone and handed it to her father. Parker shoved it into his back pocket.

A voice from the office doorway startled them. "Why is she here?"

Parker spoke over Jordyn's shoulder. "Picking up some clothes for her mother, who is in Florida."

Jordyn whirled around to see Cole in the office doorway, rubbing sleep from his eyes. She stared at Cole as though he were maggot-encrusted garbage.

"You running a homeless shelter now?" Jordyn said to her father.

"Be nice. Cole is staying here until Grace's body is released."

Cole slammed a hand into the doorjamb and clenched his fists. Jordyn taunted him, both hands signaling him forward—*Come and get me*. Parker pushed the kid into the kitchen. Victorious, Jordyn chortled.

Parker said, "Go on up and get the clothes."

Jordyn slipped around Cole, sneered at him and moved to the stairway to the master bedroom.

Cole opened the refrigerator and pushed jars and Tupperware dishes around. "You don't have a beer in this place?'

"Sorry, Paula is an alcoholic. I do have some port hidden in the laundry room."

Cole chuckled and shook his head. "Port? I should have known. That's a sissy British thing, isn't it?"

"You're right, Cole, it's far too sophisticated for you."

Cole ignored Parker, pulled lunch meat, mustard, and a can of Coke from the refrigerator. "Bread?"

"In the cabinet to your left."

Cole made the sandwich and took a seat at the kitchen table to eat it.

When Jordyn came downstairs with the repacked suitcases, it felt to Parker as though Paula were moving out of the house. Parker offered to take her to dinner, but Jordyn demurred. "I've been back and forth to Florida, and I'm going to do it again tomorrow. All I want is one night in my own bed."

She let her father hug her again and drove away to her apartment.

***

Parker was dead asleep when his burglar alarm went off at 3:04 a.m. He crept down the stairs to the ground floor, turning on lights as he went.

Awakened by the screech of the alarm, Cole burst out of the guest room stood at the top of the stairs. "What's going on?"

"Stay up there," Parker yelled.

Through the family room, he quick-stepped to the garage, where he grabbed a baseball bat. Back in the house, he went to the security panel on the kitchen wall and saw that the light representing the sensor in the French doors to the deck was flashing red. The solid wooden doors couldn't be jarred by anything less than a purposeful tug. He flipped on the backyard spotlights and watched for movement. He saw nothing. Parker ran to the front of the house and surveyed the cul-de-sac. Like a madman, he moved from window to window, peering through slots in the blinds, gaps in the curtains. Lights appeared in the front windows of neighbors' homes. A pair of taillights faded away as a car climbed the grade toward the entrance to his subdivision. The car was big and dark in color, not orange like that sedan he'd seen the other day, and it didn't have a loud muffler.

Back at the alarm panel, he keyed in the secret code and suppressed the blaring siren.

"Damn, Parker, how many enemies do you have?" Cole said.

The kid sounded insolent, happy that Parker was being harassed, but Parker thought he had asked a very good question. "Go back to bed," Parker said. "False alarm."

Fully twenty minutes later, the security company finally rang him. In a thickly accented voice, an operator in a foreign country asked a couple of questions and concluded the incident was a false alarm.

Parker didn't think so. Parker now believed that Meredith's accomplice drove a big and shiny black car. He slept with his bat under the covers.

Parker strode through the bullpen carrying Shaw's group picture and daring anyone to question him. Sabrina joined up with him and followed him into his office.

"Someone will tattle to Jack that you have his picture."

Parker took a black magic marker from his desk drawer and drew a circle around his mother's image. Then he placed the picture in his closet. "If he wants it, he can come and get it."

She took a seat at the conference table. "Tweaking Jack's nose is not a good idea, Parker. We need to stay under the radar until we have evidence of fraud."

"This is personal."

Sabrina sat back, folded her arms across her chest. "I have a personal question, too. According to your daughter, your wife thinks I'm your girlfriend. Is that how *you* feel about me, Parker?"

The last thing Parker wanted to do was discuss feelings that he was very unsure about. Clearly, Sabrina had crossed some imaginary boundary of intimacy since their trip to Columbia.

He motioned at his open office door. She was about to close it when Carolyn Burke barged into Parker's office.

"Oh, good, I can kill two birds with one stone," Carolyn said.

Sabrina gave Parker a fearful look and sat at his conference table. Parker suspected Carolyn had come for Jack's picture.

"What can I do for you, Carolyn?" Parker said.

"Would you mind working from home? Just until things quiet down?" The local news, she informed Parker, had corrected the identification of the body recovered from the river, but the other sister was still missing. Word of Meredith's call and her lawsuit had spread from Human Resources, where secrets go to be leaked indiscriminately, to the rest of the Shaw Technology employees. The optics, she said, were awful. She didn't want any more cops at the office, and she wanted to curtail the gossip and rumors. Productivity had suffered.

"We've disabled your keycard. Temporarily, of course. It's HR policy, Parker."

He was not surprised to be convicted in the court of public opinion, but the speed of the verdict astonished him. Idly, he hoped his judgmental colleagues weren't the "peers" selected for his jury.

"I'd like to speak with Mr. Shaw."

"Don't waste your time. He'll back me up."

"It's not about my keycard, Carolyn. I have something for him."

"You mean the picture you stole from him?"

Parker deduced that Jack wanted him out of the office so he could retrieve the picture without talking about it. He opened his closet door and pulled out Shaw's picture.

"I just borrowed it." He handed the picture to Carolyn. "Can I keep my keycard now?"

"No."

"Fine."

Parker began packing as Carolyn sat next to Sabrina, leaning in close and speaking in a low voice. "Could you do me a big favor, Ms. Mitchell, by wearing your hair up, uh, pinned down or something? When you wear that … ah, Afro out to here," she spread her hands outward from her ears as though her head had exploded, "you look like a '60s revolutionary in a protest demonstration. Makes people uncomfortable."

"What people?" Parker said. He didn't suppress his anger.

"Stay out of this, Parker," Carolyn said. "It's a Shaw Technology matter."

"My hairstyle is natural, what I was born with," Sabrina said. "Can you show me in the employee handbook where it says I can't wear my hair natural?"

Sabrina waited calmly while Carolyn searched for politically correct words.

"The handbook," Carolyn said, "requires that everyone appear professional. You should think of it as part of the dress code."

"Uh-huh. And who's the arbiter of professional appearance, Carolyn? You? The 1940s called and asked for your hairdo back."

Parker laughed out loud.

Carolyn turned red. "I was hoping for some cooperation."

"Cooperation? I'll wear my hair any damn way I please. And, if you do outlaw it, I promise you'll hear from the ACLU and every civil rights organization in this city."

Carolyn sat back as though she had been slapped. "I told Jack you were a mistake." She got to her feet and left with Shaw's picture.

"You like antagonizing them," Parker said.

"So do you," Sabrina said.

"Bring Steve to my house and tell me what you've found."

***

Parker brewed a cup of coffee and took it onto the deck where Cole slouched in a lawn chair. Parker's house guest looked at him with a beady-eyed smile and canted his head toward the thicket. An army of cops was conducting a sector search of the thicket. Parker had hoped Ron would get into the thicket first, but Rawlings had beaten Ron to the punch. Parker counted eight men, dressed for fieldwork, walking slowly abreast through the underbrush. They had started at his property line and were moving inexorably toward the park. His face flushed with heat while a solid block of ice formed in his stomach. Would they find Meredith's decaying body out there? Would they find two spent casings from Paula's pistol somewhere in that thicket?

The cops covered the area from the footpath to the river's edge in an intense search for objects large and small, every other man equipped with a metal detector, similar to the things old codgers use to find nickels on the beach.

Cole fiddled with his cell phone as it repeatedly made the annoying chirping sound that notified him of arriving text messages.

"You don't seem worried about what they'll find," Parker said.

Cole stood, craned his neck and watched the searchers for a minute. "I'm not worried." His two thumbs resumed typing rapidly.

How could the kid be this nonchalant? Parker sifted through the possibilities and arrived at the only logical conclusion: the cops wouldn't find Meredith's body because it wasn't out there. Meredith was alive, and the kid knew it.

As Cole paged through his messages, he turned green around the gills. With a hand over his mouth, he mumbled, "I have to use the toilet," and stumbled into the house.

Parker sipped lukewarm coffee and worked his way through the ramifications of the cops finding Meredith before Ron did. When he set his cup down on the small table between the chairs, he noticed that Cole had left his cell phone behind. Before it could time out and require a passcode or fingerprint, he went to the text message queue. Parker opened the conversation with a Colorado area code and saw a picture of two bandaged wrists held over a bathtub with fresh blood smears. No face or body was visible. Parker forwarded the picture to his phone.

Cole stepped back onto the porch and caught Parker with the phone in his hand. He snatched it and looked at the screen.

"Damn it, Parker, is nothing sacred?"

"Looks staged to me."

"Christ, Parker, that's her blood!"

Parker jumped to his feet, and in one long stride, towered over the shorter kid. Before Cole sensed the imminent onslaught of violence, Parker grabbed two handfuls of the kid's shirt and lifted him off the deck. "Where's your mother hiding, Cole?"

Cole looked like a puppy that fears a spanking for peeing on the carpet. "She won't tell me; says she's safe."

Hiding with her accomplice. "Why is she hiding?"

The kid blinked rapidly behind his thick glasses. "She wants her money, or she'll testify, and you guys will be fucked."

Parker gave the kid a playground shove in the shoulders. "Testify to what?"

"To what she saw in the thicket."

Parker shoved him again. "You mean what she saw in my backyard."

"She said in the *thicket*."

Parker's worst fear had become a reality. Meredith and her accomplice had seen Paula shoot Grace. Bile rose from his stomach and leapt through his esophagus. He swallowed air to keep it down, then almost lost it as his cell phone rang. The caller was another Florida number he didn't recognize. He turned back into the house to answer in privacy.

"Parker," Paula whispered, breathless.

"Hey, I thought you only got one call."

"I'm in the men's room. A new girl is checking in, and her boyfriend is taking a leak. I'm using his phone."

"Don't peek."

"He's got a nice one, you want to know. That cop who sent you to prison was just here, the guy who looks like he sleeps in his clothes."

The cops had done their legwork. "Lieutenant Monahan. What did he want?"

"He took my official statement. I told him what we told the Atlanta cops: nothing happened in our yard, and we never left the deck."

"Good girl."

"He wanted to know if Meredith had a gun when she came to see us."

"And you said …"

"Maybe, but I didn't see one."

"Good enough. Anything else?"

"He asked where my gun was. I had to tell him about Uncle Melvin."

"Will your uncle remember what to say?"

"Maybe." Parker heard the flick of her Bic lighter.

"The cops are searching the thicket with metal detectors as we speak. If they find your spent casings, they'll be all over that pecan grove."

"Jesus Christ. We have to go through this again?"

"Yes, Meredith is alive and claims she saw you shoot Grace."

"She's lying."

"If you're so innocent, why did you run away?"

"To get away from you! I can't stand to be blamed for something I didn't do."

Me neither. Parker decided to take it easy on his fragile wife. "Okay, if Monahan comes back, refuse to answer questions without an attorney present."

He heard a gulp, Paula swallowing fear. "He's all zipped up, wants his phone back." The line went silent.

From the deck, Parker could no longer see the cops in the thicket, but he heard their occasional shouts. He jumped when his doorbell rang. Cole heard it and followed Parker through the house.

"The cops are here to question you about your mama," Parker said. He enjoyed sadistically tormenting the kid and was rewarded with a frightened look on Cole's face.

Parker held up a hand—stay back—and opened the door. He should have known it wasn't the cops. Cops pounded on doors and threatened to break them down. Sabrina and The Wookiee stood on his porch holding laptops and files. Terry Horan ambled up the walkway behind them. Parker sighed with relief as he let them in and directed them to his office.

"Are you going to give me the money?" Cole asked.

"We'll talk about it after I work with my team. Stay out of the way and keep the noise down." Cole slunk away.

Parker followed his team into the kitchen, where Steve stopped at the refrigerator and helped himself to a soda. Sabrina opened cabinets until she found the coffee pods for the Keurig and brewed a cup. Terry declined a beverage, shuffled this way and that to let people maneuver around him.

In Parker's office, Sabrina walked around his desk and peremptorily plopped into his executive chair. She kicked off her sandals, propped her bare feet on the edge of his desk, and put her red readers low on her nose. With her hair natural, she did resemble a '60s revolutionary. Parker and Terry sat in the side chairs.

Steve drew a diagram on the whiteboard beside rows of bullet points. Sabrina dug through Parker's desk drawer and found his supply of Snickers bars. She tossed one to Terry, one to Steve, and one to Parker. Parker flipped it back to her. His queasy stomach was not ready for candy.

Sabrina unwrapped the candy as she spoke. "Ravi's test case files are much larger than the original Midwestern Assurance files."

"They gave us five hundred cases and Ravi's file is about twenty percent larger. His program code files are bigger than ours too," Steve said, as though any intelligent being would intuit deep meaning from his discovery.

Parker shrugged. A question.

"Steve reverse-engineered their program code to see what Ravi did," Sabrina said. "It's your damned machine learning routine, Parker. The machine learns to make the numbers better and better."

"Ah," Terry said.

"That's what it's supposed to do," Parker said.

"In a normal operation, your routine learns from the current cases and teaches the machine to refine the rule base for the next set of cases. What Ravi did is put the test cases and your routine in a loop." Sabrina let that sink in.

"A loop?"

Terry, the computer engineer, said, "I get it."

Sabrina looked at Parker like a tutor about to impress a student. "After a run, Ravi duplicates the test cases then reruns the process against the same test file, which refines the rules once again. He repeats the process until the rule base is perfect. Wash, rinse, repeat. Like washing the same load of clothes over and over until they come clean."

"Brilliant, really," Parker said.

"Brilliant, maybe, but not operationally feasible," Sabrina said. "You can't run the same cases over and over in real life, so it's not a fair test of Alexi's code and not a fair use of your code."

"Can you replicate what he did with the loop-de-loop and see what he got?"

"Steve is working on it."

"Should finish this afternoon," Steve said.

"We need a plan," Sabrina said.

"You're getting ahead of yourself," Parker said. "The loop-de-loop thing doesn't constitute major fraud. Actually, it shows the power of machine learning over time. We don't have Ravi's results or Dennie's proposal or the stolen ASC proposal. If Ravi's numbers and Steve's numbers are wildly different, I'll confront Kumar," Parker said.

"You think he's going to say, 'Oh, sorry, honest mistake?'"

"We need Jack's help," Terry said.

"We can't trust Jack Shaw," Sabrina said.

That Sabrina had drawn Terry into their rebel group made Parker nervous. "We have to keep our information a secret until I spring it on Kumar in New Orleans."

"Kumar will run you down like a snowplow in Chicago. He's pure evil," Terry said.

Parker never subscribed to the theory that some people were inherently evil, an idea originated by religious zealots to sell the concept of a fearsome devil. In his mind, there were only evil *deeds*, committed either by the mentally defective—God's mistakes—or by ordinary people with selfish motivations and pragmatic rationalizations for their behavior. Parker would have explained his theory to Terry were it not for the melodic chime of his doorbell. The muscles in his neck and shoulders tensed involuntarily.

"Sorry, that has to be the police."

"Jesus save us," Sabrina said. Her feet found her sandals, and her eyes betrayed her fear.

Parker feared the cops had found Paula's casings. He grabbed Paula's phone from his desk drawer and put it in his pocket. He thought he might now have to play a trump card.

As he walked to the foyer, Terry followed, and Cole hovered in the background. From the porch came clichéd shouting: "Police! Open the door, or we'll break it down."

Parker peered through the pebbled glass window in the door, and there they stood again: Rawlings and Conroy. A blue unmarked sedan and a black and white SUV with police markings on every panel crouched on the lawn since his visitors' cars blocked the driveway.

He opened the door. "Sorry, I forgot to buy the donuts."

Conroy had ditched his discount-store sports jacket and Christmas-present tie for paramilitary garb intended to intimidate Parker. Rawlings wore his usual cheap detective clothes.

"We have a warrant to confiscate computers and files," Conroy said.

"Any device that can connect to the Internet," Rawlings explained.

Terry said, "Excuse me. I was just leaving," as he averted his eyes and slipped past the cops. They gave him the once-over but didn't stop him.

Rawlings sent the uniformed cops upstairs again. Cole looked as though a monster had slithered out from under his bed.

Rawlings walked to Parker's office with a swagger befitting a man who owned the place and found Steve and Sabrina cowering.

"Pack up your shit and get out of here."

"Jesus can't save us," Sabrina said. Reluctantly, she and Steve unplugged and stashed equipment in their backpacks.

"How about we put our run results in a document and send it to you by email so you can read it when you're less … distracted?" Sabrina said. She snapped a picture of the whiteboard with her smartphone. "We'll leave the whiteboard for you to look at when you read our mail."

Rawlings backed through the kitchen and moved into the family room. Parker slid past him into the doorway and caught Sabrina's attention.

"Don't forget that one," he said as he jabbed a finger at his personal laptop. He didn't want the computer he would use to expose Kumar's fraud to be locked in some police evidence locker until the case was closed. "Put all the files on that one."

In the space of microseconds, Sabrina's face morphed from bewilderment to cognition to brave complicity. Sabrina stuffed Parker's computer in her backpack, swallowed her fear, and zipped it up.

Rawlings came back from the family room. "Hurry the fuck up."

Sabrina grabbed her half-eaten candy bar, gave Rawlings a wide berth, and followed Steve through the house without looking back.

Rawlings followed Parker into the kitchen as Conroy walked out the French doors and jogged toward the thicket.

"I see you have a house guest," Rawlings said.

"He's got no money, didn't know he'd be stuck here waiting for a body to be released."

"So you're just a good Samaritan?"

"He's just a sad kid."

"Where is he? I need to ask him a few questions."

He shrugged and yelled the kid's name. A minute later, Cole inched into the kitchen. Parker didn't move. He wasn't about to let Rawlings question Cole alone.

Rawlings gave Cole his most threatening interrogator's look. "Have you heard from your mother?"

"Not me," the kid lied.

Rawlings cupped his chin and stared at the kid. The kid stared back. "We can pull your call logs at the phone company, you know, so you may as well tell me if you've heard from her."

Parker thought Rawlings was bluffing. The kid wasn't a target of the latest search warrant and a new warrant for the kid's call records would be hard to get. He signaled his doubt to Cole with pursed lips, drooping eyes, and the slightest shake of his head.

The kid understood the signal and shrugged. Rawlings let the silence weigh on Cole, like the airtight lid on a pressure cooker, but the kid didn't break. Rawlings conceded the battle with a thumb jerked over his shoulder and Cole disappeared again.

"I already have a warrant for your call logs," Rawlings said to Parker. "It's easier than making the tech guys analyze your phone, so you may as well tell me if you've received any communications from the missing woman."

"No, I haven't. You don't seem to understand that I don't want to talk to her because she's just after my money."

The detective's immobile face, like a bronze bust in an art gallery, concealed whatever he was thinking. Parker marveled at the power of the detective's pauses, as though he were leaning his considerable bulk on his suspect. Parker withstood the pressure.

"You think she's alive?" Rawlings said. The cop seemed genuinely interested in Parker's opinion.

"I didn't harm her; maybe someone else did."

"If she's alive, where would she be? Does she have friends here, relatives in the area?"

"I have no idea. She has no connections to Atlanta that I'm aware of." The truth.

"So, a hotel then. We'll find her. If she's dead, we'll be back with an arrest warrant. If she's alive … well, then we'll all know what happened, won't we?"

Rawlings ambled into Parker's office and took a seat behind Parker's desk, guarding the rest of his belongings against tampering. The sound of doors slamming and drawers banging wafted down the stairwell as the cops desecrated Parker's private spaces. After a short while, the uniformed cops came downstairs with an iPad that Parker kept on his bedside table so he could read a few pages of a book before turning out the lights.

In the home office, the two uniformed cops detached Parker's business computer and put it in an evidence box for transportation. They opened the file cabinet and rummaged through household bills and correspondence, work project files, and voluminous tax records. They boxed it all up.

"The desktop computer belongs to my employer and contains information confidential to my employer. You'll need their permission to access the files," Parker said.

Rawlings grunted a you-can't-question-my-authority sound and stepped from behind the desk.

Parker edged in front of him. "My paper files contain privileged communications with my lawyer. You can't read them."

"We'll decide what we can and can't read, Mr. Parker."

After the cops carried the boxes away, Parker told Rawlings to open the middle desk drawer and look at the top piece of paper. He opened the drawer and pulled out the fake bill of sale for Paula's gun. After one glance, he dropped it on the desk.

"Your wife's uncle, strange old guy, said he lost it in your mother-in-law's orchard. The Lakewood Police Department searched the pecan grove but couldn't find the gun. They think the old man led them on a wild goose chase."

"No telling where he lost it."

"The old guy said maybe one of the migrant workers found it and kept it. Of course, your mother-in-law's employee records weren't helpful. Hard to tell who had been in that pecan grove."

Every morning pickup trucks full of day laborers arrived at Lillian's farm, and she chose the ones she wanted to work that day. After a grueling day in the fields, black and brown men in every state of decomposition gathered on her country porch and were paid in cash by the woman they called "Miss Lillian." There were no records whatsoever.

"I'm not familiar with my mother-in-law's business practices."

Rawlings dismissed Parker's concern with a wave of his hand. "They'll keep looking."

Rawlings levered himself out of the chair, then froze. He put a finger to his radio earpiece, pushing it closer to his eardrum to hear the transmission. "They've found something," he said.

Rawlings grinned as he led Parker out to the deck where they stood side-by-side. One hand cupping his chin, Rawlings gazed at the thicket as though he were clairvoyant and able to imagine what had happened out there on the Fourth of July.

Soon Conroy burst out of the thicket holding two evidence bags daintily in front of his chest as he approached the deck. One bag, with a large number 2 on it, held a shell casing, and the other, bag number 3, held a woman's sandal. The casing appeared to be high caliber. *Boom.* Conroy intentionally let Parker see some of what they'd found—but not everything. Evidence bag number 1 held something the cops were keeping secret. If Parker had to guess, he'd guess that evidence bag number 1 held a .45 caliber pistol since evidence bag number 2 held its expended casing.

Rawlings took a closer look at the distinctive, sequined sandal. Meredith wouldn't have discarded the designer size seven. She was a collector of footwear as acquisitive as Imelda Marcos. From Parker's vantage point, he didn't see any blood.

"Recognize it?" Conroy asked.

Parker shook his head. "My wife has better taste."

"I'm tired of this guy's smart-ass remarks," Conroy said to Rawlings.

Rawlings sighed. "Was Ms. Walker wearing that sandal on the Fourth of July?" he asked Parker.

"No idea. If you saw her you wouldn't be able to take your eyes off her chest, detective."

Rawlings' head bobbed slowly up and down. Calmly, he switched to the bag holding the large-caliber casing. "Did Ms. Walker have a gun that night?"

Parker's stomach clenched. *They may think Meredith had the .45. It's too soon to play a trump card.* "We were pretty far apart. She was down there by the firepit and gesticulating all over the place. It was dark."

"Is that a 'No?'" Conroy asked.

Parker shrugged. "If she had the big gun that fired that round," he said, pointing to the large caliber casing, "I think I'd have noticed it."

Rawlings's chest heaved up and down, but he made no remark. In the cat-and-mouse game with the cops, Parker was the mouse, doomed to tell more lies to cover the first lie.

Rawlings handed the evidence bags back to Conroy and sighed again. There would be no arrest today. Two cops from the search party strung yellow crime scene tape across the thicket from the river's edge to the corner of Parker's house. They went back the way they came, toward the park, where they must have staged for the search.

Parker thought the search was over until Conroy pressed his fingers to his earpiece and yelped. "They found the car, Sarge!"

Rawlings grinned again. "Get it to the motor pool."

Conway jogged back through the thicket. Rawlings elbowed Parker into the doorjamb and bulldozed his way through the house. Parker traipsed after him like a smitten puppy. As he got into his car, Rawlings yelled, "Next time, there better be donuts."

A woman glared at Parker from her porch at the house next door. Parker waved and stepped back into his house.

"Can we talk about money now?" Cole said.

Startled by the kid's sudden appearance, Parker said, "Christ, kid, you're like a ghost, now you see him, now you don't. The money isn't stashed under my mattress, Cole. I'll get it tomorrow."

Parker slid past him, bumped the foyer table, and knocked over the tall stack of soggy bills and junk advertisements. As he gathered them up, a plain brown envelope caught his eye. It had just his name on the back, no return address. He tore it open and found a postcard depicting the Civil War carvings on Stone Mountain. In block letters, someone had written: "Sign the settlement, or I'll tell the cops everything. Leave it in your mailbox."

When was the last time Paula had collected the mail? Maybe Saturday, maybe not since Friday. An old orange car, out of place in the neighborhood, had sped up the street as the cops searched his house on Sunday afternoon. Someone tripped the burglar alarm Monday night. That was a shiny black car. *How many enemies do I have?*

Thoughts tumbled through his mind like dice on a baccarat table. The postcard had to come from Meredith, the only person who knew he had the settlement agreement. The postcard had been her first attempt at blackmail. Now she had Cole to communicate her demands. If her accomplice drove the orange car, who drove the shiny black car? Which car did the cops find?

Parker sat at the kitchen table, perusing a Florida law known as the Baker Act, when the security system dinged, alerting him to an opened door, and a deep bass voice yelled, "Knock, knock!"

Ron Gardner ambled into the foyer and grinned. Wearing boat shoes, no socks, faded jeans, and a filmy long-sleeved shirt rolled to the elbows, he appeared to be the fishing buddy he was posing as.

"You're early. Good, good," Parker said.

"Finished the other job this morning. Flew up first-class on your dime." Carrying a twelve-pack of Negra Modelo beer in one hand he gave Parker a one-armed bear hug. Taller and heavier than Parker, he moved to the kitchen with the ambling grace and rolling shoulders of a former defensive end for the University of Florida and shoved the beer into the refrigerator.

"Didn't figure you'd have a supply at your house," he said. Ron knew of Paula's affliction.

Ron handed Parker a bottle of beer and grabbed another from the refrigerator. Parker led Ron onto the deck.

Ron took in the river view, the expanse of lawn, and the firepit. "Nice place," he said.

Parker believed he could live in a shoebox—a prison cell had been adequate—but Paula had needed the status of an upscale home. She'd found it difficult to balance envy for what they didn't have with gratitude for what they did have.

"Is that where it happened?" Ron asked as he pointed to the thicket.

"Yes, it all happened in the woods."

"Bring me up to date."

Parker glanced over his shoulder to ensure that Cole wasn't eavesdropping. "The body they pulled from the river is Meredith's sister, Grace."

"Saw that on the news."

"Meredith's son identified the body and now he's staying here with me until he can claim the body."

"Keep your friends close and your enemies closer."

"Yup. Meredith is alive and she's been texting with Cole."

Ron sagged into a chair and made a sound like a leaking steam pipe. "So she's a witness, too."

"While Meredith and I were down there by the firepit, her accomplice took two shots at us from the tree line over there." He pointed to a spot near the far corner of his house.

"Two witnesses make a strong case."

"That's the threat, but now she's blackmailing me."

"Clever girl. What do your witnesses say?"

"Paula and Jordyn both say they saw nothing. During the chase in the woods, Jordyn heard two shots, one like a big dog barking and the other like a little dog yapping."

"What caliber is Paula's pistol?"

"It's a .32 Tomcat."

Ron pursed his lips and nodded. "A yappy little dog. How many shots did you hear?"

"I was here on the deck," Parker lied. "The fireworks were going off overhead, so I can't be positive, but I think there were several more shots."

"I'll have to crawl through there, see what I can find."

"Too late. The cops had a whole team out there today. They showed me a sandal they think Meredith lost and .45 caliber casing. I'm sure they have that gun."

"The big dog. The cops probably have a lot more they didn't want you to know about."

Ron stood, guzzled his beer and surveyed the thicket as though he could see through the thick vegetation and locate the evidence. "Any hint as to how I can find her. Or her accomplice?"

Parker told him about the orange car and the black car, the Fulton County hotel, and the fake suicide picture. "The cops think they're in a hotel."

"I'll start tomorrow—" Ron stopped midsentence, raised his eyebrows, and canted his head toward the door—hush—as Cole stepped onto the deck.

Cole stepped onto the deck and waved a hand at Ron. "Who's he?"

"This is Ron, my buddy from Florida," Parker said. "He's on his way to the North Georgia mountains for a little trout fishing."

"Can I have one of those?" Cole meant the beer the men were drinking.

"You can have as many as you like," Parker said.

The kid drank three beers as they ate delivered pizzas. They didn't talk much, each of them harboring private thoughts about what had happened in the thicket. Ron said goodnight and left in the rental car paid for by Parker to go to the room also paid for by Parker at the Hilton on Peachtree Industrial Boulevard. Cole meandered upstairs to bed. Parker poured himself a double shot of port and thought about what a mess he had made of his life. Then he had an idea.

Parker took the stairs two at a time and pounded on Cole's bedroom door. The kid opened the door a crack, his hand over his cell phone's microphone. "I'm busy."

Parker said they needed to see where the cops found the evidence in their search this afternoon. There would be markers that matched the numbers on the evidence bags. The kid rose to the bait like a trout to a fly and hung up on his mama.

Parker's Florida attorney, Vince Romeli, had opined that all behavior is contextual. When trapped in a moral dilemma, he'd said, self-interest determined all behavior. He had used abortion as the example. People who were opposed on moral grounds to abortions often changed their minds when their teenaged daughter got pregnant. Parker came to agree that the sort of morals one learned in church were an extravagance affordable only for people without real problems. His personal code now determined his behavior. His prison buddies had told him that the only way to stop a blackmailer was to blackmail the blackmailer. He wanted to see if there was a way to blackmail Meredith.

Parker pulled on jeans, hiking boots, and a long-sleeved shirt to protect himself against the briars and bugs in the thicket, not to mention the copperhead snakes that frequently make Georgia thickets their home. The kid didn't have anything very suitable, just shorts and sneakers. They walked out the back door, around the firepit, to the spot where Meredith had first appeared. Parker ducked under the crime scene tape and entered the thicket, thinking of the inadequate barrier as a red light at a deserted intersection. Never trust an ex-con at a deserted intersection.

In the beam of Parker's flashlight, they stumbled through underbrush until they reached the footpath. Where a straightaway began, they found an evidence marker, a thin wire stalk topped by a triangular red pennant with a yellow 4 stenciled on it. Thinking back to the bags Conroy had shown him, Parker remembered that number 2 held a .45 casing and therefore number 1 would be the gun. This spot had to mark a different shell casing. Someone had fired up the straightaway, toward the fallen tree. Parker heard a boom-bang exchange from this location, so the smaller pistol had been fired from this spot. One of Paula's missing shells. Why hadn't the cops questioned him about it?

"What did they find here?" Cole said.

"One of your mama's spent casings." Parker tried to sound authoritative. "Grace fired your daddy's gun at her, and she shot back."

"Aunt Grace wouldn't do that," Cole snapped.

"It was dark. No telling how two scared two women reacted."

They continued down the straightaway and found evidence marker number 5, just short of the fallen tree roots. "Another one of your mama's shell casings. She fired a shot from this location."

Parker pointed to evidence marker number 1, down the bank on the park side of the fallen tree. "That's where the cops found your father's gun. Your aunt was standing in that area when she was shot." *Probably true.*

"Are you saying that someone shot her from here?"

"Yes, your mama shot your aunt right here."

"No fucking way."

"The cops have the casings to prove it."

Cole muttered something under his breath as he soaked in the scene. Parker hoped Cole considered the possibility that his mama had lied to him and had indeed shot his aunt. Parker, at the same time, imagined that Grace had fired the .45 caliber gun at

Paula down the straightaway, and Paula had returned fire and missed. When she reached the fallen tree, after Meredith was long gone, Paula fired again and hit Grace. Two bullets were missing from her gun. In that case, Meredith's accomplice had witnessed the murder and the cops had found Paula's casings. If the cops ever found Paula's gun in Florida, she'd go to prison for life.

Parker left the kid to his painful ruminations, stepped around the tree roots, and followed the path around a big bush. Evidence marker number 3 was planted at the edge of the path, marking the spot where the cops had found Meredith's sandal.

His moment of reflection was interrupted by the sweep of a flashlight coming toward him from the park. Parker hustled back around the big bush, put a finger to his lips signaling Cole to be silent, and dragged him down the straightaway toward his backyard. They hurried, but the flashlight was about to come around the big bush that blocked the park end of the straightaway, and they would be lit in its beam. Parker pulled Cole down the bank and into the surging water, holding onto branches to resist the river's malevolent attempts to sweep them downstream. In the darkness, the river was opaque under the flashlight beam. Parker switched it off and waited.

The cops had posted a night watchman in the thicket, which meant they had settled on a theory they would take to court. Either the watchman was making his routine rounds, or he had seen Parker's flashlight beam moving through the thicket. The guard's flashlight swept left and right as it came casually down the path, and Parker could see that the man was a rent-a-cop, not a policeman. The guard continued out of sight toward the ambush point. The flashlight did not reappear for several minutes, implying a search of the backyard. If the watchman found Parker's car in the driveway and the lights on in the house, but no one responded to a knock on the door, he would try harder to find snoopers in the thicket.

Figuratively holding their breath, Parker and the kid waited. Cole gripped Parker's forearm like a white-knuckle flyer strangling his armrest. Finally, the flashlight beam reappeared, moving slowly back up the path. It paused at evidence marker number 4, moved up the straightaway, and paused at evidence marker number 5. Slowly, the flashlight made a 360-degree sweep of the area around the fallen tree. The fact that none of the evidence markers had been disturbed may have convinced the watchman that he had no reason for concern because the flashlight moved toward the park, around the big bush, and out of sight.

Cole started up the bank, but Parker stopped him and dragged him back into the water. Parker wanted to be sure the watchman didn't double back. After five agonizing minutes, Parker said, "Okay, move fast." They scrambled up the bank and sprinted to the ambush point.

Leaving nothing to chance, Parker peeked out of the bushes and looked for cops in his yard. No one was there to see them. Hunched over, they skittered to the firepit chimney and stopped to watch the house. There were no signs of movement in the house where the lights were still on, so they dashed inside, feeling foolish but justified.

"Strip naked and toss your clothes in the washing machine." Parker pushed the kid toward the laundry room.

Cole passed him coming from the laundry room, wearing an embarrassed look, but making no attempt to cover his genitals, acting like he was a grown man now. As Cole ascended the stairs, Parker called after him, "Better let Mama know what we found."

The kid groaned, tired of playing intermediary between two recalcitrant people.

Parker stripped in the laundry room, added dirty clothes from the hamper to make it look like a routine clothes-washing cycle, and started the washing machine. Then he went upstairs to shower and put on dry clothes.

In the swank offices of Morrison & O'Brien, Attorneys at Law, in Tower Place in Buckhead, Parker sat in a small, glass-walled conference room with the blinds open, at a small round table hunched over a speakerphone. In his office, Tim Morrison was busily amending Meredith's settlement agreement to reflect a settlement amount of seventy-five thousand dollars and to include a provision to bar Meredith from testifying against Parker or Paula.

"I told you before it's a waste of time." Noah Friedman was a psychiatrist and part of the "gang of four" friends from before Meredith Walker had ruined their idyllic world in Florida. Along with Ron, the private investigator, and Vince Romeli, the attorney, they had been golfing and boating and drinking buddies. When Vince took two weeks to get Parker bailed out of jail and couldn't get the charges against Parker dismissed without a trial, Parker had fired Vince. In his place, he'd hired a slick, expensive defense attorney from Tampa who'd preened in front of the press cameras. That move had cost him his friends. The gang of four had disintegrated, and Parker went to prison anyway.

Once upon a time, Noah had been in private practice but had found it difficult to make ends meet. No one submits to long-term, deep psychoanalysis anymore—psychologists are cheaper and less emotionally demanding—so Noah had been reduced to writing prescriptions for the psychologists who counseled the patients. Now Noah had taken a job at state-funded West Florida Psychiatric Center in Tampa and had become a government bureaucrat overnight.

After thirty seconds of social niceties, Parker had broached the subject of a Baker Act petition to have Meredith involuntarily examined by psychiatrists at a Florida mental institution. He had made the same suggestion when his trial had ended with a conviction, but Noah had demurred. That, in turn, had led to Parker's despicable act of revenge: sending Meredith to prison instead of the funny farm, an outcome Parker had thought less than perfect.

"I'm a real MD and not a shoulder-to-cry-on clinical psychologist, Parker. From what I've seen of her behavior, I'd say she's psychotic, but we don't involuntarily commit psychopaths. In their infinite wisdom, the legislators in this fine state exempted psychopaths from the Baker Act because we can prescribe anti-psychotic drugs and treat them as outpatients."

"Just listen to my story, please. As I read the Baker Act, there are three reasons why a court can order someone to be examined involuntarily. The first is the risk they might harm themselves. She just attempted suicide, sent her kid a picture of slit wrists. I have a copy of the picture."

Noah sighed down the line. "Unless there's a record of hospitalization after a suicide attempt, we'd disregard the gesture as a symptom of common depression. Psychopaths usually practice before going for it. We wait until they're serious."

"Your empathy is overwhelming. Okay, the second reason is the risk that they'll harm other people."

"You have any proof?" Noah asked.

"I have pictures of her with a gun in my backyard."

"Did she shoot at you?"

"No, I didn't give her a chance. What about a complaint we made to the authorities here in Atlanta because she harassed us? I can send you all the details."

"You have pictures of her doing that?"

"Okay, dammit. The third reason you can involuntarily evaluate a psychopath is if they are self-neglectful. That's the term in the law—self-neglectful. You could check her medical records, see if she takes her meds and makes her outpatient appointments."

Beaten into submission by Parker's relentless badgering, Noah said, "Alright, Parker, I'll see what's in her records."

"Thanks, pal. One more thing: if she qualifies, in your expert opinion, for an examination, could you write the petition, make it persuasive for that Judge Williamson who rubber-stamps them? A psychiatric professional can petition the court for an involuntary examination."

Noah had a rather unprofessional interest in Meredith's physical charms. Once at a pool party at Parker's house, he had kidded Meredith about wanting to see the butterfly tattoo on her butt, and she had pulled her bikini bottom aside to show him. Noah had nearly fainted. Now Parker hoped that Noah could summon some professional interest in Meredith's abnormal behavior.

Noah was silent for a full minute. "It's just an examination by your objective colleagues," Parker added. "If she doesn't qualify for commitment, you let her go, and there's no harm done. If she does need in-patient care, you take a dangerous person off the street. It's your civic duty."

"Civic duty?" Noah said. "That's rich coming from a guy with your history."

Despite Parker's repeated pleas of innocence, his incarceration for shooting a man was a stigma he couldn't wash away with soap and water.

"All I'm willing to do is check her records and review your material. Send the stuff to my personal email account, and I'll have a look." He gave Parker his email address.

When they hung up, Parker used the law office computer to send the package of evidence, including the pictures of the fake suicide attempt and Meredith brandishing a gun in his backyard.

To complete the preparations, Parker called another erstwhile friend—Vince Romeli. The lawyer's paralegal, Melissa, answered the office phone.

"He says he's not your lawyer."

Apparently, Melissa had been trained to screen Parker's calls. "It's not for me. Noah Friedman will be his client. He'll want to hear the story."

"Maybe," Melissa said.

She placed Parker on hold, and he stared at the phone's speaker as though Vince might materialize like a genie conjured from Aladdin's lamp. Tim broke Parker's concentration with a rap on the glass wall. He waved a sheaf of papers, and Parker motioned for him to enter the tiny room.

"This won't stand up in court," Tim said. He dropped two copies of the amended agreement on the table. "The court can subpoena her and force her to testify as a hostile witness."

Parker turned to the third page and read the inserted declaration. "True, but her testimony can be impugned since she has to swear here that she had no knowledge of our movements."

The attorney's left eyebrow danced upward toward his hairline. "You a jailhouse lawyer, now? She signs both copies, you sign both copies, one copy to her lawyer, one copy to me." He turned on his heel and left Parker to stare at the phone's speaker.

After a minute, Vince said, "What do you want now?"

Vince was as reticent to socialize with Parker as the psychiatrist had been, so Parker explained the situation.

"She's paid her debt to society," Vince said. "Why not leave it at that?"

"Meredith is harassing us again. You know where she belongs, Vince."

"Okay, okay already. I'll do it for my friend—*Noah*. If he writes a Baker Act petition, I'll submit it to Judge Williamson. I'll do it for him, but I'm not representing you, Parker. Clear?"

"Crystal. Noah will let you know if he wants you to proceed," Parker said.

He breathed a sigh of relief as he escaped the claustrophobia-inducing conference room. Walking down the hallway toward the reception area, a skinny guy wearing a checked shirt with rolled sleeves and a clashing striped tie popped out of an office.

"If you're John Parker, I'm your defense attorney, Connor O'Brien." The man stuck out a hand.

Parker noticed Connor's straight white teeth and Johnston & Murphy wingtips. *Nearly Americanized*, he thought, shaking Connor's hand.

"Let's have a word," Connor said. He showed Parker into his office.

On a wall the color of day-old blood, he had hung undergraduate and law diplomas from a Cambridge college, and a plaque commemorating his acceptance into the Georgia bar six years ago. The other wall held a blown-up picture of a British court scene, Connor in white wig and black gown gesticulating to a panel of judges who wore the same clownish attire. Parker chuckled at the antiquated and exaggerated theatricality. "Putting on a Shakespeare play?"

"That's the Old Bailey, I'll have you know. Your courts still feel like the Wild West to me. They lack gravitas."

"But they're so efficient, Connor. More prisoners per capita in America than anywhere else in the world."

"You're all descended from convicts, as I recall." The lawyer took a seat behind his desk. "I'm glad you stopped by. My 'deep throat' in the police department called me with the status of your case."

"Good news or bad?"

"Both. No surprise, you're a person of interest. They checked with the St. Petersburg police, a lieutenant named Monahan, and know the history you have with the Walker sisters."

Before he'd seen Grace on a cold slab, Parker hadn't seen her in the flesh since Meredith had gone to prison, but Grace had appeared in a recurring nightmare, the twisted end of a noir movie. In the scene, Cole pushes his father down the street in a wheelchair as Grace walks alongside with an arm around her "son." As they pass the camera, they look directly into the lens, and Grace's evil smile conveys her triumph. Grace had coveted her sister's husband but ended up caring for a cripple instead of marrying a war hero. Naturally, she'd blamed Parker for that.

"Detective Rawlings has developed tunnel vision, and I'm the light at the end of his tunnel."

"Common occurrence, mate. They start with those closest to the victim instead of following the evidence trail, and that causes the tunnel vision. Every cop detective in the country uses the same approach and that's why *Dateline* and *20/20* have so much material for their TV shows."

"But I'm not closest to the victim; her sister is."

"The sister is nowhere to be found, mate."

"Do they have scientific proof that Grace went into the water at the park beside my home?" As he'd tossed and turned in sweaty bedsheets, Parker had composed a speech he fantasized delivering to a jury: "The water level has been up and down several times since the Fourth, so the river has run at different speeds. It's full of rocks and fallen trees where a body might get stuck. Hard to say how far she floated. Water temperature is a problem too. The river water is colder when the water is up and coming from the bottom of Lake Lanier than when it's down and getting plenty of sunshine. That complicates any estimate of how long she'd been in the water. She could have been kidnapped and taken somewhere else to be murdered. By someone else."

Connor leaned back in his chair. "I had forgotten that you're a scientist, Parker. Unfortunately, your jurors will be simple-minded citizens, and they'll want to hear a simple story. Grace's van was recovered at the park; ergo, she was killed at the park."

That's what Conroy and Rawlings had been so excited about. They found Grace's van and now they're examining it for clues. If Meredith came to the park with her sister, why didn't she drive the van away? Because Meredith left with her accomplice.

"Doesn't mean she drove the van. They have any witnesses?" Parker wanted to know if the cops are aware that Meredith had an accomplice.

Connor sighed. "They don't have a witness just yet, but you'll see them canvassing your neighborhood to find people who were at the park."

That was unwelcome news for Parker as the cops would hear stories about what regularly went on at the Parker home. Paula had gone barhopping one night and failed to come home at all. The next morning a neighbor—Parker had no idea which house this woman occupied—had knocked on his front door. When he'd opened the door, the woman pointed to Paula sprawled on the front lawn in a drunken stupor. She'd said, "You don't belong in our neighborhood," and walked away.

"Terrific," Parker said. "I'm persona non grata at the office, now I won't be welcome in my own neighborhood. When they searched the thicket yesterday, they found a spent shell casing and a sandal. Showed it to me for identification. Can you follow up on that?"

"They've already processed the evidence. The lab is chockablock, but they put a rush job on it because the murder is getting so much attention in the press. You know they found a Colt .45 pistol too? Fired once."

"No," Parker said, but he knew evidence marker 1 represented the big gun. *Boom.* The surprise was that it had been fired only once. So, what gun was used at the ambush point? And what about the other booms he'd heard when he was crawling through the thicket?

"The fingerprints on that gun belong to Grace Walker, and the prints on the casing were traced to someone called Duncan Hardy, former Navy Seal … lives in Florida. They'll be lookin' 'im up."

Parker snorted. "Hardy didn't shoot anybody. He's in a wheelchair, paralyzed from the waist down. Lives with Grace, who takes care of him."

"*Took* care of him," Connor said. "That means the dead sister brought the war hero's gun to Georgia. Curious that she would do that."

Parker didn't want to go down that rathole, so he changed the subject. "Was that all they found? A gun that doesn't belong to me and was fired by someone else and a sandal that could belong to anyone?"

Connor surprised him. "That's all the cops found but they have a working theory based on pictures of a broken window, scratches on Paula, and the bruise on your face. The four of you had a big dustup in the backyard. Meredith and Grace ran into the woods, trying to reach their car. They hid behind a tree and defended themselves, but you were the better shot. You shot a man in Florida. This time you winged Grace with your wife's gun, and she fell into the water. Eventually, her body washed up in Martin's Landing and Bob's your uncle."

An icy chill slithered down Parker's throat, through his stomach, all the way to his genitals. "They think I did it?"

"Sure, who else?"

Connor's "deep throat" had neglected to mention two other casings the cops found in the thicket. "Can they identify the caliber of the bullet that caused Grace's wound?"

"That's the sticky wicket, isn't it? They're convinced it was small caliber, like your wife's gun." He paused to let that sink in.

"Maybe Meredith had a gun and shot her sister by accident." Parker knew he was skating on thin ice, sharing that theory with an officer of the court.

Connor shook his head. "There's no record of Meredith owning a gun. They checked with the boyfriend in Florida, and he confirmed that he doesn't own a gun either. So, after eliminating all other possibilities, you had your wife's missing gun."

"Do the cops have any leads as to Meredith's whereabouts? Dead or alive?"

"Her boyfriend Wade Gilbert's credit card was swiped yesterday at two convenience stores down near the airport. The cops had asked the professor to leave it active in case that happened."

That idiot! She's going to get caught. "I told you I didn't kill her."

"Maybe you stole the credit card off her dead body. Maybe you buried her body in the north Georgia mountains. This morning someone turned in a sandal floating down the river that matches the one the cops found in the woods. Since Grace had laced trainers on both feet, they're guessing the sandals belonged to Meredith. Yesterday someone turned her phone on again and tossed it in the back of a pickup truck that went all the way to Jacksonville, Alabama. Six patrol cars surrounded the poor bloke near Fort McClellan, and he shat his knickers."

That made Parker laugh.

Connor laughed too. "It's funny until you realize that the cops think that you pulled that little stunt. Now the geniuses in blue think you offed 'em both."

"Bloody cops." Parker used the British profanity to help Connor understand his frustration. "They couldn't find their ass with two hands and a flashlight."

"American colloquialism? Haven't heard that one before. Chin up, Parker. All in all, their case is the dog's breakfast. They'll have a hell of a time proving her bruises and abrasions were suffered before she went into the water, and they don't have a murder weapon."

Under ordinary circumstances, being suspected of a double homicide would be bad news. Since Parker knew Meredith was alive, he considered it good news. It meant the cops had to search for both a dead body and a live one. It meant he had time to stampede her to Florida and into an insane asylum.

"Thanks, Connor." Parker rose to leave.

"Ah, if you don't mind, I'll take my retainer now," the lawyer said.

Parker gave him an aw-shucks smile. "Of course." Parker wrote Connor a check for $10,000 from his dwindling checking account.

***

Parker passed Rawlings' unmarked police cruiser as he traveled down the street to his house. In his rearview mirror, Parker watched Rawlings disappear over the hilltop. A beige minivan with its hood and doors open blocked Parker's driveway, so he eased to the curb. The van wore a Florida license plate.

Parker climbed out of his car and approached. Cole. Cole pressed a button and operated the wheelchair lift. With a rag, the kid wiped white dust from the apparatus.

"Is this your aunt's van?" Parker asked.

The kid was all smiles. "Yeah, the detective said they found it in the parking lot on the other side of those woods. It's covered in fingerprint powder, so I'm wiping it down."

"How did it get here?" The kid gave Parker a questioning look, didn't understand the question. "I mean how were they able to drive it?"

The kid's smile faded. "Aunt Grace left the keys in it. A guy from the motor pool drove it and the detective gave him a ride back to the motor pool."

Grace left the keys in the van so they wouldn't get lost in the thicket. Meredith would have driven the van away if she had come to the park with her sister.

Did Rawlings ask you any questions?"

"Why are you so paranoid? Rawlings said I can drive it to the morgue tomorrow. I have to sign some papers for…to pick her up, I mean…" His hands flopped to his sides.

"Did he ask for me? Did he want to know where I was?"

"No. Shit, Parker, you're not the center of the universe. He only wanted me to have the van. Aunt Grace's clothes are in it."

Parker inhaled deeply and exhaled slowly. "Sorry, Cole, I didn't mean to sound unsympathetic. When you're done, let's talk about money."

The kid closed the hood and the doors and followed Parker into the house.

Parker took a seat on the back deck and Cole stood, staring into the inscrutable thicket.

"When the cops pull your phone records," Parker said, "they'll find those texts from your mama and they'll be back to sweat you until you give her up."

"I don't need a lecture, Parker. Just give me the money."

"The cops found your mama's phone—her real phone—in a pickup truck in Alabama, so they know she's alive and hiding."

"The money, Parker."

"Your mama can have the money after she signs a set of papers." Parker laid the settlement agreement that Tim Morrison had prepared on the tiny table. He lit a Macanudo cigar, slender like Parker himself, and waved it at Cole. "Turn to the third page and read it."

Cole blinked rapidly behind his thick glasses. In slow motion, he turned the pages and read the new clause, a sworn statement that Meredith Walker has no knowledge of John and Paula Parker's actions after she left their backyard on the Fourth of July, and therefore she has no factual testimony to bring against Paula or John Parker in the matter of Grace Walker's death.

"We can't accept this," he said and dropped the document on the table. "It's not enough money."

Parker noted that the kid was now invested in the negotiation—*we* can't accept this, he'd said. Maybe Meredith had bribed the kid with a chunk of the loot. "Small problem; I don't have one hundred fifty thousand dollars. I've paid for a lawyer and rehab for Paula, so you can have what's left—seventy-five thousand dollars."

Cole shook like a man in the electric chair feeling the first blast of retribution for his crimes. "What she saw in the thicket is worth more than seventy-five thousand dollars. If she signs this, she loses all her leverage."

"Leverage? She lost her leverage when the cops found her casings in the woods."

"She says those markers were for your wife's casings."

Probably true. "You're playing poker now, Cole, pushing all your chips into the pot and hoping for an ace in the hole based upon the lies of a mother who never loved you."

Parker thought the kid was about to cry.

"She loves me," the kid insisted.

"She has a funny way of showing it." Parker pointed to the affidavit. "Tell her no ticky, no laundry."

Cole made the "oof" sound a little kid makes when the schoolyard bully punches him in the belly. He grabbed the settlement agreement and ran into the house—presumably to confer with his mama.

Parker slouched in a lawn chair and puffed on his cigar. Engulfed in aromatic smoke, he imagined the scales of justice with a little bit of good news perched on one small tray and a heap of bad news clumped on the other. As he waited for his houseguest to return, Sabrina tapped on the French door behind him. He waved her onto the deck.

"Don't you lock your doors?"

"Don't want the cops to have to break them down."

She plunked his laptop down on the little circular table. "It feels radioactive in my backpack."

He shrank away from the machine as though it were a snake ready to strike. "Too dangerous to have it here in my house. Can you keep it at your place?"

When she didn't move, Parker said, "I know what you're thinking: how far am I willing to go for a guy who's been to prison and is suspected of murder?"

"That's not—" she stammered.

"It's okay, you're being smart. But there's nothing incriminating on that box, and you're just prepping it for legitimate work reasons. I don't want the cops to take it away before we foil Kumar's fraud. Put the computer in your car. Please."

Sabrina sighed and rose and ambled through the house to take the computer out to her car.

While he waited for her to return, his phone rang. Another Florida number. "I thought you only got one call."

"Borrowed a phone from Jim."

"Who?"

"One of the counselors. He likes me."

"Everything okay there?"

"Peachy-keen. Is she with you?"

"Who?"

"Who? Who? You sound like a fucking owl. Jordyn said your girlfriend was in my house. Are you fucking her in my bed?"

"No. I've been kicked out of the office because of the murder investigation so we're working here."

"Get her the fuck out of my house, Parker!"

"Fine, we'll move to a seedy motel." He hung up.

"That went well," Sabrina said. "You want me to leave?"

"No, stay. Cole is negotiating with his mama, and my private investigator is about to show up."

"You have a private investigator?" Sabrina said.

Parker put a finger to his lips. "Shh, don't want Cole to know. Ron is just a fishing buddy passing through. He's going to figure out what really happened on the Fourth of July."

She declined Parker's offer of alcohol and selected a bottle of sparkling water from his refrigerator. She brought him a beer.

"You still haven't told me everything, Parker."

"About what?"

"It doesn't make sense for Meredith to kill you when you owed her money. And what did the other sister have against you?"

Parker took a long draft of his beer, decided to tell Sabrina a little more of the truth. "When our company ran out of cash before we could go public, Meredith falsified the beta tests of my algorithms so she could entice new investors. I refused to participate in the fraud."

"It's déjà vu," Sabrina said.

"Meredith came to my house that evening three years ago to have me killed so she could own my algorithms and entice investors to relaunch the company—her company. She was going to trick Duncan Hardy, who was her ex-husband, into believing I was raping her. He went full commando and I shot him. But here's the twist: Grace was in love with Hardy and after his divorce from her sister, she thought he'd be hers. But then I crippled him."

Sabrina made that perfect O with her lips and said, "So Grace had motive to kill you. Grace came here for revenge."

"Meredith wanted revenge, too. After I went to prison, I tattled to the FBI and testified against Meredith. She was convicted of conspiracy to defraud investors and went to prison. I'm ashamed of myself for the petty payback, but she tried to kill me and got away with it. I'm sure Meredith would like to see me dead, but she wants her money first."

Sabrina took a minute to think about it. "If you didn't kill the sister, there's only one reason you'd hire a private detective to figure it out—you think your wife did it."

"No, it's because the cops think I did it," he lied.

"And they're wrong as usual."

Before Parker could respond, Ron lumbered onto the deck. "Interrupting anything?"

"No," Parker said, and he made the introductions.

"Pleased to meet you," Sabrina shook Ron's hand.

"Grab a beer, Ron, and I'll tell you what the cops did today."

"Bring you a fresh one?" Ron said. "I restocked with Labatt Blue, worsening America's embarrassing NAFTA trade deficit."

Parker chuckled. "Yeah, just keep them coming."

Ron sat the beers on the table, shuffled down to the firepit, and hefted one of the heavy wrought-iron chairs.

"Bring them both," Parker said. "Cole will be down soon. He's negotiating with his mama."

Ron lugged them to the deck, sat in one, took a long swig of beer. "Go ahead."

Parker told Ron and Sabrina about Duncan Hardy's .45, one .45 casing, two unidentified casings, and one of Meredith's sandals. "Her other sandal was found in the river, so the cops have to account for the possibility that she's in the river too. But she's not. She and Cole have been texting."

"You were right, there were more shots fired in the thicket," Ron said. "One from the big dog and two from the little dog."

Parker tested the theory he would tell a jury if it came to that. "It was dark out there, and they were scared, so Grace and Meredith got confused and shot at each other."

"Meredith shot her sister?" Sabrina said. "What an awful accident."

Parker wanted Sabrina on his jury.

"The cops will have to find Meredith's gun to prove it," Ron said.

Leading the conversation away from who-shot-Grace, Parker said, "My lawyer says the .45 was fired only once, so Meredith's accomplice used a different gun from the ambush point. Do you have any leads on him?"

Ron started at the beginning to recount his day of sleuthing. At the motel on Holcomb Bridge Road where Dr. Wade Gilbert had rented a room for Meredith, Ron had shown the desk clerk pictures of the sisters, side by side. The clerk had said that Meredith had been there for a couple of days, but then the maid had reported the room empty even though Meredith hadn't checked out. She'd come back, though—he'd thought she was Meredith, anyway—but now the clerk realized it had been the other sister who had stayed there the last two days. "They're the same but different, you know?" is what he'd said.

"Were Meredith's clothes still in the room?"

"No, not a thing."

"Was she with anyone?"

"Yeah, a tall guy. I asked him what the guy looked like, and he goes, 'He was a white dude, man.'"

"Meredith is shacking up with her accomplice." Parker oscillated between doubt that Paula could have stepped up to the fallen tree and shot Grace in cold blood and the acute fear that there were multiple witnesses to what had happened in the thicket.

Meredith's burner phone, Ron went on to report, had been purchased with cash at a convenience store in south Atlanta, near the airport. "The clerk said the surveillance tapes had already cycled—they only keep twenty-four hours—but he found the cash register receipt from Sunday. Then he remembered the buyer was a white male, tall, baseball cap and sunglasses, driving an old orange Japanese sedan. He bought half a dozen burners."

"Aha!" Parker said. He retrieved the Stone Mountain postcard and showed it to Ron. "The orange car dropped this note in our mailbox last Sunday. The car must belong to her new boyfriend." That left Parker to wonder who belonged to the shiny black car.

Ron continued. "I found the hotel where Meredith and her boyfriend stayed over the weekend. The boyfriend hasn't been seen since yesterday morning. Meredith skipped out on the room charge this morning."

"Last night, Gilbert's credit card was swiped twice near the airport. I'm sure the cops have pulled the ATM video. My guess is the boyfriend has abandoned Meredith, scared to get in any deeper. So where's Meredith now?"

"Not in a hotel down there around the airport. I checked them all. The hotel manager said to let him know if I find her. Trashed her room, red hair dye stains in the bathroom sink, and dried blood in the bathtub."

"She sent Cole a photo of her bandaged wrists over that bathtub."

Sabrina turned her head from one man to the other, following the conversation like a spectator following the ball at a tennis match.

"At a nearby convenience store, a woman with short red hair got into a fight with the clerk and ran out with stolen scissors, bandages, and razor blades," Ron said.

"For the fake suicide to convince Cole to help her."

"By ignoring the threat, you called her bluff. She's just trying to get away with murder."

"Gotta be the boyfriend who took the shots from the ambush point."

Ron sat upright and pointed his chin over Parker's shoulder at Cole, who was making his way back to the deck. Ron offered the kid a beer, and he declined but took a seat.

Cole jerked a thumb at Ron. "What's he still doing here?"

"He decided to fish the Hooch before going up north. What did your mama say?"

Ron and Sabrina leaned toward Cole. The kid sneered at them and said, "Mama said to stick your papers where the sun don't shine."

"Whoa!" Ron jerked back in his seat.

Now Parker felt like he was the one playing poker, holding two pair—Paula's gun was lost in a pecan grove and he had pictures of Meredith waving a gun. He hoped Meredith didn't have a full house. "If that's the way she wants to play it," Parker said, "I'm willing to call here bluff."

"Yes!" Ron said with a fist pump. "Call her bluff."

The kid blinked behind his thick glasses, stood uneasily. "You have twenty-four hours to come up with all the money or she'll go to the cops."

Parker slapped his knees and said, "Sure, give Rawlings a call, see if he believes her. Of course, she gets no money that way."

He offered to take everyone to dinner at J. Alexander's at the Forum in Peachtree Corners.

Sabrina demurred. "I'll let you boys talk." She paused. "About fishing."

Cole said he wasn't hungry. "Can I have another beer?"

"You can have as many as you want," Parker said.

***

Ron and Parker ate Rattlesnake Pasta at the bar. A TV above rows of liquor bottles played the late evening news as they ate. The anchor talked over pictures of Grace and

Meredith. The cops wanted to know if anyone had seen Grace at Jones Bridge Park on the Fourth of July. They wanted to know if anyone had seen Meredith anywhere at any time since the Fourth of July. They splashed a tip line number on the screen.

"That's Grace's van in your driveway, right?" Ron asked.

"Yeah, she came to Atlanta to find Meredith," Parker said, "and she brought Duncan Hardy's Colt .45 with her."

"But Grace wasn't the person who shot at you from the edge of your yard."

The thought of Grace as a sniper, like a Navy Seal stalking Osama Bin Laden, was ludicrous. "No. She was an accountant, Ron, and her gun had only been fired once."

"But Meredith didn't drive the van away from the park, so she left with someone else," Ron said.

"Grace's clothes are in her van. She may have been backup, but she was ready to leave for Florida. Meredith came with her accomplice and now she's on the run with her accomplice."

They watched the news in silence, sipping their beers, until Ron said, "One thing bothers me: Why did the accomplice shoot at you before you had a chance to sign the settlement agreement?"

Parker thought he had to be very careful with Ron who was a professional detective. He couldn't reveal that Paula had preempted the signing of the settlement agreement by shooting at Meredith first. "I guess he saw that we were arguing. I wasn't accepting the agreement; I was yelling at Meredith to get out of my yard and let the lawyers handle the agreement."

"So, it was sign or die, you're saying?"

"Yeah, and maybe the shooter lost his cool. He took a shot at Paula and Jordyn on the deck, too."

Parker had the sudden chilling thought that the bullet that went through the window of the French door might be lodged in the siding on his neighbor's house.

"So, he's not a pro." Ron slid off the barstool and wrapped an arm around Parker's shoulders. "When you get home, keep the kid inside until I give you the all-safe. I want a close look at that van before the kid drives it."

Back at the house, Parker found six empty beer bottles lined up on the kitchen table like soldiers at reveille. Cole was no doubt passed out upstairs. Parker loitered in the kitchen a while, uncapped another beer he neither needed nor wanted. Finally he moved to the foyer and risked peering through the blinds. He saw a flashlight moving around under the van. Ron was thorough. Finally he received a text from Ron: Meet me in the backyard.

Parker turned on the marina lights but not the spotlights and snuck out the back door. When Ron came around the side of the house, wiping his hands on a shop rag, they met at the firepit and hid behind the tall chimney.

Ron leaned close and whispered, "The kid has his mother's gun, taped to the firewall of the van."

Parker leaned toward Ron to whisper back. "How the hell did it get there? Cole hasn't left the house since I brought him home."

Ron craned his neck around the chimney, looking for Cole. When he was sure the kid wasn't eavesdropping, he said "He was alone while we were at dinner tonight. His mama must have told him where she hid it."

"You think he crawled through the woods in the dark? I don't think he has the cojones."

"You have a better explanation?"

Parker thought about his time with Cole and reached a conclusion. "The other day, when the cops searched the thicket, Cole wasn't worried about what they'd find. He had already been talking to his mother. She must have told him where she dropped her gun. I think he had already moved it to a spot where the cops wouldn't look. Tonight he moved it to the van."

Ron rubbed his chin. "I don't think he's stupid enough to hide it in the house, so where was it?"

Parker replayed the scene in which he and Cole had watched the cops' search the thicket. Cole had craned his neck to see where the cops were searching. Then he had relaxed. "The cops searched the thicket from my house to the park, but they never searched my property. Maybe it was right here, like maybe up in this chimney. Tonight he retrieved it."

"Smart kid," Ron said. "Either way, he thought the van was safe because the cops wouldn't search it again after they'd just returned it."

Ron glanced around the chimney, then pulled a plastic baggie out of his pocket and handed it to Parker. In the low ambient light Parker couldn't see what was in the baggie but he felt hard cylindrical shapes.

"Bullets?"

"I unloaded the gun," Ron said. "Can't have that kid running around with a loaded gun."

Parker tried to count the bullets by feel.

"Three bullets are missing from the clip, and one round was in the chamber, so Meredith fired two shots out there," Ron said.

"Meredith did shoot her sister."

The cops didn't mention the two casings they found or accuse me of firing the shots because they don't have a matching weapon, whether Paula's or Meredith's, Parker thought.

"Put those where the kid won't find them but you can get to them. There will be fingerprints," Ron said.

"I have a spot."

"The gun wasn't the only thing I found," Ron said. "There's a tracking device stuck to the rear driver's side wheel well of that van."

"The cops are playing both hunches: they'll look for her dead body, but if she's alive, they want Cole to lead them to his mother."

"When his aunt's body is ready, let the kid walk into the trap."

"She won't tell him where she is until she has a deal for the money, so I'll have to lure her into the open so the cops can catch her," Parker said. Not really a lie, he thought, just a little subterfuge. He wanted Meredith in an insane asylum, not a prison. If Meredith were in an asylum, her testimony against Paula would be discredited.

"One way or the other, I'll find Meredith tomorrow," Ron said.

"Look for an accomplice before the cops do, Ron."

"Sure, buddy."

Ron loped around the side of Parker's house and disappeared into the night.

Parker crept to the house and into the laundry room. He hid Meredith's bullets above the cabinets, where he had hidden liquor from Paula.

Noah called at the crack of dawn and Parker made him hold as he scampered downstairs to his office. He closed the door and locked it.

"Top of the morning to ya, Noah. What's up?"

"You were right," Noah said. "When Meredith was inside, the prison shrink diagnosed her as having all five personality disorders: antisocial, narcissistic, avoidant, histrionic, and paranoid. That's a royal flush in my profession. The prison shrink got to examine the perfect lab specimen, lucky guy. He prescribed anti-anxiety and anti-depressant medications, but she complained that the meds made her sluggish and caused her to gain weight, which happens all the time. She stopped picking up her prescription at the pharmacy, but it wasn't reported because they don't give a shit. Following her release, she never filled her prescriptions and never made a single outpatient appointment, but it wasn't reported—"

"—because government employees don't give a shit. Is that enough to get her examined?"

"It's pretty flimsy but I included all the other stuff you sent me. I wrote up the petition and sent it to Vince. Judge Williamson likes to protect the public welfare by putting people through the examination process so there's a chance."

"Thanks for working so fast, Noah. Tell Vince to hand-carry the petition to Williamson. If the judge orders an examination, let me know ASAP. I'll be down in a couple of days, and I'll look you up. Buy you a beer for old times' sake."

"Sure, but I have to warn you that even if the judge orders an examination, her personality disorders won't get her committed. We'll put her through the ringer for seventy-two hours, but if we find no more serious conditions, we'll have to put her back on the street."

"Noah, the woman is a psychopath. Even your eggheads should see that."

"Millions of people are functioning psychopaths. We've had psychopathic presidents and psycho CEOs driven to exceptional performance by their psychoses. We'll prescribe anti-psychotic drugs and monitor her outpatient appointments, make her submit to blood and urine tests to ensure she's taking the medication."

Parker realized that Noah was cooperating only because he could examine a royal flush lab specimen and not because he could take Meredith off the game board for Parker. "Noah, someone has to make up for the incompetence of the state legislators who wrote the Baker Act."

"The law is the law, my friend."

Parker relented. "I'll be grateful for anything you can do, Noah."

Seventy-two hours of involuntary examination wasn't likely to discredit Meredith's testimony, but Parker had no other cards to play.

As a delaying tactic, Parker made Cole breakfast—scrambled eggs using sour cream instead of milk, mixed with diced jalapenos. Breakfast foods were the only things Parker could cook. He had a well-documented history of destroying hotdogs and hamburgers on the grill, a disappointment for Paula, who cleaved to stereotypical gender roles.

They ate in silence, Cole's head nodding in rhythm with whatever was playing in his earbuds, the kid connected to a millennial fantasy world that was more tolerable than the real world. A buzzing sound wafted through the open French doors and halted Parker's fork in midair. He dropped his fork, moved onto the deck and climbed onto a wobbly lawn chair to peer over the bushes at the bottom of his yard.

The bumblebee sound came from the outboard motors on two heavy rubber police rafts—one dragging the bottom, and the other fifty yards farther downriver, poised to collect whatever was dredged up. The cops' level of commitment to this search impressed him. Many shallow runs and rocky rapids blocked boat traffic between Jones Bridge Park and Martin's Landing. The cops would have to pull the boats out, portage downriver, and launch them again many times on the twenty-four-mile journey.

It reminded him of a scene from *Butch Cassidy and the Sundance Kid.* Butch and the Kid were on the run from a posse led by Lord Baltimore. No matter what devious tactics the outlaws employed, the posse found their trail and tracked them relentlessly. Over and over, an exasperated Butch Cassidy asked, "Who are those guys?" Detective Rawlings was Parker's Lord Baltimore.

He dropped to the deck, strode inside, and yanked the cords from Cole's ears.

"What the fuck, Parker?"

"Hear that?" Parker pointed at the French doors.

The kid perked up his ears like a fawn in the forest and slowly rose to his feet. He got on his tiptoes to look through the window above the sink but couldn't see over the vegetation at the bottom of Parker's yard. "What is it?"

"They're dragging the river, looking for your mama's body. When they don't find it, they'll know she's alive and they'll be back to grill you."

"They're looking for your wife's gun," Cole said.

Possible, Parker thought, *if they haven't bought the Florida pecan grove story.* "They're looking for your mama's gun." Parker enjoyed torturing the kid.

"She didn't have a gun."

Now that he had his mama's gun, Cole's strategy was to play out the lie all the way to the end. Parker's cellmates would have been proud of the kid.

Parker patted Cole on the back. "We'd better take care of Grace before the cops come to get you."

"I can take care of Aunt Grace by myself." Cole started for the front door.

"Well, there's a complication: you can't drive the van."

Cole stopped in his tracks. "Why not?"

"Ever hear the story about the Trojan horse?" Parker slipped past Cole and walked out the door.

Perplexed, Cole followed him onto the driveway. Parker knelt next to the rear driver's side tire and pointed to the wheel well. "See for yourself."

Cole squatted next to Parker and bent his neck to have a look at a black metal magnetic box affixed to the wheel well. There were no flashing red lights like you see on bad TV shows.

"The cops planted a GPS tracking device so they can follow you to your mother."

"Can we turn it off?"

"No, this beauty sends a message to the police monitoring station if switched off or detached." Ron had told him that. "I looked it up on the Internet."

"I don't appreciate you snooping around my van." Cole's face dissolved like melting cheese. "How am I going to get back to Florida?"

"You can drive my car. Leave it at your father's house, and I'll pick it up when I'm in Florida next week."

Cole gave him a hangdog look. "Give me your keys, and I'll take care of Aunt Grace."

"You shouldn't claim the body alone, Cole. I'll tell them where to send her and pay for the embalming and the flight to Florida."

Cole shuffled over to Parker's car, stunned by yet another turn of events. Thankfully, no media vans were parked in the cul-de-sac. They must have been in the park, waiting for the search to be completed.

At the morgue, Parker asked for Detective Rawlings, but a woman in ankle boots, black jeans, and a man's button-up shirt soon appeared in the morgue lobby with a sheaf of papers in her hand. The detective, probably Rawlings's partner, didn't look happy to see Parker accompanying the kid. When she heard that the body would be claimed by a local undertaker, the detective said, "Here? Once you sign for the body, we can load her in a hearse for the trip, ah, home. Why not have her funeral as soon as possible?"

Rawlings had expected the kid to come alone so that Rawlings could tail him to his mama right here in Atlanta.

"We want to embalm her and then fly her home," Parker said. "I'll pay for that and the casket."

The detective huffed, a frustrated sigh. She allowed Cole to sign the release papers while giving Parker the evil eye. When he finished, she took the kid aside to ask him if he had heard from his mother. Cole made brief eye contact with Parker and sidestepped the question by shaking his head and saying he had no idea where his mother might be. The kid had learned to dissemble.

***

The cops weren't waiting for them at Parker's house. A car he recognized as Sabrina's white BMW sat in his driveway next to Grace's van, but Sabrina wasn't in it. He turned his key in the front door lock and found it already unlocked. He stepped into the house, unnecessarily wary. "Hello?"

"In the family room, Parker," came the shouted reply.

He found her lying on the couch, head on one armrest, bare feet on the other, munching a Snickers. Her hair was kinky curls style today.

"Found the spare key under the flowerpot. Pretty obvious, Parker."

Parker chuckled, felt an intimacy with Sabrina that was both alarming and thrilling.

Cole trailed behind Parker. "Give me the damn money so I can get out of here."

Startled, Sabrina swung her feet to the floor and sat up straight. "Your house guest isn't very polite, is he?"

"He doesn't know when to be thankful for my help."

Parker couldn't let the kid leave until he'd heard the results of the Baker Act petition. "Convince your mother to sign the settlement agreement and you can whisk her away to safety."

"She won't do it."

"Well, now you can tell her the cops know she's alive and that they're trying to trick you into leading them to her."

"You ripped her off once before, and now you're doing it again. She's not going to let it happen."

"I need to work, so go play in the traffic." Parker shooed him away with a backhanded wave of his hand.

"This is work?" The kid stomped his foot like a recalcitrant teenager and slinked away.

Sabrina had a smile on her face. Parker thought she had begun to savor the drama.

He sat beside her on the couch. "Is this a social call or have you developed more results?"

Sabrina said, "We finished the runs and loaded your laptop with the test reports."

"And the reports say ..." Parker's voice rose an octave, like a game show host waiting for the answer to flash on the big electronic board.

Sabrina played along, slapped the couch cushion as though slapping the red button. "We ran Alexi's app one time against the testbed, and we got a six percent savings in claims payments. If you wash, rinse, and repeat five times, you get twelve percent for claims. The rules get marginally better."

Parker shook his head and pursed his lips, considering. "Decent results, actually. The claims savings go straight to the bottom line."

"But it's not what Dennie needs, so the loop-de-loop machine learning can't be the only change Ravi will make."

"They'll have to commit fraud." In the excitement of the moment, he reached out and grabbed her arm, near her wrist, and felt the electric pulse of her heart. He forced his heart to slow. "What about Ravi's test results?"

She covered his hand. Touching had become something to do whenever the opportunity presented itself. "They're not on the Google drive I have access to. You'll have to wait for the big reveal in New Orleans."

"A difference in savings calculations won't be enough to prove fraud."

They sat in depressed silence while Parker thought about the process the crooks had to follow. "To commit fraud," he said, "they'll change the test cases or change my machine learning code. Are those files on the Google drive?"

"Nope. There's nothing new out there."

"Shit! They know you hacked their drive."

Sabrina's eyes grew wide at the thought of getting caught. "Steve did it," she protested.

Yeah, Parker thought, but you're the one they suspect is my girlfriend.

"Okay," he said, "manipulating a huge test bed or changing unfamiliar code in a large program is too hard to do by looking at a small computer screen and scrolling up and down. There must be printouts."

"I thought of that. Ravi's filing cabinet is locked."

He leaned back in on the couch and concocted yet another scheme. "Go back to the office and take a picture of Ravi's filing cabinet and text it to me. Stay late at the office tonight, and when everyone has left, text me. I'll come over, and you can let me in. I'll do the rest."

"Jesus, Parker, I don't want to get caught."

"All you're doing is letting me back in the office. I'll take the blame." This is just as dangerous as last time I took the blame, he cautioned himself. "I'll also need a spreadsheet showing the base numbers for one run of the original test cases and for five loops of wash-rinse-repeat. Put it all in a proposal on my laptop."

"No offshore outsourcing?"

"No outsourcing."

After Sabrina left, Parker went to the spare bedroom he called his home office, closed the door and the blinds so Cole couldn't eavesdrop, and sat behind his nine-foot-long trundle table desk in the cherry-red leather executive chair Paula had bought him for his birthday. He called Connor and was put on hold for ten minutes. He waited, persistence and patience two qualities he'd acquired in prison.

"I was just about to ring you up." Connor sounded cheery.

"Yeah, I think you forgot a few details when we spoke yesterday."

"Not sure what you mean. The cops are done with your computer and files," he told Parker. "They want you to pick them up as soon as possible, downtown."

The cops are trying to get me out of the way so they can follow the kid. "Okay, thanks for letting me know. What I'm calling about are the two pieces of evidence the cops found in the thicket that your 'deep throat' didn't tell you about."

"Righto. Do I want to hear how you know about that?"

"No, you don't. What's the deal, Connor?"

"My guy just wanted to wait for the lab results. The Fulton County boys found two .25 caliber casings lying about. Seems there was an old-fashioned shootout in those woods next to your house."

Parker let out a sigh of relief. Meredith's casings, not Paula's. Not those of the accomplice, either. "All we heard was fireworks and firecrackers. I guess some of them were gunshots."

"Sure. Are there any records linking you to the purchase of a .25 caliber gun?"

"Nope. I can't own one."

"'Course not, convicted felon and all," Connor said.

The lawyer was starting to annoy Parker. "Whose fingerprints did they find?"

"They haven't released that information."

"Meredith's," Parker said with some intensity.

"You'd love that, wouldn't you? They haven't figured it out yet, is all."

That stumped Parker for a moment. Either the cops didn't want to reveal that the prints were Meredith's or the prints belonged to … the accomplice!

Parker told Connor about *Butch Cassidy and the Sundance Kid* and the relentless Lord Baltimore. "Lord Baltimore dragged the river this morning," he said. "Looking for Meredith or her gun, I assume."

Connor hesitated, cleared his throat. "Looking for your wife's gun, too. They did a thorough search of that Florida pecan grove and didn't find the gun. Or any snakes."

"Did they find any guns in the river?" To sound innocent, he had to ask.

"They used sonar and underwater cameras, but all they found were fishing lures, mate. I'll let you know if they plan to charge you with any crime. Won't happen till they find a gun. Or Meredith."

After he hung up, Parker considered the mystery of Paula's missing casings. Maybe the cops found them but wanted to keep that information to themselves. If so, why weren't there any evidence markers for her casings?

*****

The sucking sound of the airtight door on his refrigerator being opened alerted Parker to the presence of someone in his kitchen. "Cole?"

"It's me," Ron said.

Parker joined him; the big man was chugging a beer, sweat stains visible under his arms.

"The cops found Meredith's casings in the thicket, but they didn't find the accomplice's casings at the ambush point," Parker said. "What's that tell you?"

"The accomplice wasn't a pro who'd retrieve his brass, so his gun was a revolver."

"The cops may be tracking him from the ATM video. Have you found any trace of him, the tall white guy in the baseball hat?"

"Nah, man, I've looked everywhere. He dumped the crazy lady and skipped town."

"He should be easy to spot in that old orange wreck. Let's wind the kid up." Parker led Ron through the foyer and stopped at the bottom of the stairs. "I have some bad news for you, Cole," Parker yelled.

"What?" the kid peeked out his bedroom door.

"Those two evidence markers we saw last night, numbers four and five? My lawyer says the casings were for .25 caliber bullets, not the .32 caliber bullets from the gun my wife once owned. They're checking the fingerprints."

"Caught your mama red-handed," Ron said.

Cole became combative. "Aunt Grace's wound could have come from any gun."

"So, you admit she had a gun?" Parker said.

"No! You're trying to trick me." Confused and frustrated, the kid blushed. "I just mean they can't match casings to a wound without a bullet."

"Contrary to what you were taught in civics class, prosecutors have no burden of proof," Parker said. "Trials are storytelling contests, and they have a helluva good story. Grace's wound was caused by a small caliber gun and they found small caliber casings. When they match your mama's fingerprints to the casings, she'll be back to wearing pinstripes."

The kid moved onto the landing, clenched his fists. Parker's favorite line from *Reservoir Dogs* came to mind: *"Are you gonna bark all day, little doggie, or are you gonna bite?"* "Are you crying, little boy?"

"I'm not crying," The kid choked back a sob.

"If it weren't for that damn lawsuit I'd just let the cops hunt her down and put her away. But I want out from under. She should kiss my ass for helping you guys out."

"She just wants her money."

"Go give her the news, Cole. She knows how to get her money."

Parker and Ron sat at the bar table, drinking their beer until Cole reappeared. Standing beside the table, the kid said, "Okay, she'll sign the agreement if you give her the one hundred fifty thousand dollars she asked for in the first place."

Parker's lips spread in a self-satisfied smile. "It's a deal, Sportsfans. Where do we meet?"

"She's not going to walk into a trap. I'll take her the money, and we'll drop the signed agreement at her lawyer's office."

"Too late to do that today. The lawyer's office is already closed, so we'll do it tomorrow morning. Anyway, I have an errand to run and I can't have the cops following me in your van."

Parker nodded to Ron, signaling he should follow him and walked through the house and out the front door. He lit a Macanudo cigar, like Michael Jordan celebrating a basketball victory. Although Meredith's spent casings were valuable circumstantial evidence, he knew they weren't enough for the DA to make a murder case. Secretly, he also doubted that Meredith had killed her sister in cold blood. He still had to protect Paula.

He didn't think of himself as amoral; he had an innate sense of fairness, like hammered copper forged by calamitous experience. Meredith's commitment to the funny farm would be a fair ending for her, whether Paula had murdered Grace or not.

"Early tomorrow morning, hide somewhere up the hill until you see Cole leave in my car." Parker pointed vaguely up the street. Finding a hiding spot was a PI's job. "Then zip down here and pick me up so we can follow him."

"Why don't we just tell the cops the plan and let them do it?"

"Not yet, Ron. I want her signed statement and settlement agreement before the cops get in the way."

Ron shrugged. "Should be fun."

Parker guessed that Meredith wouldn't want to show up at a police station with a gun hidden in her sister's van and no accomplice to corroborate her story, so he felt it safe to leave the kid alone in the house.

Parker drove to the office supply store where Shaw Technology purchased its equipment and supplies and located the aisle where the desks and filing cabinets were displayed. He matched the picture Sabrina had texted him to a tin two-drawer model that fit under a desk. There were two such cabinets in the aisle; two were all Parker needed. A pair of silver keys on a metal ring dangled from both locks. He took the keys from the locks, separated them, and mixed them up in his hand. Then he tried all four keys in each lock. Every key worked on both cabinets—all the locks on the cheap filing cabinets were the same. He replaced three keys, slipped one key into his pocket, and casually walked out of the store.

Traveling against rush hour traffic, he made good time, reaching Technology Park in Norcross as high-tech employees headed home for the evening. Slowly, he glided past the Shaw Technology building where some lights were still on and a few cars rested in the parking lot. He pulled into the lot across the street, parked facing Shaw's building, and waited for Sabrina's text message. Parker was checking his phone for the tenth time when it magically rang.

"Judge Williamson just issued the order. Last thing he did before his court closed for the weekend. You owe Vince for this one." Noah said.

It surprised Parker to realize that it was Friday and after business hours. He had been so preoccupied with his problems that he had lost track of the day and time. Probably a good thing, he thought, or he'd have been freaking out over the court order.

"What happens now?"

"You bring her to me, or the cops do, I guess. I don't know. Ask Vince."

"Okay, I'll figure it out. Thanks, Noah."

"My pleasure. I'll be waiting at the front door," Noah said.

After waiting more than an hour, Parker's legs were cramping, and his lower back was protesting, but finally, Sabrina's BMW was the only car in the lot and she texted him a thumbs-up emoji.

He eased out of his car and crossed the street, then stopped to survey the situation. Two cameras hung above the main entrance, one pointed at the parking lot, the other at the sidewalk leading to the double glass doors. Parker avoided both by creeping around the side of the lot, through pine straw flowerbeds, out of the cameras' peripheral vision. He crept to the corner of the building, constantly glancing over his shoulder, alert for passing cars. The side street was deserted. His back pressed against the building wall, he shuffled toward the doors like an escaping convict dodging the searchlights in a prison yard.

Sabrina opened the door when he rapped on the glass. "Hurry," she whispered as though they could be overheard by lurking spirits.

Parker stifled a laugh and followed her through the interior doors. Sabrina took a circuitous route through the maze of cubicles, stopping at one with computer printouts stacked on the floor, on the desk, on top of a bookshelf. The tin two-drawer cabinet squatted under the desk.

"This is Ravi's cabin," she said.

Parker flipped through the listings on the floor and found nothing that looked like his code or test cases. He inserted his key into Ravi's cabinet and turned it smoothly.

"Where'd you get a key?"

"At the office supply store."

Sabrina's lips made her trademark perfect O.

Parker pulled out the top drawer and let out a loud, "Ha!" He leaned aside so Sabrina could see. "Look what we found."

From the drawer, he lifted a bound document with a clear plasticine cover, gold lettering on a red cover page.

Sabrina's lips formed that perfect O again. "The ASC proposal. Dennie should have kept that in her office."

"She wanted plausible deniability if someone found it. She'd let Ravi hang for the theft."

He handed the proposal to Sabrina and pulled the lower drawer open. A four-inch thick, green-and-white lined computer printout lay in the drawer. Parker lifted it out and flipped through the pages.

"The test cases. More than five hundred, I'd guess."

"That's why their file is bigger than ours."

He spread the listing open on Ravi's desk and looked at it together.

"See those strikethroughs?" he said. "Cases they deleted."

"They pulled the outliers, the ones that don't conform to the rules and therefore diminish the savings."

"And yet, I'll bet the total number of cases added up to five hundred so it looks like the MA test bed. Where did the replacements come from?"

"They must have dummied up cases that conformed to the rules."

"There appear to at least one hundred strikethroughs. Lot of work."

"Okay. What now?"

"We take all of this to New Orleans."

"They'll know it's missing."

"No sign of forced entry. For a while, they'll blame Ravi for losing it."

Parker handed her the printout. "Let me out. Wait for me to leave before you leave." He stood, his back creaking from the effort, and started for the door.

"I thought you said you need this stuff in New Orleans."

"I do but it would be safer if you brought it to New Orleans."

"You want me to be your partner-in-crime?"

Always looking for an opportunity to joke his way out of a serious conversation, he brightened and said, "Yeah, like Batman and Robin."

Sabrina played along. "Excuse me?" Hands on hips, elbows out. "No woman wants to be a wimpy-assed boy." Gallows humor.

"Batgirl then! I like that outfit. And the mask."

"Pervert. Nope, I'd be Shuri, from *Black Panther*."

"Cool. I'd be T'Challa."

"You wish, white boy. You wish."

Before Sabrina could object, Parker quick-stepped out of the cubicle and back to the front door.

***

Overtired and anxiety-ridden, Parker tossed and turned until another unrecognized Florida number rang his phone.

His first thought was that the recovery center was calling about an emergency. "Is she okay?"

"It's me," Paula said. A snuffling sound and a deep inhale of breath. "Ah can't sleep, and they won't give me a pill, Parker."

Parker rolled out of bed, more comfortable on his feet, pacing, as he spoke to his wife. "How are you calling me this time?"

"House phone in the visitors' center. I snuck out of my room."

"They'll kick you out if you break the rules."

"They won't kick me out if you pay the bills. They're whores like everyone else."

Parker hoped she was right. "Well, you can relax, Paula. The cops didn't find your casings."

"You are so tone-deaf, Parker. Aren't you worried about me?"

"I'm worried that you won't finish the program."

"I can't do it, Parker. If you love me, come right now and get me out of here."

"We have to get you through the program. I'll be down to see you this weekend."

"And you'll take me home?" Her voice quavered. "I promise I won't drink, Parker."

"You're kidding yourself."

"You prick. This is your last chance."

"Finish the program, Paula."

"You don't care about me. Has your girlfriend moved into my house?"

"Maybe I should let you go to prison this time," Parker growled. "See how you like it."

"Fuck you. I want a divorce."

Before Parker could respond, he heard a scuffle and a male voice: "It's after curfew, Paula."

"Leave me alone," Paula said.

More scuffling, someone manhandling Parker's wife, followed by the sound of the telephone handset banging against the wall.

"Stop it," Paula said.

"Paula? What's happening?" Parker said.

Muffled male words, and then the handset was slammed onto its cradle. After that, Parker couldn't sleep.

As Parker drank a second cup of coffee, Cole came down the stairs with his backpack slung over his shoulder.

"Give me the money, Parker."

"Good morning to you, too. Want to have some breakfast before the long journey?"

"Stop stalling, Parker. Hand over the money so I can get out of here."

"Sure." Parker led Cole into his office and made a big show of crossing out $75,000, writing in $150,000, and signing both copies of the agreement. Then he wrote a check for $10,000 to Meredith Walker. As though it were a solemn ceremony, Parker handed Cole the check and papers.

"What kind of scam is this? We agreed on $150,000," Cole said.

"The agreement says $150,000, but I'm not about to give your mama all the money before she signs the document," Parker said. "She's guaranteed the rest by the courts when the agreement is filed."

Cole hung his head in despair. "God, I hate this, Parker."

Parker took his hand and shook it as though sealing the deal, and the kid shuffled to the front door.

"Remember: Your mama signs both copies and drops them at her lawyer's office or she won't get the rest of the money."

Cole didn't move. *Probably fearing his mama's reaction when he shows up with a $10,000 check,* Parker thought. He took the kid by the arm, pushed him around his SUV, opened the door, and shoved him into the driver's seat. "I'll drive the van around here, so the cops will think you're still in Atlanta. Good luck, kid."

As soon as Cole was out of sight, Ron screeched into Parker's driveway. and Parker got in, but Ron got out. The investigator dropped to his knees, rolled onto his back, and shimmied under the van. A moment later, he slid out from under the van, dusted himself off, and climbed into the driver's seat.

"He has the gun," Ron said.

As Parker had anticipated, the kid had taken the gun from its hiding place in the van while Parker was stealing Ravi's files.

Ron sped up the street. He needn't have hurried. Down I-85 South and then across the top of Atlanta's perimeter on I-285 West, the kid drove at legal speeds. He wouldn't want to get stopped with a wanted gun in his pocket.

At the Powers Ferry exit on Atlanta's northwest side, Ron followed Cole through the intersection at the top of the exit, four cars back. Cole went left across the expressway overpass and then turned right onto Powers Ferry Road, toward the river. A mile or so down the road, he turned left into the Riverfront apartment complex, drove down to the last building on the left, and parked. Ron stopped short, pulled into a spot from which they could watch the kid. Cole got out of Parker's SUV and, without so much as a glance at his surroundings, made a beeline for the stairwell in the 300 building.

The apartment complex stood on the banks of the Chattahoochee River, the rearward-facing units having a river view and the forward-facing units overlooking a greenbelt. Cole walked into apartment 319, on the third floor, facing the greenbelt. Parker opened his car door.

"We should let the cops do this," Ron said. "Her accomplice could be up there."

"I need a signed document before we have her arrested, Ron. If I don't come out of there in fifteen minutes, call the Atlanta cops." Parker got out of the car and walked around the back of building 300 and then down the riverbank, hoping no one would report him as a stalker. The complex was nearly deserted, everyone at work. Nonetheless, Parker nearly peed his pants when his cell phone rang. Paula had found another way to make an unauthorized call.

"I can't talk, Paula."

"I'm done with you, Parker, because you won't believe me. I wanted to let you know before I file for a divorce."

"We can work this out. Call me later." Parker disconnected before she could say anything to keep him on the line and silenced the phone's ringer.

At the stairwell Cole had used, Parker peeked around the corner and looked up at the door of apartment 319. The sounds of a heated exchange emanated from the cracked-open door. Mama was seriously pissed off at her weakling son. Scratching his back on the pebbled building wall, Parker inched to a spot beneath the stair landings and waited until he heard a door close and a key turn in a lock. She's not locking her accomplice in there, Parker thought. She said something, and Cole answered. "I've got them, Mama."

The cement and steel stairs shook as Mama and her deluded son descended to the second-floor landing. When they started down the last flight, Parker popped around to the foot of the stairs and hopped up three steps, blocking their egress. Meredith looked as though she'd been living on the street—soiled, rumpled clothing, hair chopped into uneven spikes and dyed a comical shade of orange.

Cole dropped two suitcases, and one rolled heavily and noisily down the steps. Parker sidestepped it, and Meredith used the moment to run for it. She almost got past Parker, but he reached out one long arm, caught a bandaged wrist, and yanked her backward. She fell to one knee on the cement steps and squealed.

"Hush," Parker hissed in her face. "You want the cops to catch you?"

Parker dragged Meredith as he ascended the stairs. Cole started down for the suitcases but Parker stopped him. "Leave the suitcases. You can get them on your way out of here."

With more urgency, they climbed the third flight. At the door to apartment 319, Meredith took a key from her purse and, her hands shaking, tried without success to insert it in the lock. Parker yanked it away from her and opened the door. The key went into his pocket.

Cole placed a protective arm around his mother. He tried to mimic the defiant look on his mama's face, but his lower lip quivered. "We weren't skipping out. We just came to get the rest of Mama's clothes."

Parker gave them a condescending smile. "Of course. You were going to drop the signed agreement at your lawyer's office, right? I'll do it for you." Hand outstretched.

Sheepish looks. Meredith and Cole studied their shoes.

"Oh my. You were going to cash the check, tell on Paula, then move forward with the lawsuit." Parker shook his finger at Meredith. "You see Cole, that's what blackmailers do."

"I want the rest of my fucking money," Meredith said.

"No worries," Parker said. "I don't want you to sign that one. I want you to sign this one."

He pulled two fresh copies of the $75,000 settlement agreement, laid the documents side by side on the coffee table, and placed a pen on top.

A muscle in Meredith's left cheek twitched, causing her left eye to blink like a caution light at a pedestrian crossing.

"Not gonna do it."

"I know everything, Meredith. Your Atlanta boyfriend abandoned you, stole your Florida boyfriend's credit card, and left you to face the music. Guess he got tired of fucking you."

Meredith lunged at Parker, claws first. He caught her arms, spun her around, and clamped her hands to her chest. Something hard brushed his hip. Cole tried to pry her away, but Parker gave him a hip check, and he sprawled on the couch.

"That was your deal, right? You traded sex for help with things like loosening all my outdoor light bulbs, so it was dark when you came into our yard."

Meredith bent her head to bite Parker's arm, so he dumped her on the couch next to her blushing son. "Spray-painting a message on our front door, killing Paula's cat."

Meredith wore the look of a woman who'd been scammed by the guy she thought she was scamming. "I didn't do any of that."

In plotting against his mother, Shakespeare's Othello says he will "Put out the light, and then put out the light." "Of course not, your boyfriend did it for you."

Meredith laughed derisively. "He's afraid of his own shadow."

"You left a note in our mailbox. I know your handwriting."

She gave him a desultory look. "One time was all he was good for."

Indicating the documents, Parker said, "Your John Hancock, please."

"You can't make me sign this. I saw Paula shoot Grace in the thicket."

"Nobody is going to believe you, Meredith. They haven't found a gun or casings that can be traced to Paula. They do have the casings from the shots you took."

Cole clenched his fists, gathering the courage to attack Parker. "You lied. Mama's prints aren't on the casings in the thicket or on the bullets in the gun. She borrowed the gun."

"Aha! From her boyfriend. You think the gun is registered in his name?" Parker chuckled. "When he's caught, he'll say your mama used that gun."

Meredith jerked to her feet and swore at Parker. Cole tried to pull her back down to the couch, but she pulled the little .25 caliber gun from her back pocket and pointed it at Parker's chest.

"Mama!" Cole screamed. "Don't!"

She pulled the trigger. The pistol made a dry, metallic clicking sound. Confused, she shook the gun and smacked the bottom of the grip as though it were a bottle of ketchup that could be forced to belch its contents. She pulled the trigger again. Click. And again. Click. Meredith threw it at Parker. He sidestepped the missile, and it struck a tall gold trophy on a buffet table and bounced off the wall.

"You think I'd leave a loaded gun in the hands of a psychopath?" Parker pulled a one-quart plastic freezer bag out of his pocket and dangled the bag in front of their shocked faces.

Meredith swore again. "You didn't know it was unloaded?" she asked Cole.

"How was I to know?"

"It's light, dipshit."

"Hey!" Parker yelled and the mother-son spat stopped. "Cole has done everything you asked of him. Take the money and run." Tim had warned him that the statement in the settlement agreement would be challenged in court, but Meredith might believe she couldn't tell on Paula.

Defeated, Meredith sank into the couch. She gave Parker a fierce look, then bent over the table and picked up the pen.

As she signed the documents, he said, "I'll need the other settlement agreement, please." Cole dug the papers out of his mama's purse and dropped them on the table. "And your signature as the witness." Cole reluctantly scribbled a few lines and swirls on the paper.

Parker picked up the documents and put them in his pocket. The five small cartridges from Meredith's pistol made a resounding clatter when he tossed the plastic bag onto the glass-topped table, and the apartment key made a sound like an ice cube clinking in a glass.

"Okay, kids," he said. "Nice doing business with you." In case they got other ideas, Parker gave them instructions: "A check that large will have to be cashed at my bank in Florida." *In other words, don't stop on the way to Florida.* "Leave my car at Duncan Hardy's house, and I'll pick it up next week. Lock this place up and drop the key in a storm drain. You were never here."

They stared at Parker, calculating their next move or memorizing the instructions. The odds were 50/50 that they would believe he was helping them escape.

Parker stepped into the doorway, then turned around and said to Cole, "On the long drive, maybe your mama can explain why she didn't have you move your daddy's gun to protect your aunt."

The kid was speechless as he thought about it. Parker smiled and nodded and closed the door behind him as another intense argument erupted in the apartment. He trotted down the stairs and climbed into Ron's car to watch their getaway.

"Did you get it signed?"

Parker patted his pocket and nodded.

"And she has the gun?"

Another nod.

"You have to call the cops. I'm not licensed here."

"We can't do that, Ron," Parker said. "All the cops know is that her gun was fired twice in the thicket. They can't prove that a bullet from her gun struck Grace and caused her to fall in the river. Your buddies Noah and Vince have gotten a court order to have her detained for an involuntary examination under the Baker Act. The woman is deranged and belongs in an insane asylum. In Florida. Ask Noah."

Ron gripped the steering wheel so tightly that Parker thought he might yank it off its column. "She's wanted in connection with a murder in Georgia, and she needs to be arrested by the Atlanta cops."

Parker persisted. "If the shrinks keep her, she's where she belongs. If they let her go, you can turn her over to the cops. No harm, no foul."

Ron had been fired from his position as a St. Petersburg cop after some questionable arrests, but he treasured his investigator's license. The P.I. took a minute to think. "I can turn her in?"

"Follow them to Florida, make sure she ends up at Noah's hospital."

"You used me, Parker. I won't forget it."

"You're going to take a bad person off the grid, Ron. You've done a good job."

"I feel used."

"Get over it. When a court order is issued in Florida—a bench warrant, I guess—where does it go? Who serves it?"

Ron wore a confused look. "County. Sheriff's deputies execute the warrant."

"So, Pinellas County cops and not St. Pete city police?" If Lieutenant Monahan hears about this, he'll rat me out to Rawlings.

"Yeah. Why?"

"You have any friends at County?"

"Sure. Used to work there."

"Tell your best friend to get his hands on the warrant and wait for your instructions on where to catch her. When they catch her, make sure they find that gun in the car in case we have to give her to the cops."

Ron mumbled something under his breath.

Several minutes passed before Meredith and Cole came out of the apartment and locked the door. Meredith used her T-shirt to wipe her prints off the doorknob. Cole retrieved her suitcases and put them in Parker's SUV. As instructed, Meredith dropped Luke's key down a storm drain before climbing into the driver's seat. *Lots of evidence swirling around in the Atlanta sewer system.*

Meredith pulled away, and Ron said, "Get out."

"If Meredith stops to cash that check, call the Atlanta cops and have them search the car."

"Don't worry, I'm like Velcro."

Parker stepped out of the car, and Ron burned rubber in hot pursuit.

Sabrina's white BMW pulled up to the curb forty-five minutes later. In the small cabin, her warmth made Parker shiver. He seemed to have a different effect on her. She said, "You need a shower."

"Hot chasing criminals out there."

She snorted as she skillfully navigated the entrance lane for I-285 West and then the exit for I-75 South. It was clear that she enjoyed making her car perform, got a thrill out of its agility. "Did the cops arrest her?"

Parker took a moment to gather his thoughts. As in his conversation with Ron, his explanation for Sabrina had to be carefully crafted. "No, Ron is following her, and she'll be arrested in Florida."

"Florida? Why Florida?"

"My psychiatrist friend Noah has sworn out a warrant to have her detained for a psychiatric exam under the Baker Act."

"My, how you love playing God. I'm very conflicted about you, Parker. It's one thing to live in your own little world, by your own rules. It's another to impose your beliefs on the rest of us."

"Crazy people belong in asylums, not prisons."

"I can see right through you, Parker. You're trying to have her committed because her testimony wouldn't be useful against your wife."

Parker wasn't happy with how this conversation was going. "She's lying about the Fourth of July but the cops might believe her. I can't let this situation turn go wrong like it did the last time, in Florida."

"When you shot the Navy Seal."

An unaccustomed feeling came over Parker, the feeling he thought Catholics must have after confessing their sins, a feeling of unburdened relief. "The truth is I didn't shoot Hardy. Paula did."

Sabrina gasped.

"I feared Meredith was setting me up, so I had Paula hide in the boathouse with her gun, I thought she could even the odds against Meredith, but I didn't guess Meredith would have backup, much less her ex-husband. Duncan Hardy couldn't figure out how I got the drop on him because Paula lost her cool and without a warning, she shot Hardy from behind."

Sabrina's free hand flew to her mouth. "You went to prison for her."

"She saved my life."

"And you're willing to go back to prison for her?"

Of course, Parker hadn't guessed he'd end up in prison in Florida. But Duncan Hardy had been shot in the back so the jury didn't buy the Stand Your Ground defense. This time he wasn't sure he could save his wife and he was tired of being the scapegoat. He settled for, "No one should go to jail for a crime they didn't commit."

He didn't know if Sabrina believed him, her eyes locked on the road, her hands positioned at ten o'clock and two o'clock on the steering wheel. He didn't know if he believed himself. He clung to the single exculpatory piece of evidence in the case against Paula: The cops had not found her spent casings in the thicket.

Miles passed as Parker sought a way to break through the icy atmosphere in the car. "Have you heard any reaction to what we did last night?"

"Oh, yeah. They called me in for a bogus Saturday meeting, and while I was away from my desk, they searched my office and computer."

"Who's they?"

"Dennie and Ilya."

"What do they know?"

"They know everything. They have the key card logs, so they know I was the last person to leave the office last night. I think I'm going to be fired."

"Well, that's one way to get out of Shaw Technology."

"I can't have a dismissal on my resume, Parker."

He was sorry he had been flippant. "The crooks can't fire you for stealing evidence of their fraud."

Sabrina gave him a disgusted sigh. "I should resign and put this mess behind me."

"But the evidence is safe?"

"Glad you're worried about me. It's at my apartment, not the office. I read the ASC proposal last night. They offered twelve percent in immediate labor arbitrage plus ten percent year-over-year labor cost savings, and fifteen percent in claims payment reductions."

"Is that possible?"

"They're the eight-hundred-pound gorilla in the insurance software business, more customers than Shaw, and they don't need a partner, can do the work on the cheap at their own offices in Ireland, South Africa, Poland, and Romania. They appeal to certain executives because the work would still be done by white folks." She cleared her throat in a way he interpreted as "ah-hem."

"Those places aren't as cheap as India and Manila, so they're cheating, too."

"Probably. ASC will absorb any loss to prevent Kumar from gaining traction in the US."

"And this deal is Kumar's last chance to buy Shaw Technology because his outsourcing is failing at New England Indemnity."

"Yep. Steve found a second download of test cases from Midwestern Assurance on Ravi's Google drive. Had a fictitious name. The cases are simple, rules-abiding claims. Ravi didn't have to dummy-up cases to replace the ones that were ruining their savings numbers. He just replaced the tough cases with the easy cases."

"Hoy shit. Midwestern Assurance is in on it. They supplied those cases."

Sabrina pointed her index finger at the sky and blew on it, as though blowing the smoke from the barrel of a pistol. "That's the smoking gun."

At Tower Place, Parker gave the two countersigned copies of the settlement agreement to Tim Morrison and told his lawyer to hold the document until he gave him permission to file.

Back in the car, they headed to Parker's house. Impulsively, Parker squeezed Sabrina's hand, and she smiled.

Ron called to say, "We're past Macon. They're going to Florida."

Parker told Ron to stay with them all the way so he could give the deputy an exact location for the arrest. "You can stay at home in Florida. I think we're done here."

Ron thanked Parker. "Good luck leading the cops on a wild goose chase."

"Go Gators!"

Sabrina pulled into Parker's driveway, and he opened the car door. "Don't answer your phone for anyone but me. Bring everything to New Orleans and get a room at the Wyndham Grand on Royal Street. I'll meet up with you on Monday afternoon."

"Aren't you staying at the team hotel?"

The team would stay at the Marriott on Canal Street. "Too dangerous." He was about to close the car door when he thought of one last detail. "And Sabrina? Bring your gun."

Her lips formed her signature O. "What are you going to do now?"

"I'm going to St. Pete to return the van to Cole."

"Will you see your wife?"

"Yeah, we have a lot to talk about."

"You're not Mother Teresa. Caring for an alcoholic isn't a job for everyone."

Sabrina's insight annoyed him because he knew she was right. He hadn't been any help to Paula. He nodded and closed the door.

Sheriff's deputies lay in wait for Meredith in Pinellas County, which left Parker the job of diverting the cops' attention until Meredith was wearing a straitjacket. He spotted the tail as he wound through fast, heavy traffic on I-75 in Atlanta. The cops had waited patiently for the van to move and the tracking device had functioned properly.

The tail car mimicked Parker's lane changes, never allowing more than two cars to ride between predator and prey, ensuring that Parker didn't slip away down one of the numerous exits. Past the city center, the traffic thinned, and the tail car dropped back, occasionally accelerating into view and then melting into knots of tractor-trailer traffic. The tracking device wouldn't allow Parker to evade them entirely, but the cops in the tail car were taking no chances. Parker guessed they'd want to be on the scene the moment Cole picked up Meredith.

Beyond McDonough, urban sprawl transitioned to rural farmland with widely spaced exits, and the tail receded from Parker's view. Undoubtedly, they'd watch him on a GPS monitor in their squad car, but they were too late to counter his subterfuge. He received a text from Ron: *In Florida. Go Gators!* He settled in for the long ride at five miles under the speed limit, a shit-eating grin on his face.

As he neared Macon, Parker received a call from an Atlanta number he didn't have stored in his contacts. "Enjoying your vacation away from the office?" Dennie's throaty Carolina drawl made him shiver. "Kumar and Jack want to have dinner tonight. Meet us at the office."

"I can wait till New Orleans to see Ravi's numbers."

"Tonight, Parker, and bring your girlfriend."

That they wanted to include Sabrina distressed Parker. "I wish I could, but I'm on my way to Florida to see my wife, who is in alcohol rehab and raising hell because I'm not there. I'll go to New Orleans from there."

Dennie covered the mouthpiece with her hand to exchange words with a man in the background. Parker couldn't understand the words but was certain the voice belonged to an American male, not Kumar.

"Be in New Orleans on Tuesday. We'll let you know where and when. Got it?"

"Got it," Parker said, but Dennie had already disconnected.

Parker pulled into the rest stop just before the Macon bypass, partly to see if the cops were still on his tail and partly to use the restroom. He stretched and walked inside. When he emerged, he stood in the shadows and surveyed the surreal scene. The cop car blocked him into his space, grill lights flashing, attracting rubberneckers. The female cop from the morgue leaned against the van's driver's door, her hand on her holstered gun. Her partner, a young, lanky guy with a buzz-cut and mirrored sunglasses, the kind the guard wore in *Cool Hand Luke*, stood between the cop car and the van. He had his hand on his gun too.

When Parker moved out of the shadows toward the van, the female cop recognized him and exclaimed, "Damn it!" Shock, combined with anger, contorted her cute face. "Unlock the door."

He pushed the clicker. "Need my license and registration?"

She jerked a thumb over her shoulder. "Walk back to my partner."

He slid out of her way, and she stood on tiptoe to see the empty passenger seat. As ordered, Parker sauntered to the back of the van with a friendly smile on his face.

"Who are you?" Buzz-cut asked.

"I'm John Parker, US citizen."

Buzz-cut gave Parker a quizzical look, not sure how offended he should be by Parker's smart-ass attitude.

The female cop threw the van's sliding door open, took a moment to verify that no one was hiding under the seats, and slammed the door shut. She started toward the building, toward the restroom, no doubt, then remembered that she was a female. She pointed to the restrooms and said to her partner, "Go see if he's in the shitter."

Buzz-cut jogged to the restroom. A minute later, he returned, shaking his head.

"Where's the kid?" she asked Parker.

"He didn't want to come along."

"Where are you going?"

"St. Pete. See my wife in rehab."

"Shit." She leaned into the cop car and got on the radio. A couple of minutes later, she bullied her way past Parker, stooped beside the rear wheel well, and yanked the tracking device off the van. "Get out of here," she yelled at Parker.

Parker got back into the van and watched in his rearview mirror as the cop car squealed out of the parking lot.

Within seconds his phone rang. Parker flinched but forced himself to remain calm. He was pretty sure no one had ever been arrested over the telephone.

"Where is he?" Rawlings said.

"Who?"

"Don't fuck with me, Parker. Meredith's kid."

"I have no idea. Cole was in Atlanta when I left." Close to the truth.

"There's no one at your house."

"Well, I guess he's running errands in my car, Detective." Not *that* far from the truth.

"Why are *you* driving the van?" Rawlings spat.

"Gets better gas mileage than my SUV. I have to see my wife before she divorces me."

"Aiding and abetting a fugitive is a felony, Parker."

"I have no idea what you're talking about, Detective."

Rawlings made an angry sound in Parker's ear and hung up. Parker wondered how long it would take Rawlings to issue an APB/BOLO for Parker's SUV.

***

He was on the long, boring stretch of road between Macon and Valdosta when Ron called.

"Bad news, buddy. She ditched me."

"What the hell, Ron?"

"They got off at an exit in Pasco County, and she went into a convenience store. After a while, the kid left her, just drove away. I went into the store and no Meredith. She went out the back door and left with someone else."

Why didn't I think of this? "Her parents live in New Port Richey. Her daddy rescued her. She'll go to the branch of my bank in New Port Richey. Catch her before she cashes that check."

"No can do, buddy. The Sheriff in Pinellas would have to go through the Sheriff in Pasco County, and by then, your money will be gone. I followed the kid the rest of the way. He dropped your car at the Tampa

~ 254 ~

airport parking garage, red side, and took an Uber to his father's house, Grace's house, in St. Petersburg."

"Okay. Stake out Grace's funeral tomorrow."

"Sorry about this, boss. If she doesn't turn up, I'll have to call the Atlanta cops, let them know she's down here."

As Parker crossed the Florida state line, he received a fraud alert text from his bank: Meredith was attempting to cash the large check, and the bank was making her wait for Parker's approval. Parker pulled onto the shoulder, turned on the flashers, and slapped the dashboard. "Fuck!" He had to admit that Meredith had won another round in their fifteen-round fight. He didn't want to draw attention to Meredith before she could be detained for the psychiatric exam, so he typed his approval for the bank to cash the check. He had to hope that Ron could pick up her scent or find her at Grace's funeral.

Dismayed by Meredith's chicanery, Parker called Jordyn and reached voicemail. "I'm on my way. Staying at the Don Cesar on St. Pete Beach. Let's meet for dinner."

As the hours slipped by, it became obvious that dinner with dad wasn't Jordyn's idea of a relaxing evening.

He parked the van in the Tampa airport garage, red side, and left the keys on the passenger side front tire. Walking up and down aisles, clicking his spare remote, he finally located his SUV, backed into a spot up against a wall. With a sigh, he let himself into the SUV and looked for a parking ticket above the visor, in the console, under the seat. Nothing. He thought about going back to the van and throwing the kid's keys away, then he decided he could be the better man.

He drove to the hotel and skipped dinner, carried a CC&7 cocktail from the lobby bar out to the veranda, and sat in a rocking chair listening to the Gulf surf. The cocktail had been his mother's favorite, and he drank one whenever he reminisced about her. He wondered how she'd feel about the shape his life was in, which he imagined as a trapezoid with sharp angles and edges. He imagined she'd be disappointed in him. He moved away from a young couple to the far edge of the veranda, so he could smoke a cigar without inspiring millennial outrage. He had just gotten it lit when his phone rang. He hoped it was Jordyn, but when he got it out of his pocket, he saw that it was Connor.

"I think the gods have intervened in your case."

"How so?"

"The cops have arrested a man named Luke Braun. Someone phoned in an anonymous tip that he owned an orange car and lived at the Riverfront Apartments. A detective named Conroy spotted the car at a hotel in Gwinnett County, near your place, I think."

Parker stifled a scream. He thought back to the apartment where he had cornered Meredith and remembered that the room was decorated with a dozen trophies. *Lacrosse trophies!* How common was it to win Lacrosse trophies? Uncommon. Could you find them in just anyone's apartment? No. Like the tumblers in a lock falling into place, the clues fell into place for Parker: that was his half-brother's apartment. "Luke of Duke," they'd called him, the Lacrosse star at the school known as much for its Lacrosse teams as for its basketball teams. Luke had fallen on hard times since his wife Susie, an insurance agent, and the real breadwinner in the family, had been convicted of vehicular homicide. By that time, Luke had lost his job as—ironically—a pharmaceuticals salesman, after missing work while procuring drugs and caring for his opioid-addicted wife. Apparently, he had sold his expensive house—or had it repossessed—and moved to that apartment, just inside the perimeter highway. Luke could almost see his former house from his apartment's window, could almost feel how the good life had slipped away.

Parker let the ramifications of this discovery wash over him like a wave breaking on a beach. If Luke was the boyfriend, then *he* was the ambush shooter. His own brother had tried to kill him.

Connor didn't seem to know that Luke was his brother, and Parker thought it better to keep the secret until Connor divulged everything he knew. "Why did they arrest him?"

"They found the murder weapon in his apartment."

Parker jerked in surprise. *That wasn't an anonymous tip; Meredith turned him in.* He'd assumed Meredith would take the gun to Florida to drown it in the Gulf of Mexico. He had wanted Meredith to be caught with the gun when she was apprehended. Instead, she'd planted the gun in Luke's apartment to frame him, her former lover. Poor

Luke, Parker thought, literally in bed with a crook, and this is what happens. Parker's prison buddies had told him that the trouble with being a criminal was that all your coworkers were untrustworthy criminals.

"How do they know the weapon in his apartment is the murder weapon?"

"The prints on the gun had been wiped but prints on the bullets in the clip match prints on the casings at the scene, and ballistics matched the casings found at the scene to the gun."

Luke loaded the gun and loaned it to Meredith. He must have had another gun to use at the ambush site.

"You still there?" Connor said.

"Yeah, just shocked is all. Why were they looking for an orange car of all things?"

"Braun was on ATM video using Wade Gilbert's stolen credit card and a convenience store clerk IDed the orange car. Can't miss it."

Ron had only been a baby step ahead of Rawlings in tracking the accomplice. "Was the car Japanese? Old and beat up?"

"Korean, actually. The model favored by Hispanic gang members. They're still looking for Meredith Walker."

So am I. "Maybe Braun can tell them where to look."

"They think you helped her get away." Connor sounded serious. "I hope that's not true."

"I left for Florida and loaned my car to the kid. Can't say what happened after that."

"They're looking for her in Florida. Stay away from her, Parker." Connor disconnected.

In his mind, Parker mounted a corkboard, the kind cops use to diagram their cases with pictures of suspects and victims linked by strands of yarn. On it, he pinned photos of Meredith, Grace, Hardy, Paula, Jordyn, and Luke; a .45 caliber gun, a .25 caliber pistol, a .32 caliber pistol, and a revolver; casings from the .45 and the .25; a photo of apartment 319; and pictures of an orange car and lacrosse trophies. Then he added one more picture, one that didn't fit—a picture of a big, shiny, black car.

If Parker applied Occam's Razor, ignoring the piece that didn't fit the puzzle, the corkboard told a logical story. Luke brought Meredith to the park, and when the plot to extort money from Parker fell to pieces, he helped her escape. Then he got scared, Grace was dead, and he was harboring a madwoman. He stole the professor's credit card to finance his hideouts and ran as far from Meredith as he could get. But why did he shoot at Parker from the ambush site?

Ron was a believer in karma, and that's what he'd have called the apprehension of Lucas Braun for a murder he hadn't committed. Parker's view was less mystical. When he'd been in prison, a guard he'd become chummy with had grown tired of hearing Parker protest his innocence. "What you don't get," the guard had said, "is if we can put a bad guy behind bars, we don't give a shit what crime we use to do it. It all evens out in the end.

You're a bad guy, Parker, and we got you inside, so get over it."

The Atlanta arrest rate for homicides is sixty-two percent, a failing grade on any school test but one of the best percentages among America's big cities. Parker had looked it up. Luke was a bad guy who deserved to be inside, but the case against Luke was shaky. Rawlings couldn't prove that the gash in Grace's arm was caused by a .25 caliber bullet from the gun in his apartment.

Nonetheless, Connor's news had ruined an already disastrous evening. Parker flicked his cigar into the sandy beach and made his way to his room.

The visitor's hall at the rehab facility, a cavernous space with beamed ceilings and wood-burning fireplaces at either end, overflowed with visiting families on this Sunday morning. The area was organized into a dozen conversation pits—a couch, two armchairs, and a coffee table—supplying the afflicted with a bit of privacy as their loved ones commiserated with them and encouraged them to get sober.

Parker walked the perimeter of the room, nervously searching for familiar faces, breathing in through his nose and out through his mouth to relieve stress. He spotted his family near one of the fireplaces, and his trepidation was justified. When she saw her father, Jordyn helped her Grandma Lillian to her feet and guided her to a hard-backed chair beside the fireplace. Paula and a stranger sat side-by-side on the couch. She looked scrubbed in clean clothes, and her eyes were alive, the green color so deep that the pupils were barely distinguishable from the irises.

Parker walked into the middle of their pit. "Who the hell is he?"

"This is Harley Scott, and he's helping me through this," Paula said.

"Is he a … what? A patient?"

"Yes. He knows what this is like." Meaning Parker didn't know what it was like to undergo rehab. Parker did know that the counselors encouraged the drunks to find new friends, but then the new friends turned out to be the other drunks in rehab.

"You're sober, and I'm glad to see that."

"You never understood, Parker. Sobriety isn't a permanent cure. Alcohol addiction never takes a rest. That's why they say, 'one day at a time.'"

"Well, I'm here now, so Harley can crawl back in his hole."

"Are you here now, Parker, or am I just a waypoint on your journey to somewhere else?"

That sounded to Parker like an actor's rehearsed lines. "I can't stay long," he admitted. "I have to go to New Orleans for business."

"And after New Orleans there'll be something else. There's always something else." Paula now held Harley's hand in both of hers, her knuckles white as she gripped him.

Suppressing a gnawing irritation, Parker said, "I had to fix your problem. Luke has been arrested for Grace's murder."

Paula relaxed and let out an exaggerated laugh. "Your brother is an asshole. You should have believed me when I told you I didn't do it."

"Luke is in jail for it, but we both know he didn't do it. You took a shot at Meredith in the backyard and fired your gun two more times in the thicket. You still need my protection."

Harley flinched. Parker guessed that she hadn't told him that part of the story.

"I don't need anything from you," Paula growled. "You like having problems so you can solve them. My counselor, Jim, calls it oppositional defiant disorder—ODD. I don't want to be your problem anymore."

Parker's agenda disintegrated into wet chunks like a watermelon dropped on pavement. "Paula, sit tight and don't talk to the cops. I'll be back, and we can work this out."

"You're not hearing what I'm saying, Parker: You're the reason I'm an alcoholic."

Tired of being blamed for Paula's relapses, Parker neglected to filter his response. "Blame me if it makes you feel better, but you're the drunk."

Nearby patients and their families heard him and looked their way. A security guard moved in their direction, monitoring the exchange. Jordyn tensed, her body tilted toward them, waiting for the tête-à-tête to reach a climax.

Paula shook her head. "Enjoy your time in New Orleans with your mistress. I have Harley to keep me company, know what I mean?"

It's one thing to imagine your wife with another man, quite another to see it in person. Conversations in the nearby family groupings had halted, and people were watching the skirmish. Parker wavered between walking away in shame or crushing Harley's skull.

Harley made the first move. He leapt to his feet and got in Parker's face, the top of his head reaching only to Parker's chin. "You need to leave," he said. He gave Parker a push. Paula looked on, her eyes bright, her lips spread in a smile.

Parker cocked his arm to take a swing at Harley, and the smaller man recoiled, fell over the coffee table, and landed at Paula's feet. Paula slid off the couch to sit next to Harley and put her arm around his neck.

The security guard rushed into the conversation pit, placed his hands on Parker's chest. "You're upsetting the patients," the guard said. "Time to leave."

Parker shrugged the guard off, causing him to stumble. "This is none of your business."

Fists clenched, Parker stepped toward Paula and Harley. Before he could make matters worse, Jordyn hustled into the pit, grabbed his arm, and marched him toward the double doors. Over his shoulder, Parker shouted, "Keep your filthy hands off my wife!"

Jordyn pushed one door open and forced him outside into the glare of Florida sunshine. "You should have talked to her yesterday. She's just trying to get your attention."

"She has my full attention, but I'm still worried the Atlanta cops will find Meredith and get her to testify against Paula. Or they could find your mother's casings in that thicket."

Jordyn's body went slack. Her eyes downcast, unable to look her father in the eye, she said, "There's nothing to find, Dad. I found Mom's casings, one just beyond the fallen tree where the path curls around the big bush, and the other in some bushes at the start of the straightaway. I saw what you did with the casings on the deck and I, ah, did the same thing before I went home that night."

Jordyn's behavior now made sense to Parker. "That explains why you took so long to get back to our house. And that's why you thought it was okay to give the gun to Uncle Melvin. Why didn't you tell me?"

"She didn't shoot anyone, Dad. If I had told you about the casings you wouldn't have believed her. You still don't believe her."

"It's the cops who won't believe her if Meredith was a witness." He wouldn't say it out loud, but Parker still suspected that Paula mistook Grace for Meredith and shot her. "Can you stay here a while longer, take care of your mother?"

"Sure, I'll stay with Grandma till Mom gets through the program."

"Good. I'll fly to New Orleans in the morning. Keep my car for me till I get back." He tossed her the keys. "Lunch at Sloppy Joe's?"

***

Jordyn declined Parker's invitation, so he camped alone at Sloppy Joe's bar in Treasure Island, drinking beer, not CC&7. It wasn't a celebration; it was a wake for innocence and righteousness. He considered asking Noah to join him for a drink, but he guessed the psychiatrist would decline, a state employee reluctant to be seen in public with an ex-con. Ron was an option, but Parker didn't want to deflect Ron's attention from the search for Meredith Walker. In truth, he knew he was there to drown his sorrows over his failure to supply the love and comfort his wife needed.

He lost count of the beers he drank, the bartender's refusal to serve him another drink the only indication he had of his condition. Pretending to cooperate peacefully, he slid off the barstool, wobbled out to the veranda where the bartender couldn't see him, and sat at a table under an umbrella. A waitress brought him the menu, which contained a history of Hemingway's publications and travels. He knew it by heart.

"Sloppy Joe, no cheese, sweet potato fries, and a Tecate," he told the waitress.

The sun had traveled to its apex, making him shade his eyes and squint to survey the broad expanse of beach. This beach was not the sugar sand of the Florida Panhandle but rather thick gray glop, something close to wet cement, infused with crushed seashells that made walking barefoot a challenge for all but the sun-worshipping regulars. That's why he took note of the large man loping in his direction.

Ron wore shorts, a Hawaiian-print shirt, and a grin. He didn't see Parker until Parker had scrambled down the ramp to the beach.

Excitedly, Ron pointed toward the ocean, toward a navy-blue canvas cabana. "See her?"

Parker shielded his eyes and saw orange spikes and a skimpy yellow bikini on a voluptuous woman fifty yards away. Next to her sat a tall, dark man—Professor Wade Gilbert—whose condo was one hundred yards to the north. Parker thought that he and Duncan Hardy and the boyfriend all looked remarkably similar. Meredith definitely had a "type" she gravitated to.

"Cole and his dad buried Grace today," Ron said, "but Meredith didn't show up. I came down here to question the professor, see if he'd heard from Meredith, and like magic, she appeared."

"Your friend the Sheriff's Deputy on his way here?"

"No, he's on another case, real police work." Ron's face radiated pity, and maybe a touch of shame but no regret. "I called Lieutenant Monahan to come get her."

"Ron," he said, disgust dripping from the single word. "You should have trusted me."

Ron held his hands palms out, the surrender position. "My license. She's wanted for murder."

"Not anymore. My brother Luke has been arrested for Grace's murder."

"Your brother did it?" Ron asked, surprised.

"I think he was her accomplice. The apartment where we trapped Meredith was Luke's apartment. Meredith phoned in an anonymous tip and the Atlanta cops found the murder weapon in it."

"You mean the gun that the kid hid for his mother? She's framing your brother, but I have a picture of that gun in Grace's van. We can make the kid squeal on his mama. I'm glad I called Monahan."

Before Parker could sort through the obvious complications—he hadn't reported Meredith to the police, had allowed the kid to tamper with the evidence, and had facilitated Meredith's disappearance—two police cruisers pulled into the space between the Bilmar hotel and the restaurant. Their flashing lights alerted the diners, and everyone jockeyed for position at the wooden railings. Inside, the barflies flew to the restaurant windows, noses pressed against the glass like magnets on a refrigerator door. Hotel guests climbed out of the pool to watch the unfolding drama.

Monahan crawled out of the lead car, and two uniformed cops emerged from the trailing cruiser. Paula was right; the lieutenant looked like an unmade bed. Parker hurried into their path, put a hand on Monahan's chest, stopping him. "There's a—"

Monahan swept Parker's hand away and gave him a stiff-armed shove. Parker landed on his backside in the sand amid a mixture of cheers and jeers from onlookers.

"I should arrest you for aiding a fugitive, Braun," Monahan said.

Parker struggled to his feet. "My name is Parker now."

"Whatever." Monahan waved an arm at the uniformed cops like a platoon sergeant ordering his troops to follow him into battle.

Ron stepped in the way and flipped open his ID wallet. "Ron Gardner, Private Investigator. I made the call."

"You work for him?" Monahan jerked a thumb toward Parker.

"Yes, sir. The situation has changed: an arrest has been made for the murder in Atlanta, so Meredith Walker is not a suspect."

"I know that, Mr. Gardner. Get out of the way."

Monahan tried to move around Ron, but Ron blocked his path. "There's a bench warrant for the woman's apprehension—Baker Act. Judge Williamson ordered her delivered to the West Florida Psychiatric Hospital for an involuntary examination."

Ron queued up the bench warrant on his phone and handed the phone to Monahan. "The original is at County, waiting to be served."

"Fuck the Baker Act and fuck County. This broad is wanted for questioning in connection with the Atlanta homicide."

Parker feared that Meredith would hear the commotion at the bar and slip away. Over his shoulder, he checked on her, her back to them, catching the midday rays of the sun. Nothing Meredith liked better than to bake in grease like a Thanksgiving turkey.

"You screwed up when you arrested me the last time," Parker said. "You owe me, Lieutenant. You know you do."

"I don't owe you shit." Monahan pushed Parker out of the way, then repeated the "follow me" arm motion and led his troops away as though they were landing on Omaha Beach. A murmur grew to a cacophony as they strode across the sand to confront Meredith and her lover.

Parker and Ron were too far away to hear what was said, but they saw Meredith dig her heels into the sand and push herself away from the cops on her backside. She looked like a little child skittering across the floor before she learned to stand and walk. As Monahan spoke, Meredith's lover bounced to his feet and backed away from her. At a nod from Monahan, he turned and hustled up the beach.

After a brief shouting match, Monahan motioned to the uniformed cops. They grabbed Meredith, rolled her over on her blanket, and cuffed her behind her back. Meredith squirmed like a hooked fish. The gawkers cheered.

Meredith refused to do a humiliating "perp walk," so the cops lifted her off the sand, carried her face-down to a cruiser, and stuffed her unceremoniously into the backseat.

Trailing the parade of cops, Monahan walked up to Parker. "If you're still here when I get back, I'll throw you in the drunk tank, Braun."

Parker nodded and smiled. "Sounds like the Old West, Lieutenant. You should get yourself a cowboy hat and some boots. Don't forget the spurs."

"We're gonna find your wife's gun, too, asshole. Rawlings knows what you did."

Ron covered Parker's mouth with his hand before Parker could make the situation worse. The cops departed and Ron dragged Parker away to his table. The waitress brought Parker's food and beer. The smell of the food made Parker gag.

"Murder is more important than your vendetta against Meredith," Ron said.

"They only want her as a witness, Ron. They could interview her at the hospital. Now she's going to pin it on Paula and Luke."

"She's mixed up in it. I had to turn her in, Parker."

"Your license. Sure." *Betrayal is so banal.*

Parker didn't touch his sloppy joe but he drank the beer. When the sun fell off the far edge of the Gulf, Ron drove his drunken buddy to the Don Cesar Hotel and got Parker into his room, where he passed out.

Parker awoke with all the common symptoms of a beer hangover—throbbing temples, roiling belly, foggy brain, aching muscles, and wobbly legs. Drinking himself into a stupor had not changed his circumstances. On one tray of his mental scales of justice, he balanced the negative facts: Paula was with some addict named Harley; Meredith had his money; and his plot to put Meredith away had been wrecked by Ron's betrayal. On the other tray, he balanced the positive facts: the cops would never find Paula's casings; the Lakewood cops had not found Paula's gun; Meredith signed a sworn statement that she'd seen nothing in the thicket; and Luke had been framed for the murder. It occurred to him that since Meredith had framed Luke, she wouldn't have to accuse Paula.

As he waited for the in-room coffeemaker to brew his hangover antidote, his phone rang: a St. Petersburg number.

"This is Mr. Whitman at the funeral home. Just following up on the funeral of Ms. Grace Anne Walker?"

"Did the charge not clear?"

"Oh, it cleared fine, Mr. Parker. I'm just checking to see if you thought everything went to your satisfaction yesterday."

"Oh. I couldn't attend, unfortunately. I'm sure it was okay."

"We did our best with her; all the bumps and bruises and gunshot wounds were a challenge. The swollen head was impossible to make lifelike, I'm afraid."

"Mr. Whitman," Parker cut in. "Did you say gunshot wounds, plural?"

"Of course, the one in the arm and the one in her leg."

Oh my god. That's why the female cop at the morgue didn't want the body to go to a local undertaker. They didn't want me to know about the second gunshot wound. "Was it through-and-through?"

"Beg your pardon?"

"Was there an exit hole on the back of her leg?"

"Back of the leg? No, sir, the bullet went *into* the back of her upper leg, near her, ah, buttocks. Made a small hole, and beside it was a clean incision. Guess that's how they got the bullet out at the autopsy."

"No wound on the front of her thigh?"

"No, sir."

"Thanks for your call, Mr. Whitman. Everything was fine, but I've got to let you go."

Parker hung up and thought about Grace being shot from behind. Evidence marker number 5 had been beyond the fallen tree, beyond Grace's position. That was in the same area where Jordyn had found one of Paula's casings. Either Meredith or Paula had intentionally shot Grace Walker.

He dialed Connor's number and was told that Connor was in court The paralegal passed Parker to voicemail. The message he left was blunt and terse: Get a copy of Grace's autopsy report. ASAP. The cops had hidden evidence that Grace was assassinated from behind. Parker knew of three suspects—Meredith, Paula, and Luke—and of that trio, Paula was the most likely perpetrator. No matter what Paula had done, no matter what Paula was doing with Harley, he couldn't abandon her the way Karl Braun had abandoned his mother. Alcoholism never takes a rest, but neither does childhood trauma.

***

On the flight to New Orleans, Parker feigned sleep, his eyes closed, his seat tilted all the way back. A potpourri of clues danced behind his eyelids as though on a video screen he couldn't control. Paula had seen a big car with blacked-out windows in the cul-de-sac, but Luke drove a beat-up Korean clunker. Meredith had said that Luke was afraid of his own shadow, and Parker believed her. If Luke fired the little .25 caliber pistol and Grace only fired the big .45 caliber gun, Meredith had another accomplice who shot at Parker from the bushes. By ratting out Luke,

Meredith may have been protecting someone else. Sifting through clues that wriggled and shimmied like Jell-O gave Parker a headache.

He taxied to the Wyndham Grand on Royal near Canal. The hotel lobby was small and cramped, stuffed with sofas and easy chairs occupied by tourists planning their day, charting their routes with phone apps, and reading brochures for attractions and tours. Sabrina popped up from a couch when Parker entered and ran into his arms. She didn't try for a kiss but held on tight for a long minute, provoking scattered applause. Parker was embarrassed by the feeling of her body pressed against him. He imagined this was how it would feel to have an affair—acute excitement tinged with fear and guilt that intensified the emotions. He understood why some men were addicted to cheating.

They separated, and Parker noticed people watching them. The white men looked envious; the black men scowled. Parker had heard that at the core of racism was a fear that black men would steal white women. That the fear worked both ways amused him. He went to the reception counter, presented his driver's license and a credit card. As the clerk searched for his reservation, Parker asked for a room on a different floor than Sabrina's.

She gave him a quizzical look "They don't know you're here, but they'll be looking for me. If they find me, we can't let them find the evidence, so we'll keep the evidence in your room."

She took a step back and scanned Parker's face. "You're just using me to hide the evidence?"

"Dennie called while I was on the way to Florida and wanted to meet with me." Parker didn't mention that she had wanted Sabrina to be at the dinner. "I think they were going to cut me out of the meeting with Midwestern Assurance. If they do that, you'll have to stand in and drop the bomb on them. So, we need to keep the evidence safe."

Parker saw the doubt in her eyes. "That's tomorrow. Today, let's enjoy the French Quarter before they get here."

Sabrina gave Parker a look of resignation. "Okay, let's go."

After he dropped his bags in his room, they met in the lobby. Sabrina wore a silky multicolored blouse, jeans with no designer rips or tears, and pink three-inch heels. In shabby jeans, no socks, old loafers, and a faded black T-shirt, Parker betrayed his casual Florida roots. They walked one block down Royal Street to the Hotel Monteleone. A slow smile spread across Sabrina's face as she took in the lobby's brown-checkered floor, crystal chandeliers, frescoed ceiling, walls of decorative windows, and a ten-foot-tall grandfather clock. Up the steps to the right, they entered the Carousel Bar.

She squealed with delight at the sight of the carousel, slowly rotating, stools on its edges surrounding the circular bar itself. Colored like a calliope and emitting carnival music, lit by dim circus lights in an otherwise darkened room, and topped by oval mirrors and paintings of clowns, the Carousel was crowded with insurance conventioneers off to a fast start on happy hour. Parker surveyed the room, saw no one he knew, and asked a tipsy woman to move one seat to her right so that he and Sabrina could sit side by side.

Parker had never seen Sabrina drink alcohol, but now she ordered a French red wine in honor of being in the French Quarter; Parker asked for a local beer, Abita Turbodog.

"Would it be prying to ask how it went with your wife at the rehab facility?" Sabrina said.

"She's found a boyfriend inside. Taunting me."

"I'm sorry, Parker, but maybe it's fate."

Parker nodded as though accepting her opinion.

They whiled away the afternoon window shopping on Royal Street, Parker checking reflections in the shop windows in an amateurish attempt to detect suspicious characters on the opposite side of the street. He had learned to do that from reading John LeCarré novels. Parker saw no one from the IBS team, recognized no one else. After browsing in the antique shops and admiring fancy estate watches—Parker resisted—they cut through Pirate's Alley and stopped into Faulkner Books, on the ground floor of a building in which William Faulkner had written one of his early novels. He bought a signed copy of Larry Brown's *Dirty Work* and told Sabrina he'd let her read it when he was done with it. "It contains some interesting insights into race relations," he said.

"Your only valid insight will come from hanging with me," Sabrina said.

He checked her facial expression and body language and decided she was serious about her advice. "Walk a mile in my shoes," she said.

He watched their backs as they passed St. Peter's Cathedral, where a brass band played upbeat music, and they walked alongside Jackson Square, where a mime painted silver from head to toe posed as a statue. He saw no would-be assassins.

As they waited on the curb to cross Decatur Street, a black woman dressed like a hooker collapsed on the opposite sidewalk, foam sputtering from her mouth. Tourists glanced at her and stepped around her as though she were an inconvenient impediment to their progress. Parker jogged up to her, stood at her head, and directed foot traffic around her. As he called 9-1-1: "We have an overdose, down on the sidewalk, at the corner of St. Peter's and Decatur—" Sabrina stooped beside the woman and urged her to "stick with me." The first responders' reaction time was reasonable—less than fifteen minutes—but the woman was unresponsive when they arrived.

The paramedics jostled Parker out of the way, but he couldn't take his eyes off the woman; his sister-in-law Susie could have easily ended up this way. "No one cared," Parker said.

"That's how she ended up in this life," Sabrina said.

As the ambulance pulled away, no lights or siren, Sabrina started toward the French Market then stepped off the curb to pet the nose of a tired old horse pulling a gaudily decorated carriage. Before Parker could join her, a young black man dressed in baggy denim shorts, a basketball jersey, and sneakers with no laces, jumped off the bleachers, sprinted across the sidewalk, and tore Sabrina's purse from her shoulder. He ran into the crowd on the street, and Parker gave chase, yelling at him to stop. The young man barged into people and bulldozed his way ahead, just out of Parker's desperate grasp. Despite Parker's cries to stop the thief, tourists shrank away from the absconder and opened a path for his escape. Parker was about to attempt a shoestring tackle when a burly biker—full beard, do-rag, tattoos, motorcycle gang jacket— stuck out a heavy leather boot and tripped the fugitive. The young thief sprawled on the dirty street, squealing in pain as his elbows and knees scraped across the pockmarked road surface. Sabrina's purse tumbled end-over-end, ejecting her pistol, which skittered to the biker's feet. The biker picked the purse off the road but did not touch the gun as Parker staggered up, out of breath.

"My girlfriend's," Parker gasped, hands on knees.

Sabrina trotted up to the men, not even winded. The biker tilted his head toward Sabrina, a question on his face. Parker nodded. The biker gave Sabrina a gap-toothed smile as he handed her the purse.

The young thief scrambled to his feet and tried to sneak away, but the biker whirled and kicked him flush in the stomach with his heavy leather boot. The thief doubled over and sank to his knees.

"Don't guess you want to involve the police," the biker said. He nodded at the pistol.

Parker picked the pistol off the street and dropped it in Sabrina's purse. She reached for her wallet. "Let me—"

The biker stopped her with a hand on her wrist. "Just being a good citizen, lady."

The thief scurried away, bent at the waist, holding his bruised diaphragm. The biker joined his buddies, who were leaning on their bikes in front of a row of tourist trap storefronts. He bowed and absorbed their gleeful applause.

Parker and Sabrina waved to the men. Parker wrote the incident off as random crime and not some plot to disarm him.

"Do you think the biker would have stopped the thief if he knew the purse belonged to a black woman?" Sabrina asked him.

"I think so. Bikers have a code of conduct."

"Would he have helped if the thief was white?"

"Hmm. Good question." A pause. "A question for you: With all the white women parading down that sidewalk, why you? Did the black thief target you because you're a black woman?"

Like summer lightning that heralds a crack of thunder, a bolt of anger flashed in her amber eyes and quickly dissipated into a tilt of the head, a wry smile. "Touché."

She slipped an arm through his and turned him back toward the French Market, but Parker resisted. "I'm hungry, and I have a favorite spot."

They shambled back through Pirate's Alley and up Bourbon Street in the torrid heat, stopping to watch the street performers who were returning to the Quarter in significant numbers for the first time since Hurricane Katrina. On one corner, a comic told jokes from the top of a tall stepladder while juggling oranges. At another intersection, an all-female band played hillbilly music. In the middle of a block, a man wearing only a camouflage Speedo and a camouflage jungle boonie hat played the saxophone.

On the corner with Bienville, Parker dragged Sabrina into Arnaud's restaurant. At the hostess stand, an attractive woman dressed for cocktail hour unashamedly looked them over: a shabbily dressed white man with a black woman, albeit a nicely dressed black woman. Parker thought the hostess might deny them entry, but she snapped her fingers, and a young woman in a white waistcoat and black bowtie responded immediately. The hostess whispered to her, and then the young lady led them to a table for two, along the wall in the back corner of the Jazz Room, farthest from the band stage.

"Did we get stuck in the corner because of me?" Sabrina said.

This is the way it would always be with Sabrina, he thought. "No, they hid me because I'm not properly dressed," Parker said. "Look around."

She did. Men in suits and women in dresses occupied the tables. A tuxedoed waiter bent over them and handed them menus. Bald with combed gray sidewalls and a gray goatee, he introduced himself as Jimmy and offered refreshments. Jimmy probably lived in a rundown, three-story walk-up apartment with a nagging wife on Social Security and three cats whose excrement overpowered the smell of imminent death, but in this castle, Jimmy was king. He exuded just the right degree of indignation at having to serve unworthy interlopers a feast that their palates weren't sophisticated enough to relish.

Parker ordered a bottle of Pouilly Fuisse to show Jimmy how sophisticated they truly were, then laughed behind his back. To prove it again, Parker ordered Arnaud's signature shrimp cocktail and Fish Meuniere for Sabrina, escargot, and Pompano Duarte for himself. Jimmy gave them an approving nod and backed away respectfully.

Sabrina toasted him with her glass. "I love you, Parker." Embarrassed, she fanned herself with her hand, blushing at the admission.

Once again he tried to bypass an emotional moment by joking about it. "It's okay, all the girls love me because I can dance," he said.

"You're a shit. I know how you feel about me."

Unlikely, since he wasn't sure of his feelings for Sabrina. He was afraid Paula was right, that he was addicted to problems, to chaos, maybe to impossible challenges. Paula's alcoholism made her an impossible challenge. Sabrina's skin color might be an impossible challenge as well. You can't be blamed for failing at an impossible challenge, right? What he knew about Sabrina was that he was a better man than before he met her. Was that love or gratitude? He had promised himself never to say those three words to a woman unless he was certain he would be with her forever. "You know I'm attracted to you," was all he was willing to admit.

Sabrina sighed. "Would you be attracted to me if I was white?"

"Hunh? What kind of a question is that?"

"Am I a novelty, a new toy that will hold your attention for only a short while?"

"No!" shaking his head. "I'd like you if you were purple."

"Don't make light of it. Am I the poster child for another thing to fix—something on a grandiose scale—or a way to thumb your nose at the world?"

"That's silly. I wouldn't use you that way."

"I hope not."

Jimmy saved him further irresolute circumspection by delivering the appetizers, positioning plates and utensils. As though his momentary embarrassment had never happened, Parker coerced Sabrina, who had never eaten escargot, to try one of the snails. She took the challenge and chewed tentatively, then spat it into her napkin and covertly dropped the snail under the table. "It was growing in my mouth, Parker."

They laughed. "Don't let Jimmy see you do that," he said.

Jimmy brought the entrees, and they were magnificent. Afterward, they sipped coffee and finished the meal with Baked Alaska.

Parker left Jimmy a tip that would keep the lights on in his apartment for a month. Then they strolled up Bourbon Street, staying in the crowd of conventioneers, arms around each other's waists, skirting women baring their breasts for beads thrown from balconies. Sabrina playfully shielded his eyes from those sights.

Parker took Sabrina's hand as he led her into The Blues Club. For ten minutes, they stood between the bar and a jukebox, on the side of the dance floor farthest from the club's entrance, as Parker scanned the crowd, alert as a bloodhound to anyone who might know them.

"No one from IBS," Parker said.

Comfortable that they were among strangers, they took a table, ordered beers, and listened to the live band until Parker dragged Sabrina onto the dance floor. She threw her head back in laughter, worked hard to follow Parker's moves.

Between sets, they returned to their table, and Parker saw that Kumar had texted him: *Arnaud's. Use the Bienville entrance. Upstairs room. Sunday, 7 p.m.* A chill slithered up Parker's spine. He showed the text to Sabrina.

"It's a secret room that Presidents use when they're in town," he said.

He imagined Kumar interrogating him in the secret room: *Where's the proposal, Parker?* Finding Parker uncooperative, they would tie a cement block around his feet and throw him in the Mississippi River.

When he became rigid and stared at the message, Sabrina said, "You're not scared, are you, Parker?"

The definition of cool that Parker had learned in prison was to never show fear. Faking it now, he said, "Not scared. Just not sure of the best approach."

"You know what you have to do. You saw what happened in Hartford. You saw what happened in Columbia. You know what will happen in Iowa. You have to stop them."

"I know." To change the subject, he tried to pull Sabrina back onto the dance floor, but she resisted.

"You've had enough, white boy," she said. In the wee hours of Tuesday morning, Sabrina led Parker out of the club. "Time to go home," she said. Parker knew what she meant.

They walked back to the hotel in the light of the streetlamps and neon signs reflected in the black mirrors of dew-sheened streets. Denizens of the night scurried to their hiding places like vampires fleeing daylight. It was a changing of the guard from the night people, certain their lives were seasoned with more fun, to day people, up early and feeling superior about their productivity. Parker had his arm around Sabrina's waist, and she had hers around his as they walked casually.

Two ladies of the night stood on the corner of Royal and Iberville, looking for last-chance customers. One wore a blonde wig, a halter top that pushed her breasts toward her chin, cutoff jean shorts over fishnet stockings, and four-inch pumps. The other had her hair in cornrows, wore a sequined jacket, unbuttoned—no blouse or bra—and a miniskirt. There was no mistaking what they were selling.

As Parker and Sabrina approached the women, blonde wig said, "Wanna have a good time, handsome?"

Cornrows parted her sequined jacket and flashed bare breasts at Parker. "Two for one sale, handsome."

"You're reinforcing the black stereotype." Sabrina pointed a manicured finger at Cornrows.

Blonde wig said, "Say what? You doin' it for free is ruinin' bidness." She jabbed an inch-long fake nail at Sabrina.

Parker and Sabrina scurried across the street and into the shelter of the hotel lobby.

"Can you believe how brazen they are?" Sabrina said.

"It's the free enterprise system at work."

As the elevator rose toward Sabrina's floor, she leaned into him, her eyes as shiny as a kid's marble. "Wanna have a good time, handsome?"

Sweat beads formed on Parker's brow. He feared he would give in to temptation—and he feared he wouldn't. Which decision would make it harder to sleep?

When the elevator reached Sabrina's floor, she grasped his hand, pulled him out of the car, and led him down the hallway. Parker chuckled uneasily and halted, like a recalcitrant horse digging in its hooves and straining against the reins.

"I'm not ready for this."

A snort. "You're kidding. You confess your love and then you back out?"

Parker put a finger to his lips. "Shh." Sabrina's loud voice threatened to wake the whole floor. "I'm still married."

"Your wife doesn't think so. How married men cling to their disastrous wives. It's a chromosomal flaw." Arms crossed, sure of her opinion.

Am I doing this because I'm a married man or because Paula's with Harley or because I'm afraid of my emotions?

A door opened; a plump white face topped with bedhead peeked into the hallway.

"Shut your damn door. Nothing to see out here," Sabrina said to the man, her voice harsh, commanding. The door closed.

Parker had never faced this sort of problem and he was all out of smart retorts. "Paula is still in trouble."

"What's that got to do with us? You going to jail for Paula again? Mister tough guy going to play the hero?"

He didn't want to admit it. "This can wait," he said. Immediately, he knew it had been the wrong thing to say.

Sabrina's nostrils flared. "You're a coward, Parker. You tiptoe into my world, but then you play it safe and back away." She turned and walked past two doors, slid her key card into the slot at the third door. Parker hurried along behind her, searching for words to repair the situation. He held her door open, stopped just outside the threshold, unwilling to violate a moral boundary. Sabrina picked up his laptop, the computer printout, the new proposal, and the red and gold American Systems Corporation proposal off the desk and shoved them into his arms.

She leaned on the door, pushing him into the hallway. "All I am to you is a hiding place for this stuff. Deal with it however you like." The door clicked closed.

Bedhead popped out of his door again. "If you try to bust in there, I'll call the police."

Parker faked a lunge at the eavesdropper, and the bedhead disappeared like a turtle's head retracting into its shell. Nonetheless, Parker scampered down two flights of stairs to his own floor before bedhead could do something rash, like call the cops.

Parker shooed the maid away when she barged through his door at noon. He swung his sore, cramping legs over the side of the bed and rang Sabrina's cell phone. He wasn't surprised to receive no answer, his call echoing in the space reserved for what might have been. The front desk confirmed that Sabrina had checked out. Did his refusal to sleep with her earn him brownie points on some mythical moral scoreboard, or did it make him a stupid chump?

While passed out, he had missed a call from Cole. Parker queued the message and listened on speaker as Cole launched into an angry diatribe reeking of disgust for his mama. Parker dialed Cole's number.

The kid was apologetic. "I had nowhere else to vent. Mama didn't even come to Aunt Grace's funeral. What kind of person doesn't say goodbye to her sister?"

"She was on the beach with her boyfriend when the cops arrested her. Was it okay, Cole? The funeral?"

"They opened the casket for Daddy and me to say goodbye to her, but we closed it for the service. She was all beat up, you know?"

"All I can say is that I'm truly sorry for your loss."

"Tell me the truth, Parker, did that guy they arrested kill my aunt?"

Parker was reminded of the conversation he'd had with the prison guard. Luke had conspired with Meredith. He was a bad guy. "No, your mama had that gun in the thicket."

"You're sure Mama shot Aunt Grace?"

"There's a bullet in Grace's leg that came from your mama's gun." Was that the biggest lie he'd ever told? "She had you hide her gun but leave Grace's gun in the thicket so she could blame Grace and Luke for a shootout with Paula. All lies to protect herself."

"She can't go back to prison, Parker." She had to … do things to the guards so they'd protect her from the other inmates."

"She doesn't have to go back to prison. You know she's sick, don't you?"

Parker had touched a nerve. He heard the kid suck air.

"I know about the diary."

"She kept a diary? What's in it?"

"It's disgusting. Goes back to when you were partners. You're all over it. She hated you and wanted to hurt you."

"Like the journals they find after mass murderers kill a bunch of people. Where is it?"

"I don't know. Aunt Grace kept it while Mama was in prison."

"To keep the prison shrinks from reading it."

"Now I wish she had gotten help in prison."

"That's the problem with our penal system: we incarcerate the mentally ill, throw them in with violent criminals, and then we wonder why we have high recidivism rates. If they send her back to Georgia she'll never get help. She'll be back to giving blowjobs to the guards."

The kid moaned.

"Listen, I left Grace's van on the red side at the Tampa airport. Your keys are on the passenger-side front tire." Parker hung up.

He ordered breakfast for lunch and ate unenthusiastically while he compared the numbers in the three proposals: the ASC proposal, Dennie's fraudulent proposal, and the valid proposal prepared by Sabrina and Steve. ASC's numbers were exaggerated, Dennie's were a bigger lie, and the valid proposal numbers, good enough to make most CIOs salivate, looked anemic in comparison—five percent in labor cost savings plus twelve percent claims savings.

But so what? He couldn't change the world by derailing one corrupt deal, stopping one unscrupulous entrepreneur. If he was honest with himself, Kumar and Dennie scared the pants off him. Sabrina was gone, and he'd made his choice—cooperate with Kumar, sell Dennie's deal to Midwestern Assurance, keep his job, fight to protect Paula, and save his marriage. As for

Midwestern Assurance and the nice folks in Iowa? *Caveat emptor.*

If he were to play Kumar's game, he had to protect himself. He couldn't be caught with the ASC proposal or with Steve's numbers on his laptop. Using the maps app on his smartphone, Parker found the Spring Hill Suites on Canal Street, on the opposite side of the French Quarter from his room on Royal Street. The hotel was near St. Louis Cemetery No. 2 and within easy walking distance of Arnaud's Restaurant. Local myth had it that the cemetery was haunted. Maybe he could relax in the arms of the undead, commune with spirits enjoying their final reward. He called the hotel and made a reservation.

He spent the afternoon daydreaming, wondering where Sabrina was, whether she would accept an apology, give him another chance. No, he had chosen Paula over Sabrina, and Sabrina was too prideful to give him a second chance.

His daydreams were shattered by a call from Rawlings. "I asked Monahan to pick you up but he couldn't find you. Where did you go?"

"In New Orleans for business meetings today and tomorrow."

"Get your ass on the next plane and turn yourself in at my office."

"You arresting me? What's the charge?"

"You'll see when you get here. Be in my office tomorrow morning or I'll have NOPD pick you up."

"I have no reason to rabbit, detective. I'll be there after my business meetings." Parker disconnected before Rawlings could issue any more threats.

***

At 5:30 p.m., Parker stepped out of the elevator into the lobby, leaving all the evidence and his key in the room. For fifteen minutes, he chatted with the doorman on the sidewalk, ready to scurry back into the hotel if he spotted any IBS employees.

Up to Canal Street and westward, he trundled in the heat of the late afternoon, his blazer slung over his shoulder. Every now and then, he stopped to survey the crowds around him. No one seemed to be following him. Once past Bourbon Street, he was beyond any route to Arnaud's that Kumar and his entourage might take from the Marriott, so he relaxed. After checking in at the Spring Hill Suites, he slipped the key card into his breast pocket then walked past St. Louis Cemetery No. 1, north to Bienville, and back eastward toward Arnaud's.

He watched the plain brown building's unmarked side entrance from the shade of an abandoned storefront and saw no one he recognized enter or leave the restaurant. At 6:45 p.m., he took a deep breath and walked across Bienville to face his adversaries. Inside it was dark, the sound of boisterous conversations coming through a doorway to his right. He waited for his eyes to adjust before peeking into the Richelieu Bar to survey the plush carpet, the pictures on the sumptuous wood paneling, and the heavy chairs upholstered in a leopard print. Most of the tables and all the barstools were occupied by tourists and conventioneers, having a swell time in the Big Easy. At the far corner table, Dennie, Alexi, and Ravi sat with Kumar while Mani stood to one side, listening raptly to Kumar's proclamations.

Two waiters wearing white waistcoats crisscrossed as they wound their way through the tables, blocking his view of Kumar's table and Kumar's view of the doorway, giving Parker a chance to slip across the threshold undetected. He ascended the steep, carpeted staircase, flanked by polished wood handrails and paneled walls, to pause before a solid steel door with a push bar. He shoved the door open, revealing Ilya standing guard outside the secret room, hands clasped in front of his crotch like a funeral director standing beside a casket.

Parker advanced to the secret room's doorway, and Ilya stopped him with a meaty hand on his chest. "You wait," Ilya said.

Parker ignored him and looked into the room where another waiter in a white waistcoat stood beside a dining table that had not been set for table service. An overhead projector hummed on the table, and a pull-down screen crouched in the corner behind the waiter.

"Aren't we having dinner?" Parker asked the waiter.

"You only ordered A/V equipment, but I can fetch refreshments from the bar if you like," the waiter said.

"You wait," Ilya said.

"I'll wait," Parker said. He smiled at Ilya.

A full head taller than Ilya, Parker shifted position to stand beside the thick man, with his hands clasped in front of his crotch to mimic Ilya's pose, staring at the closed steel door. The waiter raised an eyebrow, then moved discreetly out of sight around the corner.

Ilya grunted. Or maybe it was a snarl.

Ten minutes later the steel door swung open on squeaky hinges, and Mani appeared first, followed by Ravi, carrying a laptop case, then Alexi, Dennie, with a carryall bag slung over her shoulder, and lastly, Kumar. One by one, they filed into the room, looking at Parker as though he were a Christian to be fed to the lions. No Gentleman Jack Shaw, Parker noted; the man must want to keep his hands clean. When the others were seated, Ilya shoved Parker into the room and closed the door behind them.

"Where's your laptop?" Ilya said.

"Why do I feel like I'm at the Lubyanka prison?" Parker said. "The Atlanta cops confiscated it."

Kumar signaled Ilya to back off. "Are you here to join the team?" he asked Parker.

"I am. May I sit?"

Kumar waved a hand at the empty seat. To the waiter, he said, "Come back and check on us in fifteen minutes, please."

The waiter nodded and left as Parker sat, crossed his legs, and leaned forward, expecting induction into the "team."

"Have you checked in?"

"I have."

Ilya shook his head. "Nyet."

"Wrong, Ivan." Parker pulled the Spring Hill Suites keycard from his breast pocket and flashed it at Kumar, who squinted at the unfamiliar color and logo on the card.

"Where the hell is that?" Dennie said.

"Why aren't you at the team hotel, the Marriott?" Kumar said.

Parker shrugged. "Guess I didn't get the memo."

Kumar gave a dispirited sigh, as though Parker were a disobedient pet. "Tell us," Kumar waved a hand around the room, "what you've been up to since you haven't come to the office this week."

"Carolyn asked me to stay away from the office while the cops investigate the murder of Grace Walker, which worked out well since I had to deal with a thieving ex-business partner and a wife in rehab. I traveled to St. Pete to visit my wife and got here today."

Kumar leaned back, watched his subordinates consider Parker's explanation. "Have you spent time with your team?"

"Steve? Nope. He's working on the New England Indemnity numbers like you asked."

"What about Sabrina?"

Parker shrugged. "She works for Shaw, not me."

"You can't believe anything he says, Kumar," Dennie said.

Kumar ignored her. He snapped his fingers, and Ravi, who had booted his machine and plugged it into the overhead projector, tapped a few keys, and a spreadsheet appeared on the screen. Parker rose and walked around the table. Ilya reacted by moving in front of the door, but Parker bypassed him for the projection screen to get a closer look at the rows of numbers as Ravi slowly paged down through the spreadsheet.

Parker shook a finger at Alexi and made a goofy smile. "I know what you did."

Kumar tilted his head, waiting to hear what Parker knew.

The bottom-line numbers were a fifteen percent labor cost savings due to labor arbitrage and a twenty percent savings in claims payments, exactly the lie that Dennie wanted to tell the Midwestern Assurance execs to beat the ASC proposal and win the deal.

Parker tapped his temple with an index finger and constructed a look of admiration. "I know what you did because I invented it."

"You invent shit," Alexi said.

"I invented the machine-learning loop, Comrade."

Kumar chuckled, enjoying the repartee.

"You invent shit," Alexi said again, half rising from his chair.

Kumar placed a hand on Alexi's arm. "It's okay. Let him continue."

"Wash, rinse, repeat."

"Huh?" Alexi, unfamiliar with the American idiom.

"You replicated the test cases, I'd say about five times, and used the machine learning loop after each replication to make the rules better and better, the savings bigger and bigger. Brilliant, really, but I want credit for it. We'll call it the 'Parker Loop' and trademark it."

"That's outrageous!" Dennie screamed. "You've been opposed to us the whole time, and now you want credit?"

Kumar gave her a settle-down signal with both hands. "You're living up to your reputation, Parker. One look at the numbers, and you immediately figured them out."

Parker shrugged. "It's what I'd have done. You came up with bigger savings than I might have predicted, but the technique you used is my technique. Of course, we'll explain this to Midwestern Assurance tomorrow, am I right?"

"No way," Dennie said. "They won't understand it."

"We can explain that their test cases were representative of the kinds of claims they will receive, but not the volume. So, we increased the volume to show the power of machine learning—the Parker Loop. We don't have to hide things to win the deal."

"You show remarkable integrity for an ex-convict," Kumar said to Parker.

"He is crazy man," Alexi said.

Parker knew that Alexi—or Ravi—had tampered with the test cases, with Midwestern Assurance's help, but he wanted to find out just how far he would have to go to save his job.

To Kumar, Dennie said, "If you must have Parker do this, just make him present the numbers so we can win the damned deal. Or else I'll present the numbers."

Kumar folded his hands on the table and gave his subordinates a lecture. "Parker is the only man who can present the numbers. He has the prestige and credibility in the world of numbers. Salespeople," he said directly to Dennie, "are only good for picking up the check."

Dennie huffed but said nothing.

Kumar turned his attention to Parker. "You can tell them about the Parker Loop, but you have to assume our numbers are more accurate than your guesstimate. You good with that?"

"Oh, fuck this," Alexi said.

Parker pursed his lips and mimed a thoughtful stance. "The number I can't figure out is the one for labor cost savings. How did you come up with that?"

"I invent it," Alexi said, and Parker chuckled at Alexi's poor grasp of English nuance. The number had indeed been "invented." The accurate number, according to Steve, was five percent.

"What he means," Kumar said, "is that he's developing a software robot to operate the system and eliminate human operators and their exorbitant cost."

"RPA, Amerikanski," Alexi said. "Robotic Process Automation. We call it the Petrov Robot. We trademark."

"I invested the money, and we kept it a secret, like the Manhattan Project," Kumar said. "Alexi hasn't finished it yet, but our friend, Peter Thorndike at Golden West Insurance, has agreed to test it when it is ready."

That's why Alexi posted a guard on his lab door. "What about the jobs that were supposed to be retained in Iowa?"

"They can go back to their villages and herd pigs," Mani said.

Now all the Americans lose their jobs. "You'll cannibalize the Indian jobs too."

"Let them eat cake," Mani said.

Parker laughed at the reference to Marie Antoinette. He turned to Kumar. "Alexi will present this part, right? I'm a numbers guy, don't know anything about robots."

"We're not explaining the technology, just presenting the numbers," Dennie said.

"She's right," Kumar said. "Just make them believe our numbers so we get selected for due diligence."

Parker figured it out then. Kumar's game was to leverage Parker's credibility and set him up as the scapegoat when IBS/Shaw Technology failed to produce the savings. If he revealed Steve's accurate numbers to the Midwestern Assurance executives, he was certain to be fired for insubordination, and he wondered if he'd feel self-righteous when he was shucking oysters in a Florida dive bar.

"Okay," Parker said. "There's some 'art of the possible' involved in this, but the AI numbers are solid."

Kumar stood. "Looks like you'll save your job, after all, Parker."

At his signal, Dennie slid the IBS/Shaw Technology proposal document across the table to Parker, as though she were dealing cards. "Study it, Parker. The meeting is at the JW Marriott on Canal Street at 9:30 a.m. tomorrow, so don't sleep in. Midwestern Assurance will reserve a meeting room. Check the event board for the room name when you get there."

"Mani and I have another meeting to attend now," Kumar said, "but I've made reservations for the five of you downstairs in the Jazz Room. Dennie can pick up the tab."

The five of you. Dennie, Alexi, Ravi, Ilya, and me.

As soon as Kumar and Mani departed, Parker moved toward the door, saying, "I'm not hungry."

Ilya blocked the exit. "You stay."

"Where's the ASC proposal, Parker?" Dennie said.

"I don't know what you're talking about."

"Where's the test case printout?" Alexi said.

"It's in his hotel room," Dennie said. "Get his key."

Roughly, the Russian brute pulled Parker's room key from his breast pocket. "I keep," Ilya said.

"Can't take ya both. Y'all are too big." The skinny pedicab driver wore a red bandana and a gold hoop earring. His pedicab, with a tucked-and-rolled red leather seat reminiscent of '57 Chevys, was the only one parked at the curb beside the side entrance to the restaurant.

"Get yourself a different ride, Ivan," Parker said. Outwitting Ilya, he jumped onto the seat and commandeered the pedicab.

"You wait," Ilya said to Parker as he blocked the cab's departure.

The kid stood on the pedals of his pedicab and waved an arm at the other cabs waiting in front of the restaurant's main entrance. He flashed two fingers, and two of them moved toward the side entrance. Ilya and Dennie slid down the sidewalk toward the other cabs like anxious passengers in a taxi queue, giving Parker a chance to talk privately with his driver.

"I've got to lose these people," Parker said.

"Which way we going?"

"Straight ahead, toward the cemeteries. They think I'm staying at the Spring Hill Suites on Canal."

The driver sized Parker up, decided to play the game. "You got fifty dollars?"

Parker showed him three twenties.

"Hang on. I can ditch 'em."

Ilya and Dennie took seats in their cabs, and the procession started off at a gentle pace down Bienville and through two stop signs before approaching the busy intersection with Rampart Street. As he neared the stop-and-go light, the driver stood on his pedals and surveyed the cross-traffic. He coasted for a few seconds, timing his move, then pumped hard, ran the red light, then hit the brakes, fishtailing like an eighteen-wheeler in the median. He straightened, paused, then dodged speeding traffic coming from the right. The chasing pedicabs stopped at the red light, prompting Ilya to shout at his driver like a jockey whipping a horse on the home stretch.

Pumping hard, the kid opened a hundred-yard lead on Ilya as he raced through the green light at Basin Street, away from streetlights, into the darkness.

The driver craned his neck to look at Parker. "When I stop, jump off and run into the cemetery. Run straight down the center path, and I'll circle the block and meet you on the other side."

Parker nodded in respect for the driver's street smarts. The young trickster held out a hand, and Parker gave him the money and tensed for his exit. They glided past St. Louis Cemetery No. 1, famous for its guided ghost tours, but gated and locked at this hour to deter vandalism, and stopped beside derelict and foreboding St. Louis Cemetery No. 2, donated by the Catholic Church in 1823.

The driver skidded to a halt, the only light the stuttering glow of headlights on cars whooshing by on the elevated I-10 expressway, less than a block ahead. Parker alighted from the pedicab, all too aware of Ilya speeding toward him, eighty yards away. He skipped around the front of the pedicab. Before entering the graveyard, he looked back up the street as the driver pedaled away and saw that Ilya and Dennie were closing the gap.

Parker dove into the shadows, the light absorbed by narrow aisles between sepulchers and mausoleums fraught with mold and mildew. He sprinted down the center aisle toward the Iberville entrance, where he expected to find his pedicab. It wasn't there. He had been scammed by the streetwise kid who wanted no part in a graveyard execution. He turned around and several rows deep into the graveyard, he cut into a grassy alleyway and stooped beside a filthy, cold tombstone to watch the Bienville entrance to the cemetery.

Ilya's pedicab stopped at the entrance and waited for Dennie's cab to catch up. A loud conversation ensued and Parker heard Ilya bellow, "You go round. I drive him like cow to slaughter."

They split up, Dennie riding her cab around the back of the graveyard to the entrance on Parker's left, Ilya stomping into the graveyard from his right.

Parker crept down the row to a narrow path at the front of the cemetery and through the fence, he saw Dennie's pedicab arrive at the Iberville entrance. Dennie climbed down and her pedicab driver pedaled swiftly away. She moved toward the opening in a crouch, a big silver pistol pointed at the darkness. Parker was trapped between a deranged gunwoman and a frantic madman with muscles.

Parker moved back down the outer path, staying ahead of Dennie's pace on the center path, looking for a hiding place. The sound of a horse-drawn carriage moving toward him down Robertson Street chased him into the shadows of a grassy row. The horses clopped slowly across Bienville and toward the section where Parker hid, their smell pungent, the rushing sound of their breath ominous. He scurried away from the specter, deeper into the darkness.

In the middle of the row, he chose a wide mausoleum, it's flat top a foot and a half higher than the top of his head. Hands flat on its top, Parker tried to pull himself up with his arms and failed. His second attempt began with bent legs and a standing jump, as though rebounding a missed basketball shot, aided by feet, knees, and ankles seeking purchase on the smooth sides of the building. Every body part he could bring into contact with the cement wall scrabbled and scraped until he had both elbows on the flat top. With a heave, he levered himself upward on his forearms until his stomach teetered on the edge like a fulcrum. Maintaining momentum, he swung his legs, threw a knee atop the tomb, then rolled to the right to lie flat. An involuntary yelp escaped his lips as his lower back contacted something sharp. Gulping the pain, he rolled onto his stomach. Off to his right, Ilya grunted a wordless yet eloquent response that meant he had heard Parker and was coming for him.

The top of the crypt had decayed into splintered chunks of cement, jagged and angular. He ran his hand over the surface beside him until he felt the chunk that had stabbed his back, a loose mass the size of a soccer ball with one sharp edge pointing up. Parker's large hands could palm a basketball, and this lump was smaller, easier to wield as a weapon.

As he waited for Ilya, he sensed rather than saw Dennie move past his row, a combination of the Doppler effect and the displacement of stagnant air. Ilya mumbled something incomprehensible to her, then tromped down the aisle to Parker's right, less than six feet away.

Squatting on his haunches like the baseball catcher he once was, and gripping the cement rock in his hand, Parker tensed for Ilya's appearance as the horse-drawn carriage rolled down Robertson toward Iberville. Ilya rushed around the corner into Parker's aisle, unmindful of threats from above, a bull charging the matador's red cape. Parker sprang from his perch, arm cocked like a catcher, ready to throw to second base to catch a base stealer. The cement rock smashed into Ilya's face an instant before Parker's knees slammed into his chest.

The immense Russian toppled with a pained, guttural grunt and an outrush of air from his lungs. Parker scrambled to his feet and stood over the inert body for a moment, then sprinted down the outer path toward the graveyard opening on Iberville, hoping to outrun Dennie's bullets.

He halted beside the mausoleum on the edge of the center path, stooped, and peeked around the corner. He could see no movement on the path in the inky night. *Run, Parker, run!* his mind urged his paralyzed muscles, as he plotted a course to the right, toward the interstate and away from the carriage somewhere to his left.

Mentally crossing himself, he darted through the opening then froze as he saw a man shuffling down the road from his left.

"This way, Parker. Come with me," Jack Shaw said.

Parker slunk back into the graveyard opening, fearing that Shaw was half of a pincer movement to trap him.

"Come on!" Shaw urged him. "You've got to get out of here."

Parker searched the older man's face for a clue as to his intentions, and the pause was a fateful delay. Dennie emerged from the right, three rows away from the entrance. "How convenient. The gang's all here."

Her hand outstretched, a look of serious concentration on her face, she aimed her weapon and the pistol barked at them. Instinctively, Parker ducked, and Shaw moved around him, between Dennie and her target.

"Don't shoot, he's—"

"I know," Dennie cut Shaw off. She fired another gunshot, and the old man crumpled. Parker caught Shaw under the arms and was dragged to the ground behind him.

Ilya staggered out of an aisle beyond Dennie, his eyes white holes in a bloody red mask. He glanced at Dennie's outstretched gun hand, Jack sitting on the ground, bleeding, and he wobbled in the opposite direction toward the Bienville exit.

Dennie took a purposeful step toward her cowering prey, careful not to trip over the loose gravel in her red high heels. She was only twenty feet away. "I'm better off without you, Parker. I have your room key."

Shaw moaned. Parker gathered himself into a sprinter's crouch, hoping she'd take one more step before firing her weapon. She wouldn't be very fast in those high heeled shoes, so he could zigzag toward the heavy traffic on Rampart Street where Dennie would be less inclined to commit a public execution. He hesitated. He couldn't leave his father to be murdered. He had to drag Jack Shaw to cover. As he rose, a hand on his shoulder pushed him down, and a shot rang out above his head.

Dennie stumbled as she jerked to her right, and the bullet whizzed harmlessly past her. Parker turned to see Sabrina, shock on her face, the gun wavering in her hand. *She came back!* A bullet struck the stone column beside Parker and a fragment stung his cheek. Dennie's arm was raised, a look of concentration in her eyes. Sabrina was paralyzed with fright. Parker grabbed her gun, swung it toward Dennie, and pulled the trigger repeatedly, not aiming, just pointing at the woman. Bang, bang, bang.

Dennie stiffened, a small red dot appearing on her forehead, just right of center. Three heartbeats later, like an imploded building, she collapsed in a heap.

Jack Shaw shuddered, as a pained wail escaped his lips.

Alert now, Sabrina reached for her gun. "It's legally registered in my name."

Shaw regarded Parker and then Sabrina, the confusion ebbing from his eyes. "You can't be a black woman who killed a white woman in Louisiana," Shaw said. He reached for the gun.

"I shot her. I'll face the music," Parker said.

"As an ex-con, you'd be in just as much trouble," Shaw said. He grabbed the gun from Parker. "It's self-defense. She shot me and I shot her."

"With Sabrina's gun. How did that happen?"

"Just the way it happened. Sabrina took a shot and missed, and Dennie kept shooting, so I grabbed the gun and shot Dennie."

Parker hesitated, watching blood ooze from Shaw's right leg.

"Get out of here and call 9-1-1, Parker. You're a complication."

"I'm Jack's witness," Sabrina said. "Terry is holding a carriage up at the corner. Go!"

"Go," Shaw croaked.

"Wipe the gun down then put yours and Sabrina's prints back on it." Parker ran. He avoided the carriage, wanted no witness to his presence at the cemetery, and crossed Conti toward the river. The sirens of emergency vehicles wailed in the night. He stopped and watched the ambulance and police cars head toward the cemetery to save Jack.

Parker hid within milling crowds on Bourbon Street and as he shuffled to the Wyndham Grand Hotel. He retrieved his key from the registration desk although he wasn't sure his room was a safe hiding place. The NOLA cops could be hunting him down for Rawlings; Jack might tell the cops the truth; Sabrina might cave under questioning. Or the cops might arrest her for murder. No matter what happened, he had finally unmasked the identity of his birth father and could thank the man for saving his life.

Several times he tried Sabrina's cell phone without success. He did not leave messages. He remained dressed, in case the authorities came knocking, and lay on top of the bed covers. Without meaning to, he dozed off.

Parker woke stiff and sticky from sleeping in his clothes, his head aching from lying on the too-soft pillow. He popped off the bed and found a phone book in a dresser drawer. The throwback to analog days might very well have been out of date but the yellow pages contained a list of hospitals that wasn't likely to have changed. His third call went to the Tulane Medical Center, the hospital closest to the cemeteries, and a woman confirmed that Jack Shaw was a patient.

From the lobby he scanned the street once again and neither did he spot Sabrina, nor did he see any NOLA cops. He took a pedicab down Canal Street to the hospital and received directions to Shaw's room from a distracted nurse who was in a heated discussion with a doctor.

Parker was relieved to find no police guard standing watch outside the room. He peeked into a room with brilliant white walls that suggested the bright light reputedly at the end of the tunnel between life and death. A nurse busied herself at a medical cart with her back to her patient. The head of Shaw's bed was raised into a sitting position. Propped up by pillows, Shaw held a folded newspaper he didn't appear to be reading. Parker eased into the room and caught his attention.

"Jelani, honey, can you give us a minute?" Shaw said.

The nurse whirled around, saw Parker, and said, "Family only. Sorry."

"He's my son," Shaw said without hesitation.

"Oh. Of course, Jack," the nurse said. "Not too long now." She shook a playful finger at her patient and left the room.

Parker closed the door and moved to the foot of the bed. "You going to be okay?"

"Thankfully, the bullet didn't hit anything important. They stitched me up, and I'll be out of here in a day or two."

"Have the cops been here?" Parker said.

Shaw nodded slowly, as though a quick shake of his head would disrupt the delicate balance between pain and comfort. "They were waiting for me when I came out of recovery, took my official statement. I told them the fable we concocted before you left the cemetery. They tried to get me to say that Sabrina did the shooting or loaned me the gun, either of which would have been a crime. They wanted to bring a murder case against a black woman, but I insisted I took the gun from her when Dennie started shooting and Sabrina was too scared to defend us."

"Probably helped that Dennie fired several times and you had one of her bullets in your leg." Parker had thought through the questions the cops were likely to ask Shaw and Sabrina and now he wanted to know the fabricated answers in case he had to rescue Sabrina. "Did they ask why you were at a cemetery?"

"Oh, yes, that was tricky. After dinner, Dennie lured us to the cemetery with the promise of an after dark tour of haunted graves. Sabrina and I arrived separately in a horse-drawn carriage, which is true, unaware that there was no such tour, and we fell into her trap. She figured my murder would be dismissed as just another crime in a crime-ridden city."

"So it was a planned ambush and Dennie wanted to kill you. Why?"

"She wanted me out of the way so she could become CEO of my company."

"Did the cops believe that?"

"If they bother to review the minutes of our board meetings they'll find Dennie's opinion that time had passed me by and that I should retire and let her take command. The cops must believe me; I'm free to go."

"What about Sabrina? Where is she?"

A phlegmy cough erupted from Shaw. "They took her to the police station and brought me here. I took all the credit for …" He let his voice trail off. "I'm sure they've released her."

Parker wasn't sure about that. Sabrina hadn't answered her phone. The story Shaw told the cops seemed flimsy. Then again, the truth was incredulous as well. "What the hell were you guys doing at the cemetery?"

"We were coming to join the meeting at Arnaud's—Sabrina knew where it was taking place. When we saw you being chased. We followed."

"You knew you had to save me, didn't you, Jack?" Parker nearly called him "Dad."

Shaw recoiled. "Sabrina was worried about you."

"What did you hope to accomplish at the meeting?"

"Sabrina wanted to kill the deal and end the partnership, of course."

"But that's not what you wanted."

Shaw gazed at the ceiling, stalling for time. "No, that's not what I wanted. I was hoping to find a compromise to keep the deal alive."

Parker felt like a lawyer who had trapped a witness as he delivered the unexpected question. "Did you know about Dennie's fraud?"

Shaw grimaced, whether from pain in his leg or mental anguish, Parker wasn't sure. "A little birdie told me."

"Sabrina."

Shaw nodded, too pained or too tired to speak.

Parker found it hard to believe Shaw. He had seen the surreptitious huddle between Shaw and Dennie in Iowa, before Dennie acquired the ASC proposal from the Midwestern Assurance exec.

Parker rose and meandered around the spacious private room, searching for a nonjudgmental way to ask the questions that had been on his mind since he first read the IBS/Shaw Technology contracts.

"Spit it out, Parker," Shaw said.

Parker stopped in front of the window, the early morning sun endowing him with a saintly aura. "Why did you do it, Jack? Why did you make the deal with the devil?"

"It was my exit strategy. I was going to fish my way around the world," Shaw said with a wistful smile on his face. "We had fallen behind the times in our industry, needed the AI apps—Alexi's work—to become competitive again. But I ran out of capital because Alexi is damned expensive. Kumar bought stock on the condition that the proceeds were invested in Alexi. Then he brought you and your analytics to the table to complete the strategy."

"Alexi participated in the fraud so Kumar's money would keep flowing."

"The mad scientist? He wants to be famous, so he convinced Kumar to make secret investments and expand into robotics," Shaw said.

"But Terry threw a monkey wrench in the works, sabotaged Alexi's installation at New England Indemnity and his demo in Iowa."

Shaw grimaced again, whether in pain or in reaction to Terry's sabotage, Parker couldn't be sure. "Terry is no politician. He's a bulldog, doesn't know how to compromise."

"He wants to save fifteen hundred jobs in Iowa," Parker said.

"Those jobs can't be saved," Shaw said. "If we don't get the deal, MA will award the contract to American Systems Corporation."

Nurse Jelani stuck her head in the door and said, "Time's up. I gotta work."

Shaw raised a finger in the air. "Another minute, pleas," Shaw said. Jelani tried unsuccessfully for a cross look and closed the door.

Shaw seemed drained of all energy. He moaned, but Parker pressed on like a callous prosecutor badgering a vulnerable witness. "Did you steal my coffee mug, have it tested for DNA?"

"No. Why would I do that?"

"To confirm our relationship."

"Ah, now I get it." Shaw coughed, shuddered with pain. "You stole my picture, showed it to your uncle, didn't you? Think you know something?"

"Yes, I know you lied about my mother."

Shaw recoiled again. "I didn't lie. Just didn't remember her because so many young interns worked for my father."

That's not what Irene said. "You're saying you're not my father?"

"No, Parker, I'm not your father. You're like a dog chasing its tail." Shaw's face contorted with a stab of pain, and he pushed a red plunger connected to the drip bag over his head and the IV in his arm. As the painkiller reached his bloodstream, Shaw sighed and relaxed a bit.

"Terry will be my proxy in the meeting today. I've incentivized him to make the deal for me but I'm not sure I can trust him to hold the line when he's under pressure. I need you to support him, be the steal in his backbone."

Parker didn't want to be co-opted into a scheme by a man who lied about being his father. "You don't trust faithful Terry but you trust me?"

"I don't trust you but I don't think you want any complications for your girlfriend and I don't think you want to go back to prison. Your safety is based upon the statement of a man recovering from anesthesia who might remember things differently when he's not drugged."

Parker's face turned red. "You're blackmailing your own son?"

"Look," Shaw said, trying to sound reasonable. "Those jobs are gone and the cheater is dead. Play ball, Parker."

"Play ball, how?"

"The easiest way is to certify Dennie's numbers and lock up the deal."

Parker shook his violently. "I can't certify fraudulent numbers. I'll take my chances with the cops."

Shaw let his arms flop down on the bed in exasperation. "Make a deal, Parker, however you have to do it. But make a damn deal."

***

Parker rode a pedicab from the hospital to the Marriott, where he would meet the Midwestern Assurance execs. On the way, he replayed his encounter with Jack Shaw and reached two conclusions: 1) Shaw may not have known the extent to which Dennie was committing fraud, but he had given her free rein to win the deal by any means; and 2) If he believed Shaw, the only person who could have stolen his coffee cup was Dennie. She had been on the floor when Parker was in Shaw's office and she must have had a key to Shaw's office. Dennie must have suspected the relationship and apparently confirmed that Parker is Jack Shaw's son. Although murder seemed an extreme solution for her problem, she wanted Parker dead to prevent Shaw from naming his son CEO instead of her.

When he alighted in front of the Marriott, he rang Sabrina's cell phone again and once again reached voicemail. Either she did not want to be reached, or she was still being questioned by the police. Scared and depressed, he walked through the entrance to the Marriott.

Terry was waiting for him in the lobby. The two men searched one another's faces for clues as to their intentions, but neither said a word as they walked to the meeting room.

They arrived first at a modern, soulless meeting room that seemed out of character for New Orleans. Parker poured them coffee from a silver decanter into china cups that would cool the fortifying liquid to a chilly, undrinkable temperature in minutes.

Cold sweat beads formed at Parker's temples. He wiped them away as Kumar walked through the door with a smile on his face. The smile faded when he saw only Parker and Terry at the modern table. "Where's Dennie?"

"No idea," Parker said. Not quite a lie. He had no idea where the New Orleans morgue might be.

Mani and Alexi followed Kumar into the room and gave Parker loathsome looks.

"Have you seen Jack?" Kumar asked.

"Yes," Terry said. "I spoke with him earlier this morning. He's indisposed and he's appointed me to lead this meeting as his proxy."

Kumar looked puzzled. "You? I own Shaw Technology."

"You own a minority stake, Kumar. I represent Shaw's majority shares. I'm in charge of this meeting."

As Kumar digested this turn of events, Parker asked Alexi, "Where's your bodyguard?" He needed to know where the last witness was.

"Ilya was mugged last night. Fucking American criminals."

He'd reported it as a mugging. *Good, good.* "Yeah, our muggers always pick on the soft targets, like fat Russians."

"Not funny, Parker. In hospital they must rebuild his face."

"Maybe it will turn out better this time."

"Stop this nonsense," Kumar bellowed and jumped to his feet, as though he was a referee in a prizefight.

Kumar was still on his feet when the Midwestern Assurance execs, Roberto Gonzalez and Nancy Maddox, entered the room. A third man, tall with neatly parted black hair, followed them into the room. Parker recognized the man as the one Dennie had danced with in Iowa, the man she had kissed, the man who had given her the ASC proposal. Gonzalez introduced him as Ted Cummings.

Kumar extended a warm welcome, and all parties took their seats.

Cummings inquired as to Dennie's whereabouts, and Kumar said that she was expected shortly, a drowning man reaching for any scrap of flotsam to keep himself afloat.

"We need Dennie for this discussion," Cummings said. He looked to the door, willing it to open and reveal his paramour.

"We don't have time to wait for her," Gonzalez said.

That suited Parker. "Terry here is Jack Shaw's proxy and I'm Kumar's numbers guy, so we'll start with this." Parker slid the IBS/Shaw Technology proposal Dennie had prepared across the table.

Gonzalez flipped through the pages, reached the climax, and smiled. "Excellent. IBS/Shaw wins the bid."

Kumar rose and extended his hand across the table. "Welcome to our customer family."

Gonzalez hadn't needed any explanation of the numbers from Parker. He knew what the numbers would be. Parker decided he couldn't make a deal for his father without an admission of malfeasance.

"I have to make an unfortunate admission," Parker said. He pulled the ASC proposal from his briefcase and pushed it into the middle of the table.

Cummings recoiled as though a poisonous snake had dropped from the ceiling. Gonzalez regarded the proposal with something like regret. Cummings reached for it, but Parker pulled it back.

"What are you doing, Parker?" Terry said.

Explaining for Terry, Parker said, "Mr. Cummings here gave our competitor's proposal to Dennie, which gave us an unfair advantage." To the group, he said, "That disqualifies her proposal from the bidding."

Kumar inhaled noisily. "I didn't know."

Cummings froze. He and Gonzalez traded looks.

"Dennie's numbers are falsified, Kumar," Parker said. "That proposal is off the table."

Kumar emitted a breathless, "What?" His hand hung in midair, unshaken. Cummings looked around the room for a potential hiding place.

"Falsified how?" Nancy Maddox asked.

Parker pulled the green and white computer printout from his briefcase. "Dennie and Alexi here deleted eighty-six cases that ruined the test results and replaced them with simple cases to make the numbers look good. You can run a file compare to confirm I'm right. The simple cases were drawn from a separate file download. We're tracing the source of that file but I think we can guess where it originated." He stared at Cummings who failed an attempt to appear innocent.

Drunk on counterfeit power, Parker continued. "Mr. Shaw told me this morning that he will fire Alexi for falsifying the test case results. You may as well pack up and get out, Alexi." As the attendees digested Alexi's public humiliation, Parker delivered the second of his one-two punches: "Mr. Shaw will fire Dennie for unethical behavior when she turns up."

"He can't do that," Kumar said. "Alexi and Dennie are the only valuable people in Shaw's shit-pile."

Terry said, "We should talk about this, Parker."

Ignoring Terry, Parker turned to Alexi who was dumbfounded and paralyzed in his seat. "Why are you still here? Move your ass back to Stalingrad and take Ilya with you."

Reluctantly, Alexi gathered his materials, stuffed them in his briefcase, and moved toward the door. "Russians never forget, Parker. Watch your back."

Parker waved him goodbye. Gonzalez tilted his head, reached a cold-hearted conclusion. "How you manage your staff is your prerogative. It doesn't matter to me that Dennie somehow came into possession of the ASC proposal. Her proposal is excellent and we accept it, Mr. Parker."

"I can't let you do that," Parker said. "That proposal is so big a lie," he said, his voice dropping and slowing dramatically, "that it constitutes corporate fraud."

Cummings covered his face with his hands, and Nancy Maddox squirmed in her seat. Fraud was not a word she wanted to hear.

"That's an unfounded accusation," Kumar said.

Parker slapped the table to counter Kumar. "You're so ignorant you don't realize that Dennie's proposal would produce huge losses for you. She was taking you for a ride."

Kumar clenched his fists and his teeth, but Mani whispered something in Kumar's ear.

"I knew none of this," Kumar said.

"Let's go," Cummings said.

"Wait," Maddox said. "Is there a proposal you'd like to put on the table, Mr. Parker? Or have we wasted our time?"

"Yes," Parker said. "Mr. Shaw urged me to make a deal we could all be happy with." He handed Gonzalez a spreadsheet. "These numbers represent your honest outsourcing savings and a single pass of the original test cases through Alexi's apps."

Gonzalez flipped through the pages, his face growing taut, his lips pulled down at the corners. "Not acceptable, Mr. Parker. There's only a five percent labor cost savings. Dennie assured us she would do far better than this."

When Gonzalez dropped the spreadsheet on the table, Maddox picked it up and perused it.

"That's a vanilla proposal from IBS/Shaw Technology," Parker said to Maddox.

He dealt a copy of Sabrina's new proposal to Gonzalez. "This proposal uses what we call the Parker Loop against five iterations of the testbed. It shows the power of machine learning over time. It's a gainshare deal: we'll promise a level of savings and share with you the savings over and above the guarantee. With our analytics and AI apps, you can be the best in the industry at what an insurance company does—process paperwork and adjudicate claims."

Gonzalez flipped through the pages. "I like the Parker Loop," he said, nodding his head appreciatively, "but there's no outsourcing, no labor arbitrage at all."

"You already have low labor costs in Iowa. We'll make up the difference with our other AI and analytics apps."

Terry caught on to Parker's stratagem. "It's not worth fifteen hundred jobs to get a five percent savings, which is all you'll honestly get."

Kumar glanced at the document and bared his teeth. "There's nothing in this deal for IBS. I saved you from being a garbage collector, Parker, and you do this? You're fired. And take that big lug assistant of yours with you."

"I expected that. You only brought me on board to facilitate fraud."

Mani stood, and Kumar followed suit.

"Stay," Gonzalez commanded. "We came to hear a proposal that contains outsourcing," Gonzalez said. "You have one chance to make such a proposal, or we'll accept ASC's proposal."

Kumar and Mani waited for Parker, but it was Terry who spoke. "According to Jack, Shaw Technology will not facilitate the movement of these American jobs to foreign countries." Parker had become the steal in Terry's spine.

"Americans are so naïve." Kumar slammed a fist into the tabletop, and an image of Khrushchev pounding his shoe on a lectern flashed through Parker's mind. "The American middle class is undereducated and overpaid — spoiled children. American companies can't survive by employing American workers."

Gonzalez said, "You don't seem to understand how this works, Terry. I've promised my board an immediate labor cost reduction through offshore arbitrage followed by robotics to eliminate all human labor in the future."

Ah, Parker thought. Kumar was counting on robotics to reduce his labor cost and hit Dennie's savings projections for Midwestern Assurance.

"We're not offering any robotics," Terry said.

Mani whispered to Kumar again. They stood to leave.

"You can tell Jack Shaw that our partnership is over," Kumar said to Terry. Turning to Gonzalez, he said, "Don't let these bastards push you into a corner. Go with ASC." Kumar and Mani left the room.

"They cheated too," Parker said to Gonzalez. "I'm giving you a chance to do the right thing."

"My board only cares about the money, Mr. Parker."

Gonzalez stood to leave, and Cummings made another attempt to grab the ASC proposal, but Parker held tight.

Nancy Maddox didn't leave until she had scooped up all three versions of the IBS/Shaw proposal. She gave Parker a slight nod of her head as she left.

What is special about America, Parker thought, is not that you can come here and get rich, but that ordinary people can build a decent life in an affordable house with two serviceable cars in a safe neighborhood. *That's the middle-class American Dream that is slipping away.* Parker developed a self-righteous glow, felt an adrenalin rush from the irrational exuberance of martyrdom.

"Jack is going to kill me," Terry said.

"Blame it on me." As they crossed the lobby, Parker wondered if he'd go to jail for two women now. If Jack recanted his statement, he could be tried for Paula's murder of Grace Anne Walker and for his shooting of Denise Davison. After the failure of his stand-your-ground defense in Florida, he didn't trust it to work in Louisiana. When he exited the hotel, Parker asked the doorman to find him a pedicab.

Terry crossed his arms over his thick chest. "Where are you going? We need to see Jack."

"You see Jack. I'm going to the police station to find Sabrina."

"You don't need to do that, buddy. She left in her car hours ago. Halfway to Atlanta by now."

"You talked to her?"

"She texted me after the cops were done with her. Said she was driving home."

"She drove her own car down here?"

"Only way to get her gun here. You asked her to bring it."

If the NOLA cops heard that he had asked Sabrina to bring a gun, Dennie's murder would sound premeditated. Parker told the doorman to cancel the pedicab. Instead, Parker called Enterprise Rent-a-Car and asked them to deliver something cheap to the Marriott. A getaway car would be safer than passing through security to board an airplane. His name could be on a no-fly list already.

"I have one question for you," Terry said. "Since Midwestern Assurance was in on it, why did Dennie need to kill you?"

The question stopped Parker in his mental tracks. After a minute, he said. "Kumar didn't know Dennie had cheated. She wanted to keep that quiet until he gained control of the company and promoted her to CEO. She didn't want me to out her in the meeting."

"So she was pulling the wool over Kumar's eyes. I guess it could be that simple." Terry shuffled from one foot to the other. "What am I supposed to tell Jack?"

"Tell him to do whatever his conscience allows him to do."

Terry looked confused, then sulked away.

Minutes later, a small purple sedan to the curb and a uniformed woman stepped out. "You the one asked for a rental car?" she asked Parker.

Parker signed her forms, tossed his briefcase in the back seat, and slid into the driver's seat. "Thanks for the car." He closed the door and squealed away toward the I-10 expressway which would take him to I75 south and a rendezvous with Paula. Going to Florida instead of Atlanta risked Rawlings' wrath but Parker figured Rawlings had no evidence other than what Meredith had told the cops. Atlanta could wait.

***

At a red light, Parker texted Sabrina with the news that he had exposed Dennie's fraud but that Midwestern Assurance would contract with ASC anyway. No response. He called her cell phone and was greeted with the number-out-of-service message. Sabrina was off the grid.

Parker had too much time to think about Sabrina as he drove eastward on I-10 toward Florida. He cared about her and could understand and empathize with her feelings. That was something, right? They worked well together on their adventures, had the same drive to fix things. Was that just physics, two bodies pressed together by shared compulsions? He envied her fine-tuned conscience and thought it could be his surrogate since his was defective. Was that love?

He had time to think about Paula, too. Over the course of twenty-four years of marriage, Paula and Parker often had evaluated their performances as spouses, and always pointed to Jordyn as a sign of their success. They were proud of the fact that neither of them had committed adultery. Until the incident in the thicket, they had devised ways to tolerate one another's defects. Now a fissure had opened between them and needed only a catalyst to become an uncrossable chasm. And the catalyst was Meredith. Although Paula had never given him the credit he thought he'd deserved for going to prison for her, he'd do it again. Their marriage hadn't been a fairy tale romance, but it was worth saving.

Then the question of why Dennie wanted him dead became an itch in the middle of his back that he couldn't scratch. She had it so well-wired, why commit murder?

He found an oldies radio station that played the music he and Sabrina had car-danced to on the way home from Columbia. That day now seemed like the distant past and he didn't feel like dancing.

As he cruised past the interchange with I-85 North to Atlanta, a call from Connor added to his anxiety.

"The cops were jerking your chain," the Irishman said.

Parker knew that in the US justice system, only suspects are required to tell the truth. Cops can lie all they want. "What's the big lie?"

"There's a bullet wound in Grace's left thigh. You didn't see that when you identified her?"

Parker played dumb, didn't want to reveal that he knew the wound was on the back of her leg and that Connor's source had jumbled the facts. "I only pulled the sheet down to her waist. I didn't have to examine her crotch to identify her."

"Quite."

"Get to the punchline, Connor. Was it through-and-through?" Playing dumb again.

Connor made a sound to imply he was annoyed by Parker's insolence. "No, they have the bullet. That's why they arrested Braun."

Parker heaved a sigh of relief. Either Meredith had shot her sister twice, or Paula had shot her in the shoulder, and Meredith had finished the job with a shot to the back of the leg. Intentionally. Playing along, he said, "I told you I didn't do it. It's an open-and-shut case, and Bob's your uncle."

Connor laughed at Parker's use of the British expression. "Definitely. That boy, Braun, is going to fry."

Connor still doesn't seem to know that Luke is my brother. Is his connection at the police department keeping it a secret? "It's lethal injection in Georgia, Connor." You learn all sorts of miscellany when you go to prison.

"I know that, Parker, I practice criminal law, you know. 'He's going to get stuck with a needle' didn't sound very clever."

"Meredith was detained in St. Pete. What's her story?"

"Her statement hasn't been filed as yet."

"Okay," Parker said. "Let me know if you hear anything from Florida. I guess you can brag now about keeping another client out of jail—me."

"Cheers!" Connor disconnected.

"Lethal injection," Parker muttered reverently. As children Luke had resented Parker. They had competed as students and athletes and their parents' attention, and Luke always came out second best. Karl Braun had been a hard man to please, so Luke could never be good enough. Now, Luke had cheated on his wife after enabling her addiction. Luke had collaborated with Meredith, sending Paula into an alcoholic spiral. It was possible that Luke had tried to shoot Parker. All good reasons for a bad guy to go inside. "It all evens out in the end," the guard had said.

If Luke took the blame for Grace's death, Paula would be safe. Parker wanted Paula to be safe. The odds were that Paula's gun would never be found. The odds were that Meredith would blame Luke for everything now that she had him neatly framed. Could he let his brother die for a crime he hadn't committed? Could he allow Meredith to go free?

Parker remembered trying as a kid to bait his fishing hook with a red wiggler worm. Meredith was just as difficult to impale. He had the means to send Meredith back to prison instead of to a psycho ward. He had the means to save an estranged brother. All he had to do was admit that he had lied to the police.

At the next exit, he crossed over the interstate and reversed his course back to the I-85 interchange. With one eye on the road and one eye on his phone, he typed a one-handed text to Jordyn: Change of plans.

Have to divert to Atlanta. Will be down to see Mom in a couple of days.

Jordyn's immediate response wasn't sugar-coated: You're fucking up again.

***

Parker drove to Sabrina's apartment complex and found no trace of her. The strutting little autocrats in the leasing office refused him any information about her apartment's status. He camped in the parking lot, listening to oldies, waiting for her white BMW to appear.

What the hell are you doing, Parker? She's a black woman, in case you haven't noticed, with all the inherent problems that skin color heaps on a person. You don't need the aggravation.

He stayed in the parking lot until midnight, but Sabrina never showed. The situation was clear: she had high standards, and he didn't measure up. It was also clear that when she told Terry she was driving home, she didn't mean Atlanta.

At the top of the street that led down the hill to his house, Parker pulled his rental car to the curb, watched, and waited. Darkness fell over the street like a shade drawn slowly down on an enormous window. He could see his house at the very end of the street, the one with no lights in the windows. No cop cars squatted in his driveway, and no suspicious cars ringed his cul-de-sac. Without headlights, he coasted down the road and into his driveway. Feeling foolish again, he scrambled out of the car and punched the passcode into the keypad beside the garage door. The door rose noisily on its tracks as he dove back into the car. He slipped into the garage and bent to watch the street as the door slowly descended to the pavement.

Inside, he stood in the dark in the mudroom and listened to the creaking sounds of an unoccupied home. His footfalls echoed on the hardwood floors in the hollow spaces as he moved from dining room to foyer to family room. In the kitchen, he flipped on the spotlights above the deck, scaring a small doe that had been grazing on his lawn. Most of his enemies were indisposed—Meredith and Luke were in jails; Dennie was dead; Jack and Ilya were in hospitals—but Alexi or Rawlings could attack at any moment. He hoped it wouldn't be tonight. Tomorrow he'd turn himself in.

He grabbed a brandy snifter glass from the cupboard and poured a double shot of Graham's Six Grapes Reserve Porto. Thinking of the World War II soldier's admonition not to be third man on a match because it gave snipers time to zero in on their target, Parker lit his Macanudo cigar in the dark kitchen. Then he turned the spotlights off, turned the dim marina lights on, and moved onto the back deck, carrying the bottle of port with him.

The air smelled green. He sat in a deck chair, sipping and puffing, enjoying the song of the katydids, half expecting someone to pop out of the thicket to shoot him or arrest him.

He imagined himself a World War II submariner under attack by an enemy destroyer, cowering in the dark confines of a tin tube six hundred feet beneath the surface, with no control over his own survival, cringing at every depth charge explosion, fearing the one that would cause the watertight walls of his casket to implode, crushing him under thousands of tons of seawater.

Immersed in the dilemma of odds and probabilities, like a gambler at the baccarat table, he poured another glass of port and ignored the nagging thought that he had been drinking too heavily during this ordeal.

He stopped at a Dunkin' Donuts store before checking in with Rawlings as he had promised. Carrying the pink and orange box, he walked inside the police station.

The female cop, Rawlings's partner, gave him a big smile. cooperating witnesses, citizens who supply information, are the lifeblood of any police department. She led Parker into a noisy bullpen and pointed to the detective, sitting in a cubicle against the far wall.

"There's your man, Mr. Parker."

Rawlings saw him coming and waved Parker toward an enclosed office. Parker entered the vacant room and waited for Rawlings. The detective closed the door and took a seat in a cheap swivel chair behind a government-gray metal desk.

Parker set the donut box in front of Rawlings. "For my favorite cop."

Rawlings failed to suppress a chuckle. "Always a wise-ass."

Rawlings waved Parker into a visitor's chair, but Parker remained standing, nervous. Impulsively, he discarded the speeches he had practiced and got straight to the point. "Luke Braun did not murder Grace Walker."

"That's not news, Mr. Parker. The woman drowned, so the charge will be voluntary manslaughter."

Parker was tempted to leave the office; Luke wouldn't get a lethal injection for voluntary manslaughter, but he'd spend twenty years in prison for a crime he didn't commit, and Meredith would get away with it. "Braun didn't shoot Grace. Her sister, Meredith, shot her."

"Is that the best your fancy lawyer could come up with? You're paying him too much."

"It's the only way it could have happened, Detective."

Rawlings leaned back in the swivel chair, gazed at the ceiling for a moment. A heavy sigh expanded his chest, and a self-satisfied smile formed on his lips as he savored the moment.

"I figured you'd come in, try to save your brother's ass—"

Parker made a small sound, like a door hinge squeaking, and Rawlings held up a hand for silence. "Wasn't hard to figure out that you're related, Mr. Parker. Here's the deal: we found the guy who sold him the gun, a gangbanger in Doraville. Braun says Meredith threw the gun into the river. 'Course that's a lie since it turned up in his apartment. His prints are on the empty casings at the scene."

"If Braun fired the .25 caliber, who fired the .45?"

"The dead sister."

"A meek accountant fired a big ass .45 at someone in the dark? Who was she shooting at?"

"Braun."

"You have a motive for that?"

"Don't need one. All criminals are stupid."

"You think they're all stupid because you only catch the stupid ones," Parker said.

Rawlings growled, but Parker didn't give him time to vent his rage. "Meredith fired the little gun, and Braun used the big gun, which he had gotten from the dead sister. Meredith shot her sister, but Luke didn't hit anyone."

Unlike Cole, who blinked when shocked, Rawlings became stolid, immobile. "That's your theory: one sister offed the other sister?"

"They were all in on a plot to extort money from me, but it fell apart. Meredith and Braun had a gunfight in that dark and scary thicket, and Grace got in the way."

"My ass." Rawlings sneered at Parker. "I have evidence; all you have is a fairy tale."

Poor Luke, Parker thought, walking a tightrope between denying he fired the .25 and admitting he fired another gun. He didn't know there was proof that Meredith had the .25 caliber pistol. For a moment, Parker wished he had Ron's picture of the .25 caliber pistol taped to the van's firewall. But then he'd have had to explain why he and Ron hadn't reported the evidence to the police and how they had allowed the pistol to end up in Luke's apartment. He would have to cover one lie with another lie.

Parker pulled Paula's phone from his pocket and cued up the pictures of Meredith in his backyard with Luke's pistol. "Swipe left."

Rawlings looked at them, swiped back and looked again, touching the screen and spreading his fingers to get a closeup of the gun. "You've been hiding this from us?" Rawlings rose from his chair, leaned two hands on the desk. "I'll charge you with concealing and tampering with evidence, Parker."

"That's my wife's phone. She took the pictures the night of the incident, as you can see from the date and time stamps, but she was drunk and passed out and never mentioned it. I sent her to rehab in Florida, where they took her phone away from her. I didn't know what she had till I claimed her phone when I visited."

Pointing a meaty finger at Parker's chest, Rawlings yelled, "You lied to us, said Meredith didn't have a gun in your backyard."

"I said I didn't see one," Parker yelled back, "but the camera doesn't lie. With these pictures, any moronic defense attorney can beat a manslaughter rap."

Rawlings slammed a fist into the desk, denting the thin metal and causing the box of donuts to bounce. "Dammit! You think I'm going to just open the door, let him walk away? Waste all the time we put in?" He leaned his thick mass on his desk. "Braun gave an unregistered gun to a known felon. That's a gun violation. If I believe your fairy tale, he unlawfully discharged the .45." He glared at Parker. "That's assault with a deadly weapon. He's still going to prison."

"Sounds fair to me," Parker said.

Rawlings snatched Paula's phone from Parker's hands. "I'll keep this, Mr. Parker, gives me the leverage to force Ms. Walker to testify against you and your wife. She swears your wife shot at her in your backyard and then you shot her sister. Braun said the same thing." He raised his eyebrows, a question.

Parker placed his hands on the back of a visitor's chair, leaned on it to steady himself. His mouth hung open at the thought that his brother would frame him. "One's a liar trying to wriggle off the hook, and the other is batshit crazy. Paula was holding a camera, not a gun and I never set foot in those woods."

Parker pulled the revised settlement agreement from his pocket and offered it to Rawlings. "Meredith signed this statement, witnessed by her son, that she never saw Paula with a gun, never saw either of us in the thicket."

Rawlings backed away from the proffered papers. "She showed that thing to Monahan in Florida. She was coerced, just wanted her money. It'll never stand up in court." He looked at Parker with a challenging expression on his normally poker face. "You think you're slick, but you're not. We took a bullet out of Grace Walker's leg too."

Parker gave Rawlings a congratulatory smile. "Oh, good for you," he said, as though he hadn't known about the bullet. "Meredith shot her sister twice with the gun she got from Braun."

"Where did you get that idea?" Rawlings leaned back in his chair. "The bullet in the dead sister's leg came from a 9mm gun, not the gun in your pictures." Rawlings folded his arms across his chest, waited for Parker's reaction.

Parker did sit down, and everything went dark. The world came back bit by bit, first the light, then the cool draft from the air conditioning, then the sound of Rawlings's voice. The cops had lied to Connor about the bullet they'd taken out of Grace's leg.

"You shot the dead sister in the leg," the detective said. "Then your wife delivered the coup de grace. The dead sister was balanced on one leg, didn't take much to tip her over. That's the story that fits the evidence, Mr. Parker."

"What evidence? You're missing two guns."

"No, Mr. Parker, we have everything we need: your wife's gun will turn up; Monahan has Meredith; we have your brother, we have the gun you used, and we know who gave it to you. Ballistics is testing it as we speak, and the results could come at any moment." Rawlings glanced at the open blinds on the window to the bullpen. Parker followed his gaze. A burly young cop in uniform, blond and balding, had his hands on his hips as he looked through the glass at Parker in the office.

A cold sweat formed at Parker's temples. "Meredith and Luke are framing me, Detective. Maybe Grace did fire the .45 because Luke must have had the 9mm gun that shot Grace."

"No, Mr. Parker, you're the only one coulda had this gun." Rawlings curled his fingers, signaling the uniformed cop to enter. "Show Mr. Parker to the guest suite," he said to the uniform.

"Huh?"

"Put him in an interrogation room." Rawlings used two fingers to pick a donut out of the box—chocolate icing with sprinkles. "And bring me a glass of milk."

***

Parker sat in the chair typically used by the interrogator, the chair facing the door. He did not pace. He did not look into the camera staring at him from the corner of the room. He did not hang his head in his hands in despair. He did not talk to himself. That behavior, his prison mates had told him, leads the simple-minded cops to believe the person in custody is guilty. In Parker's experience, cops weren't motivated by high-minded morality; they wanted to win the game of cops and robbers. Parker couldn't allow Rawlings to think he had won the game.

What Parker did was stare straight ahead as he formed another mental corkboard. Grace was shot in the back of the leg by a 9mm pistol. Rawlings thought

Parker had access to a 9mm gun. Ballistics was testing a gun against the bullet in Grace's leg. Sabrina's gun was a 9mm pistol, but it wasn't a revolver; it was the kind that expelled a casing after each shot, and it was in an evidence locker in New Orleans. Parker had the feeling you get in a dream when you're under attack, but you can't make your legs work to escape. The solution lay just beyond a mental border, cloaked in a funky purple haze.

After more than an hour, the door opened. It wasn't the blond uniform; it was Rawlings's partner, the female cop, who came to get him. "You can go."

She wasn't smiling. Parker realized that her smile earlier hadn't been a welcoming smile but rather the smile of the victorious. She hadn't had to lift a finger to hunt Parker down for his arrest.

"The bullet didn't match the gun in New Orleans."

Parker cocked his head, waiting for a sign. The female cop backed out the door, out of camera range, looked around to see if anyone was watching, then nodded ever so slightly. "Derrick says it belongs to your girlfriend."

Everybody thinks Sabrina is my girlfriend. "Can I pick up my computer and files now?"

"The tech guys are still working on them. Come back on Monday." She took his arm and lead him to the reception area.

Jack Shaw was restricted to working from home where he would undergo a physical rehab program for leg muscles that had been more severely damaged by Dennie's bullet than he had thought. Carolyn shuttled between the office and Shaw's house with papers to sign, decisions to make. The mood in the office was somber, some employees mourning Dennie's death, the artificial intelligence team rudderless without Alexi. In the bullpen, whispers traveled from cubicle to cubicle, employees anxious about the loss of the Midwestern Assurance account, fearful of a future without IBS as a partner.

The whispers targeted Parker, who had wreaked this havoc in a terrible performance at the meeting with Midwestern Assurance in New Orleans. That was the rumor, so Parker packed his belongings behind the closed door of his office. He advised the Wookiee of his firing and made him an empty promise that things would work out.

He worked his way through the last of his emails and found that an email from Sabrina. His finger moved swiftly to the enter key, then froze in midair as he became petrified, wondering what farewell message she had written. He castigated himself for his lack of courage and pressed the key. The email contained just two lines: "I can't work for a company that outsources American jobs. Attached is a copy of the resignation I sent to Carolyn." No explanation for ditching Parker. No x's and no o's.

So that's the end of it. Time to get on with your life, Parker. He dialed the main switchboard number at the rehab clinic in St. Pete and asked to speak with his wife. The operator asked him to hold, then shunted him to an officious administrator.

"How can I help you, Mr. Parker?"

A tingling sensation shot from the base of his neck, through his shoulders and down both arms. "Is there something wrong? I already told the operator I need to speak to my wife, Paula Parker."

"I'm afraid that isn't possible, Mr. Parker. You're on her No Contact list."

"What? I'm her husband!"

"It's her choice, sir. She said you could leave a message if the house was on fire."

"Yes, the urgent message is that I'll be down to see her on Saturday and she hold off on, uh, everything, until I get there."

"You won't be able to see her, Mr. Parker. You're on her No Contact list, but we'll give her the message."

"This is ridiculous!"

"If you love your wife, let her finish the program in peace, Mr. Parker. We'll let you know if your status changes."

The administrator hung up. Parker couldn't believe the mess he had made of his life. For hours he rocked in his chair staring at the geese on the pond behind the building. No immediate fixes came to mind.

As he packed the last of his office belongings into boxes, his cell phone rang.

"All kinds of good news for you, buddy," Noah, the psychiatrist, said.

"I could use some good news."

"Ron found Meredith in a cheap motel on 34th Street South, where the city stashes its material witnesses and delivered her to my hospital."

Ron had redeemed himself. Son of a gun. "And Ron … what? Abducted her?"

"This is funny. Her kid lured her outside. She had complained about her accommodations, so the kid told her that the County boys were moving her to a better room." Noah chuckled. "Now, she has one."

Cole redeemed himself, too? "Monahan will just walk over there and arrest her again."

"I don't think so. Paula's gun was used in the commission of a robbery by an undocumented immigrant who had found the pistol while working in your mother-in-law's pecan grove. It had been fired, and the perp's prints were all over it. You told the truth about where the gun was, and that impressed Monahan. It meant that he had no reason to chase Paula, and it meant that Meredith's statement contained lies. He seems to have decided that Rawlings' case has no merit and Meredith should be kept in Florida as a win for local cops."

Monahan redeemed himself, too? "So Meredith is committed?"

"Not exactly. We can hold her for seventy-two hours to reach a diagnosis."

"So, Rawlings could still get her out?"

"Possible, if the Atlanta cops charge her with a capital crime before she's committed, but I'd bet against it. Her kid brought us her journal. That thing is … grisly, ghastly, and obscene are the words that come to mind. The older entries, back when your company flopped, were ugly, but the newer entries are downright terrifying. She was plotting violent revenge against everyone in her life— you, her sister, her boyfriend, your brother, judges, lawyers. Had the plans all mapped out to kill everyone who was conspiring against her. She could be paranoid schizophrenic."

"I'm glad Cole had the courage to turn the journal in."

"Yeah, he said you convinced him she needed professional help and her journal is confirmation for my colleagues and me, but the complaints you filed with the Atlanta police convinced Judge Williamson to issue the emergency detention order. She killed your cat? Jesus! Making threats is one thing but following through with menacing acts got her a padded room and a comfy bunk."

Meredith had denied the terror spree, but Ron would call her detention karma. "Hurry, Noah. Hurry."

If asked, Ron and Cole and Noah would say they had acted to seek justice, but justice is based on what's legal and illegal. Right and wrong are different concepts. Meredith in a straitjacket felt right.

At home, he reclaimed his seat on the deck, smoking a cigar and sipping port, listening to the katydids until dawn, replaying the last two months, identifying all the things he could have done differently. Someone at the office had told Rawlings about his relationship with Sabrina. That had to have been Carolyn. Luke's charges would be reduced to gun violations. That served Luke right for helping Meredith extort him. Rawlings would find Meredith in the psychiatric hospital. He didn't want to be within range of Rawlings's billy club when that happened. Meredith and Luke swore Paula had shot Grace in the shoulder and that Parker had shot Grace in the leg, but the bullet didn't match Sabrina's gun. Dennie had had the Midwestern Assurance deal rigged perfectly, and yet she'd wanted him dead. His marriage was over. And he had lost Sabrina. He had made a total mess of his life and he still had no logical explanation for it.

On Saturday, Jordyn met Parker for lunch at Zapata's in Norcross after she drove his car home from St. Pete. Her greeting was less than warm. "You look like shit."

"Thanks. Been a rough couple of weeks."

"For you? How about for Mom? Rehab is no picnic."

"Is she done with it already?"

"Has a week to go but doesn't need me anymore."

"Doesn't need me either." Parker could guess why Paula no longer needed Jordyn. "Is she still with that guy?"

Jordyn squirmed in her chair, then sighed. "Harley? Yeah, they're like peanut butter and jelly. You shouldn't have let that happen."

"Wasn't my choice."

Jordyn said, her face flushed with sudden anger. "Of course, it was your choice. You dragged her up here, you never believed she didn't shoot anyone, you let her walk away. And, when you had one last chance to save your marriage, you chose to save your brother instead."

Life is nothing but fucking choices. Parker had rehearsed a line for this moment, an admission of total failure. "Now she can be with a man who is better for her."

"What? You want to play Rick in Casablanca?" She folded her arms and leaned back in her chair. "Your buddy Vince helped her file for the divorce."

"I know. I asked him to help her and I got the papers yesterday. The settlement is payback for firing him when I got in trouble the first time."

"You think you're getting screwed?"

"She gets the full proceeds of the house sale because she doesn't want to wait by the mailbox every month for an alimony check from someone she doesn't trust. Meredith and my lawyer drained our savings, so there's not much cash to split. I have to buy your mother's store back for her, and I'm happy to do that."

"She'll be back to the way she was. Before ..."

"Before I ruined her life."

"Now you're ruined, starting from scratch at your age. You should find a job in Florida, where you belong," Jordyn said.

"I've started looking." He gave her a smile that hid his pessimism about his job prospects.

They ordered food and ate ravenously. Jordyn paid the bill—"You'll need to watch your pennies now." Parker rose to leave, but Jordyn grabbed an arm, held him in place.

"Is Mom safe?"

"As safe as possible. Her gun was found by an illegal immigrant who fired it in the commission of a robbery. No way to tie it to what happened up here. Meredith is in the nut house so her lies can't be used as testimony."

She seemed to relax, gave him a rueful smile. "I was hoping you'd bring your girlfriend. I wanted to apologize for what I said when I first met her."

"She was just a colleague."

"Don't bullshit me, Dad."

"Seriously, we worked together to stop something terrible at work, and when it was done, she took off. I don't know where she is."

She watched his eyes to see if he was telling the truth, then rose for a hug. "I wish she was a girlfriend. I hate to see you alone."

***

On Sunday, Parker visited his brother in the county lockup. The hair on Luke's head was shorn like a sheep after wool harvesting, but his complexion was good, his eyes alive. His white canvas jumpsuit with blue piping fit snugly on a frame that had not withered under the strain of incarceration. Parker was not tempted to pity him.

Luke picked up the black plastic phone handle on his side of the bulletproof Plexiglass divider. "I'm sorry, Parker. Really and truly sorry for what I did to you. She sucked me into her conspiracy."

Parker figured that was literally true. "She's good at that. You look like you're surviving."

"I made a deal to plead guilty in return for a light sentence," Luke said. "No rap sheet, no history of drug abuse or mental defect, so I'll do less than two years for gun violations. I have you to thank for that. Have you seen Susie? Is she okay?"

"Yeah, she'll be released in a couple of months. I'll let her live with me till you get out. Then you guys can decide what your future will be."

Luke looked at Parker with questioning but grateful eyes. "You'd do that?"

Parker nodded.

Luke wiped a tear that had slid down the side of his nose. "Well, thanks. We don't deserve your help." Another convict belatedly inflicted with remorse.

"Actually, I'm here for your help. A couple of easy questions."

Luke waved a hand in the air. "You won't say anything to Susie?"

"It's our little secret, Luke. Let's start at the beginning: Did you paint a message on our door, kill Paula's cat, unscrew the lights in our backyard?"

Luke scrunched up his face like he'd never heard anything so ridiculous. "One time, I drove her to your house, and the cops were all over your place. Scared the shit out of me, but she was so pissed to see that you had put your life back together and lived in a nice house that she jumped out and put a note in your mailbox. She is crazy, man."

Crazy, yes, but he believed Luke—Meredith hadn't done the menacing. "Did you throw

Meredith's cell phone into the bed of a passing pickup truck?"

Luke laughed out loud. "That was her after I bought burner phones. She wanted to throw the cops off our scent."

"Okay, let's talk about the Fourth of July. Did you take two shots at us in our backyard while Meredith was talking to me?"

Luke rose up, as though offended. "I only went as far as a big tree that had fallen in the river."

There was another accomplice. "So you did come into the thicket."

Luke looked over his shoulder at the armed guard who was pretending not to listen to any of the ongoing conversations. He settled into his seat. Softly, he said, "I went in twice. At first, I followed her to watch what was going on. I wanted to drive away, but I knew Meredith would tell Susie what we were, um, doing."

"Did you know Grace was going to be there?"

"No, that wasn't part of the plan. I found her hiding behind the roots of that big tree."

Like good spies, the women had compartmentalized. Once Luke was locked into a role in the plot, he was excluded from rest of the planning. "Grace gave you the .45?"

"Yeah, she didn't know how to use the gun."

"Did you take a shot at Meredith, or did Grace do it?"

Luke chortled. "I don't think my lawyer would want me to answer that one."

That is an answer. Grace may have brought it for Meredith, but then Luke gave Meredith an easier gun to use. Luke took the opportunity to eliminate a threat to his marriage. He could be charged with attempted murder.

"You gave the gun back to Grace."

"Sure." A whisper. "I gave it back, and I ran."

"Did you have another gun of your own?"

"No, I gave my gun to Meredith."

"The little .25 caliber."

Luke nodded. The accomplice had a 9mm gun, a revolver. Parker proceeded slowly and carefully. "Had Grace been shot before you left her?"

Luke pressed his thumb and index finger into his eyes and pinched the bridge of his nose. He looked up with bleary eyes. "I'm embarrassed about this."

He asked a question with his eyes and eyebrows, and Parker nodded at him.

"Just in the shoulder. I didn't think she'd fall in the damn river. I figured she'd come out with Meredith and we'd get her fixed up."

Luke never knew Grace had been shot again, in the leg. He was only part of the boom-bang exchange everyone heard. It had never seemed logical to Parker that the shoulder ding sent Grace to her watery grave. The shot to the leg did that. Even if Paula had shot Grace in the shoulder, she was innocent of murder. "You went back in again."

He nodded. "Meredith was taking too long. I found her hiding behind that same tree that fell into the river."

"Did you see Grace then?"

"No." He shook his head. "She was already, ah, gone, I guess."

Gone between the time Luke abandoned Grace and when Luke returned to find Meredith. "Did you see Paula?"

"Nah, I never saw your wife. Meredith made up the story about Paula shooting Grace. She said it would keep us out of jail." He sniggered. "When I heard she was wearing a straitjacket in a padded cell, I laughed my ass off."

"Did you tell the cops that I shot at Grace?"

"No, I told them Paula shot her. That was what Meredith told me to do."

While Parker had thought he was tricking the cops, Rawlings had been playing him, feeding Connor misinformation intended to trip Parker up. Maybe Meredith had added Parker to the story, or maybe Rawlings had lied about that too.

"So, you never saw me, and you never saw Paula, right?"

"Right."

For Parker, it was as though a kaleidoscopic image of overlapping shards, colors, and angles finally resolved into an intelligible picture. Luke took a shot at Meredith—*boom*—and Meredith shot back, striking her sister in the shoulder—*bang*. Later, she fired back down the straightaway at Paula. Whether Paula took a shot at

Meredith at the start of the straightaway or fired into the mud when she fell was anyone's guess. Luke and Meredith never realized that Paula had fired a parting shot at them as they ran, leaving another brass casing for Jordyn to find near the fallen tree.

"So why didn't Meredith run?" Parker said.

Luke leaned back in his chair, examined the fluorescent lights in the ceiling. He sighed and then shifted his gaze back to Parker. "I've thought about that a lot. I think she was going to ambush Paula."

Afraid of what Paula may have seen. "Then she threw your gun in the river because she shot Grace with it."

Luke held his hands defensively in front of his chest. "I threw the damned gun in the river because it could be traced back to me. How it ended up in my apartment, I'll never know." He shook his head in wonderment.

Parker knew how the gun ended up in Luke's apartment. The gun may have hit a branch and landed short of the river or it was in the shallow water just off the bank. Luke didn't see where his gun toss landed, but Meredith did and later she directed her son, Cole, to retrieve the weapon. Parker tried to remember when the dam was closed and the river water low enough for Cole to find the gun but he couldn't be sure if it was the morning the cops searched the thicket or the evening he and Ron had dinner at J. Alexander's. Parker was sure that his choice to leave the gun in the van had doomed his half-brother.

Luke continued. "Then I dragged her out of there. She was hopping on one foot because she had lost a sandal, so I threw her other one in the river too."

"If it came to it, would you recant your statement, tell the cops you never saw me or Paula?"

Luke squeezed his head between his hands. "Don't make me do that, Parker. I can't add lying to the police to my time here."

Parker was sorry he had asked. Luke would be exposed to an attempted murder charge if he recanted. "Okay, we'll save that in case we need it. Did you see anyone other than Grace and Meredith in the thicket?"

"I never saw Jordyn, if that's what you mean."

"No, I mean someone you didn't recognize. A Russian, broad as any NFL lineman."

"Nope." Luke shook his head.

"Did you ever see another woman talking to Grace or Meredith, a tall brunette?"

Luke shook his head again. "Once Grace showed up, the girls spent a lot of time alone. I was just the getaway driver, you know?"

"So you drove Meredith away from the park. That's why Grace's van never moved."

"I didn't know there was a van. I drove as far as I could, to a hotel by the airport, lots of transients. After we came to your house—on Sunday, I think—she went batshit, and I dumped her crazy ass. Thought with my gun in the river, I'd be okay."

The guard walked up behind Luke and tapped him on the shoulder. *Time's up.*

Luke lifted his butt off the chair to imply he would obey the guard, but he rested on his elbows and leaned close to the glass to say, "I'm really sorry for what I did, Parker. Will you bring Susie to see me?"

Parker hesitated, then said, "Of course, I will."

The guard led Luke away, but Parker made no effort to leave. A few visitors remained, but none were waiting for his stall.

He concentrated on the scene in St. Louis Cemetery No. 2, tried to picture Dennie's gun, remembered the dark evil eye of the muzzle aimed at him. It must have been a revolver. Parker was sure that if the bullet in Jack's leg was compared to the bullet in Grace's leg, they would match.

Parker shuffled the pins and yarn around on his mental corkboard of evidence to match the latest evidence. Dennie owned a Mercedes S-class sedan with blacked-out windows. Ilya was the terrorist, chauffeured around by Dennie, trying to scare Parker into resigning and moving.

Dennie was in Shaw's office when Meredith called looking for Parker and Dennie overheard the conversation. Dennie connected with Meredith to discuss their mutual enemy. Grace arrived and joined the cabal that hatched the plot. Meredith snuck into Parker's backyard with a settlement agreement and a gun on the Fourth of July, and Dennie stationed Ilya at the ambush point in case Meredith didn't get the job done. Meredith was the patsy, a pawn in Dennie's hands.

Ironically, Paula fouled the plot by shooting first at Meredith, and then she chased Ilya from the ambush point by shooting at him. When his attempt to assassinate Parker failed, Ilya hustled to Grace's hiding spot, and between the time Luke had taken a shot at Meredith and when he returned to drag Meredith out of the thicket, Ilya shot the weak link that could have gotten them caught. The .45 was only fired once, so the last two booms Parker had heard that night came from a gun that left no casings behind—Dennie's revolver in Ilya's hands. Ilya's second boom was an attempt to murder Meredith as well. Ilya escaped, perhaps in Dennie's Mercedes, leaving Meredith to hide behind the tree roots, waiting for an opportunity to eliminate Paula.

Meredith knew she had been set up by Dennie and feared Ilya, so she'd framed her boyfriend and blackmailed Parker for the money to get the hell out of town. When she'd only gotten some of the money she demanded from Parker, she ran back into Wade Gilbert's arms. After her apprehension in Florida, she had no choice but to lie about Paula and Parker.

Parker felt confident he had that much of the story right. The loose string on the complex ball of yarn was that when Kumar insisted that Parker make the presentation to Midwestern Assurance, Dennie had made a second attempt on Parker's life in New Orleans. The question was: why?

Parker closed his eyes and absorbed a hollow feeling of wrong-headed miscalculation. Paula hadn't needed his protection from the Atlanta cops, and Meredith hadn't plotted to kill him on the Fourth of July. Had he known these facts, would he have left Paula with Harley, or would he have fought to save his marriage? Would he have had Meredith committed to a mental institution? All she wanted was the money the courts said he owed her. Yes, he decided, Meredith deserved to be evaluated. It was the same argument he had made with Ron: Either she needed long term help or she didn't. Noah would decide.

Back at the house, he wrote Sabrina another email, just to bring her up to date: Luke's charges have been reduced to gun violations; Meredith is in the psychiatric hospital; Paula didn't shoot anyone. She's filed for a divorce and I've agreed. Everything is fixed except us.

He stared at his computer for ten minutes, but nothing happened. Unlike postal mail, his email system did not return messages like "Not at this address," so he couldn't be sure if she was ignoring his mail or if his mail was lost in the ether because she had deleted her account. *She doesn't want you, Parker. Doesn't miss you, is glad to be rid of you.*

On Monday morning, Parker and Shaw sat facing a fireplace in Shaw's living room, reclining in sumptuous cordovan leather wing-backed chairs that flanked a rolling service cart on which stood two crystal decanters of rich brown liquor. Terry sprawled on the couch, at ease, facing a faded portrait of a fearsome man scowling at them from above the mantle. A tarnished bronze nameplate across the bottom read, "Buford J. Shaw." Jack Shaw had invited Parker to breakfast at his home in the toney neighborhood of John's Creek, and Parker had accepted to clear the air with his father and see if he could get a job. He considered it a job interview.

Parker declined food, his stomach too unsettled by the prospect of this conversation to eat. He tried orange juice and found the acid too harsh to enjoy.

Shaw was clear-eyed but fidgety, perhaps as nervous as Parker. "You didn't have the power to fire Alexi. Now Kumar has given him safe harbor and I can't convince him to come back. He's brilliant, you know, and without him, my AI programs will founder."

Parker felt like a child hauled on the carpet by an angry parent. "Nonsense, his staff is loaded with brilliant scientists to carry on."

Shaw huffed. "After your interference, Kumar terminated our partnership, and I'm obligated to buy back his stock at a premium."

"You're better off without a partner," Parker said. "You'll sell the AI apps and if you hire me and Steve Goldblum, we'll build new analytics apps for you. That's what will make your company competitive."

"You're never again going to walk through the doors of my company, Parker."

"You'd rather employ a fraud like Alexi than your own son?"

"I'm not your damned father, Parker. Get that out of your head."

"So why did you ask me here?"

"I wanted you to see the damage you've done. After all your misguided machinations you've lost your job and killed my company. I'm negotiating with American Systems Corporation, my hated rival, to buy my stock, at a discount, of course, just so I can retire. Those jobs you thought you were saving will go offshore despite your wrong-headed efforts."

"All you care about is your retirement. Where's your loyalty to your employees? You're dooming them to work for a huge, coldhearted company for purely selfish reasons."

"I'm taking care of my employees, Parker. I own two-thirds of the stock, which I will sell, but one-third of the stock is in a trust and that stock will be distributed to the employees. They can take cash for it from ASC or convert it to ASC stock. I'm taking care of Terry, too. He'll succeed me as CEO."

Terry had taken Parker's advice and blamed Parker for killing the Midwestern Assurance deal. Then Terry played Pontius Pilate and washed his hands of the affair so he could be promoted. Parker turned to Terry, and with a swollen tongue between dry lips, he said, "Congratulations, I guess. You've given those fifteen hundred jobs in Iowa to ASC. Does your promotion to CEO make that okay?"

"ASC is taking me on a fishing trip to Montana, my form of wining and dining, and we'll finalize the numbers," Jack said.

"The almighty dollars," Parker said.

"Jack will negotiate the number of jobs and where they'll go," Terry said. "A lot of the jobs will go to Poland and Ireland, but we can save some of them."

The jobs will go to white foreigners as Sabrina predicted. "Once upon a time, you chided me for not caring about jobs in Iowa. Did you only care because the jobs would go to brown people in India? You're a hypocrite like everyone else, Terry. Shame on you."

Parker rose, knocking over his glass of orange juice, spreading the sticky mess on the serving table. To Shaw, he said, "Fuck it. I wouldn't want you as a father anyway."

"Get out of my house." Shaw struggled to his feet, leaned on his cane, and limped out of the room.

As Parker left Shaw's house, he wondered if Shaw was vengeful enough to recant his statement to the NOLA cops and implicate Parker in Dennie's death. No, Parker thought, no matter how angry Shaw was, he wouldn't do that to his son.

Parker drove downtown to pick up his personal files from the police station. Out of spite he refused to accept his work computer, told the clerk that someone from the company would claim it. Maybe they would and maybe they wouldn't. The lethargic property clerk made him sign several forms even though Parker couldn't confirm he was getting everything back. Parker made two trips to carry his files to his car.

He was closing the trunk when he heard his name called from behind: *Rawlings,* and he didn't sound happy to see him.

"You think this is over?" the detective shouted. "It's not. Not by a long shot. It's just going to take more time to get her ass out of that hospital so she can testify. Under Florida law, a mental patient can be jerked away from the shrinks if they're charged with a crime. Did you know that?"

Was Noah wrong about Rawlings's power to spring Meredith? "You think it's a good idea to put mental patients on trial?"

Rawlings grunted. "We convict sickos all day every day. You're just afraid she'll testify against you and your wife." Rawlings grabbed Parker's arm and shook him. "Your brother, Braun, will corroborate her testimony."

Had Luke lied about what he said in his statement? Parker considered telling Rawlings what he knew about the death of Grace Walker and the reason she died. A good citizen would do that. But recounting that long, convoluted story would mean betraying a woman who had twice saved his life and exposing his wayward brother. The cops and the justice system had gotten it wrong again, but this time no innocent people would be hurt. *Ilya is in Russia; Dennie and Grace are six feet under, and the bullet that came out of Shaw's leg, the bullet that would reveal which pistol shot Grace, is buried in an NOPD evidence locker.* He couldn't let Rawlings win his little game of cops and robbers. This case would remain an unsolved blot on the cop's record, like a suppurating sore. Unless he had to tell the story at trial, of course.

Parker called the detective's bluff. "Luke won't corroborate Meredith's lies, Derrick. You can't prove what caused Grace's shoulder wound, can't identify the accomplice who shot her in the leg, sending her into the river to drown. You lied to me over and over, and my gullible lawyer dutifully passed all your lies to me, but you couldn't frame me, or Paula, because we're innocent. Your case against us is as cold as a gravedigger's ass."

"Watch your back, asshole," Rawlings muttered as he turned to walk into the building. "I'll be there."

"Cold as a witch's titty, Derrick," Parker gleefully yelled at him.

***

Parker packed up what remained of Paula's personal possessions and had them shipped to her mother's home. He hired a professional cleaning team to scrub, mop, dust, shampoo carpets, and wax floors. He cut the lawn and trimmed bushes. He did some touch up painting. Then he found a realtor he trusted and put Paula's dream home up for sale.

He went to work on his resume and filed it with three online job placement services. He left the house only to allow his realtor to show it to prospective buyers. In the evenings, he smoked cigars and drank port on his back deck. No cops bothered him.

No lawyers bothered him either, until one humid, sweltering summer afternoon, when Tim Morrison called him. "I just got a call from Meredith's Georgia lawyer. They're still pursuing a resolution to the civil case in Florida."

"She can do that from the nuthouse?"

"It's not her; it's her son, Cole Walker, acting with her power of attorney. A lawyer named Vince Romeli had Meredith sign it in case she was committed. Good advice."

Betrayal knows no boundaries. "Good thing we have the one she signed before she went to Florida, the one for seventy-five thousand dollars. She cashed the down payment check, so there will be bank records to confirm her agreement to the deal."

"That's not going to work for three reasons, Parker. Number one: That document makes no mention of a down payment so the check she cashed isn't connected to the deal you thought you made. Number two: The kid says they signed it under duress—"

"That's ridiculous. She tried to shoot me!"

"Number three: If she's committed, the court won't honor the contract."

"Son of a bitch! Her little weasel is sticking it to me."

"Revenge for sending his mother away."

"No, the kid sent her away by giving the shrinks her journal. I thought he did that because it was the right thing to do. He did it for revenge on his mama, got rid of her and got his hands on the money. He is his mother's son."

"Well, the kid and his lawyer have you backed into a corner. You owe the kid one hundred forty thousand dollars."

Parker retreated to his back deck, sweating with a glass of port in one hand and a cigar in the other. The accounting was straightforward: Meredith had gotten a chunk of his savings; Tim and Connor had charged him huge fees; he had paid the rehab facility for Paula's treatment; he had bought Paula's store back for her; he had agreed that Paula could have the proceeds from the sale of the house. He had been fired from IBS, so there was no severance check in the mail. And now, he owed Cole the money Meredith had extorted from him. There was a good chance he'd end up in that cardboard box under a bridge that Paula had feared.

The next day, Noah called with an update on Meredith's examination. "Our panel of three psychiatrists has evaluated her mental health and prescribed a one hundred eighty-day commitment. She has to prove now that she isn't insane, or she'll be here forever."

Noah's news should have brightened Parker's day. Rawlings now had little chance of reinstating any case against him or Paula. However, Parker's conscience gnawed at him like a squirrel burrowing into an attic before winter. *Meredith didn't do it*, his conscience kept saying. *Meredith was the patsy*.

"Remember when you said our police reports sealed the deal? Well, I know who terrorized us and it wasn't her. You didn't have cause to examine her." There, he said it and he felt better for it. He felt as though he was holding Meredith's hands as she dangled over a cliff.

"Too late, buddy. She's already stolen drugs off a nurse's cart, probably to commit suicide, and she attacked a doctor she thought was you come to kill her. She has trouble distinguishing reality from the addled fantasies in her brain. Does that sound sane to you?"

Meredith slipped out of his grasp. "Shit, Noah, all she wanted was the money I owed her. This shouldn't have happened."

"Your mistake was fortuitous—she's seriously ill. You don't have to feel guilty about it."

Then why don't I feel better?

***

Four days later, Carolyn called with tragic news: Jack Shaw was dead.

"My condolences, Carolyn. I know how much he meant to you."

"You knew about me?"

"I knew you were his bridge partner, thought you might be more."

With a smile in her voice, she said. "Yes, I'm in the picture."

"Hunh?"

"Sitting beside your mother, another intern. Jack thought you might have recognized me."

"No. I was too focused on my mother."

"I had a terrible crush on him, back then, but he married Donna Jane. After she passed—ovarian cancer—we became companions."

"I see. How did it happen? Jack's death, I mean."

"Such a gruesome way for Jack to pass." Carolyn stifled a sob. "He was on that trip with ASC in Montana when it happened. His hurt leg, the one that got shot, gave out on him, and he fell in the river. His waders filled up with water, weighted him down, and the current swept him away." She sniffled.

Parker was stunned. Within a week of handing the reins of his company to Terry Horan, Jack Shaw drowned while on a celebratory trout fishing trip. *The wound he suffered while protecting me caused his demise.* Imagining Jack's last moments, Parker had the queasy feeling you get when swallowing raw eggs.

"Let me know about the funeral arrangements and I'll plan to attend."

"Of course, but first I need you to come into the office and meet with the lawyer."

"The lawyer?"

"The executor of the will." Some excitement enlivened her voice. "He'd like to get it out of the way as soon as possible."

A will! A secret, Buford Shaw's assistant, Irene, had said. Jack *had* lied. The will was the final proof that Jack Shaw was his father.

***

The following morning they met in Jack's office, sitting on the facing couches beneath the picture of Jack, Carolyn and Parker's mother, Alice, at Old Man Shaw's insurance agency. The executor, a pasty-faced, primly dressed man in his thirties, pushed a pile of documents across the bare table. The executor tapped the pile. "Read the top one first."

Curious and excited, Parker read a legal document as Carolyn looked on with a benevolent smile on her face. The document described a trust in the name of Buford John Shaw—Old Man Shaw—holding one-third of the stock in Shaw Technology. The CEO of Shaw Technology was the managing trustee and held voting rights for the stock. For as long as the trust had been in place, the CEO had been one "Jackson" Shaw. The document stipulated that the proceeds from the Trust were to be transferred to "… the son of Alice Parker upon his legal identification. In the event that no such identification is made before the death of Jackson Shaw, the trust shall accrue to Jackson Shaw's children, if any. In the absence of direct descendants, the proceeds of the trust shall be distributed to the employees of Shaw Technology." At the bottom of the last page, beside Buford J. Shaw's signature, was the notary seal of Irene Richardson, Old Man Shaw's private secretary, the purple-haired lady at Brookhaven.

Thoughts swirled through Parker's mind like flotsam on a fast-running current. He had assumed Jack Shaw's formal name was John and that his mother had named him for his father, but Jackson Shaw wasn't a "John." Jack had wanted to bypass Parker and bequeath the trust stock to his employees.

Parker looked up at Carolyn. "This is the payoff for being Jack's bastard?"

Carolyn frowned like a teacher whose student had completely misunderstood a lesson. "No, Parker, you aren't Jack's son."

"If I'm not Jack's son," Parker shook his head to unscramble his thoughts, "why am I the primary beneficiary of the trust?"

"Come on, Parker, it's not that hard to figure out."

He raised his head slowly, like the big guns on a battleship seeking the correct elevation for firing at a distant target. It took a couple of minutes to figure it out. "Old Man Shaw was my father?"

"Yes."

He felt as though he had fallen through a trap door, and the beginning of his life story was flashing past him as he fell. His hands on the solid table stopped his freefall. "That's disgusting. He was twice my mother's age."

She placed a hand on his shoulder. "He was the love of your mother's life. She kept you because she loved him. He called himself John—he hated the name Buford—and she named you after him."

Parker slumped in his chair. Had Jack Shaw been his father, something he had anticipated if not hoped for, there would have been a person he knew to blame for the circumstances of his birth, a person to point to and say, "That's my dad, whether I like it or not." Old Man Shaw was just a name on a business sign. Parker had been robbed of a boy's greatest ambition: to grow up to be like Dad. Worse, Buford John Shaw had cheated on his wife to father a child and had then bribed the mother to keep it quiet.

The executor grew impatient and brought Parker's shocked ruminations to a halt. "I'll need to see your driver's license."

Parker fought an urge to sweep the papers onto the floor, to reject the bribe, and obliterate his past. He held up two hands for a moment of silence as he thought through the ramifications of his inheritance. Old Man Shaw couldn't have anticipated that Jack would sell the company. He just wanted his two sons to be co-owners of Shaw Technology.

"Did Jack consummate the deal with ASC?" he asked Carolyn.

"No, they hadn't dotted all the Is and crossed all the Ts, hadn't signed the deal. Jack was still negotiating the terms and the stock price. When it happened."

"So who inherited Jack's stock?"

"I did," she said. Carolyn, now a dowager, appeared to be pretty pleased by the windfall. "To be accurate, I inherited sixteen and two-thirds percent of the stock and one-half of the Shaw stock will be distributed to his employees. So, you and I together now own half of the company and the employees own the other half."

Parker sat back, digested the shocking revelations. "Jack didn't want me to inherit the trust, so who identified me?"

Carolyn shrugged. "I did."

"I wouldn't have guessed you'd do that for me."

"Oh, I didn't do it for you. I liked John and I liked your mother. After Jack passed, I decided it was only fair that John's wishes were carried out."

That triggered another troubling thought for Parker. "I could have inherited at any time during my life, but my mother never told me. She didn't want me to inherit either."

"Alice didn't know about the trust. John couldn't damage his reputation with a divorce, so he offered your mother the money to leave and have the baby at an unwed mothers' home. She refused to take John's money, and kept the baby, you, so he did it this way. Then she hid you, to protect John, and subsequently you were adopted by Mr. Braun and your name changed."

"Who knew about this? How did you know all these facts?"

"John's secretary, Irene, whispered it to me years ago. Until you turned up at the office, there was no conflict. I respected both your mother's wishes and Jack's. Then it became a problem and I was conflicted."

"Until Jack died."

"Yes."

Parker decided he didn't have to think of the inheritance as a bribe; he could think of it as power, the power to reshape Shaw Technology and save the company. Parker pulled his license from his wallet, and the executor compared it to his birth certificate and to the court order that changed his surname from Braun to Parker.

"Where did that come from?" Parker said, indicating the court order.

The executor canted his head at Carolyn. "I acquired a copy for Jack when he investigated you," she said.

The executor handed the license back to Parker and offered an ornate pen. "We just need a few more signatures, Mr. Parker." He indicated the places where Parker had to sign the document. Then he handed him a letter-sized manila envelope. "The stock certificates."

The executor slipped the signed documents into his messenger case. "I'm sorry for your loss, Mr. Parker." He shook Parker's hand and left.

"Big crowd." With a flick of her wrist, Jordyn indicated the long line of cars disgorging mourners who made their way slowly and respectfully toward the gravesite.

"His employees adored him," Parker said. Parker didn't adore the man, but paying his last respects was the right thing to do. His mother would have wanted him to attend the funeral.

They climbed a gentle slope that flattened out beneath a huge oak tree where a wrought iron fence encircled the Shaw family plots: Buford John Shaw and his wife Claire Marie on the left, an unused plot, then a freshly dug grave next to Jack's wife, Donna Jane, and finally a recently covered plot that had no headstone. Over one hundred people lined the fence, respectfully silent.

Carolyn, dry-eyed and stoic behind a black veil, separated from the crowd, came to Parker's side, and slipped her arm through his. "You should be with me."

Parker understood what she meant. "Everyone will know," he said.

"Good, good," Carolyn said.

The mourners parted courteously to allow Parker and Jordyn to move to the front rank with Carolyn, next to the gravesite over which a polished mahogany coffin was suspended. Many of the mourners consoled Parker and Carolyn with timeworn offerings of sympathy: "Jack died doing what he loved;" and "He lived a long, fruitful life;" and "He's in a better place." If he heard those tired clichés one more time, Parker thought he'd either throw up or punch out someone's lights.

An Episcopalian minister waited for Carolyn to take a seat on a folding chair. At her signal, the preacher began to read from scripture. The fall weather in Columbia was perfect for an outdoor service—a cloudless azure sky, mild temperature, low humidity. The mourners were comfortable in their funeral attire, standing and listening to Terry Horan's lengthy eulogy. Then Carolyn placed a spray of flowers on the coffin and kissed the wooden cover.

"Do you want to say good-bye?" she said to Parker.

Good-bye wasn't what Parker had in mind. *The son-of-a-bitch tried to deny me my inheritance all the way to his grave!* He cleared his throat and came up with a few hollow words about Jack's integrity and spotless reputation for fair dealing. He added, in case anyone was unsure, that Jack had had nothing to do with Dennie's fraud, but he wondered just how complicit Jack had been.

Had he only wanted his employees to inherit the trust, or had he been a part of the scheme to maximize his retirement payout? The minister said a final prayer, and the crowd dispersed.

They turned to walk with the other mourners. Jordyn took Parker's arm and shepherded her father toward a bench under the enormous oak tree. Carolyn sat beside Parker and took his hand and squeezed it. Jordyn stood in the shade where she could hear the conversation.

Carolyn looked at Parker like the woman at a luncheon who has the juiciest bit of gossip to share. "Have you figured out who's buried in that fresh grave?"

Parker shook his head. "I have no idea. Jack had no children."

"Well, Parker, Jack did have one child—Denise Davison."

"Dennie was his daughter?" Parker was speechless as he digested the news and recovered from the shock. Jack had taken the blame for killing his daughter? Why would he do that? At the cemetery, Jack had sent Parker to safety, but his motive hadn't been altruistic. "You're a complication," he had said. A police investigation would probe Dennie's motive for trying to murder Parker, and if uncovered, would expose Jack's secret and ruin Jack's planned disbursement of stock. Leaving Parker out of it, Jack's story was clean and simple and his plan was intact. Parker marveled at

Jack's quick thinking while pain wracked his body and blood seeped from his bullet wound.

"Why was Dennie's identity a secret?"

"Jack demanded that she keep her married name when she divorced, didn't want the Shaw name damaged by her antics, didn't want to be accused of nepotism either."

"That makes me her uncle. Dennie shot her father and Jack shot his daughter. That's the most tragic thing I've ever heard."

"She was always a problem for him. He and Kumar argued about who was to succeed Jack as CEO. Kumar wanted Dennie and Jack wanted Terry," Carolyn said.

"Did Dennie know her father didn't want her to be CEO?"

"Of course she did. She and Jack argued about it."

In the cemetery in New Orleans, Dennie said, "How convenient. The gang's all here." Had she killed us both, she'd have inherited from Jack and from her grandfather's trust. So, Dennie had two reasons to kill me: her fear that I might expose the fraud designed to make her CEO of Shaw Technology; and the possibility that I would inherit Buford John Shaw's stock instead of her. Upon her death, Jack chose to conceal her identity and protect his retirement. Parker wondered if Jack had mourned the loss of his daughter or congratulated himself for aa trip to fish around the world?

Parker glanced at the grave where two men were shoveling dirt atop Jack Shaw's casket. "Jack had a lot of secrets to conceal, didn't he? He hated me, didn't want me to have my birthright."

"Jack didn't hate you; he hated the idea of you. His father loaned him the money to start Shaw Technology but kept one-third of the stock for his other son—you. Jack despised his father for cheating on his mother and then favoring his illegitimate son. Jack was determined to undo what his father had done, so he wanted your stock to go to his employees."

And I shot Jack's daughter. My niece. Did he hate me for that too? "Thanks for telling me the truth, Carolyn."

"Dennie is buried in that unmarked grave, still waiting for the headstone. You know who that empty plot is for, don't you?" She tilted her head toward the fenced gravesite.

Parker turned to stare at the tombstones. "No."

"It's a symbol of your place in your father's life. John's dying wish was that Jack find you."

Parker imagined a life as Buford Shaw's son, Jack Shaw's brother, part owner of Shaw Technology. Would he have been a better version of himself?

Carolyn expelled a deep breath. "I'm sorry if I wasn't always ... nice."

"It's Sabrina you owe an apology."

She nodded. "I'll look her up." Carolyn hobbled off to find her car.

Jordyn sat beside him, took his hand in hers. Jordyn was smart enough not to ask him the question many women would have asked, "How do you feel about it?" Instead, she said, "If you're going to buy a Lamborghini and a yacht, I want a house and a Porsche."

In spite of himself, Parker laughed. "You'll have to settle for a purse or new shoes. I have a different use for that stock."

Terry Horan rang Parker as Parker and Jordyn drove back to Atlanta. "ASC would still like to buy Shaw Technology. They'll want to buy your stock. Will you sell it to them? It's worth something north of five million dollars. Lot of money."

"I don't need a Lamborghini. What about you and the employees?"

"We'd have to sell as a block. ASC isn't going to buy dribs and drabs."

"Get to the punch line, Terry."

"The employees will sell if you sell, but they'll hold their stock if you do. They don't want to be owned by ASC. As one-third owner, you'd vote the largest block of stock and the employees are okay with that."

"Are you inviting me back?"

"Maybe. You going to replace your old buddy as CEO?"

"No, Terry, you're the right man for the job, but I would like to be your head of analytics and AI."

Terry laughed. "A bit odd that I'd work for a man who also worked for me. But, sure, I'd love to have you on staff if you retain your shares. If we sell to ASC, I'm outta here."

"I'm not selling."

"The employees will be pleased to hear that. Can you join me for a call with Midwestern Assurance?"

"What about? They're going with ASC, aren't they?"

"She didn't tell me what it's about, but it's with the whole board."

"She?"

"Nancy Maddox. They need our permission to have ASC use our systems from offshore. The contract grants us the right to block foreign use of our systems but we'll lose them as a customer if we do. Jack would have given them permission in his deal to sell Shaw Technology."

"So, what's your answer?"

"Now that I know your intentions, I know my answer: No, nyet, never in a million years. If you agree, of course."

"Okay, let's be brave. When is the call?"

"First thing in the morning."

***

Terry and Parker sat on one side of Shaw's conference table, facing a camera.

Terry followed Nancy's instructions to dial into the board meeting using a video conferencing tool. When they were connected and facing a dozen men and two women around a massive conference table, Nancy Maddox introduced the players.

The man at the head of the table, the Midwestern Assurance Chairman, spoke first. "What is the status of your company? Will you sell to ASC?"

"No, sir, the company is now employee owned. Mr. Parker here is the largest individual stockholder with one-third of the stock."

The Chairman nodded thoughtfully. "Will you grant ASC permission to use your systems if we sign with them?"

"No, sir, we would protect our intellectual property by withholding permission," Terry said.

The die is cast, Parker thought.

"In that event," the Chairman said, "we'd uninstall your systems and install systems from ASC. That would delay outsourcing and inject risk and massive cost into the project. And you would lose a customer."

"We'd be sorry to have that happen," Terry said.

Parker jumped into the conversation. "I'm sure Ms. Maddox has apprised you of the two proposals we presented. One is pure vanilla and shows that ASC is overstating your projected savings. The other proposal is an embellished version that reflects our vision at Shaw Technology."

"Yes," the Chairman said. "We've taken the time to review both versions and to vet the ASC proposal. They've added a few interesting wrinkles you may not be aware of."

"We can match their savings without a layoff of fifteen hundred employees. So, it comes down to your loyalty to your employees."

The Chairman bristled and the board members squirmed in their seats, but Maddox touched the Chairman's shoulder and whispered in his ear and he calmed down. The Chairman asked Parker to standby while the board had a sidebar. The woman at the Chairman's elbow hit a few keys on her computer, and the screen froze, and the microphone at Midwestern Assurance's end was muted.

The sidebar lasted an uncomfortably long time. Parker stood and stretched, grabbed a bottle of water. Fidgeted. *Either this works, or I buy a Lamborghini.* Finally, the people on the screen began moving, and he could hear voices, so he resumed his seat in front of his laptop's camera.

"We've voted on your proposal and we accept it," the Chairman said.

"Good, good," Terry said.

"I have a quid pro quo," Parker said and the MA board stiffened. "I won't work with Gonzalez and Cummings."

"I just fired them."

"Good, good. We'll send the contract across as soon as we hang up."

"Will you work with Maddox?" The Chairman waved a hand at her.

"Yes, Nancy wasn't involved in the fraud."

The video conference ended, and Terry emailed Shaw Technology's formal contract.

Kumar will be furious, Parker thought, left with two orphan customers in the U.S. that he won't be able to satisfy with cost savings. It occurred to him, then, that he and Terry needed to protect themselves against Kumar.

"We need to fire a shot across Kumar's bow, Terry."

"What?"

"Have our lawyers draft a letter threatening to sue if Alexi copies any of the intellectual property he invented while an employee of Shaw Technology."

Terry gave Parker an appreciative smile. "You're beginning to think like a business owner, Parker."

The last thing Parker did that day was write Sabrina yet another email, hoping he might elicit a reply with his raft of shocking news. He told her about Jack's passing and the disquieting revelation that Old Man Shaw was his birth father, and the astounding disclosure that Dennie was Jack's daughter. "If she had murdered both Jack and me, she'd have inherited from both Jack and her grandfather." Parker related his transaction with Midwestern Assurance, saving thousands of American jobs. Surely that would prompt a reply, he thought, and he pressed *Enter*.

Over the next forty-eight hours, he closed the sale of Paula's house, sent the furniture to storage, and moved into a furnished apartment in Norcross. Each time he passed his laptop, sitting on a kitchen counter now, he checked his email account. There was never any mail from Sabrina.

Carolyn found Sabrina's parents' address in her employment file under *Next of Kin/Emergency Contact* and sent flowers and a note of apology. She passed the address to Parker—"In case you want to write to her or something."

Parker looked it up on Google Maps: a rural road just east of Fresno in a place called Big Bunch. On Google Earth, it was a large house with a gaggle of farm buildings among massive orchards and endless fields of green plants in neat rows. He asked Terry for some time off and Terry surely knew the reason.

Parker flew to Fresno, rented a car, and drove east toward the Sierra Nevada mountains and then north on a two-lane farm road. No mailboxes helpfully labeled with owners' names or street numbers guided him to his destination. While he saw the occasional farm equipment building, few homes were visible from the road, so he missed the driveway leading into a copse of trees on his first pass, reversed course when the Google Maps lady prodded him, and turned into what appeared to be a small forest. A quarter of a mile down the driveway, the trees parted to reveal a paved parking area fronting a wide California ranch home built of beveled glass and hewn wood. Sabrina's white BMW sat beside a well-used pickup truck. To the right of the house, the paved driveway became a dirt road leading deeper into the fields.

He wiped clammy hands on his brown corduroy sports jacket as he approached the front entrance under an overhanging roof. The main door opened before he could push the bell button revealing a tall woman with white cotton hair and red-framed glasses wearing a full-length apron.

She gave him a quick once-over. "Well, ya passed the first test, ya showed up."

She swung the screen door open and held it for him with an outstretched arm. Before he crossed the threshold, he said, "Is this the Mitchell residence?"

"Obviously." She grabbed an arm and yanked him into the house. "White folks sure can be slow."

"Is Sabrina here?"

"She's around somewhere." She placed a hand on his back and shoved him down a hallway of tongue-in-groove hardwood flooring and paneled walls covered in family photos. "Clarence is on the back porch, and he's got some questions for ya."

Parker felt like he was back in high school, meeting his girlfriend's parents for the first time. He stepped through another screened door onto a deep-set porch spanning the back of the house. Three spaced ceiling fans revolved slowly overhead, cooling a man in his seventies who rocked slowly in a cushioned wicker slider. A look of recognition spread across his handsome face as Parker approached him.

"I'm—" Parker began.

"I'd know you anywhere," the man said, rising from his seat. "Seen the pictures."

He had been about to introduce himself for the first time as John Parker Shaw, the name he had legally adopted as his true identity, but he realized that Mr. Mitchell wouldn't recognize the name Shaw. "People just call me—"

"Parker, I know. Like that character in *Cold Mountain*, just a last name."

"Maybe the author heard about me and liked the idea."

Clarence Mitchell chuckled. He swept a hand at an adjoining wicker couch upholstered in a yellow floral print. "Have a seat, and we'll get started."

"Where are your manners?" Mrs. Mitchell said, holding the screen door open. "Would you care for some iced tea, Mr. Parker? Before y'all get started?"

Get started? "No, thank you, ma'am."

"Alright, then, I'll keep her away till you give me the sign." And the woman disappeared.

Clarence sank back in his chair, leaned away from Parker with a canny look on his face. Wanting to preempt whatever "get started" meant, Parker said, "How big is your operation? Nothing but trees and fields as far as the eye can see."

"Three hundred fifty acres and over there, beyond those trees," Clarence pointed to a stand of trees at the bottom of the grassy backyard, "are work buildings and all the trucks and shakers and harvesters. I sold it all when I retired, but we kept this house, only house we ever owned. The dirt road leads to the equipment sheds and out into the orchards, so the heavy equipment comes right up our driveway every day. Martha hates the noise, but I welcome it. Makes me feel a part of it."

"And you grew ...?"

"Almonds, of course. Biggest cash crop in California."

How odd, Parker thought, to have been a member of a family of Florida pecan growers and now, interviewing with a family of California almond growers. From one nut to the next. "That's very impressive."

"You mean for a black man?"

"No." Parker felt he had stepped in a bear trap. "That's not what I meant. I—"

"This was a small operation, relatively speaking. But in this business, you reap what you sow, like it says in the Bible. The dirt don't care what color you are."

"Neither do I, Mr. Mitchell." Parker stole a glance at the screened door, but no one appeared to rescue him.

Clarence tapped him on the shoulder, wanting him to look him in the eyes. "Sabrina says you ditched her in New Orleans, so why have you hunted her down?"

Ditched her? That was her politically correct way of telling her parents she had been rejected by a married man.

Parker felt the heat rise from his shirt collar to his neck and then to his cheeks. Rarely had he been taken to task by someone whose opinion of him mattered. His mother had been the one person who could make Parker question himself. He said, "We had a spat. I've come to make it right."

"I don't know that she'll accept an apology. First couple of weeks she was home, she sat in that chair by the front window and waited for you. She doesn't do that anymore. Now she's applying for jobs, out here in California."

Parker swallowed hard. "I still owe her the apology."

"Let me ask you a couple of other questions, Mr. Parker. Number one," he held up a crooked index finger. "You're a smart man, but do you know what you're getting into, chasing after my daughter?"

"Yes, I've seen the subtle racism that Sabrina endures." Quotas and laws and regulations designed to combat racism will never erase bias on a personal level, Parker thought.

"Racism isn't always subtle," Clarence said. "You can ignore it for a while, but it will wear you down, son. You'll come to wonder if it's worth it."

Parker didn't give him a knee-jerk answer, took a minute to consider his last chance to run away from these complications. "No, Mr. Mitchell, your daughter is worth it."

Some of the tension left the elderly man's body. "That brings us to number two," he showed Parker two crooked fingers, misshapen from years of manual labor. "It's my faith that gets me through hard times, son. Are you a religious man, go to church?"

Parker thought the role of organized religions in a civilization was to scare heathens into behaving, a mission at which religions had failed miserably.

"I was raised Catholic. My mother used to take me."

"Used to." Clarence massaged his gray stubble. "Lotta scientists don't believe in God. Are you a believer, Mr. Parker?"

Parker had a ready answer, one that reflected the extent to which he had reconciled science and theology in his own mind. "I believe in the Big Bang because we can prove it happened, but science has yet to explain where that tight little ball of material came from."

Clarence bobbed his head. "In Genesis, it says, 'In the beginning, God created the heavens and the Earth …' I believe God created the tight little ball, Mr. Parker, pulled the trigger and planned what we have now."

"The material had to come from somewhere. We'll figure it out."

Clarence shot Parker a tight little smile. "We? Scientists? All it takes is faith, son."

If Clarence insisted upon a definitive position on the existence of God, Parker would say he leaned toward yes, there is a God, not only because of the preexistence of matter but also because of the intricacy of the universe. He found it difficult to attribute the complexity of the world to an accident. And then there were the five proofs postulated by St. Thomas Aquinas. The one that bedeviled Parker was that there must be a God since humans wanted a God, had the need for a god woven into their DNA. Humans invented gods to worship at every step in their evolution.

"I hope God does exist," Parker said.

He could tell that Clarence didn't like his answer, but the elderly man changed the subject. "She won't go back to Georgia. You know that, right?"

Parker felt stupid for not having considered this possibility. He had no particular objection to living in California but wondered if Florida was off limits for Sabrina. He could work remotely. Parker hated equivocation, was composing another evasive answer, like a politician at a press conference, when the screen door squeaked and swung open. The two men turned as one to see who had intruded.

Mrs. Mitchell said, "She ain't in the house." She pointed to the grove at the bottom of the yard. "She likes to walk in the orchard, think about things. Onliest other place she could be."

Parker rose, hoping to bring the interview to a conclusion.

"If you're half as smart as ya think you are, you'll go back to Georgia now," Clarence said. "She's settled. Leave her be."

It would be so easy, Parker thought, to walk out the door, fly back to Georgia, and forget about a black woman who would complicate his life, but he had one more chance to make a good choice.

"I can't do that, sir," Parker said.

Clarence sighed and slapped both knees with his hands. "I hope you know what you're doing."

Parker took the dirt road, a mound of weeds between two worn ruts, looking left and right down the rows of trees laden with nuts nearly ready for harvesting. After a quarter of a mile, he began to perspire in the August sun, so he removed his jacket and slung it over his shoulder. He trudged another hundred yards, the dust and dirt covering his polished loafers and sticking to the cuffed hems of his dress slacks, before he sensed movement off to his left. A long, slender shadow appeared between rows, then melted into the larger shadows cast by the trees. When he saw the long shadow again, he turned into the grove, ducking under limbs, taking long strides to catch up.

She heard him before she saw him and stood still as a heron about to spear a fish. She wore shorts and a T-shirt, had her curly hair piled into a haystack atop her head. She pivoted in his direction and located him two rows away, her expression hard for Parker to read. She looked to him like a river goddess who had come home.

He knew what to do, what to say. "I love you, Sabrina Oyawale."

She smiled. "Took ya a while to figure it out, didn't it?"

~THE END~

ACKNOWLEDGEMENTS

Thanks first to Angie Kiesling of The Editorial Attic for helping me turn a rough draft into a manuscript that a publisher would recognize as a book worthy of publication.

And finally, thanks to my wife, Angie Nemeth, who read the drafts, critiqued my ideas, injected optimism into the process, and gave me the time and space to complete the work.

ABOUT THE AUTHOR

Mike Nemeth, a Vietnam veteran and former high-tech executive, has written four mystery novels in which his characters face moral dilemmas. Defiled was an Amazon bestseller in the Crime Fiction Noir category. The Undiscovered Country won the Beverly Hills Book Award for Southern Fiction and the Augusta Literary Festival's Yerby Award. The book inspired songwriter Mark Currey to compose the song Who I Am. Parker's Choice, won a Firebird Award for thrillers and American Fiction Awards for Diverse and Multicultural Mystery, and for Romantic Mystery. His latest novel, The Two Lives of Eddie Kovacs, was released in late 2022. Mike's short pieces have been published by The New York Times, Georgia Magazine, Augusta Magazine, Southern Writers' Magazine, Deep South Magazine, and the Writers' Voices anthology. Creative Loafing named him Atlanta's Best Local Author for 2018. Mike lives in suburban Atlanta with his wife, Angie, and their rescue dog, Scout.

PARKER'S CHOICE
MICHAEL E. NEMETH
9 780996 537001
PUBLISHER
NEMO WRITES, LLC